HIGHLANDER LORD OF VENGEANCE

HIGHLAND REVENGE TRILOGY

BOOK THREE

DONNA FLETCHER

Highlander Lord of Vengeance

Cover art
The Killion Group

Visit Donna's Website
www.donnafletcher.com

CHAPTER 1

A soft knock sounded at the door before it opened. "Lord Torrance approaches, my lady."

Esme leaned against the bedpost for support, her legs turning weak. She acknowledged the message with a bob of her head and the servant hurried off.

She feared her heart would pound out of her chest it beat so wildly. It had been so peaceful here without his presence, without the roar of his anger, or the pounding of his fists on a table, or the fear that he would demand her presence in his bedchamber and...

She pushed herself off the bedpost, warning herself that she had to remain strong, that she had no choice. He was her husband and nothing would change that, not even prayer, and she had prayed, but it had been a sinful and selfish prayer.

She had prayed for his death.

Dreadful fear robbed her legs of any strength left in them and she sunk down on the edge of the bed tears threatening her eyes.

Her husband had exceptionally fine features. At first

glance, his handsome features captivated. His height stood a good head or two above others, and his fine body was sculpted to perfection. But it was only when one looked past all that that his true nature was revealed—evil.

She had seen it in the way his eyes would narrow, and his lips would curl ever so slightly in pleasure when he issued a punishment. He got enjoyment out of seeing someone suffer and even more pleasure in inflicting the suffering himself. Then there were his subtle threats dropped here and there or his hand that would strike fast for barely a reason.

Memory had her cringing, as if she could feel his hand grab a handful of her hair and yank it hard, stinging her scalp and for what? Because she hadn't responded to him quickly enough or because she dared to take a step ahead of him, or she spoke too much or not enough. Any reason was good enough to raise his wrath and leave her trembling in fear.

When she received news that her husband would not return right after a victorious battle, she almost wept with relief. She could walk through the village, enjoying the last days of autumn that had already turned cold, speak with whoever she wished without seeking permission from her husband to do so. Smile. Laugh. Sleep. All without an ounce of fear.

She had even worn what garments she pleased, plain and comfortable, not the elaborate ones her husband insisted she wear and that she now wore to please him. Always to please him so as not to give him any reason to lash out at her.

Stay strong, a warning that had become like a prayer to her.

Her mum had told her that a woman's lot in life was to remain strong no matter what fate dealt her since women had little say in decisions made for them.

Not so the peasants, Esme would argue with her.

Her mum would tell her that their lot was no better.

Whether noble or peasant, life was difficult when little choice was left to you.

Esme didn't want to believe that. She had entered the marriage with hope, believing kindness could make a difference. She learned fast that evil took pleasure in toying and tormenting kindness until it finally retreated and hid in the shadows.

The one thing she wished her mum had been more forthcoming about was the marriage bed. All she had told her was to submit to her husband. To lie there and let him have his way and it would be over soon enough. But that didn't happen, and she didn't know what she had done wrong. She closed her eyes, recalling the fearful moment. Her husband had grown so angry at her, she feared he might beat her to death. But it was his tongue that cut as sharp as a knife, and she felt its every slash.

His warning, "Fail me again and you would suffer greatly for it."

A horn sounded and she spang off the bed. The sound was close, which meant her husband would arrive at any moment and he would bring fear and darkness with him.

She brushed at the few wrinkles on her heavily embroidered tunic, silently reprimanding herself for having sat. Torrance would notice and admonish her for being unkempt. She hurried her hand to her hair to make sure that not a single blonde strand had escaped her neatly plaited hair. She refused to even give thought to her features. Many thought her beautiful, while her husband believed he had gotten stuck with an ugly wife. He insisted that her eyes were too big and the color too blue. He reminded her repeatedly that her mouth was too small, that she barely had any lips, and her nose was too wide.

She lowered her hand to rest on her stomach where by now her husband had expected a bairn to be growing, but it wasn't. Though she had gained some weight, her fault. She had been able to enjoy her meals since he hadn't been there to comment on everything she put in her mouth. He would notice and no doubt remark on it and see that she got less food.

She sighed feeling helpless, trapped, and fearful. Always fearful.

The horn sounded again—close this time.

She hurried out of her bedchamber to greet her husband, the man she hated with her whole heart. She silently prayed as she made her way down the stone stairs for strength and sneaked in a prayer that had no hope of being fulfilled—*please, please, let me be free of him.*

* * *

The wind stirred the hem of Esme's cloak as she stood atop the stone steps of the keep, her hands knotted tight at her sides. The village that spread wide before the castle was lined with clan members—men, women, even bairns clutching their mothers' skirts—all summoned at the sound of the horn. Not for celebration. Not for joy. But for duty touched with fear.

Esme watched as silence settled over the village and a chill swept through the crowd like a shadow passing over the sun as hoofbeats rang out, sharp and steady.

She forced her glance up the slope where the road cut through the last of the pines. A black horse crested the ridge, a brute of an animal, its mane flying like a war banner. Upon it sat a man clad in a dark plaid and furs, his cloak billowing behind him as if the very wind feared to touch him.

Lord Torrance… her husband.

Her stomach twisted and she turned her eyes away for a moment. She hadn't seen him in months, not since he'd ridden off to crush Clan MacLeish. Why couldn't her prayers have been answered? Why couldn't he have been struck down in battle, freeing her? It had been wrong of her to offer such a prayer, or was it? Shouldn't evil be struck down?

She turned her eyes on him again, his face coming into view, hard as granite cliffs and his green eyes, even from a distance, icy and calculating. Her skin crawled, knowing what was to come.

The crowd broke into a forced cheer as he rode through the gates. They knew if they didn't welcome him as a victorious leader they would be made to suffer for it. Not one of them avoided his gaze, knowing his warriors watched for anyone who didn't greet him enthusiastically.

Esme remained still, her chin lifted though her heart thundered. He spotted her as he drew near, and she felt it like a threatening blade to her throat. He reined in before the keep, the horse snorting clouds into the cold air.

His gaze swept the crowd once before dismounting. Then he turned his eyes on hers and they never left hers as he climbed the stairs with deliberate slowness. There was no warmth in them, no smile, not a single nod. Not a sign of affection, only possession.

Esme stood unmoving at the top, her spine rigid though every instinct screamed for her to retreat. Run! Get out of here! But she had no place to go.

His boots thudded against the stone, measured, unhurried, ominous.

He mounted the final step and stopped before her, tall and broad. His face was as handsome as ever but evil often disguised itself in fine features. Whereas the battlefield softened some and hardened others, Torrance took pleasure in it, and it showed in his bold green eyes.

"Wife," he said, holding her gaze.

Her throat had turned as dry as dust, knowing he was

assessing her and finding fault. It took her a moment to say, "Congratulations on your victory, my lord."

He appeared hesitant for a moment, then his strong voice rolled over her like thunder.

"There had better be food waiting for me and my men."

She hurried to say, "Aye, my lord, there is food, ale, and wine aplenty."

She didn't need to remind the cook. The woman had been prepared, knowing the severe consequences she would suffer for such a mistake.

He looked past her, at the heavy doors of the keep, then back. His gaze did not warm. If anything, it turned heavier, like a weight pressing down.

Esme's stomach knotted.

He looked at his warriors, gathered near, waiting in anticipation and shouted, "We celebrate!"

A cheer rang out as he grabbed her by the arm and propelled her into the keep, his words falling on her like shackles. "You will remain by my side until I say otherwise."

When they reached the dais in the Great Hall, he pulled out a chair and ordered, Sit."

Esme stared at him, a bit bewildered.

He lowered his face to hers. "Did you not hear me, wife?"

"Aye, my lord. Aye," she said confused and sat.

Why hadn't he shoved her down on the chair? He had done so many times when she had not moved quickly enough for him. Why not do so now? And how was it he seemed a bit taller, his chest a bit wider?

She cast a hasty glance his way.

He scowled at her in warning, and she quickly looked away.

The tables were ladened with food and drink and soon chatter and laughter filled the room. Tales were told about the victorious battle and how Lord Torrance would soon rule over much of the area. He had even managed to save his half-sister, Autumn, threatened by a Northern tribe and befriend another tribe's leader, promising to send him a wife.

A chill ran through her, hearing that. What poor lass would be sacrificed for his promise?

She was startled when his face was suddenly next to hers. If she turned, she was sure her lips would brush his. The thought roiled her stomach. His kisses had felt more like punishments, his lips pressed so hard against hers that she could barely breathe.

"Look at me, wife," he ordered, his voice low and touched with menace.

She turned slowly, trying to avoid their lips from touching, but he was too close, and her lips grazed his like a feather faintly brushing across them. She was surprised by the startled look in his eyes that quickly turned to annoyance.

"Why aren't you eating?" he snapped.

Esme struggled to find an accuse that would appease him.

"Have you been ill?" he demanded.

"Nay. Nay, my lord."

"Then eat," he ordered. "You are too thin."

She was glad he turned away and didn't see the shock on her face that she failed to hide. She had expected him to admonish her for just the opposite. She hurried to turn her head so as not to be caught staring dumbfounded at him. Did he not see the fullness in her face?

A servant had, Gwen, she had remarked about it one day, keeping her voice to a whisper so no one could hear her and repeat her words to Lord Torrance.

It was barely a few words she murmured but Esme heard the warning in them.

"You have rosy, full cheeks, my lady."

Later, when in her bedchamber, she pressed her hands to

her cheeks and felt the fullness and taking full stock of herself, she realized she was not as slender as when she wed Torrance, six moon cycles ago. She had feared what he would say, and yet, he had just accused her of being too thin.

The night wore on and with it grew more outrageous tales of the victorious battle, many laughing about the cowardly actions of the Clan MacLeish. They claimed that Chieftain Ryland had been carried off the battlefield half dead and now laid near death in his bed at home.

Esme cringed, knowing that her husband would wait to see if Chieftain Ryland survived and if he did, he would take great pleasure in executing him in front of his clan. She had seen Chieftain Ryland the few times he came to speak with Torrance to try and settle their disagreements and avoid a battle. She had even spoken with him and had suffered abuse from her husband for it. She was amazed at how much Ryland resembled Torrance. They could be twins and though they looked alike, they were vastly different. Both were powerful men and skillful with a sword. But Ryland had a calmer nature unless pushed. She had learned that on Ryland's last visit. His discussion with Torrance had nearly erupted into an altercation. Oddly enough, Esme believed that Torrance would have lost if a fight had ensued and she wondered if he believed the same since he told Ryland it would be the battlefield that settled their dispute.

A sudden yawn had her covering her mouth with her hand. She wished she could retire to her bedchamber, but it wasn't her choice when to take her leave. It would be a long evening of revelry for her husband and his warriors, so she settled in to make the most of her situation and tried hard to keep herself from falling asleep.

She jumped at the sudden burst of laughter.

"Wife!"

Esme eyes flashed open, and she sprang forward in her

chair and had just enough time to turn her head and brush her husband's cheek with hers to avoid their lips from meeting.

"You embarrass me," Torrance scolded. "You fall asleep while courageous tales are told about my victory."

"Please forgive me, my lord," she said, tired of endlessly asking for his forgiveness.

"Go. Take your leave. Retire to your bedchamber," he ordered. "We will speak tomorrow."

"As you say, my lord," Esme hurried to say, relieved to be spared the remainder of the evening, but mostly because her husband did not order her to his bedchamber.

Grateful for the reprieve, she wondered, as she climbed the stone stairs, why after being absent from home for nearly two moon cycles that he didn't demand her presence in his bedchamber?

CHAPTER 2

"Something is disturbing you. I can see it," Brack said and shook his head. "Didn't your wife have good news for you?"

"I had little chance to speak with her yesterday," Torrance said, glancing around his solar at the many weapons hanging on the walls.

"Are you still considering looking for another wife?"

Torrance landed his glance on Brack. "Not yet."

Brack reached for his tankard of ale. "You taught her well to be an obedient and dutiful wife."

"It is my duty as her husband to see that she obeys my word."

"But if she cannot produce an heir, she is worthless to you." Brack took a generous swallow of ale.

"Are you saying I should not waste my time with her?"

"Nay, I am saying you should not waste a moment in filling her belly with a bairn."

Torrance scowled.

Brack raised one hand as if fending off his glare, his other hand still clamped on his tankard. "The servants talk about

Lady Esme spending all last night in her bedchamber... alone. They know the importance of an heir to a clan. Do you?"

"Remember your place, Brack," Torrance warned, glaring at the man who had stood beside him no matter what, and he bore the signs of such loyalty.

Minor scars peppered his face though distracted little from his fair features. A few old scars could also be seen on his thick, muscled arms, but years of training and battle had turned him into an exceptional warrior and scars became a thing of the past.

"Always, my lord," Brack said, raising his tankard before he took another drink.

"You need a wife, Brack."

Brack's head snapped back as if he'd been punched. "I have no want of a nagging wife, and you know it, sir. There are willing women plenty enough to keep me satisfied. But enough about women. There are many matters that need your attention. Clan MacLeish being one of them."

"Quint, the infamous Monk, is overseeing Clan MacLeish until Ryland, their chieftain, is well enough to resume his command. Once that happens, I will deal with the fate of both Ryland and the clan."

"You spoke often of wanting to see Ryland dead," Brack reminded.

"Aye, and that still may be so, but Clan MacLeish, at least at the moment, is not my most pressing problem." Torrance continued, silencing Brack before he could broach another issue. "My sister Autumn will remain wed to Knox, and he will continue to oversee Clan MacFadin for me."

"A wise decision," Brack praised. "Unlike most mercenaries, Knox is a man of his word and can be trusted."

"And he will be loyal and serve me well when needed

since I can take his wife from him at any time and without cause."

Brack grinned. "A good reason for him to remain loyal." His grin faded. "What about the Northman, Hakon, the one you promised a wife in return for his allegiance to you?"

"He's an evil one. See if you can find a woman just as evil," Torrance ordered. "The other Northern tribes fear him and if I can keep him in my good graces than the other tribes may fall in line as well and I can secure their allegiance."

"And become more powerful than the king himself."

"Without it being known or the king will see my empire destroyed before I create it, and rule a good portion of the north," Torrance cautioned. "Since I have been absent from the clan longer than planned, alert the clan that tomorrow I will hear and settle grievances."

"There may not be many, if any at all, since they fear to speak their complaints."

He leaned forward, a glimmer of annoyance in his green eyes. "Are you suggesting I am too hard on those who speak up?"

"As it should be, my lord," Brack said quickly. "As you often say... both parties have a share in the complaint so both should be punished."

"Let it be known that there better be a good showing of grievances tomorrow or I will walk through the village myself and find them."

Brack nodded. "Aye, my lord."

"Now find my wife and send her to me," Torrance ordered.

"Aye, my lord," Brack said once again as he got to his feet.

"Make haste about it," Torrance snapped.

Brack hurried out of the room, nodding.

Torrance pushed himself away from the table in his solar and stood to walk around the room. He glanced again at the weapons hanging on the walls, some rusted, some barely used, as he walked over to the narrow table braced against a wall. An iron candelabra, its four candles providing good light sat at one end. He studied the crude map drawings, on the reverse side of several pelts. His empire was growing.

A rap at the door had him turning and calling out, "Enter, wife."

Esme entered the room. She kept her hands linked tightly in front of her to keep them from trembling.

"Sit," he ordered, his glance directing her to the table in the middle of the room with benches on either side.

She hurried and took a seat, grateful to hide her trembling hands beneath the table.

Torrance walked slowly around the room to come to a stop behind her. He leaned down, his face close to hers, his arm brushing her shoulder as he rested one hand on the table.

Esme could feel his warm breath on her cheek, and she silently warned herself to remain strong.

"Did you miss me, wife," Torrance whispered in her ear.

She couldn't stop the shiver that ran through her, and she quickly said, "Aye, my lord."

"Do you tremble with passion for me, wife?"

"Of course, my lord," she said, and her stomach turned at the lie.

"Then why are you not with child?" he demanded and pounded his fist on the table.

Esme's whole body cringed. "I don't know what I do wrong, my lord."

Her body remained tense even though he left her side and walked around the table to sit opposite her. She knew he wasn't finished with her, and she waited anxiously for what would come next.

"It is not a difficult task to lie there and submit to your husband," he reprimanded.

Esme didn't know how to respond to him. Did he forget what happened each time she had done just that?

He pounded the table again. "Answer me, wife?"

She swallowed back her fear and did her best to place the blame on herself. "I don't know what more to do, my lord. I am ignorant of the intimate ways between a husband and wife."

His puzzled look baffled her, and he appeared ready to speak then stopped for a moment.

"You will come to my bed prepared to get with child when I summon you," he ordered.

"Aye, my lord," she said fear curling in her stomach of when that time would come.

"Fetch a cloak," he snapped. "You will be accompanying me through the village this morning."

"Aye, my lord."

"Hurry!" he ordered when she didn't move.

In her rush to leave him, she stumbled, though righted herself.

"Good, Lord, woman, don't tell me I have a clumsy wife," he called out. "Watch how you walk."

"Aye, my lord," she said, wishing she never had to say those words again yet facing years ahead with those words spilling endlessly from her lips.

* * *

"You will not leave my side," Torrance ordered, after stepping outside, a cold wind circling them.

Esme nodded. "As you say, my lord." Another never-ending response.

Torrance took her hand to walk down the stairs, startling

her. He would grab her by the arm often enough, but never had he taken her hand in his.

"What's wrong?" he demanded.

"The cold, my lord," she lied.

He let go of her hand to grip the edge of her cloak. "Go and have a servant fetch your fur-lined cloak now. I will wait here for you."

She nodded and hurried into the keep and spotting Gwen, the one servant who didn't fear to speak to her, asked, "Gwen, please fetch my fur-lined cloak."

"Aye, my lady," she said and hurried off.

Esme shook her head. Something didn't seem right. Her husband had never cared if she was cold. He would tell her it was her own fault for not dressing properly and leave her to suffer a chill. And taking her hand? She could not get over that he held her hand and that he had not done so roughly. He had closed his hand around hers, as if with care, and held it firmly.

Gwen returned and Esme slipped off her cloak and replaced it with the fur-lined one, then rushed off not wanting to keep Torrance waiting.

He stood where she had left him, his head turning as he took stock of his surroundings.

"It took you long enough," he said when she reached his side.

"My apologies, my lord," she said, more words she often said to him.

He took her hand again and she wished she could enjoy the feel of its warmth and strength, but she didn't. His touch caused her skin to prickle with fear since she had felt pain from that same hand when it struck her. But what possibly could cause him to hold her hand now when he never did before?

The village path, still soft from the morning's rain, clung

to Esme's boots as she matched steps beside Lord Torrance. The villagers bowed as they passed, a forest of bent heads, a hush of held breath. No one wished to draw the lord's gaze.

They continued walking in silence, Torrance casting a wide glance around as if he listened, intending to catch any chatter or whispers being said. The whole time he never let go of her hand and Esme saw people's eyes going wide at the unusual sight.

They were deep into the village when suddenly there came a sharp, wet splat.

Esme jerked to a stop in surprise, looking down to find a thick glob of mud staining the hem of her cloak. A heartbeat of stunned silence followed, and then the air tightened, turned brittle.

All eyes shifted, not to Esme, but to Torrance.

Across the way, a lad no older than six years stood frozen, another mudball drooping from his small hand. His mother gripped him fiercely, terror etched deep into her face.

Lord Torrance turned, his movements deliberate, his expression carved from stone. He stared at the lad with a weight that could crush bone.

The lad's lips moved, trembling around whispered apologies too soft to hear.

Esme's heart ached. She shifted ever so slightly toward Torrance, her voice low and urgent as she gently squeezed his hand. "My lord, Daniel is but a child. It was a mistake... not a slight."

For the briefest moment, something flickered in Torrance's eyes as if he might consider her words, but it vanished as fast as it had appeared.

He turned his gaze onto Esme, not cruel, but sharp, warning her without saying a word.

Should she hold her tongue as she usually did? Would her interference only make things worse for them both? She couldn't see the lad suffer. She knew how cruel Torrance could be.

"Please, my lord, do not harm him," she whispered.

He glared at her with such annoyance that his green eyes appeared bolder in color and Esme knew to say any more could be harmful to the lad. She held her tongue.

Torrance turned slowly, like a storm gathering force. His eyes, sharp as a drawn blade, fixed on the lad. He let go of his wife's hand and took one step toward Daniel, then another.

Daniel's mum shoved her son to his knees, begging, "Forgive him, my lord! It was an accident! He meant no disrespect!"

Torrance shifted his attention to Daniel and barked a single command, sharp as a whip crack. "Stand."

His mum had to help him to his feet, his body trembled so badly.

Torrance's voice was cold and strong enough for all to hear. "You dare hit Lady Esme with a mud ball? An insult, even if born of foolishness, must be answered."

Torrance let the moment stretch unbearably long, letting fear root deep in the villagers' hearts. Then he announced his judgment.

"You will clean the horses' shelter until there is no stink left to it," he commanded, his powerful voice slicing the stillness. "Fail, and I will see you regret it."

Daniel bobbed his head furiously. "Aye, my lord. Aye."

Tears streamed down his mum's cheeks. "We are grateful, my lord. Grateful for your mercy."

The villagers sagged in relief. A beating had been expected. A maiming, even.

As his mum said, this was mercy.

Without a word, Torrance turned to Esme and once more took hold of her hand, grasping it tightly, a warning that she had displeased him.

It didn't matter to her. The lad had been spared a harsh punishment and that was all that mattered.

His hand eased his grip after only a few steps, and they continued their walk through the village whispers following them. While she couldn't hear what they said, she knew.

Mercy.

They all wondered as did she... why Lord Torrance had shown the lad mercy when he had never shown anyone mercy.

The silence grew heavy as they continued walking. Torrance was far too engaged in surveying the village than having any desire to speak with her. She didn't mind. Silence was safer for her.

Torrance halted when they reached the smithy.

He was a burly man with arms thick as tree trunks. At the sight of Torrance, the smithy quickly set down his work and wiped his hands, bowing his head in greeting.

Her husband released her hand and Esme lingered a few steps behind, grateful to slip into the background away from the smell of hot metal and thick smoke. From beneath the smithy's bench, a familiar cat emerged, a scrappy thing with a crooked ear and a bold spirit.

The cat hesitated, then darted toward her with a friendly meow—only to freeze mid-step, hackles rising as her wide eyes darted to Torrance. Recognizing him, the cat slunk back, tail low, the memory of past cruelties clear in her retreat.

Esme's heart twisted. The poor creature remembered.

Without thinking, Esme knelt and stretched her hand toward the cat, a small, coaxing smile on her lips. But her foot caught a loose stone. She stumbled, reaching out instinctively to stop herself from falling, her palm landed against a piece of hot iron. The pain was immediate, searing up her arm. She gasped and snatched her hand back, falling to one knee.

Torrance turned at the sound, his expression...

Esme thought she had caught concern in his eyes or perhaps it was what she wished to see, but it was annoyance she actually saw.

He strode toward her, his voice sharp and strong, carrying out across the village. "You clumsy fool."

He caught her elbow to lift her, his grip firm, though his touch was not rough enough to bruise. His gaze went to her hand, now red and already beginning to blister. Something flickered briefly in his eyes.

Concern?

But it vanished too quickly for Esme to be sure.

With a cold command, he raised his voice again. "Fetch the healer to the keep. NOW!"

A young boy bolted away at the order.

Esme lowered her head, her injured hand cradled against her chest, willing the tears back.

The next thing she knew she was swept off her feet and into his powerful arms. She stared at him, shocked, her mouth hanging open.

"Not a word, wife. Not a word," he warned and marched through the village with her cradled in his arms.

CHAPTER 3

By the time they reached the keep, Esme's hand throbbed with every heartbeat. She expected Torrance to leave her at the door, to pass her off to a servant without a second glance. Instead, he carried her to a table by the hearth and sat her down on a bench. Then he slipped her cloak off her shoulders and tossed it on a nearby table.

"Let me see your hand," he demanded, holding out his hand.

Esme knew better than to deny him, so she offered her hand to him.

He cradled it gently in his and cringed, seeing the blister. "You need to be more careful."

She stared at him. He sounded as if he cared that she had suffered an injury.

"I am here, my lord," the healer, called out, breathless and pale, as she hurried toward him.

"It is nothing more than a careless burn, Brenna," Esme said, not wishing to worry the healer, Torrance always threatening her if she should fail to heal.

"Careless, aye, but a burn nonetheless," Torrance said with a sharp sneer at his wife.

Brenna clutched the handle of her healing basket tightly as she dropped into a quick bow before Torrance. Then she placed the basket on the table.

"See to her hand. If it leaves a scar, you will answer for it."

Esme flinched, at the threat that was inevitable, but when she dared a glance at him, she found him watching the healer's every move with a fierceness that, for once, did not seem born of anger.

It was something else entirely. What it was she didn't know since the various look in his eyes today confused her. One moment he appeared to show concern, another annoyance, and another she did not understand at all. Her husband had returned to her a complex man and she wondered over the change in him.

Torrance stood over them, arms crossed, his gaze intense as the woman carefully examined Esme's hand.

"She will heal, my lord," Brenna said in a low, respectful voice. "There may be some scarring, but if tended well, it will be minimal."

Torrance's jaw tightened. He said nothing at first, his silence weighing on the room. Then he spoke, his warning clear. "See that she does well."

He lingered, something Esme hadn't expected, and his gaze turned frequently to her cradled hand, then to her face. She was grateful when Brack entered the Great Hall and called out to him.

"My lord, you are needed." Brack's eyes darted to Brenna. "People wait at your cottage."

Torrance turned, annoyed. "They will wait until she finishes with my wife."

"Aye, my lord, I just wanted Brenna to know she is to go

there as soon as she is done here," Brack said with a lingering glance on Brenna.

"I will see to it, Brack," she said.

Esme thought she caught a touch of a smile to Brenna's lips, but she dismissed it since she was seeing things with Torrance that were out of place as well.

Without another word, Torrance walked to the door and Brack followed.

The tension in the room eased the moment Torrance was gone.

"I appreciate your help, Brenna," Esme said, seeing the tremble leave the healer's slim hands.

She felt sorry for Brenna. She had been sent to Clan Glencairn, against her will, after her clan lost a battle to Torrance and was forced to be the clan's healer. She was pretty with soft blonde hair. She had a gentle touch, a soft voice, and cautious brown eyes. And Esme thought her to be a few years older than Torrance.

"I am here to help you, my lady, whenever you need me," Brenna said, her voice as gentle as usual.

Brenna had been there for her numerous times, sneaking behind Torrance's back to tend to the few bruises he had left on Esme after a fit of anger, and after denying her request to see the healer. It was why Esme was surprised when he summoned Brenna right away when he had denied her request for the healer many other times.

Brenna worked carefully, applying a thick coating of honey to heal the wound and help ease the pain.

Esme winced but said nothing, her mind on something else entirely and wondering if she should take a chance and speak with Brenna about it.

The healer's hands paused. "What troubles you, my lady?"

Esme managed a small, tight smile. "You are perceptive."

"Most healers need to be since many who seek our help find it difficult to tell us what truly troubles them. And we cannot help anyone if we do not know what really wounds them."

"It is nothing" Esme said, recalling her husband's threats if she breathed a word to anyone about it.

"I understand, but if you get a chance to visit me at my cottage, then perhaps we can find a solution to the problem without going into too much detail."

Her suggestion sounded promising, but the consequence of her husband discovering her betrayal was enough to hold her tongue.

"That is kind of you, but truly, it is nothing," she lied.

"As you say, my lady," Brenna said, sympathy deepening the lines around her eyes. She did not press further, only finished bandaging Esme's hand with deft, gentle movements.

Esme wished she had someone to confide in. Someone she could trust. Someone who could help with her problem.

"There," Brenna said, tying the bandage off neatly. "You'll need to keep it clean and dry. I'll leave a small crock of honey you can use to reapply when necessary."

"Thank you. I appreciate it," Esme said, and remained seated after the healer left.

The room felt larger in Torrance's absence, and much warmer too. His demanding presence overpowered, and his cruel nature was cold and calculating.

She flexed her fingers carefully, feeling the throb deep in her palm. A small wound, compared to others she carried... invisible wounds.

She turned around on the bench and stretched her legs out toward the hearth and let herself, for the first time since Torrance's return, simply sit still and breathe.

For a moment, she allowed herself to remember a time when she had dreamed of something different. A time when she had believed she could be happy here. Unfortunately, dreams often did not prove true.

* * *

"THERE IS TALK," Brack said once they stepped outside the keep. "Your contact with the northern clans worries those who have pledged their allegiance to you. They believe you intend to conquer them, not befriend them. They are concerned over your intentions."

"They worry I will be more generous to the Northern clans than to them. Greed is their major concern," Torrance said with disgust. "With Callan's death, his tribe is rudderless. There is no one to steer them, leaving them vulnerable, ripe for attack."

Brack smiled. "Hakon. You left him unharmed for just such a purpose and offered to get him a wife so he would side with you."

"Hakon is the type of man who sides with no one but if I can make him beholden to me then I can control him."

"You think a wife is sufficient to do that?"

Torrance shook his head. "It's a start. A trade deal will follow and the wealth he earns from that will settle it. In the meantime, I will make sure other clans pledge their allegiance to me and grow in strength so we can protect ourselves from the north, should Hakon gets any foolish ideas, and grow in influence and power."

"Then you better not delay any further in planting your seed in your wife and have her deliver you heir after heir, sons and daughters. Sons to keep the clan strong and daughters to wed to those who will benefit the clan," Brack advised.

Torrance scowled. "I do not need you to remind me."

"Obviously you do when your warriors whisper about their leader who fails to bed his wife on the night of his return."

"Who dares to—"

Brack didn't let him finish. "Men who have no doubts as to the strength and courage of their leader."

"Speak to me no more about it," Torrance said, his face twisting in an angry sneer.

"Aye, my lord," Brack said, wisely saying no more.

"Tell me there are many grievances for me to hear tomorrow."

"Aye. I have made it known that you expect a large turnout."

"Spread the word that there will be ale and food for those who speak," Torrance said.

Brack scrunched his brow. "You reward them for doing their duty?"

Torrance half-turned. "I look for lies and truths. Now go and do as I say."

"Aye, my lord," Brack said and hurried off.

Torrance remained where he was, on the top step of the keep, looking out over the village below. It was peaceful. A dog barked playfully with a laughing bairn. A mother's voice called out with great care for her daughter. Life resumed its rhythm around him, as if nothing had changed upon his return.

However, he knew better.

His boots struck a slow rhythm as he descended the stairs and walked along the worn path that circled the stronghold. He had much on his mind, decisions that needed to be made, changes that needed implementation, but mostly a future that had two paths and he wasn't sure which path to travel.

His heavy thoughts caused him to pause in his tracks.

A servant passed nearby, offered a quick bow, and hurried

on. The lad didn't speak… few did unless summoned to do so. He preferred it that way. Words held too much danger.

His gaze shifted to the keep, its silhouette sharp against the gray sky. Decisions couldn't be made quickly, there was too much at stake, too many lives that could be shattered. Time was needed but he didn't have much of that either, so he had no business wasting it.

He resumed his path, steps slow but steady, each one a measured effort to keep thoughts locked tight within him. As he neared the side of the keep, the scents changed, roasted meat, onions, fresh bread, kitchen smells thick in the chilly air.

He pressed on, his head lowered as his thoughts remained chaotic.

Cold water suddenly hit his boots with a heavy slap, soaking the leather and spattering his cloak. He stopped abruptly.

At the kitchen door stood a tall lass, a bucket still in hand, her wild red hair escaping a poor excuse for a braid. Her green eyes narrowed when she realized whom she'd just doused.

"You should watch where you walk, my lord," she said boldly, lifting her chin, her voice laced with a Highland burr as sharp as the chill in the air.

Before Torrance could speak, Brack appeared from around the corner.

"You reckless fool, Una!" Brack barked, storming toward her. "How dare you speak to Lord Torrance that way."

"It doesn't change the fact that I threw water out the door, and he walked right into it," Una said, unflinching.

Brack's hand clenched. "You will suffer for this."

Torrance raised his own hand to halt him. His expression never shifted. He remained calm, but there was a flare in his eyes, not anger… calculation.

He studied the lass in silence.

Una held her ground, shoulders squared. There was fire in her, the kind born of loss and stubborn pride. "I may be a prisoner of a lost battle, but I'm no broken woman."

"Not yet," Brack threatened. "It's two days in the stocks for you."

"Nay!" Torrance ordered sharply. "Her punishment will wait."

Brack looked about to argue.

"It will wait," Torrance said with a slight nod to Brack. Then he turned, the wet squelch of his boots following along with him.

Brack gave Una a last scowl and stalked after him, muttering curses under his breath.

Una stood a moment longer, bucket dangling from her hand, watching the two men enter the keep and thinking that waiting to learn her punishment might be worse than the stocks.

They walked in silence, entered the keep, and headed to the narrow corridor that led to the solar. Brack kept pace just behind Torrance.

When they reached the wooden door, Torrance paused, his hand resting on the iron handle.

"Una… tell me about her," he said without turning.

Brack stiffened. "Don't you remember?"

"Am I to recall every prisoner we keep?" Torrance said tersely as he entered his solar, whipped off his cloak to toss on a chest, and went to the table to fill a tankard with ale. He nodded for Brack to join him in a drink.

Brack was only too glad to fill a tankard as he spoke. "She's been here a few moon cycles now. Stubborn as a mule. She was tending to the wounded when we took Crosswell village. Could've run, but she didn't."

"And yet she speaks as if she regrets that choice."

Brack gave a humorless grunt. "She regrets everything. Hasn't stopped reminding us she wants to leave since the day she was brought here."

Torrance finished a swallow of ale before saying, "If her tongue grows tiresome, I'll cut it out myself."

Brack didn't laugh. He knew better than to assume jest where there was none.

"She was a healer's apprentice," Brack said. "Brenna says she knows her way with wounds and roots. But she was put in the kitchen to work, scrubbing and cleaning, since she can't be trusted to use such knowledge against us. She's no fool. She watches everything. Have you decided her punishment?"

"Not yet and I am not in a hurry to do so."

Brack's eyes suddenly went wide. "I know what we can do with her."

"Tell me," Torrance said.

Brack grinned as if proud of his solution. "Give her as a bride to Hakon."

Torrance tilted his head in thought. "I will consider it. Now walk with me. There is something you should hear."

Brack followed him into the Great Hall.

Servants bowed their heads as he passed through, and Esme hurried to her feet.

Torrance stopped at the table where his wife stood on the opposite side. "How is your hand? And I will have the truth, wife."

"It stings," she said.

"A reminder and punishment of your clumsiness," Torrance said.

"Aye, my lord," Esme said out of habit.

Torrance raised his voice for all to hear. "It is time you did your duty and give me an heir. You will remain in my bed each night until you do."

Esme's legs turned weak, but she managed to remain standing until Torrance walked out the door with Brack, then she collapsed onto the bench. She rested her elbows on the table and dropped her face in her hands.

How would she ever survive night after night in her husband's bed?

CHAPTER 4

Esme barely touched her food at supper, her thoughts on the night ahead. Would she fail again and suffer a tongue lashing or worse would he raise his hand to her? Her stomach roiled at the frightening possibilities.

"You don't eat," her husband said, though sounded more like he accused.

"I'm no longer hungry, my lord," she said, hoping he wouldn't insist. She couldn't bear to put a morsel of food in her mouth for fear her stomach would rebel.

"Then go to my bedchamber. I will be there shortly," he ordered and turned away from her.

She did as he said, her legs growing heavier with each step she took. The weight of what lay ahead of her was almost too much to bear and by the time she reached her husband's bedchamber she feared she couldn't take another step.

Memories, though more like nightmares, flooded her thoughts when she entered the room. Everything appeared overly large to her, the bed, the chests that sat against two walls, the single chair near the hearth, and... she shivered.

The shackles in the basket by the bed that her husband constantly threatened to use on her but hadn't so far. Would that change tonight?

Not if she did her best to please him.

She hurried to ready herself for him, donning her garments as fast as she could and slipping on her nightdress, Gwen had brought to the room and left on the bed. Then she used the footstool to climb into bed. It was too high off the floor for her to get in it any other way. She positioned herself in the center of the large bed, then pulled up her nightdress just below her hips and spread her legs. He would be expecting her to be like that, ready for him to have his way with her, and she prayed this time all would go well.

She tried to relax but her heart was beating so fast that she feared it trembled the bed and her body was so tense, she worried a bone would break when he touched her. She closed her eyes and ordered herself to calm down. Soon the warmth of the room and her worries took their toll and sleep fluttered her eyes.

She dozed in a light sleep until she heard her husband's heavy footfalls on the stone stairs. Her eyes sprang wide open, and her heart pounded in her chest. Then the door opened, and he walked in.

He came to a stop at the bottom of the bed and stared at her.

Had she done something wrong? Was her nightdress not up far enough or up too far? Should she apologize but for what?

"Go to sleep," he ordered curtly. "I have no desire for you tonight, though you will remain in my bed."

Esme was stunned but not relieved. Remaining in his bed meant that he could desire her at any time. What if he woke her during the night or demanded she submit to him in the morning? The thought of not knowing when his desire would strike made her more anxious than ever.

She pushed her nightdress down and slipped beneath the wool blanket, moving herself close to the edge of the bed, hoping to keep her distance from him. She was about to turn away from him when she thought better of it. It would be wiser of her to keep an eye on him in case he changed his mind. She watched as he rid himself of his plaid, but left his shirt on, then he went to the hearth and stood in front of it, staring down at the flames. He had the finest features she had ever seen on a man and his body more toned with muscles than most other men. There was no denying why women found him desirable. But it was his cruel nature that made it impossible to care for him. She had tried, hoping her kindness would conquer his cruelty, but it seemed to feed it. He took great pleasure in treating her badly, an entertainment of sort to him, and she wondered what would happen once he grew bored with her. What then would be her fate?

A yawn escaped her, and she turned on her side away from him only too glad to let sleep claim her and be free of her worrisome thoughts for a while.

Torrance dropped in the chair in front of the fire, worn out from the day. It went easier than he expected, especially with the plan having been made in such haste. In time, he felt decisions would be easy to come by and once he found what he was looking for, the matter could be settled and hopefully benefit all.

Though one problem haunted him. He turned and looked at the bed. What would he do with her? It was a question that troubled him, and he worried she would present the biggest problem to his plan.

Time.

He would give it time. He stretched himself out of the chair and walked over to the bed. His wife hugged the far edge of it and that was fine with him. She was better off there. He didn't want her anywhere near him.

He got into bed and kept to his side, grateful for the large bed and closed his eyes prepared to be gone from the bed before his wife woke in the morning. The thought remained utmost in his mind as he fell asleep.

* * *

A SWEET SCENT tickled his nose as Torrance woke, and he felt a pleasant warmth cradled against him. His arm closed around it drawing it closer to him and he ran his hand along it, enjoying the curving shape and soft feel—his eyes shot open.

His wife was cuddled against him, and she was awake, her eyes wide with shock and… fear.

He glared at her. "Go to your bedchamber and get dressed. Now!"

Esme scrambled out of bed, missing the footstool and falling hard on her bottom.

Torrance leaned over the bed and continued to glare at her. "You are the clumsiest woman I have ever known."

"Aye, my lord," Esme said and hurried to her feet with a wince and rushed to the door.

"Did you hurt yourself?" he yelled.

She didn't stop. She yanked open the door and as she flew out of the room, she called out, "Nay, my lord." And she wondered why he bothered to ask when he didn't care a bit for her.

"Meet me in the Great Hall," he yelled.

She raised her voice once again before reaching the stairs. "Aye, my lord."

Once in her bedchamber, she took a much-needed breath. She was still stunned that she woke to find herself cuddled against her husband, his arm around her, and his hand exploring along her back and down over her backside. What shocked her even more was that as she woke, before her eyes opened, she felt a strange pleasure she wished to linger in. Only for it to turn to fear, when she discovered her husband was the cause of it.

How had she felt pleasure in his arms? She shuddered at the terrible thought. Never. Not ever could she enjoy the touch of such a cruel man. But she had and it upset her.

She was grateful when Gwen arrived and helped her dress and plait her hair. She barely said a word to Gwen, and Esme guessed at what Gwen assumed and that upset her. She would spread the news that his lordship had done his duty last night and time would tell if his seed had taken root.

But no seed could root if it hadn't been planted.

However, there was tonight and all the nights to follow. It would be so much easier if they coupled, and she got with child. Then he would leave her alone. A blessing for sure. After waking in his arms this morning, she believed there was a good chance that that might happen soon.

Once finished, Esme made her way to the Great Hall to find her husband already sitting at the dais, enjoying the morning meal.

"You took long enough," Torrance snapped, then returned to his conversation with Brack who was sitting next to him.

She sat and ate, not much, but enough that her husband wouldn't complain, though he wouldn't know if she did or didn't since he paid her little attention.

Tables were soon being cleared away as the few warriors who had taken their meal in the Great Hall departed. Surprisingly, the long wooden tables were once again set with food and drink.

Esme turned to her husband and quickly drew back, surprised that his face lingered so close to hers.

"You will remain by my side while clan members voice their grievances," he ordered.

Esme nodded. "As you say, my lord."

The Great Hall soon brimmed with murmurs and the occasional cough as clan members filtered in, uncertain what to expect. It had been some time since Lord Torrance, feared for his unforgiving judgments, had opened the hall for grievances. Curious glances passed between the people as they eyed the long wooden tables set with bread, cheese, meats, and clay jugs of ale, an oddity in itself. But they dared not touch the food or drink unless permitted to do so.

All eyes focused on the center of the dais where Lord Torrance sat rigid, regal, and unbending. Brack stood to his side.

Esme remained seated beside him and kept her hands folded tightly in her lap, uncertain what she would witness here today, fairness or cruelty.

The first to approach was an elderly man with a limp, clutching his cap in trembling hands. "M'lord, it's me root cellar. Neil's goats broke in again. Ate half the stores I'd put by for winter."

A younger man, tall and thick-necked, stepped forward nervously. "The latch broke, my lord." He turned to the elderly man. "I've fixed the latch like promised, Angus."

Torrance leaned slightly forward. "Have your goats done this before, Neil?"

Neil hesitated. "Aye, my lord… twice. But never this bad."

Torrance's dark eyes swept from Neil to Angus. "How many roots are left?"

"Not enough to see me through winter."

Torrance rubbed his chin, giving the problem thought while the two men waited nervously to hear their fate.

Torrance looked to Neil and the man shrank back in fear. "You will reinforce the pen to keep the goats from ever wandering again, and you will replace Angus's root loss with that of your own."

"But I will not have enough to feed my family for winter," Neil complained, and realizing he objected to Lord Torrance's decision quickly tried to make amends. "Forgive me, my lord, but I have little ones to feed."

"And what is Angus to do… starve?" Torrance asked, a touch of anger in his voice.

A thin woman stepped forward and Neil hurried to wave her away.

"Let her speak," Torrance ordered.

The woman's hands knotted nervously in front of her. "I'm Mara, my lord, Neil's wife. I can make sure the food is enough to feed our family along with Angus."

Angus spoke up. "I don't eat much."

"I will see you are fed," Mara said.

Torrance looked at each of them. "Then it is settled and, Neil, if your goats wander again, I will see them made into a stew."

"I will make sure they don't wander again," Neil said, his face having paled.

"Eat and drink while we continue," Torrance offered, waving them off to the tables ladened with food and drink.

The three thanked him profusely and Mara hurried to gather her four little ones so they could feast as well.

A ripple of murmurs followed many not believing the gossip that food would be waiting in the Great Hall for those who shared their grievances. Everyone waiting to speak grew anxious, wanting to be heard before the food was gone.

The next person stepped forward, a broad woman with strong arms and a scowl that could curdle milk.

"My lord. I'm Gayla. My daughter, Innis, was betrothed to Fergus and he accepted her dowry gift, a fine woven plaid.

Now he says he'll have none of her, changed his mind he did, and he won't return the plaid."

Fergus, a lanky lad with shifty eyes, was shoved forward by his father.

"I never agreed to a full match!" Fergus stammered. "We talked. That's all."

Torrance crossed his arms on his chest. "Did you accept the plaid?"

Fergus looked to the ground.

Gayla's voice thundered. "He wore it!"

"Return the plaid or marry the lass," Torrance ordered.

Innes, her voice as thunderous as her mum's pushed through the crowd. "I won't have him. He's a liar. I want my plaid back to give to a deserving man."

Fergus kept his focus on the ground.

"You'll give it back, Fergus," Torrance ordered.

Fergus raised his head, fear in his eyes. "I don't have it."

"What did you do with it?" Innes demanded.

"Answer her," Torrance snapped when Fergus failed to speak.

Fergus jumped, the words rushing from his mouth. "I gave it to a lass I've been courting over at Clan MacVail."

"How dare you give my plaid to another lass," Innes said, fury rather than tears swirling in her eyes and her mum looking as furious as well.

"Do you want the plaid returned to you, Innes, knowing he gave it to another lass?" Torrance asked.

Innes shook her head. "Nay, my lord. I could not bear to look upon it now."

Fergus stepped back when Torrance focused on him with fiery anger in his eyes. "Liars are never to be trusted. You will spend two days in the stocks and afterwards you will do whatever chore Innes, and her mum ask of you… for the next three moon cycles."

"I have plenty that needs doing," Gayla sneered.

"Have him taken to the stocks, Brack. Gayla and Innes enjoy the food and drink."

Both women thanked Lord Torrance repeatedly before they went to the table to feast.

More grievances were aired, the food and drink replenished as it dwindled down, though the line seemed to grow longer.

Esme was impressed and surprised that her husband handled the complaints more fairly than she expected him to. None were as harsh as she thought they'd be. She was glad when only two were left. The wooden chair had grown uncomfortable, and she wished to stretch her legs with a wander around the village.

John, the smithy, was next and shoved a young lad, no more than ten years, he held by his arm, forward. "William stole some of my tools."

William trembled. "I, my lord, I did steal them, but I was trying to return them when caught."

"So, he claims," John sneered.

Torrance turned to Esme. "What would you do, wife?"

The room stilled. It was not the question itself that drew breathless silence, but that Torrance had asked her at all.

Esme stared at him just as shocked as everyone else.

"I'm waiting," Torrance snapped.

Esme pushed her unease aside and leaned forward. "Why did you steal the tools, William?"

"It's only me and my mum and some things needed fixing in the cottage. So, I took the tools, fixed what I could, and returned them the same day."

"Why didn't you ask John if you could borrow them?" Esme asked.

"I did... but he refused me."

Esme looked at John.

He shrugged. "Maybe the lad did, but I don't recall."

"I believe an apology to John for taking the tools without permission will suffice, don't you John?" Esme asked.

John caught the warning look in Torrance's eyes and quickly agreed. "Aye, my lady."

"And, William," she said, turning a soft smile on the lad. "You may borrow any tools from the keep you may need as long as you return them." She turned to her husband. "If that is permissible with you, my lord."

"It is, since William will begin working with the men who tend the keep and learn how to use the tools properly that he borrows," Torrance ordered.

"Aye, my lord, I am most grateful," William said, bobbing his head.

"Go eat," Torrance said, dismissing the lad and the smithy with a wave of his hand.

The lad hurried off to collect his mum so they could feast together.

The last person, an elderly woman with gnarled fingers shuffled forward and announced, "I've come to say my neighbor's singing is driving me mad."

Torrance blinked. "Is that so?"

"It's always sad songs. Dreadful weeping dirges. I haven't had a cheerful thought in weeks!"

Torrance looked at Esme again. "Solve this, wife."

Again, the room quieted, and Esme's stomach churned, fearful she would do wrong.

"Can she carry a tune?" Esme asked gently.

The woman cast a quick glance to another woman, reed thin, standing to the side and scowled. "Sadly, aye."

Esme realized then that both women were rail thin, and she only recalled seeing them on market day, and together, which meant they probably lived in one of the crofts away from the village. And with similar features, she wouldn't be surprised if they were sisters and came for the food.

Esme smiled softly. "Perhaps your neighbor can limit the singing to daylight hours. And include a joyful tune now and again."

"A fine solution," the woman declared with a smile.

"And perhaps on occasion, you and the woman would attend a feast here at the keep, and she could entertain us with a merry tune or two," Esme suggested, so they would at least eat well a few times within a moon cycle.

"Aye. Aye, she enjoys singing and would probably love to sing for you," the woman said, teary-eyed.

Torrance brought his fist down on the table and there was dead silence. "It is settled. Grievances are down. Now eat and enjoy."

A low cheer sounded, followed by chatter, laughter, and feasting.

Esme saw it, the slow blooming of trust, the way wary gazes softened. They weren't just being judged. They were being heard... fairly.

The question was... when had her husband turned fair?

CHAPTER 5

Esme lifted her face to the lightly falling snow, remembering how, as a child, she'd tried to catch snowflakes on her tongue. She had been young then, carefree. Those days were gone, though lately, she'd been granted a small reprieve. Torrance had departed unexpectedly three days ago having received a message shortly after the grievances had been heard. His absence, brief as it might be, had returned a measure of peace to her days.

Brack had been left in charge, though he paid her little mind. She made certain never to draw his attention just as she did a short time ago when she saw him speaking in whispers with Brenna in the Great Hall. She slipped by them unnoticed.

She didn't bother pulling up the hood of her fur-lined cloak as she made her way through the village with a particular destination in mind. Let the snow dust her hair. When she was young, she'd believed snow was fairy dust scattered across the land. A soft chuckle slipped from her lips at the memory. How lovely it would be to share such a whimsical thought with a daughter one day.

But the chuckle faded quickly. Giving Torrance a daughter would only bring hardship. Daughters could not defend themselves the way sons could. Torrance would want strong sons… warriors. Nothing less. She brushed the troubling thought aside and kept walking.

Villagers offered her smiles and respectful nods, but few dared speak with her. She didn't blame them. A single word, taken the wrong way, could bring Torrance's wrath. No one risked such things, not even for kindness.

The snow blanketing the ground lent the village an almost magical beauty. That was why she headed for the woods because there was where the magic deepened. The woods transformed beneath the snow's touch, dressed in shimmering white, quiet and untouched.

The woods welcomed her like an old friend. As she stepped beneath the trees, the quiet wrapped around her, soft and complete, broken only by the occasional whisper of snow slipping from a branch or the distant cry of a bird. The hush was comforting, a rare thing in her life… like being cradled by something far greater than herself.

She wandered a narrow trail, her gloved hand brushing over snow-laden branches, each touch leaving a trace of her passing. Icicles clung to the tips of pine boughs like delicate frozen teardrops, and here and there, animal tracks crisscrossed the snow—fox, hare, perhaps a deer. The air was crisp, each breath drawing a touch of frost across her lungs, and she closed her eyes, letting it settle through her like a soothing balm.

This was where she could breathe.

She came to a small clearing where snow lay undisturbed, a silvery-white canvas untouched by man or beast. A thick-barked tree with heavy limbs curved protectively overhead, and she stepped beneath it, tilting her head to watch the flakes filter down through the tangled branches. Here, in this stillness, she could pretend, for a heartbeat, that she was simply a woman on a wander, not a wife tied to a man she feared.

"You come here often?"

The voice startled Esme. She turned sharply to see Una step lightly between the trees, a woolen cloak clasped at her neck, her hair braided back but wind-tossed around her pale face. Unlike the others in the village, Una's gaze did not drop respectfully. It met hers, curious and calm.

"I didn't mean to frighten you," Una said, her tone light, almost teasing. "But I suppose it's easy to forget you're not alone, even out here."

Esme's shoulders eased. "It's quite all right. I just... needed some time."

Una gave a small nod and stepped into the clearing, her boots crunching softly in the snow. "It's beautiful, isn't it? Like the world decided to stop and take a breath."

Esme looked around again and smiled faintly. "Aye. That's exactly how it feels."

Una tucked her hands into her sleeves. "Sometimes I think the forest is the only place where truth can live. It's quiet here. Honest."

Esme didn't know what to say to that, so she said nothing.

"I've never liked the silence in the keep," Una went on. "It's a false silence, one full of secrets and watchers. Here, at least, no one listens but the trees."

Esme studied the young woman. There was boldness in her tone that made her nervous, but also curious.

Una seemed to catch her hesitation and shrugged. "I'm a prisoner, same as you. Some chains are just better hidden than others."

Esme's eyes widened slightly, but Una only offered a faint, tired smile. "One day I hope to be free. Until then, I take what moments I sneak—like this."

"You're not afraid to say such things?" Esme asked, unsure whether to be shocked or impressed.

"I'm afraid of many things," Una admitted. "But not of truth. And neither should you be. You should speak your mind more."

Esme sighed softly. "It is easy to say when you're not bound to a man like Torrance."

Una gave a low laugh. "I'm bound to your husband's rules, but I won't let my voice be silenced."

"You are braver than I am," Esme admitted.

"You have more courage than you think. You just need to embrace it," Una said then leaned in slightly and lowered her voice. "There's talk Lord Torrance is seeking another wife."

The words hit Esme like a stone to the chest. "What?"

"I don't say it to be cruel," Una said quickly. "Only to warn you. If you want something different, if you don't want to be replaced, you'd best find the courage to do something about it."

Esme stared at her, words tangled in her throat, when a voice cut through the stillness like a whipcrack.

"ESME!"

Torrance.

He stepped into the clearing like a storm, eyes blazing, jaw clenched. "What in God's name are you doing out here alone?" His gaze slid to Una. "Leave us."

Una held her ground for a heartbeat, then bowed her head, and slipped away without another word.

Torrance turned his fury on Esme. "Do you have any idea what could have happened to you? I couldn't find you when I arrived home. You vanished without telling anyone."

"I only walked to the woods as I have done occassionally," she said quietly.

He took a threatening step towards her. "You are not to walk in the woods alone. Not ever. Do you understand me?"

She nodded, too stunned to speak, her brief escape already crumbling, then she thought about what Una had said to her about courage, and she surprised herself and asked, "Why?"

He scrunched his brow as if he didn't understand her question.

"Why can I never walk in the woods alone? You never minded before now," she said to make herself clear.

He took another step towards her. "Because I command it."

She stayed as she was, though her legs weakened some, but her resolve held firm. "Am I in danger? Is that why you command it?"

His green eyes continued to blaze. "You dare question me?"

"I only wish to understand, my lord."

"You don't need to understand," he said, stepping closer. "You only need to obey me, wife, a duty you seem to be failing."

Esme's resolve melted with the way he towered over her like a bird of prey who could devour her with one bite. She took a step back, hitting the thick tree trunk. She went to move but Torrance was quicker. He stepped closer, trapping her against it with his body while he rested one hand against the thick bark.

Instinct and fear had her offer an apology. "Forgive me, my lord. I will do better."

"Is that a promise, wife?"

She kept her head down, not wanting to meet his eyes that surely raged with anger. "Aye, my lord."

"Look at me when you answer me," he snapped.

She raised her head slowly, fearful of seeing the fury in his eyes and of him seeing the fear in hers and extended an apology as she did. "Aye, my lord, it is a promise."

Esme eyes held his, not sure of what she saw in them, though she thought the bold green color softened.

"What am I to do with you, Esme?' he asked quietly.

She didn't know how to respond to him, or what he expected of her. She said what she thought he would want to hear, though it slipped out as a question. "Whatever you wish, my lord?" His response shocked her.

"I wish to kiss you," he said, and lowered his lips to hers.

She braced herself, remembering how harsh his kisses had been and was shocked.

His lips were gently against hers as if unsure, as if only becoming familiar with her. Faintly they brushed across hers causing an intense shot of pleasure to race through her. He must have felt or sensed it since his lips turned stronger against hers and surprisingly, and disturbingly, she responded. He kissed her with strength, and not a trace of harshness, and as if he could not get enough of her.

When he pressed his body firmly against her, she felt the hardness of his manhood poking her, and she gasped.

He ripped his mouth away from hers and pounded his fist against the bark. "You are a fool!"

She felt his sharp words like a slap in the face and turned her head away from him.

Torrance stepped away from her, anger returning to his eyes. Then he reached out and grabbed her arm, forcing her to keep step with his fast strides all the way to and through the village, people trying to avoid the troubling scene, and into the keep.

Once in the Great Hall, Torrance shoved her away and ordered, "To your bedchamber until I command otherwise."

Esme was only too glad to seek refuge in her bedchamber, away from his anger and glances of pity from the servants.

As she hurried off, she heard him shout, "Ale and food in my solar, NOW!"

* * *

TORRANCE PACED in front of the table in his solar, the servants winding their way around him to set food and a jug of ale on the table. He stopped pacing as soon as the door closed behind him and filled his tankard with ale and took a generous swallow.

He slammed the tankard on the table and grumbled when he spotted the scratches on his knuckles from punching the tree in the woods. He shook his head and went to the hearth to stand in front of it and let the heat wash over him.

He had called himself a fool too late. He should have done so before he kissed her, but he couldn't resist her lips, berry red from the cold. They raised an ache in him that he couldn't ignore.

It was too soon. The time not right and it might never be. He had to stick to the plan, find out who betrayed him before he could trust anyone before it was too late. It was the only way.

He buried his annoyance in the remainder of the ale, then filled his tankard again. He was glad for the interruption when a rap sounded at the door.

Brack entered.

"Let it happen again, and you will feel my wrath," Torrance yelled after the door closed. "And I assume you are wise enough to know of what I speak."

"Forgive me, my lord," Brack said with a bob of his head. "I will see that my lady doesn't go into the woods unattended again." To avoid more admonishment, he asked, "Did your meeting go well?"

"Aye, since the defeat of Clan MacLeish other clans seek

to gain my favor, fearing they will be attacked next. And with rumors spreading about what fate awaits Chieftain Ryland… none wish to take the chance of possibly being drawn and quartered."

"Is that what his fate will be… drawn and quartered?"

Torrance shook his head. "I have yet to decide his fate." He let the issue end there for now. "A message arrived while I was at Clan MacLodder, securing its allegiance to me, an invitation from Chieftain Stuart of Clan Rennoch to attend the celebration of his son, Roland's betrothal."

"He is not one to be trusted," Brack said. "He has thoughts of gaining power of his own."

"I am aware, but it would be good to avoid another battle if possible."

"The men are ready to fight and mercenaries standby eager to fight for you again."

"Because I pay them well," Torrance scoffed.

It is a sizeable army nonetheless," Brack reminded. "And you would be wise to take more than a small group of your warriors with you when you go to Clan Rennoch."

"I thought the same myself," Torrance agreed.

"I should go with you."

Torrance shook his head. "Nay. I need you here. It could be a ploy to attack Clan Glencairn."

Brack's annoyance had him speaking bluntly. "Stuart believes he can defeat Clan Glencairn."

"Him and how many others believe such foolishness?" Torrance snapped. "Have you ever known me to be a fool?"

Brack hesitated for a moment too long.

"Speak your piece," Torrance ordered, sharply.

"When a person is close to death, as your father was, they can make foolish demands. His mind was not right near the end. I never expected you to honor his foolish demand about your half-sister Autumn—Dru as she now calls herself. I believed you would keep your word and see her in a marriage that would benefit the clan, not wed to some mercenary."

"Whether my father meant it or not, he asked for my word, and I gave it. Dru will remain wed to Knox." He waved Brack away. "Leave me. I have much to think about."

"Think on a wife for Hakon," Brack advised. "He is not a man you want to keep waiting."

"Then bring me some possibilities besides, Una. Evil women who would suit Hakon."

"All women are evil," Brack said as he headed to the door, "but I will do my best to find the evilest among them."

Torrance remained focused on the closed door. It was important he remained focused, clear-headed with all the issues he faced. He couldn't allow himself to be distracted and have the smallest detail slip past him.

So, why did Esme stand out in his mind? Why did she intrude on his every thought? In the scheme of things, she was unimportant. But he knew otherwise, and it haunted him.

CHAPTER 6

Esme paced the floor of Torrance's bedchamber. He had ordered her there shortly after she had climbed into her own bed. She had remained in her room since he had sent her there and had had her supper sent to her. She didn't mind, though after the incident in the woods she had expected to be summoned to his bedchamber, and she had waited for it. When the time grew late, and she thought he'd forgotten about her, the summons had come.

The door suddenly swung open. Her husband stood staring at her, his eyes roaming slowly over her from head to foot. She realized the fire's light behind her allowed him to see the shapely silhouette of her body beneath her night-dress. Passion flared in his eyes and her breath caught for a moment, knowing what that meant. She prayed she would not fail him this time.

"Go to sleep," he ordered with a snap of his hand.

His command puzzled her. She had become familiar recognizing desire when it flared in his eyes and having felt his hard shaft pressed against her in the woods, it confirmed it. She thought for sure this time might be different. But it was Una's warning about Torrance searching for another wife that worried her. She knew what it meant... her sudden death.

She didn't know if it was fear or foolishness that made her blurt out, "I heard you search for another wife. If you tell me what I do wrong, I can—"

"Where did you hear that?" he demanded with a flare of anger.

"Whispers amongst the servants and villagers," she said, not wishing to see Una punished for revealing such information.

He stared at her hesitant as if trying to decide on a response, then it came sharp and menacing. "Be a good wife and I will not need to search for your replacement."

There was barely anything left of her courage to hold onto, but she tried. "I will be a most dutiful wife." She swallowed down her fear. "Please, my lord, plant your seed inside me so that I may give you the heir you deserve."

He crossed his arms over his chest and lifted his chin a notch after he took steps toward her and stopped in front of her. "You have failed thus far. Why would this time be any different?"

Esme stared speechless at him.

"You have no reason for your failure, wife?" he accused when she said nothing.

She hurried to say, "I will do better."

"If you don't understand your failing, how can you ever hope to do better?"

Please. Please give me strength, she silently prayed and stepped close enough to him to stretch up and plant a kiss on his lips.

He stood stiff and unmoving, then without warning, his powerful arm whipped around her slim waist, and he yanked her up against him as his lips took command.

Though powerful and demanding, his kiss was not unpleasant, not like previous ones, harsh and cruel. It was similar to the kiss in the woods as was her response, eager, to her surprise. That it stirred something in her, a spark of desire, offered some hope that this time could be different. He deepened the kiss as if it wasn't enough, he needed more, was eager to share more. And perhaps that was what made the difference, the kiss was shared, meant to please them both, something she had never felt before now with Torrance. Then she felt it, his shaft hardened against her and poked at her as if demanding entrance. She almost sighed with relief. Unfortunately, it was a brief relief.

As fast as he had claimed her lips, he just as quickly tore his mouth off hers and shoved her away from him.

"Go to bed," he ordered with an angry growl. "NOW!" he commanded when she didn't move fast enough.

She scurried away and hurried under the blanket, bringing it up to her chin. She shook with fear but beneath it, a strange tingle raced through her body.

Something was wrong, seriously wrong. There were things different about Torrance since his return. Her husband was a cruel man, but he hadn't been as cruel since his return. His solutions to many of the grievances the villagers had brought to him proved that as well as the food and drink he had offered the people that day. Or how he spared the lad, Daniel, from a far worse punishment. And he didn't raise his voice to the servants nearly as much as he once did. And that he sought diplomacy rather than battle was another difference in him.

But easy explanations could be found for them. What she couldn't understand was why he sent her to bed when he finally…

She shook her head. She had finally done something right. She had gotten his shaft to grow hard when all the other times she had failed. His shaft had remained limp, and he would grow furious with her for failing him. So why now when she was successful in her duty had he turned her away?

* * *

TORRANCE SAT SCOWLING at the flames in the hearth. He wouldn't dare glance at the bed where his wife slept. This plan had been devised quickly, unexpectedly, and under unimaginable circumstances. It had a good chance at success, except for one thing that had failed to be settled... Esme.

Now there wasn't time to waste on it. He would work it out somehow, but it wasn't a priority. Or was it?. He needed to be careful, very careful, and he needed to stop kissing her. Though she had been the one to kiss him this time and, bloody hell, if he couldn't resist her.

He threw his head back, too forceful, giving it an unexpected whack against the back of the chair and hoped it would knock some sense into him. There had been no time to question the wisdom of the plan. The pact had been made in haste and with good intention. It was only afterwards when he had a moment to breathe, to think clearly that he understood the implications it could cause. But if it succeeded it could end the bloodshed, the endless battles, and the meaningless deaths.

Still, if it was discovered before he found what he was searching for there would be only one death... his.

* * *

THE SNOW HAD BEGUN FALLING AGAIN, soft and steady, clinging to the thatched roofs and dusting the path before Esme in a quiet hush. She pulled her cloak tighter, her breath forming faint clouds in the cold morning air as she made her way to Brenna's cottage.

Torrance was gone from their bed when she woke this morning. She wondered if he had slept there at all, but warmth and his familiar forest-rich scent still clung to his pillow proving his head had rested there. But for how long?

She kept a quick pace, glad the village still slept, save for a few early risers tending to fires and livestock. She was anxious for answers, though she wasn't even certain what questions she dared ask.

She couldn't escape the feeling that something was... off.

Her husband had returned from the battle with minor injuries but without rage, without his usual sharp-edged temper. The change was subtle, but undeniable. His tone didn't threaten as often. He'd pause a moment before speaking as if giving thought to his words. Then there was a look in his eyes she didn't quite recognize. Not to mention what happened in their bedchamber last night. Something definitely wasn't right with her husband.

She reached the healer's door and knocked lightly, brushing snow from her hood.

Brenna opened it, her braid trailing over one shoulder and her eyes turning wide. "Lady Esme."

The door was suddenly yanked out of her hand, Brack appearing behind her.

"Is something wrong, my lady?" Brack demanded.

Esme found herself speechless. How did she explain her early morning visit, but then what was Brack doing there so early?

"My hand," Esme said, thinking quickly. "But don't let me disturb your visit with the healer. I will wait until Brenna finishes with you."

"She is finished with me, my lady, and you are far more important to tend to than I am."

Esme stepped aside as Brack rushed out of the cottage without saying another word.

"Come in, my lady," Brenna offered. "The air stings this morning."

Esme stepped inside, welcoming the warmth of the cottage that wrapped around her like a gentle wool blanket. The scent of herbs and damp wool filled the air, and the hearth crackled with fresh logs.

"Please sit and I will see to your hand."

"It is doing well, nearly healed," Esme said, taking a seat at the small table. "There is something else I wish to speak with you about."

"I am at your service, anytime, my lady." Brenna said. "What can I help you with besides your wounded hand?"

"It is not about me that I seek advice."

Brenna's brow wrinkled, but she held her tongue and waited.

Esme almost lost her courage, then after a silent moment, said, "You were at the battlefield, helping the wounded."

Brenna gave a nod. "Aye. Grim work. I'll be scrubbing blood from my hands for weeks, though none of it remains."

Esme hesitated, careful in how she probed for answers. "Did you tend to Torrance's wounds?"

"He chose to see to them himself since they were minor." She paused as if she suddenly recalled something. "His concern was for his warriors. He directed me to do all I could for those in need, including the wounded MacLeish warriors."

Esme's brow furrowed. "He thought of his men and the enemy warriors as well?"

Brenna nodded. "Aye, I remember thinking it strange, since he always warned me to tend first to the warriors whose wounds once seen to would allow them to return to battle."

Esme looked toward the fire, her voice soft. "That was a bit of a change for him."

The words weren't long out of her mouth before she realized she should never have spoken them.

Brenna crouched beside the hearth, poking at the fresh logs there, encouraging them to flame. "Men change in war. They see too much. Feel too much. Or stop feeling at all."

Esme wondered if that was what happened to her husband. Had he participated in too many battles? Had his thoughts on war changed? Had it softened him some? That would be difficult to believe with how much Torrance desired power and influence. So, what had caused the change she had noticed in him?

"Have you seen a change in Lord Torrance since his return?"

Esme flinched, her breath catching. "I—I didn't say that."

"You didn't need to." Brenna rose, her movements gentle. "There have been whispers, of such an important victory easing him, though many wonder how long it will last."

Esme nodded, not trusting herself to say more but glad to learn others had spotted noticeable differences in her husband as well.

Brenna smiled. "Everyone is eager for news about a future heir."

Esme forced a smile and lied. "I'm sure it won't be long now."

Brenna was delighted to hear that, and talk turned to birthing and bairns as she examined Esme's wound.

Esme stepped out into the snow once more, the chill nipping at her cheeks. The quiet from Brenna's cottage clung to her, but her thoughts churned louder than ever. She hadn't learned as much as she hoped to from Brenna. So, she made no move to return to the keep. Instead, her steps took her in the opposite direction, through the village and past the thinning rows of cottages until she reached the older structure near the edge of the trees—the one where the women stayed.

The women Torrance kept to satisfy his warriors after a victorious battle. Knowing the willing women were there waiting to please them made the men fight harder for victory or so Torrance claimed.

However, Torrance had made it clear—more than clear—that she was never to speak with them.

But what choice did she have if she wanted to learn all she could about the battle that brought her husband home a different man?

She inhaled an encouraging breath, then knocked once and pushed the door open before nerves could catch her. Inside, warmth and the scent of stale ale clung to the air and mingled with heavily sweet scents and drying herbs. Several women occupied the large room, most sleeping, while three women sat near the hearth, two mending garments, one brushing out her long hair. They turned at her entrance, startled at first, then wary.

"Lady Esme," one said, setting her needle aside slowly and standing respectfully. She had dark hair, kohl-smudged eyes, and a voice that had likely coaxed endless favors from battle-weary men. "To what do we owe the honor?"

"I don't mean to disturb anyone. I won't stay long," Esme said, stepping inside and closing the door behind her. "I... I have a few questions."

The three women exchanged apprehensive glances.

With her heart pounding, Esme asked, "I won't ask you to betray any confidences, and I will speak of my visit to no one. I was wondering if you could tell me... after the last battle, did anything seem... unusual about Lord Torrance?"

"Unusual? How?" asked the second woman, fair-haired and younger, still running the brush through her curls.

"Was he overly quiet? Did he… speak of anything strange?"

"Overly quiet? Strange?" the third one said with a dry laugh. "He never said a word. He'd be rough with us before spilling his seed and be on his way when done. I doubt he knows any of our names or which one of us he poked."

Esme could not keep her cheeks from flushing deep red.

The dark-haired woman scrunched her brow. "Come to think of it. He was rough and sometimes cruel, when he took what he wanted. You knew when he was in the mood, and you made certain to please him. After the battle, though…" She trailed off, eyes narrowing as she remembered. "He didn't want anyone of us. He just sat at our fire one night, watching. Listening."

"And when I spoke to him," the younger woman added, "he snapped at me, telling me he was there just to hear our voices, and we were to continue to talk. It made no sense. He had never done that before that night."

"That's true," the dark-haired woman said. "It was odd, like he was trying to learn something from us. After a while he got up and without saying a word walked away."

"Something's changed in him," the young woman murmured. "We all could see it."

Esme's fingers curled into the wool of her cloak. "You're all certain about this?"

They all nodded, as if fearful of saying anymore, the fire-light casting their faces in shifting shadows.

The door slammed open, cracking against the wall.

Torrance stood in the threshold, eyes blazing, snow clinging to his shoulders. His gaze locked on Esme.

"What the bloody hell are you doing here?"

The air turned to ice.

The women scattered back, falling silent. Esme's breath caught, but she forced herself to stand tall, lifting her chin.

"I asked a question," he said, his voice low, dangerously controlled.

"I wanted to speak with them," Esme replied, heart hammering.

"I forbade you to speak with them," he snapped, stepping inside. "You defy me by coming here and speaking with them."

"Forgive me, my lord," she said with a tremble in her voice.

His jaw clenched. "What reason would you have for coming here?"

His question caught her off guard, though she should have been prepared for it. Her heart began to pound in her chest as she rushed to think of a reasonable excuse. It struck her then.

"This is better left in private, my lord," she said, lowering her glance.

Annoyance sparked in his eyes. He stepped away from the door. "Outside. Now!"

As Esme stepped outside, she heard her husband issue orders to the women.

"If you discuss a word of what was said with my wife, I will see you suffer endlessly for it. Do you understand?"

Esme heard several strong 'ayes,' more than three.

"My solar," he said and took hold of her arm.

She could not help but keep pace with him, he practically dragged her alongside him. The snow fell lightly over them as she thought of what she would say to him. She worried that her explanation might cause her more harm than good, but then it was how she would explain it to him that would matter.

They reached the keep in silence, the heavy door groaning as Torrance shoved it open. Snow dusted their cloaks, melting in cold rivulets as they stepped inside. Esme had barely crossed the threshold when Torrance hurried her through the keep past startled servants straight to his solar. He rushed her into the room, slamming the door behind them with a force that made her jump.

"What reason could there possibly be for you talking to those women?" he demanded.

She responded quickly. "It was what you said to me that made me seek out the women."

"You blame your disobedience on me?" he snapped.

"Nay. Nay, my lord," she apologized, quickly. "You pointed out that I don't understand why I fail you, so how can I rectify my failings. The women are experienced. I assumed they could help me understand what I was doing wrong."

His eyes heated with anger. "You spoke to them of intimate details?"

She shook her head rapidly. "Nay, my lord. I simply asked what I could do to please my husband as was my duty."

"Accepting me between your legs is all you need to do," he admonished.

"I have tried, my lord, but…" She lowered her head unable to look at him.

He snapped at her again. "But what?"

She raised her head and if it wasn't for the spark of concern she saw in his eyes, she probably wouldn't have had the courage to say, "You turned me away last night when finally…"

She couldn't bring herself to say the rest, worried how he would react.

"Finally, what?" he demanded. "Tell me," he ordered sharply when she failed to respond immediately.

She rushed the words out. "I felt your need against me, my lord."

The thin lines in his brow deepened as he narrowed his

eyes, then as if he understood, his eyes turned wide. Though he quickly narrowed them again.

Esme jumped when his fisted hand pounded the table so hard, she heard the wood crack.

"I will hear no more from you about it,' he ordered, his voice edged with steel. "And you are never, ever to go and speak to those women again."

Esme resorted to her usual response. "As you say, my lord."

He took a step toward her. "I mean it, Esme. Those women are clever with their words and use what they hear to their advantage. You risk more than you understand."

"They were kind," she said.

His eyes darkened. "Women like that are never kind, Esme. They use what they learn to survive, gain favor, and provide information for coins. They are not to be trusted."

"Yet you keep them here."

"Out of necessity and for now." He took another step forward, his body brushing hers. "For your safety you will speak to no one else about me—about us. Not the women, not the healer, not anyone. I will have your word on it."

She was shocked seeing the depth of concern in his eyes and her response came easily. "Aye, my lord, you have my word."

"Leave me now," he ordered, dismissing her with a wave of his hand as he turned away from her, then quickly turned back. "Do whatever wifely thing you do to keep yourself busy and cause no more trouble."

Esme nodded and left the room.

Torrance wanted to roar out his anger but instead he clenched his hands and growled low in his chest. Esme's unexpected meddling could foil the whole plan. He might have no choice but to tell her the truth. But how much of the truth could he admit to her, dare admit to her. He knew this would not be easy, but he also knew it was a risk worth taking and that was all because of Esme. Though he never expected to face the problem she had presented him with, too embarrassed to go into detail. No man wanted to admit when his manhood failed him. And while Esme couldn't bring herself to say it, she made the problem known. This dilemma was definitely going to get worse if he didn't do something about it soon.

CHAPTER 7

The snow lay thick and undisturbed in the forest, a cold, white hush blanketing the world. Flakes drifted lazily from the gray sky above, melting into the dark folds of Torrance's fur-lined cloak. His stallion moved carefully, each step muffled by the snow, the beast's breath rising in slow, heavy puffs that vanished into the chilled air.

Torrance rode alone. He wanted no eyes upon him. No questions asked. No speculations made. His hands tightened around the reins.

He had heard whispers, a name spoken by an elder with a drink-warmed tongue, a mention of an old healer who had once lived in this area of the forest. A discreet healer. One who knew more than she should but kept such knowledge to herself. She would have delivered bairns around the time of his birth. If she still lived… if she remembered…

He dared not finish the thought.

The snow stung his face, small cold kisses against skin that felt too tight, too alert. Every creak of a distant branch or low groan of wind through the trees kept his shoulders taut. He did not trust these woods. But then, he trusted little of anything these days and it was imperative that he did. He had to discover the truth. He had to know. He needed to know or all could be lost.

The path narrowed, winding through a dense copse of trees crowded in close and where shadows clung to their trunks like secrets. And then he saw it, set back from the path, a squat cottage, its thatched roof sagging beneath the weight of years and savage weather.

He dismounted his boots leaving prints in the snow as he trudged toward it. The wind moaned low as if warning him back, but nothing would stop him. Nothing.

The door was cracked, half-hanging, its wood swollen and splintered. One firm shove, and it tore off its hinges and, with a protesting creak, fell back into the cottage. He stepped on it to enter and stood glancing around.

The air was cold, still, and heavy with abandonment. The wattle and daub walls were crumbling in spots and the hearth had collapsed. No tools of healing were anywhere in sight. Just shattered crockery and pieces of what might have been chairs and a table, possibly a bed. He moved through it slowly, as if ghosts might stir at his passing.

This was no healer's home. It had not been occupied for a long time.

He let a heavy sigh escape. He couldn't say he wasn't disappointed, but he wasn't discouraged. This wasn't the place, which meant he had to look elsewhere. He hadn't expected it to be easy. It had been over twenty years since his birth. His chances of discovering the truth might be slim, but he found that secrets had a way of surfacing even many years later.

He stepped out into the snow again, glad it was a light falling snow since it would not hamper his search. He would—

A sound cut through his thoughts.

To his right, though he didn't look. He listened.

The rustle of fabric, the crunch of snow beneath boots.

His hand went to the hilt of his sword.

Another sound, behind him this time.

His stallion snorted, restless. The woods grew too still.

And then they came, three figures, fast and silent, emerging from behind the trees like shadows rising from the snow. No warning, no words, just swords raised, and the sudden storm of violence.

* * *

THE GREAT HALL doors slammed open with a thunderous crack, the wind rushing in like an angry spirit, snow flurrying in its wake. Gasps echoed as Torrance strode in, blood streaking down the side of his face, his dark cloak tattered and touched with snow. His left arm hung stiff, blood dripping from the wound above his elbow onto the wood floor.

"Fetch the healer!" his voice roared through the hall, sharp and commanding, but beneath it... a strain. A fatigue from a hard-fought battle.

Esme was on her feet before she realized she'd moved. Her heart jolted at the sight of him—bloodied, breath ragged, and yet still upright with a storm-wrought scowl on his face. She hurried to him, her hands reaching out instinctively.

"You're bleeding heavily," she breathed, eyes darting over his wounds. "Let me see."

"I said get the healer!" he barked again, though his voice faltered as Esme's hands steadied his good arm and gently eased him toward a bench near the hearth.

A guard darted off and out the door to fetch Brenna.

"You should sit," Esme said, grateful that a servant had wisely fetched a stack of cloths and a bucket of water and had set them on the table. She grabbed a cloth, pressing it gently to the cut on his head. He hissed under his breath but didn't pull away.

She worked quietly, her fingers surprisingly gentle for someone who felt nothing for him but obligation. And yet... the sight of him like this—wounded, breathless, human—made something ache in her chest.

"You're lucky," she said softly. "The head wound isn't deep." Her gaze dropped to the tear in his sleeve. "But your arm..."

"Caught a blade. A minor wound," he said through clenched teeth, steeling himself against her tender touch, her soft voice, and a look of concern in her eyes as if she truly cared what had happened to him.

She felt a strange heat rush through her. His eyes locked firmly on hers and in their depth, she thought she saw something she had never seen in her husband's eyes before now. He looked at her as if he truly cared for her, as if he actually had a heart.

"Still," she said, her voice softer now, "it must be painful."

Their eyes held for a moment longer than they should have. His expression shifted, something unspoken rising between them, uncertainty, perhaps, or—

Before either could speak, Brack stormed into the hall, face dark with fury.

"What in the devil's name were you doing in the woods alone?" he demanded. "You could have been killed!"

Torrance's gaze snapped to him, cold and sharp. "You dare question me?"

BRACK REALIZED his mistake and though he corrected himself, his voice remained etched with anger. "Nay, my lord, but I cannot protect you if you vanish without a word. There are enemies who would pay dearly to see you bleed."

"I do bleed, yet the three who dared to challenge me lie dead in the forest for the animals to feast on," Torrance said, offering no explanation for his absence.

Brack growled something under his breath, but Esme stepped between them, hands firm on Torrance's arm again.

"There is time for talk later. He needs tending right now," she said quietly but firmly. "Brenna is on her way."

"My wife is right. We will talk later," Torrance said, a clear dismissal.

Brack hesitated, jaw tight, an annoyed glance at Esme, then he turned with a muttered curse and stalked off, the echo of his boots fading down the corridor.

The fire crackled in the silence that followed. Esme quickly tended to the wound on his arm, placing a cloth around it to still any blood that flowed, then she got busy cleaning the blood off his head wound so Brenna would have a clear view of it when she arrived.

Her touch soothed and Torrance closed his eyes relishing her tenderness. He felt an ease begin to wash over him and soon he found himself free of worry and turmoil. He felt—content. How long had it been since he felt at such ease?

"You should've taken someone with you," she said, not accusingly but with concern.

He kept his eyes closed as he answered her. "This task was for me alone."

She wanted to ask what task, but he looked so content with his eyes closed that she didn't wish to disturb him any further. She did, however, reach for his hand, her fingers brushing his, and found he didn't pull away.

"Whoever they were... they meant to kill you," she said, her voice barely a whisper.

Brenna's voice rang out. "I am here, my lord."

Torrance almost yelled at her to leave, preferring his wife's hands to tend to him, but he held his tongue and let the healer work. It was better this way. He couldn't allow anything to interfere with the plan.

* * *

THE WARMTH of the fire did little to ease the ache in Torrance's arm as he stood near the lone window in his solar, watching as dusk settled over the snow-covered hills beyond. A fresh bandage circled his upper arm, Brenna's work, though it pulled as he drew the shutters on the window closed, the tapestry falling over it, keeping the cold at bay. He barely noticed the tug to his wound. His thoughts were elsewhere—dark, tangled, and unwelcome.

Brack stood near the hearth, arms crossed, eyes fixed on him like a hawk, intense. "You should have taken someone with you. You may think yourself invincible but today proves otherwise."

Torrance didn't turn. "I didn't need a guard to instruct me."

"Nay. You needed one to keep you from getting killed."

Torrance finally turned and looked at him, one brow raised, eyes hard. "They failed miserably in their pathetic attempt."

"This time." Brack stepped forward, his boots heavy on the wood floor. "But what if the next blade finds your heart? You go wandering off again without a word, and I'll be the one telling the clan their chieftain died alone in the woods like a fool."

"Some of them might welcome that," Torrance scoffed.

Brack found his response odd. He expected Torrance to threaten suffering on any who would dare speak against him. It confused him and left him speechless.

A long silence settled between them. The fire crackled behind Brack, its light flickering across the worn stone walls.

Finally, Torrance said, "There are things I must do that I cannot speak of... yet."

Brack gave a snort. "Secrets have a way of biting the man who keeps them."

"And betrayal hides in the open just as easily as in the dark," Torrance countered. He moved to the table and reached for the pitcher of ale, filling a tankard with a steady hand. "Which brings us to Chieftain Stuart."

Brack grimaced as if the name tasted sour on his tongue. "As I've warned, he has a thirst for power. He's not to be trusted."

"His son's betrothal celebration is in three days," Torrance said, then took a swallow of ale.

"And you mean to go?"

Torrance nodded slowly. "Aye, I plan to attend. It's better to stand in his hall and smile with a blade hidden than leave him wondering why I didn't come at all. Besides, I can see who attends and learn who leans his way."

"You'll go with a sizeable escort," Brack ordered.

Torrance's eyes narrowed. "Is that a command?"

"I meant no disrespect, my lord," Brack said with a bob of his head. "I have a duty to keep you safe, and I do not intend to fail you."

"I know I can always count on you, Brack."

Brack studied him for a long moment. Something wasn't right. Torrance never praised or complimented anyone... not ever. "You're not the same," he said at last. "Since you returned."

Torrance's jaw tightened. "Maybe a day or two in the stocks would have your tongue being more respectful."

His response was more like he expected from Torrance. He let it go—for now—but he would keep his gaze sharp and see if there was anything to his observation.

"I will see to the escort," Brack said. "And double the

guards around the keep until then. Whoever came at you today may not be finished."

Torrance inclined his head. "Agreed. See to it."

Brack strode to the door, pausing only once, needing to have his say. "One day, you'll trust me with whatever truth you're hiding. Just don't wait until it's too late."

The door shut behind him with a dull thud.

Torrance stood alone again, the firelight catching the small scarlet stain on the bandage around his arm. He took another swallow of ale.

Who to trust? That was the question that haunted him. He didn't know yet who the true enemy was, but he had every intention of finding out.

His gaze turned to the fire that had burned low, casting long shadows around the room and one name came unbidden.

Esme.

The thought of her weaved through his mind like smoke he couldn't grasp. He closed his eyes briefly, but that only made her image sharper… her hands pressing gently to his wound, the worry in her eyes, the warmth of her touch, and the way she'd looked at him as if she cared, had feelings for him.

He shifted restlessly, annoyed by the stirring in his loins.

He cursed under his breath and crossed the room, staring into the dying embers. He should be thinking of possible enemies hiding in plain sight, of the attack that could have ended him in a quiet snow-covered forest.

But his thoughts returned to her… always to her.

He had made his decision as soon as the plan had taken shape. He would have it no other way.

He ran his hand through his hair and let out a sharp breath. He hadn't considered her part in this nearly enough, so he believed it would be easy enough to keep his distance.

Whereas he should have considered what everyone expected of him… an heir. Which meant intimate time spent with her and appearances needed to be made to reflect that. He was sure it could be done, but he had not anticipated something shifting between them, slowly and subtly. Her gaze lingered longer on him. Her words held curiosity instead of contempt. And when she had touched him today, just a simple, careful tending, he had felt it like a blow. Just as it did when he kissed her.

He scowled at the hearth. He was letting his guard down and he couldn't let that happen.

Esme was brave in quiet ways that others overlooked. She had watched him carefully at the grievance hearing, spoken up though surprised to be asked to do so. And today, she had not hesitated to go to him. Not as a wife playing a role, but as a woman moved by something she hadn't expected.

He shouldn't be thinking of this now. There was so much more to the plan that needed to be considered and followed through on. A muscle ticked in his jaw. He could not afford distraction, desire, affection, or attachment, the most dangerous distraction of all. Especially now with secrets waiting to be revealed.

He turned from the hearth, shadows closing in around him, and thoughts of Esme growing far too dangerous. Tonight, he would take supper in his bedchamber alone and sleep alone and try to clear his head.

Torrance left his solar, shaking his head. He was already thinking how he would miss his wife sleeping beside him in bed tonight.

* * *

Esme paced in her bedchamber. She had not seen her husband since Brenna had finished tending to his wounds that she was relieved were not life threatening. That she had taken relief in that news had completely surprised her. There was a time she prayed for her husband's death, but no more. What had changed?

Torrance.

He had changed. But had he? Or was he playing one of his cruel games? Could she truly trust the shift in his ways, the show of fairness now and again? If only it could be so.

She stopped pacing and sat on the edge of her bed. She had been surprised when she received word that her husband would dine alone tonight in his bedchamber and that she was to remain in her own room for the night.

She had thought, foolish as it was, that they had shared a caring moment when she had tended to his wounds. She had felt a shift inside herself when he looked at her and his eyes seemed to intimate a caring heart. It had sent a soft tingle through her like when he had kissed her. And strangely enough, she wanted to pursue that feeling, understand it, and perhaps feel its pleasure again.

Insane.

She had to be insane to think that Torrance had changed. But she was stuck with him and if there was a chance, even a small one, that they could at least care for each other then perhaps the marriage would be tolerable or dare she hope a bit satisfying?

With hope in her heart, she stood. She had to go see him and see if there was even a small chance that her marriage could prove to be… a caring one.

Wearing nothing more than her nightdress, she slipped out of her bedchamber and made her way to his. She stood outside the door and listened. She didn't hear a sound, and she wondered if he slept, exhausted from his wounds and the day's incident.

She eased the door open slowly, not wishing to wake him

if he slept. He didn't. He stood on an angle, naked in front of the hearth. The fire's glow cast a hazy light over his muscled body and her eyes widened when she saw his hand on his hard shaft, stroking it.

She gasped and he turned, desire hot in his eyes.

Esme didn't wait. She ran to the bed, dropped down on it, pulled up her nightdress and spread her legs. "I am ready, my lord. Fill me with your seed."

CHAPTER 8

Torrance was too shocked to move, his shaft too swollen, his passion for his wife too hot, to think reasonably. He went to the bed and for a brief moment sanity returned, but then desire took charge, and he dropped down over her. He settled his shaft to nestle between her legs, poking at her wetness while his hand yanked the neck of her nightdress down, tearing it, to expose her breast, plump, the nipple ripe for tasting. And he did just that his mouth sucking on the tight bud.

Esme could barely breath, the sensations rushing through her remarkable and a bit frightening. Never had she felt such pleasure with Torrance. Never had he been so gentle yet firm with her and she found it amazing at how much she was enjoying it.

He rolled his tongue across her nipple and the moan it drew from his wife heightened his desire. He shifted his shaft, so the tip penetrated her entrance while he yanked her nightdress further down to expose her other nipple and feast on it like he had done to the other. He loved how her nipple grew taut at his taste and grew even tighter when he nipped at it with his teeth.

He got the overwhelming desire to kiss her, join their lips together, let his tongue slip into her mouth and mate. His hand replaced his mouth on her breast, squeezing it gently as his thumb grazed the nipple repeatedly. He settled his lips on hers and kissed her with a hungry need that she responded to without delay. He felt it then, how her need was as great as his, her passion as hot, her desire for him undeniable.

Esme tore her mouth off his. "Please, Torrance. Please. I need you."

Torrance.

That she begged her husband was like cold water being thrown in his face and he sprang up off her. He stood staring at her, his shaft hard and aching, his desire for her unbearable. He silently cursed himself for foolishly surrendering to what? His need or his desire for her and her alone?

With thoughts of dropping over her once again, he yelled, "Get out of my bed!"

Esme was too shocked to move.

"Are you deaf, woman?" he said, his voice as powerful as his muscles that grew taut.

She sat up, her eyes wide and settling on his protruding shaft. "But you are—"

"Angry," he growled like a beast warning his prey, "that my wife refuses to obey my orders. Now—GET OUT OF MY BED!"

Esme wisely jumped out of bed, standing on the side opposite him. "I don't understand."

"Either do I. Why am I saddled with an ignorant, disobedient wife?"

Esme stared at him bewildered. "But your shaft is ready. Why do you not want me?"

"GET OUT!" he yelled, pointing to the door. "Get out now!"

Esme rushed to the door so fast she tripped over her own feet and the floor rushed up to meet her.

She never hit it. Her husband's arm snagged her around the waist and stopped her from crashing to the floor. He spun her around as he brought her to her feet, keeping his arm around her to steady her. She was shocked for a second time when she saw concern mingle with the anger in his green eyes.

"Go now, wife, before I do something I will regret," he ordered and released her.

Esme turned and with quick, yet cautious steps, fled the room.

Torrance slammed the door shut behind her, then dropped his brow to rest against the door. His chest heaved and his manhood throbbed. He would ruin everything if he did not think wisely about this. It wasn't only his shaft that throbbed for Esme, it was his heart as well. He had feelings for her, strong feelings.

What was it his da had told him about women?

You will know when you find the woman who steals your heart, for you will do anything for her, even give your life to save hers.

He felt a punch to his gut and his anger soared thinking of Esme possibly being in danger, her life threatened. She was an innocent in all this and nothing more than chattel to her father who had carelessly given her in marriage to benefit himself.

He needed to do as planned. It was the only way. He only hoped she would agree.

* * *

Esme threw herself on her bed when she reached her bedchamber and screamed her frustration into the pillow while her fists pounded the mattress. She was a fool, ten times a fool—twenty times—a fool for thinking Torrance had changed. That something had happened to him on the battlefield that brought him home a different man.

He was playing one of his games with her, but why when he needed an heir and his manhood was stiff and finally ready to mate. Why did he refuse to couple with her? She had gotten so excited to see his shaft swollen. They could consummate their marriage, and she would have a chance to get with child. She groaned. Worse was how she responded so eagerly to his touch, his kiss. She had desired him, and he knew it. That he refused her upset and frightened her since the possible reason that he would not couple with her, get her with child, shivered her cold. Could he truly be searching for a new wife? Had he already found a woman? If she got with child, she would stand in his way. Is that why he had gotten off her so suddenly and sent her away? But why then did he have her sleep with him each night? Did he want to make it look like he was doing his duty?

Nothing made sense. Nothing at all. Unless…

She rolled on her back and scrunched her face as a sudden thought hit her. A nonsensical one, or was it? Could it be possible? She shook her head. Her sudden thought was nonsense. There was no one who could disguise himself as Torrance and get away with it.

Ryland.

She sprang up, the name exploding in her head. Ryland, Chieftain of Clan MacLeish. He and Torrance could pass for brothers they looked so much alike. There were rumors that they were half-brothers, though no one dared speak it aloud. But Ryland had suffered serious wounds in the battle he lost to Torrance. He was home healing, waiting for Torrance to decide his fate.

She wrinkled her nose as if she smelled something funny.

What if it was all a lie? What if Ryland had killed her husband and decided to take his place? But what reason would he have to do that? Besides, he would be placing himself in danger with how many enemies Torrance had made and would be only too glad to see him dead.

It was a foolish thought.

But why did Torrance avoid coupling with her when he had berated her endlessly for failing to get with child. He told her it was her fault his shaft could not grow hard. That she was not attractive enough, obedient enough, that she sparked no desire in him.

Sparks had certainly flamed his desire tonight. His manhood was swollen, ready for matting and no women had been there to entice him. So, what had sparked his passion?

She had met Ryland a few times when he visited Torrance. It had been odd seeing someone who resembled her husband so much and it was even odder that he was cordial and thoughtful. She recalled during one of his visits how her shawl had slipped off her shoulders and he snatched it up and handed it to her with a smile that sent a flutter to her heart. Torrance had quickly admonished her for being so clumsy and sent her to her bedchamber and ordered supper held from her as punishment for embarrassing him.

She later learned that Ryland had had the courage to speak up to him in her defense and it had ignited an argument for which she was further made to suffer. Two days in her bedchamber with nothing more than bread and water. She was lucky Gwen had taken pity on her and snuck food to her.

Her husband had certain traits, likes, and dislikes but she hadn't paid them mind lately. She needed to pay more attention to him to see if she could spot any differences that may suggest her idea held merit.

His kiss was certainly different. She enjoyed his kisses, to her surprise and dismay. But now, there could be a reasonable explanation for it.

It hadn't been her husband who kissed her, but Ryland.

She had to be careful. Very careful. If she were wrong, and there was a good chance she was, it could prove disastrous for her. She had to make sure, completely sure about her suspicions and even then, would it be wise of her to confront him? And what of his plans for her?

Fear trickled over her that she might be in even more danger if she was right.

She needed to take it slowly and approach her suspicions with caution. That was what she had to do to find out what was going on. Had Torrance returned home to her or had Ryland taken his place?

A question she intended to find out.

* * *

Dull gray clouds hung heavily over the village and the cold air clung to everything it touched, promising more snow the next day. Esme pulled her hood low and walked with careful steps, keeping to the edges of the path, pausing often to peer at anything that may have looked to cause her interest, or she paused briefly to speak a few idle words to those she passed. But her gaze never strayed far from the tall figure ahead.

Torrance moved with purpose, cutting through the village like a fine blade, nodding to some, ignoring others. He was a man used to being watched, obeyed, feared. Esme had once feared him too. But now... she wasn't certain who she followed.

He looked like Torrance, bore himself like Torrance, and

yet... questions from last night still haunted her. Could it be Ryland, Torrance's half-brother? The resemblance between them had always been reason for wagging tongues, too much, perhaps, to be coincidence alone. But if it was true, then why? What had become of Torrance? And why would Ryland risk taking his place?

She needed answers. Answers that only he could give.

So, she followed him, doing her best to make it seem she was doing nothing more than wandering through the village. She knew warriors kept an eye on her, her husband's orders after yesterday's attack on him. She paused behind a row of baskets outside the weaver's cottage while the woman turned to speak with a neighbor. The cold wind tugged at her cloak. A few villagers noticed her loitering and she quickly knelt, pretending to examine a tear in her hem.

She rose just in time to see Torrance stiffen, his hand drifting to the hilt of his sword.

Four figures had appeared at the far end of the path. They walked with heads bowed, robes loose, and hoods drawn deep.

Monks.

At least, that's what they appeared to be. But Esme knew this village, and monks rarely passed through. They preferred more welcoming grounds—abbeys or well-traveled towns, not a remote village ruled by a man like Torrance.

She glanced at her husband.

He stood still, studying them. And in that moment, she saw it... the subtle shift in his stance, the narrowing of his eyes.

Suspicion.

She slipped closer, standing near the side of a hut. Her breath hitched as Torrance took a step forward and raised his voice.

"You there," he called out, his voice powerful, carrying through the village. "What business have you here?"

The four halted. For a moment, all was still. Then one figure raised his head.

It was no monk's face that stared back. It was brutally scarred and grinning.

The man threw off his hood and from beneath his robe drew a sword and let out a roar.

The other three drew weapons from beneath their robes. Villagers screamed, scattering. One of the mercenaries shouted something guttural and charged straight at Torrance.

Torrance didn't hesitate, he met the rush with steel and fury, blades clashing as snow began to fall lightly.

Esme ducked instinctively, backing toward the side of a hut, heart pounding as Torrance's warriors rushed toward him with swords drawn.

One of the mercenaries turned, his glance hurrying over the area. His eyes met hers and he grinned and ran toward her, his sword raised.

She stumbled backward, calling out instinctively, "TORRANCE!"

Her feet tangled in her rush and her cloak caught on a barrel, losing her precious time to get away from him.

The sword arced toward her as she yanked her cloak, ripping it off the rain barrel.

Torrance slammed into her, knocking her clear, his sword intercepting the blow with a shower of sparks. She hit the ground hard and came up dazed just in time to see Torrance drive his blade through the attacker.

Another came from behind.

"TORRANCE!" she cried out once again.

He turned and caught the attacker's wrist, twisted, and used the man's own momentum to bring him down.

Torrance finished him with ruthless efficiency, then whirled around, scanning for more.

His warriors had seen to the other two. It was over.

Breathing hard, Torrance lowered his blade.

Esme stood frozen, her hands trembling violently.

Torrance turned to her, eyes wild, face shadowed by damp strands of hair. "Are you hurt?"

She couldn't speak, fear holding her words captive.

In two strides he was before her, his hands gripping her arms. "Esme!"

His sharp, demanding voice broke her silence. "Nay... I'm not hurt," she whispered, though her voice shook. "You—he almost—"

"But I didn't," he said roughly, and then without another word he pulled her into his arms.

She didn't resist. Her body curled instinctively into his, clinging to his warmth, to the steady beat of his heart, to his confident strength. She felt him bury his face in her hair, his grip tightening around her.

"You should not have been here," he murmured, but it wasn't anger in his voice… it was fear. Fierce and raw.

She didn't respond. She couldn't.

Because whatever name he wore—Torrance or Ryland—he had just risked his life to save hers. And he held her now, his arms tight around her, like he would never let her go.

The snow fell a bit more heavily now, settling on thatched roofs and sticking to cloaks and hair. Esme remained pressed against Torrance, her breath shallow, her heart slowly returning to its normal rhythm. She wasn't sure how long she stood there, his arms shielding her as if danger still lingered or might return with the next breath.

But then she heard the tread of rushing boots. Others were approaching, villagers returning in cautious steps, whispering, peering from behind barrels and shutters. And among them, striding with purpose and wariness, came Brack.

He came to a halt beside the nearest dead body and crouched, muttering something under his breath as he pushed the hood fully back from the dead man's face.

"Damn it," Brack spat and stood, snow dusting his dark hair. He looked at Torrance. "I know this one."

Torrance's arms slowly loosened around Esme, one falling away the other remaining around her. "From where?" he demanded.

Brack's eyes never left the corpse. "North. Clan Fenrick's territory. A mercenary by the name of Osric. He fought for coins and not much else. He hired on for missions most wouldn't and connected with those foolish enough to do the same." He shook his head. "Not many would be foolish enough to enter your village, attempt to kill you, and expect to live."

"Or thought themselves skilled enough to do so," Torrance said. "But it wasn't me who drew that one's attention… it was my wife."

A chill rippled down Esme's spine that had nothing to do with the weather.

Brack's eyes shifted to her, his brow knitting with concern. "She was the target?"

"Why else would he have raised a sword to her?" Torrance asked, trying to make sense of it.

Brack glanced down at the dead man. "So, the others were a deterrent while he was here to see to a specific task. Why though? She is of no importance."

Esme saw the pull at her husband's brow that narrowed his eyes as he looked upon Brack, though Brack didn't see it, his focus on the dead man. Something he said had disturbed Torrance and gave him a moment of pause but only a moment.

"See the bodies burned before the day is out," Torrance ordered. "And put eyes on every road in and out of here. Change the sentinels more frequently so they remain sharp and don't miss anything. They failed, so they will try again."

"Aye, my lord," Brack said and moved away, barking orders to those still lingering nearby.

Torrance's arm tightened around his wife's waist. "You will go nowhere without my permission, and my warriors will keep watch over you."

"It makes no sense. I am of no importance," she said, repeating what Brack had uttered.

A storm suddenly swirled in his green eyes. "You are important—" He paused abruptly. "You are my wife and that is important enough."

Spoken like Torrance, his only consideration, himself. And yet... Torrance would have never slipped his arm around her and offer her any comfort. He would berate her for being a coward. Yet, his arm still lingered at her waist as though reluctant to let her go. So, whose arm held her?

He pulled her hood up on her head to ward off the falling snow, a caring gesture. One not familiar to Torrance.

More and more she wondered and questioned who the man was who returned to her from the battlefield.

CHAPTER 9

The warmth of the hearth soothed Esme the next—thankfully uneventful— day as she sat curled in one of the two high-backed chairs that faced the flames. Her solar was her sanctuary, a modest chamber tucked away from prying eyes. She kept it as she liked it, cluttered with quiet comforts. Baskets brimmed with embroidery, some finished, some forever waiting, tucked beside the chairs or resting on the low wooden table that held her stitching tools and usually a tankard of hot cider and, like now in the evening, wine.

Here, the world fell away. No guards. No curious glances. No harsh voice demanding obedience. Only the soft pop of wood splitting in the hearth and the occasional creak of stone settling into silence.

She cherished the solitude.

Especially now, with Torrance—or the man claiming to be Torrance—keeping his distance from her. Since the moment in his bedchamber, when he ordered her to leave, he had not sought her out nor had he summoned her to his bedchamber. There was some comfort in the space he placed between them and worry as well, depending on whether he was Torrance or Ryland.

And tonight, the suspicion gnawed sharper. At supper, he had turned his head away with a scrunched nose from the fish stew. Fish stew. The very dish he once demanded thrice in a week. She'd seen him grin over it like a child offered honeyed oatcakes. And now? He barely tolerated the smell, let alone touched his spoon to it.

That was not Torrance.

A sudden push of the door startled her, and she shot up from her chair, one hand pressing to her chest.

He filled the doorway like a storm rolling in from the hills… tall, brooding, intimidating.

"We leave tomorrow," he said without preamble, stepping into the room. "Chieftain Stuart's eldest son is betrothed, and we're expected to attend the celebration. You'll dress accordingly and keep your tongue well-mannered."

His boots thudded lightly on the rug she'd woven herself, and her breath caught. Torrance had never once stepped foot into her solar. Never.

He dropped into the chair beside hers with a grunt, his limbs folding heavily like they no longer had the strength to carry him. His head leaned back, and in the flickering firelight she saw the faint lines of wear around his eyes.

"You look weary," she said, unsure why she whispered it as she dropped down on her chair.

He yawned, wide. "I haven't sleep well."

She took advantage of the moment and asked, cautiously, "Are you not feeling well? You didn't touch the fish stew."

His eyes stayed closed, his voice sluggish. "Smelled off to me."

"But it was—" she stopped herself. She would watch and see if he continued to refuse the fish stew. Another piece that would help her confirm her suspicions.

His breathing had slowed, his hands resting loosely on the arms of the chair.

She stared at him, mouth slightly parted. He was asleep.

Torrance. In her solar. Asleep.

Not something she ever expected to see.

For a moment, all she could do was sit, frozen by the impossible quiet of the moment. She had never known him to be anything but alert, guarded, and coldly composed. And now… now he slumbered in the chair beside her, beneath the same hearth light that had warmed only her solitude.

She watched him, eyes tracing the flicker of flame across his jaw, the faint tension in his brow even in sleep. And the question returned, sharper now, more insistent.

Who are you really?

Esme sat still for a long while, the crackle of the fire the only sound daring to move between them.

He slept so deeply, so unexpectedly. The steady rise and fall of his chest, the slight parting of his lips, the faint furrow in his brow, none of it spoke of the Torrance she had known. That man never let his guard down. Not for an instant. Not with anyone.

A thought came to her. Should she do it? Was it wise of her? It could help her determine her suspicions, secure a piece of the puzzle.

Carefully, silently, and apprehensively she rose from her chair.

Her bare feet barely whispered across the carpet as she crept toward him. Each step measured, her breath shallow. She felt foolish like a child sneaking toward a sleeping wolf, but curiosity pressed her forward. This might be the only chance she had to truly see him… see if there was a difference.

She crouched slightly beside the chair, her gaze sweeping over his face.

He looked like Torrance. The same chiseled jaw, the sharp cheekbones, the strong, defined mouth that had once sneered when he'd said, "'a wife is a burden no man should shoulder.'" His dark auburn hair curled slightly at the edges, just as she remembered. But...

Her eyes narrowed and she looked closer.

There. Just beneath his right eye, a faint line, not more than a whisper of a scar, nearly invisible in the firelight.

She had never noticed it before.

Torrance had once boasted about the day he'd bloodied Ryland's face when they were young. Left a mark to remember me by, he'd told her, proud of it.

Could that be it?

Her gaze drifted lower, taking in the smoothness of his skin. He looked younger somehow. Still striking, but with fewer lines than she recalled. Less wear. Less... cruelty.

And she realized something else. She had never been this close to him before, not like this when he slept. Their few kisses had been cold, forced, his mouth harsh against hers. She had kept her eyes tightly shut, counting heartbeats until it ended, and wishing she could rush away as soon as it did. Not so his kisses of late.

But now... now she looked.

And the more she looked, the more she wondered—

His eyes snapped open.

She gasped.

Before she could retreat, his hand shot up, curling behind her neck. His grip was firm but not cruel, and in the space of a breath, he pulled her down, his face lifting to meet hers.

Their lips met... he made sure of it.

The kiss was nothing like before, nothing like the frigid, punishing pecks she had endured. His lips moved against hers with purpose, with something raw and sudden. Heat surged up her spine, her hands braced against the arm of the chair, her breath caught between disbelief and something far more dangerous.

She realized once again how much she enjoyed the way he kissed her.

It was pleasurable, not harsh or cruel, and tempting as if he wanted her to enjoy it, find pleasure in it. And she did.

He pulled her into his lap, his hand settling at her backside and tugging her close as he continued to kiss her. His lips dominated hers in a playful way, urging her to join in and, again, she did.

She didn't mind his hand intimately caressing her backside. It felt good and his kiss sparked her passion, and his touch brought it to life. Never did she expect to share such pleasure, know such pleasure with her husband. If only it could always be like this, if only this was real.

His warm hand found its way beneath her garment, over her backside, then his fingers urged her legs apart to slip between them. His fingers settled in the most intimate of places and she gasped against his mouth when his finger slipped inside her. She curled closer against him, though she spread her legs a bit more.

His lips left hers to press close to her ear and whisper, "I'm going to bring you pleasure, wife."

His fingers moved like magic over her, causing the most remarkable sensations to run through her. She moaned against his neck while her hand gripped his shirt. She never knew such pleasure existed. Her mum had warned her to lie still and let her husband have his way with her, but she didn't want to be still, she wanted to be part of it.

She gasped again when he drove his fingers deeper inside her and whatever his thumb was doing to her, she did not want it to stop.

She moaned, sighed, groaned, and felt pleasure like never before until she thought she would burst and she did, crying out as ripples of overwhelming pleasure shot through her, repeatedly.

Her breath skipped, her heart thudded, and never had she felt so satisfied.

Finally, when some sanity returned, she cast a glance up at him.

His green eyes were intense, his jaw tight. "You're mine. Don't ever forget it." He closed his arms tight around her and stood, then he placed her down on her chair, walked to the door, and without turning, he said, "I sleep alone tonight."

She stared at the closed door, unsure what to make of what had just past between them. It wasn't until sensibility returned to her that she was able to give it more rational thought. There was only one possible conclusion to the intimacy they had just shared.

It hadn't been her husband who brought her pleasure.

* * *

A LIGHT SNOWFALL blanketed the hills, the white dusting soft against the green that announced winter had not officially arrived yet. The air had turned kinder for now, cold enough to carry breath on the wind but not biting. No new snow threatened, only the hush of the day as Torrance and Esme rode side by side toward Clan Rennoch.

Torrance sat tall upon his black stallion, the beast's breath puffing in rhythmic clouds. Esme rode just to his left. She handled the reins with quiet confidence, her head held high, a thick fur-lined cloak falling from her shoulders in graceful folds.

Torrance hadn't spoken much since leaving Clan Glencairn and neither had she. What could she say to him? Could she ask him... who was it who brought me such satisfying pleasure yesterday? Where is my husband? Though I rather he never returns home. Why do you play this game with me? What do you intend to do with me?

"Esme, do you not hear me?"

She shook her head, his sharp voice cutting through her musings. "I am sorry, my lord, my mind wanders."

"Let it wander no more. You need to remain alert and remain close to me when we arrive," Torrance instructed, his tone firm. "If I must step away, one of my warriors will remain at your side."

Esme looked at him alarmed. "You expect trouble?"

"I always expect trouble, so I am never left unprepared. Besides, I don't trust Stuart," he said, his voice flat as his gaze swept the distant village. "He smiles with one hand while drawing a blade with the other."

That he shared that with her was another piece that filled in the puzzle since Torrance never shared such a talk with her.

Silence fell again, broken only by the movement of horses. Torrance meant to say no more, meant to keep his thoughts his own, but he couldn't take his eyes off her.

Wind caught the strands of her blonde hair, to sweep across her cheeks kissed pink from the cold, and her eyes, more watchful lately, now held a soft curiosity as she took in the village that came into sight. And her lips... he couldn't look at her lips without thinking of last night and how satisfied he felt seeing and feeling the pleasure, he brought her. There was a beauty about her, not only in her face or her lush body, but her nature... kind, resilient, courageous.

He glanced at her. "You look lovely."

The words had fallen unbidden from his lips like a confession carried on the wind.

Her head turned toward him slowly, eyes narrowing just slightly as if trying to decide whether to accept the compliment or question his sincerity. He didn't offer clarification.

He simply looked away, his jaw tight, as if the words hadn't left his mouth at all.

Torrance silently berated himself for saying what he did. He could tell by her look that such words were unfamiliar to her, and she was puzzled by them. He should know better, yet she had touched him in a way he had never expected and if he wasn't careful, he would ruin everything.

The gates of Clan Rennoch stood open, yet there was no sign of a welcoming party.

Torrance scowled seeing no sign of Chieftain Stuart.

A lone warrior approached as they entered the village, his posture stiff. He offered only a shallow nod. "Chieftain Stuart sends his welcome. He awaits you in the Great Hall."

Torrance offered no reply, his silence more cutting than words. He urged his stallion forward, Esme following closely behind as their escort led them along the main path with six of Torrance's warriors following behind. Villagers halted their tasks to watch, some bowing, others not bothering.

The Great Hall loomed, torches blazing at its entrance, warmth and merriment spilling from within. Inside, laughter rang out, music lifted in a lively rhythm, and the scent of roasted meat, sweet bread, and spiced wine thickened the air.

They were shown not to the high table, but to a long trestle near the side wall, barely more than a place of convenience. Torrance paused before sitting, his jaw clenched as he sent a quick glance toward the six warriors who stood behind him. It was a warning to stay alert.

Torrance sat, letting his cloak drop off his shoulders. He crossed his arms and kept his eyes sharp.

Esme sat beside him, leaving her cloak to fall around her, then rested her hands in her lap, easily detecting the brewing storm within her husband.

At last, a booming voice called out across the hall, "Ah!

Torrance, you've made it. We had nearly forgotten we were expecting you!"

Chieftain Stuart stood at the far end of the high table, goblet in hand, and face flushed from drink and merriment. He lifted the cup in mocking toast before turning his attention elsewhere.

Torrance didn't respond. He didn't blink. He simply sat unmoved by music or mirth.

"Touch nothing," he said to Esme without turning to her. "Eat nothing. Drink nothing. Something stinks here, and it isn't the stew."

She nodded, though her gaze wandered nervously over the crowd. Whatever warmth she had initially first felt upon entering the Great Hall was gone now, replaced with tension that wrapped like a tight cord around the room.

Time passed. Slow and watchful.

At last, Torrance summoned one of his warriors with a quirk of his finger and nodded at his wife. "Watch her."

Then, without another word, he stood and made his way toward Stuart, easily cutting through dancers and jesters with the chill of his presence alone.

Esme remained seated, hands folded, back straight. She felt more than simply curious eyes on her but refused to meet them. She wished they could take their leave now. The music pressed at her ears. The fire was too hot. And—

"Lady Esme."

The voice was barely a whisper, yet sharp enough to pierce through the din. An old woman, her hair long and silver, her frame wrapped in dark wool, slipped onto the bench beside Esme without invite.

Esme's eyes widened, instinct cautioning her not to call attention.

"He searches," the old woman murmured. "He seeks answers long buried beneath blood and vengeance."

Esme's breath caught. "Who are you?"

"A friend of truth. Listen well, what he seeks lies two days' ride from Clan Glencairn. But he cannot go alone." The woman's eyes—one pale, the other a stormy gray—fixed on Esme's. "You must go with him if secrets are to be revealed."

Before Esme could ask more, the old woman rose and vanished into the crowd as swiftly as she'd come.

Esme sat frozen, heart hammering in her chest, her glance hurrying to find Torrance. She kept her eyes on him eager to tell him of the old woman and worried for what might be brewing here.

Torrance approached the high table with unhurried steps, his expression unreadable. The noise of the hall masked his approach well enough that Stuart was startled slightly when Torrance appeared at his side.

"You dishonor your guest," Torrance said, his voice low, clipped. "No greeting. No proper place at the table. Is that how you show your respect for one who you will claim allegiance to?"

Stuart leaned back in his chair, a smug smile curling at his lips. "I pledge allegiance to no man. It is others who will pledge allegiance to me."

Torrance leaned closer, so only Stuart could hear. "You have always been a fool, but this… this is different. There's something foul in this hall. You've made a mistake thinking I wouldn't notice."

He let his gaze sweep slowly over the revelers. His stare paused on a serving girl too stiff in her posture. A man laughing too hard at nothing. The flick of eyes from corner to corner as if waiting for a cue. And he saw that no other chieftain in the area was present. A deep, bone-honed instinct took hold, and he knew… the celebration was a mask.

He didn't bother to bid farewell. He turned and walked away.

Stuart raised his cup, keeping his smile fixed. "Leaving so soon?"

Torrance gave a small nod to one of his warriors across the room. Without hesitation, the man slipped quickly toward the door, vanishing through it like a shadow.

Torrance hurried toward his wife, the crowd seeming thicker than only moments ago. He needed to get Esme out of here quickly.

He barely took a few steps.

"You're not going anywhere, Torrance?" Stuart bellowed, his voice booming over the music.

Everything stopped—music, laughter, the clatter of cups—held in a breathless pause. Then it shattered.

From the shadows, warriors lunged, steel gleaming in the firelight. Shouts erupted, benches toppled, and the joyful feast turned into a snare. Torrance's blade was in hand before the first blow came, and he met it with savage precision.

His eyes swept the room… Esme.

She stood near the table, his warriors drawing in to shield her, but too many enemies were between them now. Too many blades. He saw the shift, the tightening of the trap, and knew, in that instant, he would reach her too late if he didn't—

He vaulted up on a table, food, bowls, and tankards flying as he kicked them out of his way. He swung his sword, striking down all who tried to stop him with swift, precise slices.

He reached her as a sword arced toward her side.

With a powerful shove, Torrance slammed Esme back against the stone wall, his arm barring her from moving, his body shielding hers as he blocked the strike with his sword and finished the warrior with one thrust.

"Stay behind me," he growled, his voice thick with fury.

She couldn't speak. Her breath was caught in her throat, her eyes wide with fear as warriors bore down on them. They would not survive this. They would die here today.

The firelight glinted off drawn blades. The hall echoed with screams, the clash of steel, the scent of blood rising like smoke—

Then the heavy doors of the Great Hall burst open.

CHAPTER 10

The heavy doors slammed against the stone walls with a thunderous crash and in poured Torrance's warriors like a raging storm. Their roars echoed off the stone walls as steel clashed and bodies slammed into each other. The hall erupted into chaos.

Torrance kept Esme pressed against the wall, his broad frame shielding her from every angle.

A warrior lunged toward them and Torrance pivoted and drove a blade into his gut before the man even raised his arm. Another came from the side, but one of Torrance's men intercepted him, the clash of swords sparking just feet away.

Esme barely breathed, her heart pounding wildly, her head pressed against the stone wall, and the sounds of battle echoing in her ears. Cries of pain, grunts of effort, the dull thud of bodies falling, all blurred together. And then, as swiftly as it had started, it ended.

Silence settled like smoke in the aftermath.

Torrance's men stood victorious, their weapons slick with blood, the few remaining enemy warriors disarmed and forced to their knees.

Only then did Torrance turn to Esme. "Are you harmed?"

"Nay," she said, shaking her head and quickly reached to take hold of his arm.

Before she could, he pulled her into his arms, tucking her tightly against his side.

"You tremble," he whispered. "Are you sure you are all right?"

"I have never been in the midst of battle before, seen so many men fall, or heard the cries of pain and death. It is quite unsettling."

"Battle is no place for a woman. You did well," he said, anger burning in his eyes for what she went through. "You will remain strong and by my side while I see to this."

Stunned that he complimented her for doing well, being strong, rather than berate her for being weak, she barely managed to say, "Aye, my lord."

Silent and with fierce anger in his eyes, Torrance led her across the hall to the high table on the dais. He helped her into a chair, then took the seat beside her, his presence commanding the room.

"Bring Stuart to me," he bellowed, his voice hard as steel.

The disgraced chieftain was dragged forward, bloodied but alive, shoulders hunched as he was forced to kneel before the dais, before Torrance.

A heavy silence fell over the Great Hall, everyone waiting, yet knowing that Stuart would be drawn and quartered today, Torrance's favorite punishment.

Torrance leaned forward, eyes narrowing. "If this had been done to you, an ambush in your hall, your wife threatened, what punishment would you demand?"

Stuart opened his mouth.

"A lie better not slip from your lips," Torrance thundered in warning.

Stuart began to tremble as he got ready to speak.

A voice cut through the silence.

"My lord," Roland, Stuart's son, stepped forward, bruised and bloody but unbowed. "Please, my lord, I beg of you to spare my father. He made a foolish and grave mistake. I swear the loyalty of Clan Rennoch to you. Let me lead, and I will prove our allegiance."

The hall fell into breathless silence once again, all eyes on Torrance, a man not known to spare his enemies, suffering was more to his liking.

Torrance remained silent. His gaze swept the crowd slowly, then lingered on Roland, before it dropped to Stuart, who still trembled where he knelt. At last, he spoke.

"Your father did not think to spare me. Why should I spare him from dying?"

A gasp rushed around the room, knowing Stuart was doomed.

"The clan will be loyal to you. You can count on us. We will serve you well," Roland said. "I pledge my word to you on it. My warriors pledge their word."

The surviving warriors nodded, agreeing with Roland.

Torrance scoffed. "You will be loyal to me whether you do or don't, since I will have a mercenary group take control of your clan."

A fearful gasp circled the room, all knowing the danger that could bring.

Roland raised his chin and kept his voice strong. "Forgive me, my lord, but that would only turn the clan against you. Would you not rather us be loyal servants than those who seek revenge?"

"You speak truthfully, unlike your father," Torrance said, though suspicion lingered in his eyes.

"I will always speak truthfully to you, my lord, for the sake of my clan and my father's life."

Torrance leaned back in his chair and turned silent once again.

Breathes were held, tears fell silently, and prayers were mumbled.

Torrance turned to Esme. "What say you, wife?"

All eyes turned on Esme.

She surprised herself, her response spilling fast from her lips. "I think there has been enough suffering, bloodshed, and death today."

Torrance leaned forward. "You are lucky I have a kind wife, Stuart, for I would have chosen to have you drawn and quartered in front of your clan along with your son and warriors. But it doesn't mean you won't suffer for daring to try to kill me and mine."

Stuart spoke up. "I am a foolish man—"

Torrance bolted to his feet and brought his fist down on the table with a hard blow. "You are an ignorant man who will pay for his stupidity and foolishness. You will be taken to your own dungeon where you will remain until I decide to release you—if ever. You," he turned to Roland, "will lead in his stead. But know this, I will leave men here. Should you falter, should your loyalty fail me, they will send word, and I will return… and you and your father will die, and your clan left to starve."

Gasps and murmurs rippled through the room that Torrance had spared Stuart, his son, and the clan.

"See to your wounded, your dead, and keep in mind what future betrayal will cost you and your clan," Torrance said. "And, Roland, you will take your father to his dungeon and see that he remains there until I say otherwise."

"Aye, my lord. He will not see freedom without your word," Roland assured him.

Torrance remained standing and silent, his hand resting briefly on the hilt of his sword, thinking that the lot of them were not to be trusted. But also thinking that Clan Rennoch might not be in this alone.

"Fresh drink for my men," Torrance called out. "And you shall have first taste, Stuart, to make sure it is not poisoned."

"The drink and food are not poisoned, my lord, that I can assure you," Roland said. "My father would never waste good food and drink."

"I'll drink," Stuart said, and his son helped him to his feet.

He drank two tankards full, his son keeping him from drinking a third and forcing him from the room, two of Torrance's warriors assisting him.

"Drink and eat," Torrance called out to his men, "while Clan Rennoch sees to their wounded and dead.

He went to Esme, leaning over her chair. "I need to speak with my men about those who will remain here. While I do, eat, if you can. We leave as soon as I am done."

She was relieved to hear that, her heart finally slowing after all the tension and uncertainty.

"Are you sure you are all right?" he asked, his jaw clenching and his gaze scanning the hall once more. "I should have seen it sooner. The moment we were led to that cursed table."

The concern in his voice and that he continued to ask how she was, had her resting her hand on his arm and giving it a gentle squeeze. "I am good, unharmed, because of you, and I am grateful."

He met her eyes then. They were intense, unreadable. "I will always protect you, Esme. Always." He ran his hand gently over her cheek. "Rest with ease. A warrior will remain by your side until I return."

He barely stepped away from her when one of his warriors took a stand to her side, his eyes steady on all around him.

A servant lass approached cautiously with fresh food and

drink, the warrior stopping her and looking over the serving board.

"It is a chamomile brew and the best of our meat and cheese," the lass said with a gentle smile. "We are grateful you stopped more blood from being shed today, my lady, and grateful for the allegiance we now have with Clan Glencairn."

"Hopefully, you will do well under Roland's leadership," Esme said as the warrior allowed her to place the board on the table.

"Roland seems more reasonable than his da. There is hope he will make a good chieftain." She bobbed her head. "Much thanks again, my lady."

"Before you go," Esme said, stopping the lass. "Do you know of an elderly woman with long silver hair and draped in dark wool that was here?"

The lass shook her head. "Nay, my lady, I saw no such person, nor do I know of one. She may have been passing through and thought to join the celebration."

"There was never a betrothal celebration for Roland, was there?" Esme asked.

The servant looked puzzled. "Nay, my lady, Roland is not betrothed. Chieftain Stuart claimed a day of celebration, that is all. It is something he does now and again."

"Thank you for your honesty," Esme said with a tender smile.

The servant lass nodded, returning the smile and hurried off at her name being called out.

Esme wondered over the elderly woman who spoke with her. Who was she? What was she doing here? And what did she know about Torrance? She would mention it to Torrance as soon as she could. In the meantime, she discovered she was hungry and ate, though there was too much there for her to eat.

It looked like she barely touched the food when she finished. So, she turned to the warrior left to protect her and held the board out to him, keeping her half-finished tankard.

"I cannot eat another bite. Please help yourself."

His surprise showed in the widening of his eyes and his hesitation to respond, as if unsure what to do.

"Your fellow warriors are stuffing their faces," she said with a chuckle. "It is only fair you eat as well. You can continue to keep watch on me while you do."

He took the board. "I am grateful, my lady."

He remained standing as he ate, his eyes ever watchful.

Esme saw that he got a tankard of ale and that actually brought a smile to the warrior's face.

A yawn escaped her, at ease now after having eaten and calm being restored. She rested her head back against the high-top chair and closed her eyes to rest.

Torrance spotted her as soon as he returned to the Great Hall. Her beauty continued to amaze him. He had watched her a couple of times as she slept, unable to sleep himself. She purred softly now and again in her sleep and would snuggle against him, not that she realized it. He liked it when she rested against him. It soothed him.

He pushed the thought from his mind and made his way through the Great Hall, cleaned quickly of the battle, to the dais. He was about to wake Esme with sharp words but stopped.

Instead, he placed his hand on her shoulder and shook her gently. "Esme, wake, we take our leave now."

She opened her eyes and stretched her shoulders back. "I fell asleep."

"Aye. It has been an exhausting day," he said.

"It has been, and I am glad to be going home," Esme said and realized her words. Never would she have thought she would ever utter those words and yet... she had. But then something had changed... her husband.

She took his hand, he offered her, and was surprised when he stopped by a table, snatched up her cloak and slipped it over her shoulders. Then he took hold of her hand again and she walked with him out of the keep to their waiting horses.

"You will ride with me," he announced when they reached his stallion.

She tilted her head in question.

"You are tired. You can rest in my arms," he said with a hint of concern.

He lifted her onto his horse, then mounted, shifting her until she rested comfortably against him.

Increasingly, she suspected her suspicions were proving true. Torrance would never be this considerate to her and she would never feel so comfortable or safe in his arms as she felt at that moment. Soon. Very soon, she would need to confront him... Ryland. And see what he was up to. For now, she would enjoy his arms and warmth.

She laid her head on his chest and the horse barely moved when she fell asleep.

* * *

ESME SAT in her bedchamber in thought. Torrance had ordered her to her own bedchamber to sleep tonight, and she understood why. He had to be exhausted after today. Upon their arrival home he had called for Brack, but to her surprise it wasn't his solar they went to talk. He walked through the village detailing to Brack what had happened at Clen Rennoch and had instructed him to increase the clan's sentinels.

Gossip spread quickly about the incident, but it was that

Torrance hadn't condemned Chieftain Stuart to a horrible death that shocked everyone the most.

For Esme, it helped to further confirm what she thought, that Ryland, for some reason, had assumed Torrance's identity.

She dropped down on her bed with a heavy sigh. She wished she had the courage to confront Ryland but there was still a small part of her that worried she could be wrong. And if she was, that could prove disastrous for her.

Battle did change some men. She had heard her da speak of it. How some of his warriors could fight no more and how some were anxious for more battles. Her da, himself, had grown battle-worn and it was one of the reasons he had agreed to the proposal that she become Torrance's wife.

She recalled his words to her when he told her the marriage arrangement had been made.

"I have fought endlessly and with courage for our clan. It is time for you to do your share, your duty, and with courage."

The only problem was that her da didn't have to battle every day whereas she had realized on her wedding day that it would be a daily battle to survive her husband. It didn't take her long to discover that no matter what she did, she would never please him. Torrance would always find fault with her and that he actually enjoyed berating her. Never once had he ever praised her or had come to her defense. Not like he did today.

She sat up, another memory of today popping into her head… the old woman.

What was it, she had said? The old woman's voice came back to her as clearly as if she was there with her in the room.

"He searches. He seeks answers long buried beneath blood and vengeance. What he seeks lies two days' ride from Clan Glencairn.

But he cannot go alone... you must go with him, if secrets are to be revealed."

Esme bounced off the bed. She had forgotten to tell Torrance about it. Without thinking over the wisdom of such a sudden decision, she hurried out of the room to her husband's bedchamber eager to tell him. But each step toward his bedchamber chipped away at her certainty.

The urgency that had driven Esme from her own chamber faltered as she neared his door, doubt slipping in like a cold draft. What was she doing? He had commanded her to remain in her bedchamber tonight, and yet here she was, disobeying him.

Foolish, she scolded herself. And yet, the old woman's voice had echoed so clearly in her head, chilling her more than the stone floor beneath her bare feet.

She stopped at the door, raised her hand, and with her knuckles hovering mid-air, her breath caught. She could still turn back. Pretend she'd never left her room and say nothing of riddles or secrets or what the old woman had warned. But what if the woman had spoken the truth?

Esme made the decision quickly before her courage took flight and rapped on the door.

"Did I not make myself clear that I did not want to be disturbed tonight?" Torrance bellowed.

Esme cringed. This was a mistake, a terrible mistake, but since she already made it, she forged ahead.

"It is I, my lord, your wife," she called out bravely.

"I ordered you to remain in your bedchamber tonight," he said, his voice raised with annoyance.

Briefly, she thought to abandon her ill-thought plan, but determination had her, answering, "I have something important to tell you."

"It had better be very important," he cautioned. "Enter."

With her heart pounding fast, she pushed the door open

and stepped into the dimly lit room. She let her eyes adjust, the flames from the hearth casting shadows around the room. Not seeing him by the hearth, her glance shifted to the bed. He lay there, the blankets bunched at his waist, his chest bare, one arm propped behind his head, and his muscles taut and gleaming gold in the firelight. His hair was tousled, but his eyes were clear, fixed on her. A strange tingle settled over her, sending a shiver through her.

"Say what you have to say then begone," he ordered sternly.

She approached the bed, stopping at the foot of it. "It happened at Clan Rennoch when you went to speak with Stuart. A woman approached me, an old woman with long silver hair and draped in dark wool. Perhaps you saw her?"

He shook his head. "Nay, I don't recall seeing such a woman."

Esme continued. "She said something strange. That you're searching for answers long buried in blood and vengeance. And that what you seek lies two days' ride from Clan Glencairn. But she said that you cannot go alone. I must go with you."

Torrance stared at her, unmoving. "And only now does this come to mind?"

"Forgive me, my lord, I forgot," she said, reverting to her usual apologetic way when speaking with him. "Everything happened so fast. It only came back to me when I was lying in bed."

Torrance sat up. "And that was all she said?"

"Aye," she said, rubbing her arms, the stone floor chilling her bare feet and sending the cold seeping through her body.

He tossed the covers back some. "Get under the blankets, you're shivering."

Esme didn't hesitate, the chill crawling deeper inside her. She got in bed, sitting up beside him.

He threw the blankets over her. "Do you think I search for something, Esme?"

If you're Ryland, you might.

She let that thought linger in her mind as she said, "I don't know, though I believe that something weighs heavily upon you since you returned from warring with Clan MacLeish."

He kept his eyes focused on her. "Battle can do that."

"Can battle change a man?"

"Aye," he said, without hesitation. "Some men carry it like a second skin. Some grow quiet. Others hungrier for blood. Some don't make it home at all... not truly."

"Did it change you?" she probed, hoping to find out more that proved it wasn't Torrance who returned home to her.

His eyes narrowed and he reached out and grabbed hold of her chin. "You tell me, wife. Have I changed?"

The way he squeezed her chin, the familiar challenge in his tone when he set her up to fail no matter how she responded to him, sent a fright through her. This was the Torrance she knew, and her response came easily.

"Nay, my lord, you are who you have always been."

"And what have I always been?"

The glint in his eyes was familiar and she couldn't believe what a fool she had been believing him other than who he was, an evil man who spun his web and captured the innocent and foolish in it so he could devour them.

"You hesitate?" he snapped.

"Nay, my lord, you have always been a good husband, a wise leader, and the bravest of warriors."

"If that is so, then why did one of my own men betray me, try to kill me, and told me that he may have failed but the next one wouldn't?"

CHAPTER 11

Torrance detangled himself from his wife, knowing how dangerous it would be for him to remain wrapped around her. The scent of her alone tempted him. A scent he had begun to grow familiar with and found far too intoxicating. There was a touch of the woods to her, pine and earth, and a flowery scent, but it was her own unique womanly scent that tempted him the most.

After hurrying to dress, he left the room before temptation won out. It was early, the keep quiet, though the kitchen fires were probably being lit. The day would start soon enough, demand on his time and decisions to be made would follow him throughout the day. He needed this time alone to clear his head, to think. He reminded himself that time was not on his side, but then his task was not an easy one to accomplish.

He swung his cloak over his shoulders and stepped outside. A light snow had fallen, coating the ground, and left a dusting on the tree branches and thatched roofs. Early snowfalls warned of a cold winter and days on end stuck in the keep. An image of Esme naked in his arms in bed was the first thing that came to mind.

Quick steps took him down the keep's stairs as he shook his head at his straying thoughts. The day was just breaking, cloudy, not a speck of the sun to be seen. The moody weather reflexed his own temperament. He was annoyed with himself for ordering her into his bed last night, but how could he leave her standing barefoot on the cold floor, shivering.

That wasn't the true reason for his annoyance. It was that he had confided in her about the attempt on his life. He hadn't planned on involving her in it, but there was kindness to Esme, a true kindness that made it easy to trust her—and far too easy to talk with her. So, he had shared the betrayal with her, and it had started an interesting and unexpectedly helpful conversation that lasted well into the night and had her falling asleep beside him.

He thought back on their conversation as he walked through the quiet village.

"When was this?" she asked.

"During the battle with Clan MacLeish."

"And you are certain it was one of your own and not a mercenary for hire?" she asked, disbelief clear in her wide eyes.

"Without a doubt," he said without hesitation.

"Why would one of your own men be so foolish to betray you?"

"I have repeatedly asked myself the very same. What hadn't I seen? What had I missed? Had there been signs I ignored?"

"Had he fought beside you for years?" she asked. "Did you trust him?"

"As much as I could trust anyone," he scoffed. "I am not foolish enough to think that the promise of coins cannot sway a man's loyalty. But the dire consequences of such a foolhardy decision are something my warriors have seen, and it has kept them fearful enough not to betray me."

Her look was puzzled. "But this one had no such fear, which means something else had driven him, something far more powerful."

A dog's bark brought him back to the present. He had been impressed that she hadn't offered useless reassurances or rushed to false outrage to placate him. She listened intently and offered her own thoughts.

Her words about it being something far more powerful than fear of him had brought one word to mind… revenge. But who didn't want revenge against Torrance, his evil deeds left many with a bitter, vengeful taste.

His thoughts drifted back to Esme and how she had dropped back on the pillow to continue to talk with him. She had fallen asleep, and he had let her. He hadn't wanted her to leave. He wanted her there beside him. And when she turned and snuggled against him, her breath soft against his skin, he had wrapped his arm around her and fallen into a peaceful sleep.

He shook away the memory as he moved through the village with a warrior's gait, his thoughts tangled. As much as he wanted to ignore the memory, he could still feel the ghost of her touch, and it unsettled him.

Had he been wise in confiding in her? Had she noticed the change in him? Was she far more dangerous to the plan than he expected? He shook his head. It wasn't her. It was him and the feelings he always had for her that were now surfacing.

That realization sat heavier than expected in his chest, and he muttered a curse under his breath. Emotions made men careless. And careless men ended up dead.

A thought he needed to consider regarding the old woman Esme had told him about. It could be a trap he'd be walking into if he went in search of answers that the old woman claimed was buried in blood and vengeance.

Whose blood? Whose vengeance?

Would he find the answers? Or did death wait not only for him but Esme as well? The old woman having insisted that he'd find no answers without his wife.

Did he take the chance and go? Or did he have a choice?

He heard the crunch of footfalls not far behind him. His thoughts might be chaotic, but he kept his senses alert.

"Do not tell me that you bring me a problem before the day begins," Torrance said without turning when Brack got close enough.

Footfalls were as familiar to Torrance as were voices. Each were unique and allowed him to know who approached without having to look. Brack's thick body gave him a strong gait that was easily recognizable in his demanding footfalls.

"Nay, my lord, I but worried there was a problem when I spotted you walking through the village so early. Has your wife disappointed you that you rush from your bed?"

Torrance's head snapped quickly to the side to glare at Brack. "How is that your concern?"

"It would be my duty to find you another wife if Lady Esme does not satisfy you, and I would want to begin the search sooner rather than later, if it should prove to be necessary."

Torrance's glare threatened. "You will conduct no such search, Brack."

"As you say, my lord." Brack said with a nod of his head. "Then it is something else that troubles you?"

Torrance turned his gaze ahead once more. "Esme told me of an old woman, long silver hair, draped in dark garments, who approached her and spoke of things no stranger should know."

Brack stiffened beside him. "And you believe this old hag?"

"I believe there may be something worth discovering. The

woman spoke of blood and vengeance buried in the past... and that I'd find no answers without Esme."

Brack let out a heavy snort. "You see the trap then, my lord. You speak of blood and vengeance and think not that it could be your own?"

Torrance didn't hide his annoyance. "It could be. But it could also prove beneficial. I will not know if I don't go and see for myself."

Brack wasted no time with hesitation. "And, of course, this old woman, you didn't see, insisted you take Lady Esme with you. Is that so she can see her plan carried out… you dead."

"That's a bold accusation," Torrance snapped sharply.

"Lady Esme is not happy here. She never has been," Brack pressed. "She praises you out of duty but has no true words of kindness for you. She watches you like she waits for something to break. There is no warmth in her toward you, only cold civility."

Torrance's jaw tensed. "I am not interested in her trust, only her obedience."

"And is she only interested in her freedom that a dead husband would bring her?"

"She knows better than to defy me, betray me," Torrance admonished, or did she?

Brack scowled. "Or does she obey so she can dig and find your weakness and help your enemies."

"She is far too fearful of me to do anything so foolish," Torrance said, having seen such fear in her eyes. "I don't believe she's behind this. I've seen betrayal before, Brack. She doesn't wear its face."

Brack folded his arms across his chest. "So, you go chasing the whispers of an old woman who may not even exist and risk your life on the word of a wife who barely tolerates you?"

"I go," Torrance said, "because something about this... reeks of truth. And I've experienced enough to know when a stench should not be ignored."

Brack muttered under his breath, then looked him squarely in the eye. "Then I go with you."

"Nay," Torrance said. "You stay here and keep the clan safe. I will take Esme with me along with a contingent of men, since I am not foolish enough to travel without protection."

"I am not comfortable with this," Brack insisted.

"I must go. I need to know what this is before it grows teeth. I need to know what part Esme plays in it, if any."

"And if it is a trap?"

"Then I will find out who it is that wants me dead."

Brack held his gaze, reluctant but loyal to the last. "Then you will need men to travel ahead and to trail you to prevent any surprises."

"No mercenaries. They can be bought too easily," Torrance warned.

"Aye, my thinking as well. I will send trusted men along with you."

"See it done," Torrance commanded as he walked off.

* * *

TORRANCE SAT BACK in the chair on the dais, his goblet barely touched, his gaze drifting toward Esme where she sat beside him, listening politely to the servant who asked if there was any more food or drink, she might want. His wife wore a pleasant smile throughout the exchange and all through breakfast. She had a pleasantness to her, a grace that could not be feigned.

Brack had warned him not to trust her. Had said she cared nothing for him, wanted only her freedom. But watching her now, her gentle nods, the way she set her tankard down so she could better listen to the servant made it difficult to believe Brack was right. Besides, the way she responded to his intimate touches told a completely different story.

Unless, how he felt for her, always felt for her, had blinded him.

He hadn't realized how closely he'd been watching her until a strange stillness came over her. Her smile faded, her brow drew tight, and the color drained from her face so swiftly it jolted him upright.

He leaned forward, alarm rising. "Esme?"

She turned slightly toward him, lips parting, but no words came. Her eyes were wide, panicked, and then her body doubled over with a sharp shudder.

Torrance was on his feet in an instant.

He caught her around the waist, steadying her as she tried to rise. "Hold on," he murmured urgently, guiding her off the dais. "Get Brenna!" he barked toward a servant as he lifted her into his arms and rushed her out of the hall.

He took the stairs to his chamber two at a time and once inside rushed her to the clean chamber pot. He dropped to his knees beside her, holding her hair back, his other hand braced on her trembling back as her body convulsed with each retch.

"Easy," he whispered, feeling her discomfort and helpless to stop it.

She gasped in a shaky breath, the worst of it seeming to pass. Her face was clammy, her body slack against him.

"Torrance..." Her voice was barely there.

He cradled her closer. "I've got you."

Her head rested on his chest, and her fingers curled weakly into his tunic. "I don't understand. I felt fine and then—"

He stiffened.

A creeping thought slid through him like a blade drawn slowly. A sudden sickness and after breakfast.

He pulled back just enough to look at her, his mind racing. His voice turned hard. "Is there something you've not told me?"

She blinked in confusion. "What do you mean?"

"When I was away... did you lie with another man?"

"What?" she asked, thinking he couldn't mean what she suspected he meant.

His voice turned harsh with the question he hadn't meant to ask but couldn't stop himself from voicing it. "Are you with child? Is that why you are eager to spread your legs for me?"

Color surged to her cheeks despite her pallor, and anger flared in her exhausted eyes. "You think I'm ill because I carry another man's child?"

"You were not eager for my touch before," he accused. "Now you lie willingly in my bed. Should I not question why?"

She shoved weakly against his chest. "I obeyed every demand you made of me concerning the consummation of our marriage. I accepted failing you, of not being desirable enough for your manhood to rise to see the deed done. But since your return home your manhood has been anything but flaccid and still you refuse to consummate our vows. I am still the virgin you wed and if you did your duty, you would find the truth for yourself." She took a breath. "And I come to your bed now because" —she shook her head— "I stopped hating you enough to try."

The shock of her words froze him. He didn't move. He couldn't speak. The shame of his accusation coiled in his gut. And the thought that she didn't hate him was a revelation he never expected.

The door opened with a rush, and Brenna hurried in with her satchel.

"She's taken ill," Torrance said, his voice clipped as he lifted his wife in his arms and carried her to the bed to gently place her down on it.

Brenna stood beside the bed, seeing Esme's pale face and feeling the clamminess of her skin. "Could you be with child?" she asked, brushing a strand of hair from Esme's damp forehead.

Esme hesitated. Her gaze swiftly going to Torrance, uncertain, fearful of how to respond.

"There's a chance," he said before she could answer, though the words tasted bitter.

A knock sounded, and a young servant stepped inside, pale and out of breath. "My lord, I was sent by cook to tell you that one of the kitchen lads has taken ill too. Retching something awful. He admitted to taking a bit of the dried meat from the morning's meal. The same meat you refused but Lady Esme ate."

Torrance's head snapped around. "What?"

The servant spoke quickly. "He said it was set aside for you, but since you didn't eat it..."

Torrance remembered it then. He had refused the dried meat. It wasn't to his liking. Esme was surprised, claiming it was always a favorite meat of his for breakfast.

His eyes shot back to her pale face. "She wasn't meant to eat it. I was."

Brenna's eyes widened. "Poison?"

"Treat her for it... now," Torrance ordered, rage simmering just beneath the surface and without another word, he turned on his heels and stormed from the chamber.

Someone had tried to kill him, and his wife had nearly died in his place.

Someone would pay.

* * *

TORRANCE'S BOOTS struck hard against the flagstones as he entered the kitchen. The scent of salt and spices lingered, but it was the tang of fear that filled the air as the cook and kitchen servants scrambled to bow.

"My lord," the cook stammered. "We—we heard Lady Esme took ill—"

"You set aside dried meat for me this morning," Torrance snapped, his gaze drilling into the older woman's face. "Who prepared it?"

"I—I did, my lord," the cook said quickly. "I always do. That cut was from a new batch, smoked and salted as usual. No different—"

"It was different," Torrance growled. "It was poisoned."

The cook's eyes bulged. "Poisoned?"

"It would explain why one of your own is retching his guts out because he stole some of what was meant for me. My wife ate some. She could have died.... still could." The thought infuriated him and frightened him.

The servants shrank back fear causing them to tremble.

"Lots of people had hands on that meat," Una said, stepping forward to defend the cook.

Torrance advanced a step, his fury barely restrained. "Did you?"

"Nay," the cook said. "Una never laid hands on it."

Torrance glared at Una. "Then you will be the one to find out who touched that meat. From the moment the animal was slaughtered to the moment it reached my table. Every hand. Every eye. Every moment." He cast a deepened scowl at everyone there. "Answer Una's question honestly so she can find the culprit, or you all suffer for it."

Heads bobbed nonstop.

"I will see it done, my lord," Una said confidently.

"And quickly," Torrance demanded. "In the meantime, every one of you will stand in front of me and taste every bit of food that is served before it passes mine or my wife's lips." He pounded his fist on the table, the sliced kale and cabbage on top bouncing from the force. "Someone will suffer for this even if I find out it was nothing more than carelessness."

He stalked from the room, jaw tight, fury boiling. He had almost lost her, feared he still could. And whoever had come for him would soon learn just how dangerous it was to fail.

* * *

THE CHAMBER WAS quiet save for the occasional crackle from the hearth. Esme lay still beneath blankets and a couple of furs. She had remained in bed, Torrance's bed, since she'd taken ill this morning. She was feeling better, a bit weak and not at all hungry, her stomach churning now and again. Brenna had given her a potion that brought up the last of the food and ordered her to rest for the day and suggested she might be more comfortable in her own bedchamber. Torrance commanded that she remain where she was and Brenna did not dispute it and neither did Esme even though she would have preferred to be alone with her roiling stomach and thoughts.

Poison.

It didn't seem real. Yet the sharp burn in her throat, the sour taste still lingering in her mouth, the weakness in her limbs… it had all been real enough.

Someone had tried to kill Torrance, and she had nearly taken his place.

She shut her eyes, her breath catching. Not just because of the sickness, or even the brush with death. It was the moment he'd looked at her, eyes filled not with worry, then suspicion.

Have you been with another man?

His words had landed like stones in her chest, each one sinking deeper. She hadn't expected him to accuse her of that. Not after last night. Not after the things he'd shared with her. Or how she had woken during the night to feel his warmth steady against her back, his arm draped snug over her waist as if he truly wanted her there.

Had it meant nothing to him? Or was he playing one of his usual games, reeling her in, catching her unaware, then punishing her?

Even now, she wasn't sure what wounded her more, the poison or not knowing who her husband was. Himself. Or someone playing at him.

Her eyes grew heavy. Brenna cautioned her that she would probably sleep much of the day, her body needing rest to regain its strength. The problem had been that her thoughts refused to let her rest, until now. She didn't fight sleep, instead, she welcomed the peace it would bring her.

* * *

Esme didn't know what woke her, but her eyes drifted open to see her husband had moved the chair close to the bed and was sitting there staring at her.

"You should come to bed. You look tired," she said baffled that she invited him to join her.

He didn't hesitate. He shed his garments and slipped beneath the blankets and wrapped himself around her, tucking her close.

That she found comfort and safety, once again, in his strong embrace surprised her and she drifted back asleep baffled by their strange situation.

CHAPTER 12

"What are you doing out of bed?" Torrance demanded, striding into the Great Hall, his steps echoing with authority.

"It has been three days, my lord, and I am feeling much better. I simply cannot abide another day in bed," Esme said, sitting at the table nearest the hearth. The fire's warmth was comforting, and she soaked it in while her fingers curled around a tankard.

Torrance's eyes narrowed as his glance dropped to the table, seeing a half-eaten bowl of porridge. "What do you eat and drink? Who tasted it before giving it to you?"

"Brenna saw to it before she was called away to tend to a birth," she responded, hoping that he would not order her back to bed since she had left it without his permission.

"You disobeyed my orders to remain in bed until I said otherwise," he admonished, though was pleased to see her cheeks wore their usual soft blush.

She was ready to offer an apology, as usual, but he spoke before she could.

"I am pleased you are feeling well enough to be up and

about, but don't disobey me again," he cautioned with a slight scowl.

She lowered her gaze. "Aye, my lord."

Torrance dropped down on the bench opposite her at the table and a servant hurried to fill a tankard for him with hot cider from the jug on the table.

"I have given more thought to that old woman you told me about and decided to make the journey and see what we can find out. But not until you are well enough to travel." He raised his hand when she rushed to respond. "You are well enough when I say that you are. I will not have you traveling in the cold and turn worse because of it."

The situation with her husband continued to baffle her. Torrance never cared if she took ill. He would actually get annoyed at her if she wasn't feeling well. Tell her she was weak. That he had helped her, was concerned for her, when she had taken ill had shocked her. He also had insisted she remained in his bedchamber, and he had visited with her throughout the day to see how she was doing. That was something she never thought Torrance would do. So, again she questioned her suspicions. Though she could not ignore the possibility that he was playing some evil game with her. But why? To what end?

"Esme, you are not paying heed to me," Torrance snapped.

She jumped at his sharp voice.

"Are you not feeling well?" he asked, annoyed. "You should not have gotten out of bed yet."

"I am fine, my lord. My mind simply wanders."

"Not when I am speaking to you," he admonished, shook his head, then reached for her hand.

His fingers curled around hers and she watched as annoyance faded from his eyes replaced by concern. The change was startling as if a mask had dropped off his face and revealed another behind it.

"You will take care, wife, I need you," he said, squeezing her hand gently.

His heart-felt words left her speechless since she actually believed he meant it, but then his mask suddenly returned along with his cold demeanor, and he let go of her hand.

"I need you to give me an heir."

She bit her tongue ready to remind him that she was not the one failing to do her duty, but she feared the consequences of such careless words. She was relieved when Una entered the room with determined strides, her expression tight with purpose.

"My lord," Una said, dipping her head only slightly before stopping short of the table. "I have news."

Torrance's brow furrowed and his tone was edged with irritation. "It took you long enough to complete the task. Three days now."

Una planted her hands on her hips. "Aye, and it took that long because I don't go flinging blame without cause... unlike some." She met his glare without flinching.

Esme sent Una a warning look. The woman had a mind of her own and spoke it, but a free tongue would not serve her well here.

Torrance's jaw tensed. "Watch yourself, Una. I've no patience for insolence."

Una looked ready to snap at him, but she wisely took a breath before saying, "Aye, my lord."

Esme almost smiled at how Una had acknowledged his warning but extended no apology.

"You better have good news for me, Una," Torrance cautioned.

"No one in the kitchen had cause or chance to poison the food," Una stated bluntly. "I questioned them all and watched their movements. I also caught their whispers. No one in the kitchen is the culprit."

His eyes narrowed. "You disappoint me. If none in the kitchen are responsible, then who poisoned the meat?"

"I gave thought to that dilemma and recalled two monks who came by that day. They requested food. Something about them didn't sit right with me." She crossed her arms. "They were too watchful, too curious, and they never prayed before taking a bite of food."

"Monks?" Torrance's voice dropped low with suspicion. "You think they weren't monks?"

"They wore the robes, but robes don't make the man," Una said. "And they never offered a prayer in exchange for the food. It is something all monks do, offer prayer for the generosity of others. Nor did they ask if there were any ill people they could visit and pray for before they took their leave. They had no regard for anyone but themselves."

Esme's heart gave a small thud. "Do you think they poisoned the meat?"

"I'd not wager against it," Una said. "They left well before nightfall, said they were heading north."

Torrance's gaze turned stormy. "Why didn't you tell me sooner?"

"It took time to talk with everyone in the kitchen and make sure it wasn't any of them. Then I had to think on who it might be as well as question others who saw or spoke to the monks to gather more information. I didn't want to come to you with foolish nonsense."

"You did well, Una," Esme praised, hoping her husband would express the same appreciation for a task well done.

"She is a servant who completed a task I set for her. She needs nor deserves praise," Torrance said with a scowl.

The door suddenly burst open and a strong, cold wind followed Brack in along with several of Torrance's warriors who immediately took a stance along the sides of the hall.

"He comes unannounced," Brack called out.

"I don't care if I arrived without warning," came the deep voice from the doorway.

Hakon, a massive Northmen with shoulders the width of boulders and long dark hair that fell in tangled waves strode into the Great Hall as if he owned it. The jagged scar running down one side of his face warned he was a fearless warrior. Four of his warriors followed like shadows, silent and menacing, and the room's warmth seemed to chill.

Torrance, remained seated, glaring at the mighty warrior. "I warned you not to come on my land without summons."

"My unannounced arrival would not be necessary if you had kept your word," Hakon said with an angry grunt. "You promised me a wife, a Highland lass. Strong and fierce. And what do I get? Silence and delay."

Torrance stood and rested his arms over his chest, displaying his annoyance. "Perhaps I was ensuring I did not send you someone you'd kill on the first night."

Hakon let out a bark of laughter. "I want a woman with fire in her belly, not one who simpers and trembles. Don't insult me with that weak talk."

"Ignorant savage."

"Who said that?" Hakon demanded, turning his head to cast a glance at everyone there. His eyes settled on Una and her eyes narrowed. Her wild red hair had fallen loose from its braid, and the tilt of her chin spoke volumes. "You," he accused with a nod at her.

All eyes turned to look at Una.

"I won't deny the truth," Una said boldly.

"Hold your tongue, Una," Torrance commanded.

"Who is she?" Hakon asked with interest.

"No one of concern," Torrance said, not looking her way.

"She's got the look of a hellcat," Hakon muttered, stepping closer. "You said you had no suitable match, and yet this one prowls your hall?"

Una crossed her arms. "If you're looking for someone to chain to your bedpost, try the stables."

Murmurs rippled around the room. Brack froze in shock, Torrance shook his head, and Esme cringed waiting for either her husband or Hakon to explode in fury.

Hakon stared at Una, his expression unreadable, then slowly, he grinned. "I've broken warriors with gentler tongues."

"I've made warriors cry with my sharp tongue," she shot back.

He laughed, a low sound that rumbled in his chest. "You've spirit. I like that."

"I don't care what you like, savage. I'm no concern to you."

"Take your leave now, Una," Torrance ordered sharply.

"Nay," Hakon said, still watching her. "Let her speak. I'm beginning to enjoy her company."

Una rolled her eyes and strode past them all toward the kitchen again. "You're all mad," she muttered. "Best you not drag me into it."

As the door closed behind her, Hakon turned back to Torrance. "She'll do. I'll take her with me."

Torrance didn't answer at once. He watched the door for a moment longer.

Esme worried what he might be thinking and silently prayed for Una, her heartbeat catching at his response.

"I'll consider it." Torrance turned to his wife. "Go rest. I have matters to see to."

"Aye, my lord," Esme said and left the room reluctantly, her worry for Una growing.

Food and drink were brought out for Hakon's warriors to enjoy but Torrance's warriors remained standing guard. Torrance and Hakon retreated to the table on the dais while Brack remained nearby.

Hakon took the tankard filled with ale from the servant with a grunt, his eyes fixed on the door Una had disappeared through. "She'd bite before she'd bow."

"Then you'll need a strong hand to hold the leash," Torrance said, not partaking of the ale.

Hakon's lips curled. "I don't leash women. I challenge them, but most don't have the stamina or courage to deal with me."

Torrance studied him. "Una is no docile woman. She'll claw your eyes out if you corner her."

"She can try." Hakon looked over. "You've been slow in keeping your word, Torrance, whereas I am ready to keep mine and fight for you when necessary."

"An unexpected and dire situation has come up," Torrance said, realizing Hakon's unexpected visit just might prove beneficial.

"Tell me," Hakon said eagerly.

"There have been attempts made on my life."

Hakon laughed. "That happens to me often. All men of power have that problem. Kill a few people, innocent or not, and it will stop."

"Nay, I believe the two men left and fled north. They posed as monks."

"I could find out about them."

"What will that cost me?" Torrance asked but already knew.

"A wedding when I return."

"Una was taken prisoner after a battle. She does not beg for freedom. She watches, listens, and she learns. I have no doubt she plans to attempt to escape one day."

"Perfect," Hakon said with a grin. "I want a wife who'll keep me sharp. Just make sure she doesn't escape before I return."

"We'll see what information you bring me."

Hakon narrowed his eyes. "Careful, Torrance. I know how much you like games, but I didn't ride all this way to play games."

"And I won't fail to keep my word," Torrance warned.

"I want Una, no other. Don't disappoint me, or you won't like the consequences."

Torrance leaned closer to Hakon and kept his voice low but powerful. "Don't threaten me or you and your men will never make it home."

* * *

THE FIRE in the hearth crackled softly, casting shifting shadows across the stone walls of Torrance's bedchamber. Esme sat on the bench beside the hearth, a shawl wrapped around her, staring into the flames. She had no chance all day to speak with her husband to find out what he spoke with Hakon about. She feared her husband may have agreed to give Una to Hakon and it disturbed her to think that it could be Una's fate.

The door suddenly swung open, causing Esme to hurry off the bench and turn to see her husband enter. He had a commanding presence that always managed to fill a room when he entered it. His broad shoulders were always drawn back, his chin held at a slight angle, and his distinct green eyes seemed to devour everything around him as if nothing could be hidden from him. She tucked her shawl tighter around her as if somehow it could shield her.

Torrance shoved the door closed as he said, "You should be in bed."

"I wished to speak with you."

"Did I just say you should be in bed, wife?"

She almost cringed at his familiar sharp tongue. This was when she thought herself mad for even considering Torrance was Ryland. But it still continued to nag at her. For now, she would be cautious and that meant knowing she would get nowhere arguing with him. And he certainly wouldn't tolerate her disagreeing with him, so she dropped her shawl on the bench and took quick steps to the bed and slipped beneath the blankets.

However, she bravely said, "We can talk in bed."

Torrance glanced her way, thinking how unwise it was to keep her in his bed, and yet how right it felt. Besides, with threats on both their lives, he felt better keeping her there with him. He also slept better with her cuddled against him. Though he was treading a very thin line with her and he wasn't sure what would happen when it snapped.

Esme sat up in bed and tried averting her eyes as her husband shed his garments, but it wasn't easy. He was a fine specimen of a man, strong and muscled, born of endless time on the practice field and in battle. She squinted for a moment, the fire's light catching his naked body, highlighting it, and she thought there was something different about him, but she couldn't quite grasp what it was.

Torrance turned his back on his wife, seeing how focused she was on him, and it wasn't passion he saw in her eyes. She looked puzzled, and that was not good.

He dropped his garments on top of a wood chest and turned her attention elsewhere. "What did you want to talk about."

Esme shook her head, clearing it. "Did you tell Hakon you would consider giving him Una?"

Torrance walked to the bed. "I did."

Esme stretched out beneath the blankets as Torrance joined her in bed. "I don't believe that is a wise thing to do."

He turned his gaze on her, his brow lifted in challenge as he stretched out beside her. "Why not?"

"Hakon is not a good man. He may be useful, even honorable in his own way, but he's cruel. You can see it in the way he looks at people, in the sharpness of his tongue, in how he enjoys being feared."

Torrance's mouth twitched, not quite a smile. "And Una is gentle and as sweet as a spring bloom?"

"You know she isn't," Esme said, worry in her words. "But that doesn't mean she should be used to tame a brute."

"I'm not using her," he said, his voice firm. "Hakon asked for a wife. Una is no meek lass who'll weep over harsh words. She's sharp-witted, strong and, I suspect, no stranger to men like him. If anything, she might be the one woman capable of being his wife."

Esme turned on her side to face her husband. "That may be, but just because she can fight him doesn't mean she should have to. You don't pair two blades and expect peace."

Torrance turned his head toward her. "You see danger. I see potential. She's spent her life wielding more than kitchen knives. She thrives on challenge, and she has no illusions about men or marriage."

"So, for that she should be stuck in a heartless and brutal marriage?" Esme asked, softly.

"Do you empathize with her, wife?"

She almost bit her tongue for having spoken so foolishly and for finding herself growing more comfortable with her husband that she had voiced her opinion without thinking about it.

"Do you believe you are in a heartless and brutal marriage?" he asked.

Esme's stomach churned anxiously, and she met his eyes, surprised not to see anger in them but more curiosity.

However, she decided not to take any chances. "Nay, my lord, I am grateful I have a good husband."

"You do not think me heartless or brutal?"

"Any powerful, respected leader must have such traits to lead successfully, my lord."

"You speak of a leader. I speak of a husband. Do you care for me, wife? Does your heart feel for me?"

"Does it matter?" she asked befuddled by his question.

Torrance had made it known from their first meeting that he expected her to do her duty as a wife. That he would tolerate nothing less. So, why ask her that?

He tossed the question back at her. "Does it matter to you?"

Did she dare voice her thought? Was he setting a trap for her? Waiting for her to say something foolish so he could berate her for it?

Her stomach continued to roil, and her heart beat a bit faster, thinking about what she should say, and she couldn't hide her surprise when his hand reached out slowly and stroked her cheek.

"Am I such a heartless husband, wife, that you fear answering me?"

"Nay, husband, I cannot answer since I truly do not know you?"

A scowl crossed his face.

She hurried to explain. "Only now, since you returned home from battle, do I feel that I am getting to know you. Before that your words were few to me and we spent little time together."

She didn't think it was wise to remind him that his words had been mostly hurtful and demeaning from the start. But then maybe it wasn't that he failed to realize that. Maybe he didn't know because it wasn't Torrance lying beside her in bed. Did she dare continue to think that?

He ran his finger faintly and slowly across her lips. "It is time we change that, wife."

His hand fell away, replaced by his lips that brushed across hers as faintly as his touch.

His whisper, soft kiss sent a pleasant shiver through her. That her body responded so easily, instinctively both pleased and frightened her, for she still didn't know if she could truly trust him.

He left her lips tingling as he rolled on his back. "Go to sleep, wife. You need rest. We leave in two days on our journey."

Esme turned away from him not knowing what to make of him. At times, he was a far different man than the one who left her and at other times she could spy the ruthlessness in him.

Who was he? And what would she do if she discovered it was a stranger in her bed? She knew little of Ryland, had seen him a handful of times, had maybe two brief encounters with him. He seemed mannered and kind enough, but he was still a stranger to her and one who looked far too familiar to Torrance. But her greatest worry... what would her fate be at his hands.

CHAPTER 13

Patches of snow clung stubbornly to the ground, the last remnants of a light snowfall that had dusted the keep two nights ago. Esme drew her cloak tighter across her chest as she walked the narrow path near the animal pens. She was looking for Una and knew that this time of day she would be emptying the scrap bucket in the animal pens. The pungent odor stopped her from going any further as did Una's bold voice.

"That's all there is, fellows. We had a hungry lot yesterday."

Una emerged from behind the last enclosure, the empty scrap bucket swinging from her hand. Her braid hung damp against her cloak, her cheeks flushed from the chill. She paused briefly when she saw Esme.

"Are you looking for me, my lady?"

"I am," Esme said, falling into step beside her as she continued walking.

"Does this have anything to do with that brute of a warrior called Hakon?" Una asked and chuckled, seeing the surprised look on Esme's face. "Tongues have been going strong since he made his presence known and many assume it might be a barter Lord Torrance would consider."

"Torrance did speak with Hakon about you," Esme confirmed.

"I imagined as much," Una muttered. She slowed her steps, then stopped entirely. Una turned to face her, her eyes angry. "He offered me to Hakon like I was—what? A prize for good behavior? Payment for a debt?"

"Nay. He said he'd think on it. That's all."

Una scoffed. "He has no intentions of thinking on it. His mind is made up. I hold no value to Lord Torrance but if I can benefit him in some way, he will not think twice on it." She blew out a breath that misted in the air. "I am nothing more than chattel to be bartered between men who think battle-forged bruises and a blade make their word law." She nodded at Esme. "You're no different, bartered in marriage to benefit your clan. We're condemned at birth being born a woman, but I for one will not hold my tongue. I will speak my piece."

"As you should," Esme encouraged. "It is not fair."

Una scoffed again. "Life is not fair, never has been. But I will no longer yield or submit obediently."

Esme smiled. "I don't believe you have ever yielded, Una."

"I made sure I didn't," Una said, keeping her anger from flaring any further. "Because if I did yield, I would lose what little of myself I have left."

"You have no chains to hold you. You walk freely about. Why not simply walk away from here and never return?"

She paused, glanced up at the gray sky, and shrugged. "Where would I go? I have no coins. No clan. No name worth remembering. There is no place for a woman like me beyond this keep. You may not see the chains, but they are there. I feel them every day. Some days more than others." Sorrow filled her eyes. "Have your chains not grown heavier by the day, Lady Esme?"

UNA CONTINUED to the kitchen while Esme remained where she was, lost in thought long after Una entered the kitchen. Una was right. The chains could be felt, not seen, and they were heavier some days more than others. And like Una, she had no place to go. The marriage had committed her to Torrance until death. She would never be free.

Why at that moment it should upset her, leaving her feeling hopeless, she didn't know. She silently chastised herself for dwelling on it and forced the upsetting thought from her mind as she hurried and turned intending to take a brisk walk through the village to clear her head and heart.

She would have collided with her husband if Torrance hadn't grabbed her by the arms and prevented their collision.

"What's wrong?" he demanded, seeing the upset in her eyes.

Caught off guard, she reverted to instinct. "Forgive me, my lord. I wasn't watching where I was going."

"That doesn't answer my question, wife. You are upset." His eyes settled firmly on hers. "Why?"

Again, he caught her off guard. Why would it matter to him? He never cared how she felt about anything. Why now? The fierce look in his eyes warned he would have an answer.

"Need I remind you that I am not a patient man?" he snapped.

She went with the safest response, casting a quick glance at the gray sky. "I worry how the weather will treat us on our journey."

His eyes narrowed. "Do you take me for a fool, wife?"

"Never, my lord," she said, realizing she had made a mistake and worried over the consequences.

Torrance lowered his face close to hers. "Then I will give you one more chance to tell me the truth."

"Chains!" Una shouted. "I asked her if her chains, like mine, grow heavier by the day."

"And what was her reply?" Torrance demanded.

"I didn't wait for one," Una scoffed. "I already knew the answer. You are lucky that Lady Esme has the strength and courage to bear the unimaginable weight of your shackles."

Gasps were heard from the people who had gathered upon hearing the heated exchange.

Esme froze, knowing Torrance would not let her remark go unpunished.

"It's the stocks until morning for you," Torrance ordered with such coldness that it shivered Esme.

"Please, my lord," Esme pleaded, aware that Una had spoken up out of concern for her. "The nights have been bitter. No one can survive such cold."

"She should have thought of that before opening her mouth," Torrance said and signaled one of his warriors with a snap of his hand. "Put her in the stocks and she's not to be released until I say so."

"Aye, my lord," the young warrior said and went to Una, grabbing her by the arm to take her to the stocks.

"You save me, my lord," Una called out with a laugh. "Freezing to death is a far better fate than becoming Hakon's wife."

Esme was the only one who could hear the firm yet quiet oaths that fell from her husband's lips. Esme wanted to smile with admiration for Una. She had set Torrance up perfectly for that, unless he had no intention of giving Una to Hakon.

"Since you find that fate more distasteful, Una. I will gladly give one devil to another. You shall be given to Hakon on his return."

Una laughed. "It takes a devil to know one, Lord Torrance."

Gasps rang out once again.

"Two nights in the dungeon with no food may have you thinking differently. She can wait for Hakon there," Torrance ordered and cast a wicked scowl on those gathered around them. "Get back to your chores. NOW!"

Esme was relieved. Those in the kitchen would not let Una go without food. They would sneak some to her. She watched everyone disperse and as soon as she was alone with her husband, she wasn't surprised at what he asked.

"So, what would your response have been to Una, about chains?"

Esme was prepared. "I entered this marriage freely. I wear no chains."

Torrance leaned his head down, pressing his cheek against hers as he whispered. "Ah, but you do, wife. You are chained to me forever."

"My lord!" Brack called out.

Torrance stepped abruptly away from her. "Go into the keep and stay there."

Esme turned and hurried toward the keep, casting a quick glance back to see him speaking with Brack, though turning as if he knew she looked his way, and he pointed to the keep as if reminding her to do as she was told.

His whispered words still rang in her ear.

You are chained to me forever.

He sounded so much like Torrance. Had he returned to her? She couldn't help but pray that it was an act, though for what purpose she didn't know. She only knew it was her only hope of being free.

Esme headed to the keep but his powerful, commanding words halted her.

"BRING HIM TO ME!"

Someone had been caught at something. Could it be the one who poisoned her? She turned and seeing her husband's back to her, she hurried forward to hide on the side of a dwelling where she could watch without being seen... she hoped.

Her eyes rounded when she caught sight of a warrior, wearing the Clan MacLeish plaid being shoved toward Torrance. His bottom lip was split and bleeding, one eye swollen purple, and he cradled one arm in the other.

Brack kicked him in the back of his legs, sending him to the ground when he almost reached Torrance.

"On your knees in front of Lord Torrance," Brack ordered, and the warrior struggled to get to his knees. "He spies on Clan Glencairn."

Esme watched the way the warrior kept his eyes on Torrance and though he looked worried, she didn't see the fear in him that everyone had when Torrance was about to determine one's fate.

"I am not spying, my lord. I was just gathering the courage to present myself to you and beg for mercy for Chieftain Ryland. He is a respected leader, a good man, and beloved by his clan. He would do anything to keep his clan safe."

"Will he die for it?" Torrance asked with such coldness that it shivered Esme.

"He still may, my lord, but if he survives, I beg of you, please allow him to lead us."

People had gathered around, whispering and waiting to see the warrior's fate.

"Draw and quarter him," someone shouted.

"Make the enemy suffer," another called out.

The voices weren't those of the villagers. The shouts came from Torrance's warriors. The villages held their tongues and some of the woman wiped at their eyes so their tears wouldn't be noticed. The clan was tired of senseless death, war, and suffering.

"How is Ryland?" Torrance asked.

"His fate is still unknown, my lord, and his clan continues to pray for him."

"I do hope he lives to face his punishment for even daring to think he had a chance against Clan Glencairn," Torrance said, his voice raised with strength.

His warriors cheered him on, and the crowd joined in out of fear.

"Get the healer, Brack," Torrance ordered.

Puzzled, Brack scrunched his face. "The healer?"

"Did I not speak clearly enough?" Torrance snapped harshly.

"Nay, my lord. I will fetch the healer." Brack turned and hurried away.

"It is your lucky day, warrior," Torrance said for all to hear. "You will return home with a message to Chieftain Ryland. Tell him I continue to be the most powerful, victorious leader—just as I was when we were young lads sharing adventures in the woods. And as his fate was in my hands then, it is in my hands now."

"Aye, my lord," the warrior said with a respectful bob of his head.

Esme caught sight of Brack rushing toward Brenna, a healing basket in her hand as she stepped out of a cottage. His hand went to her arm, and he leaned his head down close to hers. Brenna did not look at all upset or fearful that Brack touched her, and Esme wondered over it as Brack kept hold of her arm, hurrying her to Lord Torrance.

"See to his wounds, Brenna," Torrance ordered, then turned to Brack. "Then send him on his way and make sure it is known he is not to be harmed. I want my message to reach Ryland."

With the confrontation ending, Esme slipped away, hoping to reach the keep unnoticed. She had only taken a few steps when a rough hand suddenly clamped over her mouth and an arm locked around her waist. Her muffled cries went unheard as she was dragged back, fighting fiercely.

"Keep struggling and I'll snap your neck here and be done with it," the man growled into her ear.

Panic surged. She clawed at his hand, kicked at his shins, but it wasn't enough. Then her frantic glance landed on Daniel, the young lad who'd once splattered her with mud. His eyes went wide with alarm.

"HELP! HELP! LADY ESME NEEDS HELP!" he shouted, running off.

The man cursed under his breath and tried to quicken his escape.

Esme needed to slow them down, so help could reach her. She let her body go limp, pretending to faint.

Torrance's fierce roar split the air. "LET HER GO!"

The man froze at the sound and all color drained from his face leaving him to look like a ghost.

Torrance stood like a storm barely contained, his face a mask of lethal rage. His eyes burned cold and hard as steel, jaw clenched so tightly a muscle ticked. There was no mercy in his glare, only the promise of swift, brutal death. The look alone was enough to make the man shudder.

Esme felt it too, not fear, but something deeper, something that gripped her chest and stole her breath. The power in Torrance's stance, the fury ignited by her endangerment, sent a chill through her. In that moment, she realized there was nothing he wouldn't do to protect her.

And she wasn't sure what unsettled her more, the danger… or how safe she suddenly felt.

The man yanked her upright and shifted his hand from

her mouth to her neck. "Come any closer and I'll snap her neck," he warned, his grip tightening.

A loud thump sounded suddenly, and the man stumbled, his hand jerking away from Esme's throat.

He cried out, staggering back, his arm still coiled around Esme's waist.

Daniel stood several feet away, another stone clutched in his hand, his small chest heaving, and he hurled it at the man. It struck his shoulder, and his hand loosened around Esme.

Torrance lunged, closing the distance in a blink. He yanked his wife away with one hand while he drove his sword through the man with his other hand.

The man fell and Torrance caught Esme before she hit the ground.

Daniel crept closer, his face pale but determined.

"You are a true warrior, lad," Torrance said, his voice low with pride. "Your bravery helped save Lady Esme and for that you will be rewarded."

Daniel stuck out his small chest and grinned.

Brack stormed forward, sword still drawn, his fury barely leashed. It is the MacLeish warrior's fault. He distracted us." He turned and stormed off to confront the warrior.

Torrance shook his head, his jaw tight with annoyance as he tucked his wife in the crook of his arm, keeping her at his side as he went after Brack.

"You kept our attention while your accomplice crept off to abduct Lady Esme," Brack accused. "That was your plan all along, wasn't it?"

The warrior's eyes widened in alarm. "Nay! I swear it on my life. I had no part in that treachery. I came to deliver the message, nothing more. Clan MacLeish has no quarrel with Lady Esme. We would never bring harm to her. That is not our way."

"Enough," Torrance yelled.

Esme could feel the tension held in the strength of his embrace, and the way his body remained poised between her and any lingering danger. She didn't want to move. Every time she breathed, she inhaled the scent of him—earth, wind, and steel—and with it came the unshakable sense that nothing could reach her while she remained in his arms.

Brack's glare didn't ease when he looked at Torrance. "Then how does he explain being here at the exact moment of the failed abduction?"

"I cannot," the warrior said, and glanced at Torrance. "But I give you my word, my lord. I rode here alone. I do not know the man who attacked Lady Esme. And I would never betray Chieftain Ryland's name by allowing such cowardice to happen under it."

Torrance finally spoke, his voice calm but laced with steel. "Let him go. If I find he speaks falsely, he will suffer for it."

Brack hesitated, then lowered his blade.

Esme turned her head slightly, enough to glance up at Torrance. His gaze was still on the warrior, sharp and unyielding, but when he looked down at her, it softened but only for a moment, then it turned harsh.

"You disobeyed me, wife, and you will answer for it."

CHAPTER 14

Esme paced Torrance's bedchamber, wringing her hands in front of her nightdress. The hour had grown late, and still he hadn't come. Not since he'd looked at her with fury in his eyes and warned, "You disobeyed me, wife, and you will answer for it."

He'd ridden off with a handful of warriors soon after, scouring the woods for any sign of lingering enemies. They'd returned empty-handed, and the MacLeish warrior, his wounds tended to, had been released with Torrance's message to Ryland.

But what message, truly?

Her thoughts circled back to that strange exchange between the two men. Something had passed between them. Something unsaid. Could it have been a coded message meant not just for Ryland, but for those who truly knew him?

She'd heard tales over the time she'd been at Clan Glencairn of Ryland and Torrance as lads, once close as brothers, always in competition. And more often than not, it was

Ryland who bested Torrance. That part had always stood out to her.

And now, she wondered…

Had Ryland truly assumed Torrance's identity? If so, why?

But even if the suspicion held weight, it was quickly tangled by the memory of his parting words. He'd spoken not as Ryland pretending to be Torrance, but as Torrance would. *You disobeyed me, wife.* That warning had not come from a stranger.

Now she waited, heart thudding, uncertain of what was to come, or who would walk through that door.

The latch clicked and the door creaked open.

Torrance filled the doorway. His eyes immediately settled on her.

She stood by the hearth, wringing her hands, her pacing halted the moment he entered. Worry etched her brow, and though she tried to appear composed, he saw the tension in her shoulders, the way her breath caught as their eyes met.

She was nervous as she should be.

He had come intending to scold her for disobeying him, for endangering herself. She had nearly been taken, nearly killed, because she'd chosen to disobey him and not return to the safety of the keep. If not for young Daniel…

His jaw tightened. The lad's brave act had saved her life and that thought turned to another. How he felt when he saw that man's arm around her neck. Her fragile neck. One wrong move and it could have ended. He could have lost her before he ever truly got to have her.

The memory of that fear hit him like a blade to the chest, cutting through his fury and pride and everything else he thought he was going to say.

The ache in his heart returned, sharp and unbearable.

He crossed the chamber in a heartbeat.

Esme barely had time to gasp before he reached her, his

hand catching her waist and pulling her flush to him. She opened her mouth to speak, to explain, maybe to plead.

But he silenced her with his mouth. His lips found hers in a kiss that was not gentle, but not cruel either. It was fierce and raw, born of fear, relief, and something deeper neither of them dared to name.

And in that moment, Esme realized she no longer feared what he might say. What she feared… was how much this man—whoever he truly was—had come to mean to her.

He tore his mouth off hers. "You put fear in me, woman, when I see you in danger and I cannot have that." He rested his brow to hers. "I cannot lose you. I will not lose you."

His lips touched hers briefly, a faint brush, and then it was as if something broke, a barrier he had kept rooted in place that was never to be crossed.

He crossed it.

His intense kiss felt like he had claimed her, accepted her as his wife and she couldn't help but feel at that moment that their hearts joined as one, locked together never to part. A strange sensation for sure since she believed Torrance didn't have a heart. But was he Torrance?

His hand gripped her backside, giving it a squeeze and keeping her pressed firmly against him as he continued to kiss her. Urgent kisses. Gentle kisses. Possessive kisses. And with each kiss his manhood swelled against her.

Again, his lips left hers and he whispered harshly, "Bloody hell, I want you so badly."

Esme wanted him just as badly, her body humming with passion and a relentless need. She could easily allow her desire to rule, and possibly her heart, but there was much more at stake here. She had to be cautious and ponder, with great difficulty, the consequences of her decision. If he was Torrance and she coupled with him she would finally have a chance to get with child. If it was Ryland she coupled with, she believed him to be an honorable man who would do right by her.

With that thought, her response came easier than she expected. "I'm yours. I'll always be yours."

He stared at her as if trying to make up his mind. He raised his hand and ran his fingers faintly over her lips, shook his head, and his arms dropped away from her, then he walked toward the door.

She felt a jab to her heart and anger rose in her as well. How often had he walked away from her, blamed her, made her feel a failure.

The words sprang from her mouth. "Do I disgust you that much that you refuse to plant your seed in me?"

"Watch your tongue with me, woman," he warned with a growl, reaching the door.

She felt as if she was pushed over the edge, falling, and feared where she would land. With nothing to lose, she called out, "I am not at fault in this marriage. Your manhood is the culprit. Whether limp or hard your shaft is useless!"

He turned, a fierce rage glowing in his green eyes and it took only a few strides to reach her even though she backed away from him in fright.

"Let's find out how useless it is," he challenged and scooped her up to carry to the bed and drop her down on it.

Her unexpected courage began to fail her. She had been in a battle with Torrance since the day they wed, and she was exhausted from the fight. She wanted it done and over no matter the consequences and if he was Ryland, he would be the one who would need to explain. She spread her legs ready to do her duty.

Torrance dropped down over her, pushed his plaid out of the way and positioned himself between her legs, his shaft hard, its tip resting just a bit inside her when he looked into her eyes. Her strength was waning, her fear growing, and surrender uncertain.

He wasn't looking for surrender.

"I'll not have it like this," he snapped.

Where she got the courage, she didn't know but she swung her hips up so hard that it drove his shaft into her in one deep plunge. She cried out as pain radiated through her.

"Esme!" Torrance cried out, seeing her lovely face cringe in pain.

"It is finally done," she said, then bit at her bottom lip in an attempt to stifle the discomfort.

"It is far from done, wife," Torrance said, feeling the pain he saw in her eyes.

"Then finish it," she urged, "and you will need to touch me no more."

"We'll see about that," he said and began to move slowly in her.

At first, she felt discomfort, then it slowly faded, replaced by a lovely sensation like she had felt when she rested on his lap in her solar. And like then, it began to grow in pleasure and soon all pain was forgotten and all she could think about was how wonderful he felt inside her."

"Does it hurt, Esme?"

"Nay. It feels quite pleasurable." She shut her eyes and allowed herself to drift off in a haze of passion. And as his thrust took on a more forceful tempo her pleasure grew and she found herself instinctively responding, raising her hips to meet his rhythm.

Her moans came unbidden, natural, and felt so right, so good that she didn't want it to end, didn't want it to be the last time she felt such an exhilarating sensation that continued to build. She was sure she would burst or come to the end of her fall, and she did in the most explosive way, screaming out in pleasure she would not believe existed if she hadn't felt it herself. And she found she took even more pleasure in seeing, hearing, Torrance do the same.

Torrance collapsed on her for a moment and whispered in her ear, "Now that you captured me between your legs, I intend to rest there often." He raised his head, his eyes catching hers. "You are mine and nothing will change that."

He said that so often to her that she wondered if he was trying to convince himself of it and not her.

He rolled off her onto his back and laid there silent for a few moments. Then he got off the bed and as he walked to the door, he said, "Sleep. We leave early in the morning." And with that he walked out of the room.

Esme stared at the door. She hadn't known what to expect afterwards when it was finally done, their vows sealed. She expected relief but instead got confusion. She simply did not know what to make of her husband. One moment, he seemed like Torrance and the next he felt like a stranger. One moment he showed concern, the next indifference.

At least her duty as a wife was done, though according to Torrance it would not be the last time they coupled. That she actually enjoyed coupling with him made her think he couldn't be Torrance. She could never have enjoyed such pleasure with Torrance.

She shook her head. She would drive herself insane if she continued this guessing game. She needed to observe, pay close attention, and once and for all find out the truth.

A thought struck her. Not once upon entering the room had he called her wife.

* * *

TORRANCE SAT in the Great Hall at a table in front of the hearth that was burning bright, having just been fed for the night. Intimacy with Esme had not been part of the plan and yet he worried that it would be the most difficult part of the plan, to ignore her, resist her. That was something that had gotten more difficult to do.

He scrubbed his hand over his face, annoyed with himself. He shouldn't have coupled with her. It was not the way he meant it to be. What way had he meant it? She was the thorn in his side that dug deeper and deeper into him just as he feared she would.

That thorn would forever jab at him if he refused to admit the truth... he loved her. And that was not going to change. He had loved her from the first moment he laid eyes on her and he would never stop loving her.

How to resolve this he had no idea, but one thing was for sure... she belonged to him now and he would never let her go.

He heard the footfalls that moved quietly into the room and said, "What brings you here so late, Brack?"

"My duty, my lord," Brack said, stopping in front of the table. "I wanted to make sure the keep had no unwanted nightly visitors after today's incident. But what brings you here? You should be—"

"Do not remind me again of my duties to produce an heir. It has been seen to and news will not be long off," Torrance said, realizing there now was a chance that she could be with child and if not now soon enough since he had every intention of resting between her legs again... only the next time would be far different from tonight.

"I am glad to hear that it goes well, my lord, and your wife has finally learned how to please you."

He wanted to lash out at Brack, defend Esme, but that wouldn't be wise, instead he asked, "Is all ready for tomorrow?"

Brack nodded. "Aye. The first troop will leave at dawn to

ride ahead and clear the way. Another will trail behind to make certain no one dares follow. And ten of your finest warriors will remain close, guarding you and Lady Esme at all times."

Torrance gave a curt nod, though his jaw remained clenched.

Brack studied him for a moment. "What do you expect to find when you get there?" he asked. "And what do you hope to accomplish?"

Torrance didn't answer right away, his gaze drifting off as if he needed to give it thought.

"I expect truths," he said finally, his voice low. "And I hope they don't come at too high a cost."

Brack raised a brow. "Truths that change what?"

Torrance's gaze returned to Brack. "Everything… or nothing at all. I'll not know until I stand on that ground." He paused, then added more solemnly, "But whatever waits, I'll see it through—with Esme beside me."

Brack gave a short nod, not pressing further, though a shadow of concern lingered in his eyes. "You should sleep, my lord. You have a long ride ahead of you in the morning."

"You worry too much about me, Brack."

"I take my duty seriously, my lord, and always will."

"I expect nothing less of you, Brack," he said and turned to face the hearth, stretching his long legs out for the fire to warm them.

"Sleep well, my lord," Brack said and with a bob of his head walked toward the door, a figure slipping out of the shadows to grab Brack's hand and hurry out with him.

Torrance lingered a while longer, reluctant to return to his bedchamber, to Esme, but with the journey looming tomorrow, he knew he needed to sleep and be prepared. He finally stood and made his way upstairs.

He eased the door open so as not to disturb her if she

slept and to his relief found her asleep. Tomorrow would be soon enough to talk about tonight, if they discussed it at all. He had allowed his frustration and anger to rule, and the night had not gone as planned. The next time would be different.

He slipped out of his garments and into bed beside her and she turned in her sleep to rest against him as had been her way of late. He wrapped himself around her as had been his way of late and the one thing he intended to change about that was to have her in his arms naked.

With a soft smile on his face, he fell asleep.

CHAPTER 15

The sky stretched gray above them, a slate canvas that promised winter had no intention of delaying its arrival. Esme rode beside Torrance, her mare's hooves crunching through the hardened earth. They had been traveling since early morning and not at a leisurely pace. They had covered much ground and would probably make camp not long from now.

She recalled his warning just before they departed.

"This journey is a dangerous one, especially with those meaning us harm. You will stay close to me, not leave my side."

Several of Torrance's warriors kept watch. None spoke, they were too busy being vigilant. The road north was long and uncertain, and none among them dared take a chance with their safety.

Esme pulled her cloak tighter around her as a cold wind cut across the open land. She wanted to discuss last night with him, but she hadn't gotten the chance. He was gone from their bed when she woke this morning, and he had been too busy seeing to their departure to catch even a brief word with him. And now was not the time with his warriors so close around them.

"You never did tell me," she said, breaking the quiet and shifting in her saddle. "What did the old woman mean when she said what you searched for was buried in blood and vengeance?"

Torrance didn't look at her, his gaze fixed ahead, but he had caught her shift in her saddle.

"Are you uncomfortable?" he all but barked at her, annoyed at himself for being the fault of her discomfort. "And do not lie to me."

"A bit, but only since traveling a while," she admitted and hurried to move their discussion away from anything intimate so the warriors would not hear. "I am curious. Tell me what the old woman meant."

"What I search for… what drives all this… it was born in blood, and vengeance buried so deep, even I don't know all the truths."

Secrets intrigued but they also could prove dangerous, so she asked, "What secrets were buried?"

"That," he said, meeting her gaze, "is what I aim to find out."

A chill ran through her, not from the wind, but from the weight of what she heard in his voice. Not fear, nor doubt, but purpose sharpened by something far more important than duty. And still, she wondered… was she riding beside a man searching for truth, or one who feared what truth might do to him?

Silence fell between them again. The chill wind tugged at Esme's hood as her gaze drifted to Torrance, or rather, to the way he scanned the land around them. His head would shift slightly at any sound. His shoulders would tense, then ease, when they passed a grove of trees or a formation of boulders.

He was ever alert, as if expecting trouble to rise from the land itself.

She angled her horse a bit closer to him, her concern growing. "You keep watch as if you expect an attack."

He didn't answer right away. "One can never be too careful or too complacent."

"But you didn't bring many men. If you truly feared an attack, wouldn't you have brought more?"

A hint of a smile tugged at the corner of his mouth, but it never reached his eyes. "There are more than you see."

She frowned, glancing behind them. "What do you mean?"

"There are men who ride a distance ahead and behind," he said. "Not close, nor obvious. They stay in the woods and the shadows. No one will surprise us."

It should have comforted her. Instead, it made her all the more aware of how dangerous this journey could become and just how vigilant he was in keeping her safe. He had not let her stray far from him and she had done her best not to. It continued to amaze her how concerned he remained for her safety. He had never been that way with her.

Esme let her gaze drift ahead, the path winding like a ribbon through the bleak landscape. She couldn't say why, but something about this journey, this search, felt like the start of a reveal of things kept secret far too long.

"Stay close," Torrance said.

Her husband had reminded her of that countless times since they had begun their journey. That he intended to protect her was obvious and oddly enough, it made her feel safer.

It wasn't long before they found a clearing tucked in the forest and set up camp. Esme couldn't be more relieved after a day of riding endlessly with barely an occasional respite.

The campsite fires crackled softly, casting flickering shadows across the clearing. Night had settled deep around them, the sky a dark veil studded with stars. The small camp was quiet, but not unguarded. The men moved with the practiced ease of warriors who knew peace was often a moment's illusion. Swords remained close and eyes kept watch on the trees beyond the firelight.

Esme sat on the thick blankets that had been laid out for her and Torrance, the fire warming her face as the cold night pressed in around them. She found comfort in the quiet, in the muted sounds of horses shifting, leather creaking, the low murmur of warriors sharing brief words before sleep.

Torrance joined her without a word, sitting beside her on the blankets. The firelight danced over the hard angles of his face, and she let her gaze linger there. Though she told herself she was being foolish, hope continued to let her be a fool and think Torrance was anyone other than her husband. She couldn't find anything different in his face and who besides him had such bold green eyes?

Ryland.

His and Torrance's eye color were identical, but how did that help her? The rumor could be true. Torrance and Ryland could be half-brothers. And it would make it that much easier for Ryland to assume Torrance's identity.

Miracle.

She was hoping for a miracle.

"Are you still… uncomfortable?" he asked quietly.

She smiled softly. "The cold that seeps through the blanket eases it."

"You should not be riding—"

"It is not that bad. A minor irritation, that's all," she assured him surprised again that he showed concern. Torrance certainly wouldn't care. He would tell her it was a woman's lot in life, and she should bear it. So, her suspicions continued to nag at her. Who truly sat beside her?

Before he could say more, she asked, "You said you expect to uncover truths on this journey. What else do you expect?"

He turned his head toward her. "Secrets. And secrets rarely come without a price."

She held her hands out to the fire. "Hopefully, not too high of a price."

Torrance reached out and took her hands in between his two.

She caught the gasp that rose up in her throat before it could escape, the reaction of the friction of his warmth against her cold startling her. It settled a warmth low in her belly that startled her even more. Why had her husband suddenly become appealing to her? It continued to frighten, delight, and confuse her, and she had no idea what to do about it.

"We need to sleep. We leave early," Torrance said, releasing her hands. "I small, insignificant clan, Clan Stott, will provide shelter for us tomorrow night. So, you need only suffer the cold ground tonight."

She spoke without thinking. "You will keep me warm enough."

He leaned his head close to hers. "You like my warmth, wife?"

She would not deny the truth. "I have come to favor it."

She spotted the shift in his eyes and knew he would kiss her, and she could not believe that she welcomed it.

He leaned closer to steal a kiss, a safe one since it could go no further but a kiss here in the camp, when suddenly a sound tore through the night. The roar was so loud, so inhuman, that Torrance shot up on his feet, dragging his wife along with him.

Esme planted herself against his side, her heart slamming against her chest in fear.

Torrance had his sword in hand, his warriors following suit, their hands going to their swords without hesitation once on their feet.

A warrior burst into the firelight, breathless and bloodied but recognized, the warriors' eyes rounding at the sight of Torrance.

"We've been betrayed!" he said, his breath labored. "By our own kind. I barely got away!"

Shock and uncertainty had warriors backing away from each other. Barely, a moment later, a warrior rode into camp from the opposite end, reining his horse hard, and yelling, "We've been betrayed."

Torrance's eyes narrowed, as he looked at every warrior in camp. "If you mean to betray me, do so now."

Not one warrior stepped forward.

Even as he spoke, the night filled with distant shouts and the clash of steel, the sounds growing.

Torrance turned to his men. "We separate in twos, so they don't know who to follow. Head back to the keep and whoever gets there first alerts Brack. Have him send only the most trusted warriors to search for those who don't make it back and to see who we lost and who it was who betrayed us."

His warriors hurried to do as he commanded.

Torrance summoned one of his warriors and they shared whispered words before he took off. Then he turned to Esme, his hand already reaching for her. "We ride one horse." Her puzzled look had him explaining. "They will have no interest in following one rider."

She nodded, understanding that they would be searching for Torrance and her, riding two horses, not one.

The warriors began to disperse but not before Torrance's horse was brought to him. He lifted her up onto his stallion, then swung himself up behind her and tucked her tight against him. She wrapped her arm around his waist as he led them into the forest, the firelight fading behind them as the darkness closed in around them.

CHAPTER 16

Torrance rode with caution, keeping one arm locked around Esme as she slumped against him. She had finally surrendered to exhaustion. Her head rested near his shoulder, her whisper warm breath tickling at his neck.

It wasn't easy maneuvering through the forest in the dead of night and only half a moon to light the way. But his stallion, dark as the night itself, moved with relentless purpose through narrow trails and over uneven ground, guided by Torrance's steady hands on the reins. He barely noticed the biting wind or the way branches clawed at him. He was too busy keeping his eyes focused in the dark while his thoughts continued to spin darker than the path ahead.

How was it that his men had turned against him?

It wasn't beyond belief. He had cultivated fear with ease, given reason for many to hate him, and trust was a luxury long stripped from his life. But to know betrayal was within his own ranks... it made him realize how desperate and dangerous the game he played could be.

He had risked much more than his life. Esme was now bound to that risk, and that weighed heavier than any blade.

By the time he spotted a low ridge nestled beneath a tangle of trees, the cold had seeped through his bones. He slowed the stallion and guided him off the trail to a narrow hollow, mostly shielded from the wind. There, between ancient trees and thick bushes, was space enough to hide for the night.

Torrance dismounted with care, cradling Esme in his arms as he slid to the ground. She stirred but didn't wake, murmuring something unintelligible against his chest. He tucked her close to him, led the stallion to a patch of grass, then lowered Esme to the leaf-covered earth and joined her there. He took her into his arms wrapping his cloak around them both. With Esme beside him, her warmth pressed close, he kept his hand on the hilt of his sword, and waited for a light sleep, if sleep would come at all.

Above, the trees whispered secrets, and the stars remained hidden. As the fire of betrayal burned low in his chest, one thought lingered… time was running out. If he did not learn the truth soon… all would be lost, much more than he ever expected.

* * *

TORRANCE URGED his stallion into a steady trot the next morning. The weight of the night clung to him, Esme's warmth against him, the silence that bred too many thoughts, and the knowledge that time was slipping through his fingers like rainwater.

Esme wasn't surprised when he had barely said two words to her this morning upon waking. He rushed her up onto his stallion and swung up behind her, and they were off. His tense body and the way his eyes continually scanned the area had her realizing they were not out of danger yet.

She had to ask, "Where do we go?"

"Clan Stott," he said, never taking his eyes off their surroundings. "We're not far from it."

She blinked against the dull light, pulling her cloak tighter around her. "That's where we were meant to take shelter today, is it not?"

He gave a short nod but said nothing more.

As the forest thinned, the land dipped into a small valley, and there a modest village sat tucked neatly against the hills... Clan Stott. Wisps of smoke curled lazily from thatched rooftops, and a few figures moved about busy with morning chores.

Torrance slowed the stallion to a stop, his eyes sharpening.

Esme followed his gaze, then felt him go rigid against her.

At the entrance to the village stood a mam, his aging frame still commanding, who Esme assumed was the clan chieftain. But it was not the chieftain Torrance watched, it was the man speaking with him.

The breath caught in Esme's throat. "That man... isn't he the one who rode into camp and warned of the second betrayal?"

"Aye, it is. Gavin." The name left Torrance like a curse. "He rode with the group that took the lead to make sure no danger awaited us. He was ordered to return home and seek help."

Esme's stomach churned with fear. How many men had betrayed Torrance? Had any warrior gone home for help? Or were they completely on their own? Watching the easy familiarity between the two men below caused worry to churn her stomach.

The way Torrance's grip whitened around the reins and

how a storm brewed behind his eyes, she believed her husband was thinking the same.

"Is that Chieftain Eagan who Gavin speaks with, and do you think the chieftain is part of it all?" she asked.

"I don't know, though from here it certainly looks that way" he said. "I'll not ride into a place where betrayal might be welcomed with open arms."

While the situation frightened her it also confused her, and she voiced the sudden thought that came to her. "Could it be that those who favored Ryland as the victor, now tries to turn defeat to victory for him?"

"Don't be a fool, wife," he snapped. "Anyone who shows Ryland any mercy knows the consequences of such folly."

Her heart thudded, realizing this could be a chance, one more attempt to crack the mask he wore, if he wore one. She could see how he reacted to the mention of Ryland and how this might be more about him than Torrance.

She edged a bit closer to danger with her next remark. "What if there are those who believe Ryland is entitled to rule Clan Glencairn?"

He turned and looked at her and calmly, though firmly as if he was declaring it an edict, said, "Clan Glencairn will always be ruled by a rightful heir of Glencairn." He grabbed hold of her chin. "And your duty is to produce one."

And finally, there was a chance she would.

His hand fell away from her chin, and he turned his head, just slightly. The sharp line of his jaw was taut. His voice, when it came, was a low growl. "I will not beg for loyalty nor chase the favor of cowards. But any man who dares betray me, any man," —he glared at her— "or woman who seeks to raise a hand against me, will know pain before he or she finds death."

That he confirmed only a rightful heir would rule Clan Glencairn would be something her husband would say, something he and his father were adamant about. And she had heard Torrance say many times that no half-blood would ever have the title of Lord of Clan Glencairn. She had believed that it was part of the reason he went to war with Ryland. He wanted him dead, never able to lay claim to the title.

And why would Ryland even want it? He had his own clan and from what she heard he was content with no aspirations of ever ruling Clan Glencairn. So, why would she think it wasn't Torrance who returned home to her but Ryland?

Torrance was different. There was no denying it. If he wasn't Ryland, then what would have changed him? And would that change last?

"You would show no mercy?" she asked, though knew how her husband would answer.

He gazed at her then, not cold, not angry just... resolute. "Only a weak woman would ask such a foolish question. Mercy is wasted on traitors."

She looked away, staring at the distant village, thinking she was losing her mind, and wondering if that was her husband's plan all along. To drive her mad and be rid of her. Perhaps he already had a woman in mind for his next wife. But then why chance getting her with child?

He grabbed her chin again, fiery anger in his eyes that burnt out quickly and he rested his brow to hers. "No matter what happens, I will not see you harmed. I will keep you safe."

That was it. He was trying to drive her mad and she, like a fool, was falling for it. One moment he was cruel, the next tender. She couldn't let herself be tricked. She couldn't fall into his trap, since she was sure death awaited her there. But how... how did she ever survive?

Torrance turned the horse away from Clan Stott and led them once again into the forest.

* * *

THEY HAD BEEN RIDING for some time, clouds growing darker as they followed overhead. The air remained heavy, as if the trees themselves were holding their breath. Each hoofbeat echoed in Esme's ears, but still Torrance said nothing. The silence between them had grown thick, stretched so taut she feared one word might snap it.

Esme kept her hands resting in her lap, having no desire to wrap her arms around him. Her worrisome thoughts continued to grow. She silently continued to berate herself for being so foolish. Torrance enjoyed laying a trap for people, though he more enjoyed the punishment he inflicted for being caught in one. She had seen him do it time and again. She should have realized it. She had dug her own grave.

Her voice broke the silence, soft and unsteady. "Where do we go now?"

Torrance's grip on the reins tightened. He did not answer her, did not look at her.

Esme swallowed the lump rising in her throat and tried again. "Will we return home?"

Still, he said nothing.

"Or do we continue on to complete the mission?"

Her only response was a snort from the stallion.

She kept her voice firm, but she could not prevent her unease from being heard. "Or are you not sure what you'll do with me yet?"

That brought a response. She felt his entire body shift, muscles tense, though he maintained his silence.

Dread coiled in her chest. The way he had dispersed his warriors so fast and rode away with her and how he wouldn't dare approach Clan Stott… it all gnawed at her. She couldn't shake the feeling that something more than betrayal haunted him. The fear that she had made the most dreadful mistake clawed at her.

What if this was the trap? Not just for her but for warriors he felt weren't loyal. It was an easy way to get rid of them. And what of her? Did he bring her this far just to be rid of her?

She wanted to believe it wasn't true, wanted so badly to believe he had changed. But evil didn't change and Torrance was an evil man capable of anything, especially deception.

Had she been a fool? Had she wanted to be free of Torrance so badly that she had conjured some reckless suspicion in her mind to free her of evil?

A sharp rustle to the left, in the woods, had Torrance drawing his stallion to a halt. Then a rustle came from the right.

Esme barely turned her head before men stepped from the woods—one, two, then more, surrounding the trail like wolves closing in. Their weapons were drawn and their eyes already locked on Torrance.

The stallion reared slightly beneath him, apprehensively.

Torrance swore beneath his breath.

Esme didn't wait. This could be her only chance, and she took it.

She threw herself off the horse, hitting the ground hard. Pain jolted through her palms and knees, but she pushed herself up and ran straight into the forest. Branches whipped at her face, roots caught at her feet, and cold air tore at her lungs. But she didn't stop. She ran as though the devil himself gave chase... and he did.

Fear pounded in her head louder than her heartbeat. He led me here. He knew. This was always the plan to get me alone. Get rid of me, so he could find a new wife.

The woods blurred around her, panic turning everything to shadow and sound. Then she heard it, the crunch of leaves behind her. Someone chased after her. The heavy footfalls grew louder, drawing closer.

She veered left, her heart thundering, her breath ragged. A branch snapped behind her. She didn't look back. She couldn't. She didn't want to see who chased her, didn't want to know how little time she had.

It came suddenly, shockingly. A heavy weight struck her from behind. She hit the ground with a cry, breath driven from her lungs. Still, she struggled as best she could, fighting until the very end, kicking, clawing, the world spinning.

"STOP, ESME! STOP!"

His voice was so fierce that it froze her, giving him enough time to pin her.

Torrance.

He loomed above her, his breath hot and fast, his hands tight around her wrists, holding her pinned to the forest floor. His hair hung loose over his brow, his eyes wild—not with rage, but something else. Something raw.

Then he said, "You know... don't you?"

CHAPTER 17

"Ryland." Esme whispered, shocked that her suspicions had been accurate.

"I knew you'd be a problem." Mumbling, he pulled her up on her feet. "Far more of a problem than I ever imagined."

"I don't understand," Esme said relieved, though only briefly, not sure what Ryland intended to do with her since he considered her a problem.

"I have no time to explain it to you right now. You're not hurt, are you?" He took hold of her hand and started moving her along.

"Nay," she said, shaking her head. "But those men who stepped out of the woods—"

"Are faithful to Ryland," he said.

"You. You're Ryland," Esme said, needing to say it aloud, needing to hear him admit it.

He brought them to an abrupt halt and yanked her against him, keeping her locked against his chest. "I need to remain Torrance for now. I cannot have you mistakenly refer to me any other way. And, at the moment, I have no time to explain it all to you."

Her racing heart slowed, seeing concern rather than anger in his eyes. "I need to know one thing."

His concern deepened and he spoke as if he had stepped into her mind and knew what she was thinking. "Aye, Torrance, is dead."

Relief turned her legs weak, and his arm tightened around her. Tears tickled at her eyes, not out of sadness but joy that she was free and would no longer live in fear... unless.

She looked up at Ryland.

Confusion showed in his eyes. "You shed tears for him?"

"Nay, I shed tears of relief that I am free of him, but tell me, what fate awaits me with you?"

Ryland wished he had more time to talk with her, explain what he could, ease her worries, and do what he wanted to do most... kiss her. He really had to quell his desire for her. Bloody hell. He knew it was much more than that. He loved her with all his heart and if he wasn't careful it would get in the way of the plan.

"That has yet to be decided, but you have my word that no harm will come to you. You are safe with me," he assured her. "Now, we must go. We can talk more when it is safe to talk."

Ryland led Esme through the woods, his grip on her hand firm and his pace quick, as if time itself were nipping at his heels.

Esme noticed that he didn't return to the spot where the men had surprised them but instead, he took her near the bend of a shallow stream, were a handful of warriors were gathered.

These were the men Ryland had spoken of—men loyal to him, not Torrance. Relief was short-lived. Strangers, no matter whose name they answered to, were still strangers.

A lean, tall, though not as tall as Ryland, warrior stepped forward at the sight of him.

"Finally," he breathed, with relief. "I was beginning to worry that you were dead since we haven't heard from you after receiving your first cryptic message."

"I'm a difficult man to kill, Nug," Ryland said with a grin.

Nug closed the distance between them and pulled Ryland into a fierce embrace, slapping his back as if proving to himself that he was real.

"Thank the Lord," Nug said, stepping back after giving Ryland's arm a firm squeeze. "You've no idea what it's been like. Not knowing, worrying, praying."

"I had no choice. The opportunity presented itself and I could not turn away from it," Ryland said. "I thank you for trusting me and keeping my silence."

"That was never in question. Need I remind you that we have been friends since we were young, Ryland? If you cannot trust me, who could you trust?" Nug said, then his gaze swept over to Esme. "I recall seeing you on a visit to Clan Glencairn. You are Torrance's wife."

The men behind Nug were all watching her now, silent, curious, waiting for her response.

"Widow. I am Torrance's widow," she corrected, surprising herself.

The silence that followed made her question her choice of words.

Then Nug arched a brow at Ryland. "Is it true? Torrance is dead?"

"Aye," Ryland said with a nod. "I watched him take his last breath, though I had no time to bury him."

"Then how can you be sure he's dead," Nug argued. "Evil is hard to kill."

"I'm no fool, Nug. I went back when time allowed," Ryland said. "The forest animals left enough trace of him for me to be sure."

Before Ryland could respond, hoofbeats sounded nearby. Esme's head snapped toward the sound, unease stirring in her again.

Two riders emerged from the dense forest, one barely big enough to ride the horse, and the other large and formidable.

"Dru," Ryland said under his breath, and sure enough, the petite, young woman flung herself off her horse the moment it halted. Her red, wind-tossed hair was as fiery as her nature.

"I knew it!" Dru marched straight up to Ryland and jabbed a finger at his chest. "You lied to me. I knew something wasn't right about Torrance. He would have never allowed Knox to wed me, not unless he meant to have Knox beheaded the next day!"

Knox dismounted with far more restraint, his gaze sweeping the area, then settling on Esme. He gave a polite nod as he came to a stop near his wife.

"You're welcome," Ryland said.

Dru softened. "I do owe you for recognizing and declaring Knox and my marriage valid. But tell me… was there any truth in what you said about my father telling Torrance that he was to find me a good husband, a safe one? Or was it an excuse you used to confirm my marriage?" She shook her finger at him. "And I will have the truth."

"Are you sure of that, Dru?" Ryland asked with a quick glance at Knox.

"Aye, I'm sure," Dru said, and Knox stepped close behind her.

"Your father cared only that your marriage benefitted the clan, and Torrance said the same to me."

Dru tried not to show her disappointment, but Knox felt

it and slipped his arm around her waist, and she leaned back against him.

"That's not true," Esme said to everyone's surprise. "I heard Torrance's father make his son promise to find a good man to be your husband. A man who would treat you well. He didn't want to fail you the way he failed your mother. Impending death has a way of making people realize their mistakes and giving them a chance to make amends. Your father wanted to see you kept safe. Torrance did not care about you or the promise he made to his father."

Dur smiled and squeezed her husband's arm coiled around her waist. "I am grateful to you for telling me that."

"My condolences you got stuck with her, Knox," Nug said with a laugh.

Dru chuckled. "Funny, Nug, but at least I have someone who loves me." She stretched her neck to gaze about. "Where's the woman who loves you?" She chuckled. "I forgot... she only exists in your dreams."

The men around them laughed.

One called out, "She's right about that."

"There are plenty women who favor me," Nug argued.

"So, you dream often then," another called out.

Esme watched the humorous exchange, uncertain what to make of it all. These were people Ryland clearly trusted. People who spoke to him with ease, without fear. It was jarring, after endlessly being watched, judged, and commanded since marrying Torrance. They laughed and teased, as if no danger lingered nearby, no past haunted them.

Yet she couldn't shake the ache in her stomach. These people were strangers to her. Loyal to Ryland... but what did that mean for her?

Ryland stepped back beside her, sensing her unease. His

hand gently brushed her arm. "Trust me. You are safe with me, with them."

Trust. Safe. There had been moments she had felt safe with him, and she wanted to believe that she could continue to do so. But trust was another matter. She hadn't trusted her husband, and she truly didn't know if she could trust Ryland. And the reason for that? Why had he coupled with her when he wasn't her husband?

"You're Torrance's wife?" Dru called out to her.

"Widow," Esme corrected.

"I am happy for you. You've suffered worse than most. Torrance was a cruel bastard. Good riddance to him."

Esme was caught off guard by her blunt compassion, but managed to say, "Thank you. It is a relief."

Nug grew impatient. "It's time we—"

"Talk," Ryland finished, "And for you all to return home before you're spotted and my identity revealed. But we need a safer place where we can be sure no eyes can see us or ears can hear us. And we have little time. I have no doubt at least one of Torrance's warriors will make it to Clan Glencairn. Brack will waste no time in coming to find me."

"Unlike others," Dru said with a grin at Nug. "I figured we might need a safe place to meet, and for Ryland to stay if necessary, so I found one."

"No clan around here can be completely trusted," Nug said. "Nor abbey as well, since Torrance pays a good yearly stipend to many."

"And you think I don't know that, Nug?" Dru asked, wrinkling her nose at him.

"I forget you know everything," Nug shot back.

Dru grinned. "Finally, you admit it."

Nug glared at her. "One of these days—"

"You will learn not to challenge her," Knox said and glanced at his wife. "Tell them where we go."

"There is an abandoned keep not far from here," Dru said.

"Purdom Keep?" Nug asked anxiously and nervous whispers began to spread.

"Aye, Purdom Keep, a place where no one will venture," Dru said.

"And for a good reason," Nug argued. "It's haunted."

* * *

THEY HAD BARELY SET a good pace, everyone dividing to meet at Purdom Keep avoiding any chance of them being seen together, when Esme spoke.

"Was this meeting with your friends planned?"

"Aye, though it didn't go as expected. I sent a cryptic message to someone who could decipher it and who could make sure Knox and Dru also got the message. I intended to see you safe at Clan Stott and then sneak away to meet with them. I knew once my friends learned of the betrayal of Torrance's warriors that they would know enough to alter the plan. They knew I would do my best to be in this area near the specified time so all they had to do was wait."

Her eyes lingered on his face, trying to see if she could spot the difference between him and Torrance. It was difficult to find one, they looked so much alike, though his features didn't seem as harsh, his eyes as cruel but that could be because she knew he was Ryland. "You look identical to him."

"And here I thought you would first ask about the haunted keep," he said with a slight smile.

The light tease in his voice and a hint of a smile did much to ease her misgivings and speak bluntly.

"That can wait until later as can the reason you coupled with me knowing I wasn't your wife. It is Torrance I wish to know about."

He was relieved she would wait for that intimate discussion since he wasn't prepared to hold it now with her. But he did give her what she asked for. "That we looked so much alike was always a thorn in Torrance's side. He assumed we were half-brothers, believing that my mother had an affair with Torrance's father. As we grew older, the thorn dug deeper, and I believe he always worried that I would try to lay claim to Clan Glencairn."

"Do you think it is why he went to war with you?"

Ryland tried to stay focused, but her lips, chilled rosy by the cold, were too inviting to ignore. Of course, it hadn't helped that they had coupled and not the way he would have had it for their first time together. But since they had, he now was eager to share more with her and as Ryland, not Torrance.

He finally gathered his senses and nodded. "I believe it was part of it, but Torrance also had a thirst for power, wealth, importance. And he believed growing his holdings would bring him all that."

She asked the question that she desperately wanted to know. "What happened to him?"

Ryland hesitated.

She rested her hand on his arm at her waist. "Please, Ryland, I need to know."

He nodded and acquiesced. "Clan MacLeish was being defeated, far too many of my warriors dying. I called for them to retreat but, the mercenaries Torrance hired were relentless. I managed to get some of the wounded off the battlefield to start their journey home. I carried a badly wounded warrior to one of my warriors who was good at mending battle wounds. I returned to the battlefield to get more of my men when I came across Torrance out of sight of the battle, one of his own warriors having turned his sword on him. I could see Torrance was badly wounded, but he continued to fight, and he managed to deliver a fatal blow to his opponent before collapsing to the ground.

"I went to him and his first words to me were… 'Though I die today, I will see victory and you will see me revenged.' He then went on to explain that I was to become him, assume his identity and find out who in his clan wanted him dead. He warned me that there would be more attempts on his life… on me."

"And he expected you to take such a dangerous chance, live such a lie?"

"He told me I'd be a fool to refuse and that it was my duty since no doubt we were half-brothers and though I am not a full-blooded Glencairn, at least a Glencairn would rule and that was all that mattered. He demanded I give him my word."

Esme shook her head. "That makes no sense. Torrance would have no way of knowing that you would keep your word."

"You underestimate him."

"Sadly, you're right," she agreed, recalling her husband's relentless determination.

"By assuming his identity, I could end the battle and keep my clan safe, which was what mattered to me the most, and he knew that."

"But you would forfeit your own life to live the life of a cruel man."

"My only thought at the time was saving more of my warriors from dying and my clan from suffering. There would be time to figure out the rest. But the attempts on my life, and yours, made me realize that if I was to protect my clan and you, I needed to survive and to do that I had to find out who wanted Torrance dead. And I did give him my word that I would revenge his death."

"Why would they want me dead?"

"An heir. With my return they assumed you would get with child, and they hoped to prevent that."

"Why not tell me the truth from the start?"

"I did not know who to trust, for all I knew you could be the one who wanted Torrance dead, and for good reason, though it became obvious quite fast that it wasn't you."

"You could have told me before I foolishly threw myself at you to get with child."

"That was not easy for me," he admitted, then thought better of it.

"It was far from easy for me—" She tilted her head slightly. "Why wasn't it easy for you?"

"I've said enough for now," he said abruptly. "You should know about Purdom Keep."

Esme grew quiet. Was it that Ryland found her as repulsive as Torrance that made it uneasy for him? But why kiss her? To keep up the pretense? She wanted to ask him, but she didn't have the courage, thinking his response might be too hurtful to hear.

"Do you believe in ghosts, Esme?"

She sighed. "I don't know what I believe anymore."

"Is that why you ran?" he asked.

His heart had slammed into his chest when she slipped off the horse and disappeared into the woods. He had frozen for a moment, she had so shocked him. Then fear of losing her had him rushing after her, his friends calling out letting him know where to meet them. He was confident he could easily gain on her, his speed far faster than hers. He would catch her and not let her go.

"I am not even sure why I ran," she said, thinking on her sudden action. "I had no place to go, yet I didn't know if I was safe with you. Worries rushed through my head and I," —she shook her head— "I reacted without thinking."

"Don't do it again," he demanded.

Her brow puckered. "You sound like Torrance, cold and commanding."

Anger sparked in his eyes, and he snapped, "I am not Torrance."

Esme drew her head back, his remark striking like a whip... as Torrance would do.

Anger fled his eyes. "I don't know how many times I must tell you. You have nothing to fear from me. I will not harm you."

She gathered her courage and voiced her concern. "So, you say and while you might not intentionally harm me, this lie you live may leave you little choice and leave me more a prisoner than I had been."

"Unlike Torrance, I speak the truth and keep my word. You need to trust me on this," he said and with such conviction that it was difficult not to believe him.

But as Esme had said to him, she didn't know what to believe and she certainly didn't know who to trust.

"Let's get back to the ghosts," he said to avoid the more difficult conversation.

But ghosts were not her concern. There was more she wanted to learn. "Is it Torrance's truths and secrets we search for or yours that brings us here?"

"Both," he said, "but that talk is better left for later. Now about the ghosts."

CHAPTER 18

"The keep has been unoccupied for some time. Rumors say it is filled with such sadness that no one can live there. Weeping is heard, fires cannot chase the cold, and shadows move where there shouldn't be any."

Ryland's words echoed in Esme's thoughts as Purdom Keep came into view, its silhouette etched starkly against a bleak winter sky. The chill in the air hinted that snow might be near. The landscape bore the waiting hush of the season's approach, bare trees, hardened ground, and a sullen wind carrying the scent of frost.

The keep crouched atop a knoll, more like a forgotten monument than a dwelling. Its stone walls were streaked black with age, and the main tower stood proud and tall as if daring anyone to approach it. A few narrow windows gaped like empty eyes. Even the forest seemed to keep its distance, the bare limbs of the trees not brave enough to reach too close.

Esme shoulders tighten beneath her cloak, intimidated by the uninhibited edifice. "It doesn't look abandoned," she murmured. "It looks alive and like it's waiting."

Ryland gave a faint nod. "Aye, waiting for something to wake the sorrow sleeping within. It looks like the others arrived before us. They'll have a fire waiting to warm us."

The keep itself appeared far from inviting but that a warm fire waited, and others as well, had Esme eager to enter the place.

Inside, the cold bit deeper. The fire in the large hearth barely warmed the air in the long-deserted hall. Nug stood by the hearth, poking the logs to flame brighter while Dru sat at a table with Knox, tucked in the crook of his large arms for warmth. Two warriors waited outside the front door and a few others were positioned near the keep but out of sight to watch for any uninvited guests.

Ryland walked with his hand at Esme's back, directing her to a table close to the heat of the hearth and once he saw her seated, he said. "We need to make this brief. The longer you all stay, the more chance of you being seen and word spreading."

"So, now with your life in danger what do we do and is there anyone you suspect?" Nug asked.

Esme watched shadows brush across Ryland's handsome face as if masking and unmasking him and she thought how appropriate, having spent time being two men.

"A suspect list would be long. Torrance made enemies, some obvious, some hidden," Ryland said. "But with his own men betraying him, there is a chance that the source comes from within Clan Glencairn itself. Hakon is tracking two men dressed as monks. I believe they may have been the ones who poisoned the food meant for me, but Esme ate and suffered instead."

"Thank the Lord you survived," Dru said, and Esme smiled her appreciation for her thoughtful remark.

"Does Hakon know who you are?" Knox asked.

Ryland shook his head. "Nay, he nor Brack know. Best it stays that way... for now."

"Then we move fast before it is too late for you and Esme," Dru said. "I'll get word to my contacts. See if any rumors surface, coin for information usually works faster than blades."

Nug rubbed at the back of his neck. "I hate to agree with Dru, but she's right. We need to move fast before it's too late."

Dru turned her head, her hand going behind her ear to push it out as if to hear better. "What was that you said, Nug. I didn't quite hear you. Something about me being right?"

"You heard it well enough and it's the last time you'll hear it," Nug said and glared at Dru, hearing her chuckle. "I need to get back to the clan. Make sure that our warriors stand ready should the worst come. And I am sure you want The Monk to know."

"The Monk is no fool," Dru said. "I bet he's already figured it out and is just waiting for conformation. And if you can trust anyone, it's The Monk."

Esme had heard of The Monk, a fierce and exceptionally skilled mercenary who her husband had admired. She had heard that Torrance, though it was actually Ryland who had placed The Monk in charge of Clan MacLeish not long after the battle and until he ordered otherwise. Ryland had made sure to see to the safety of his clan as soon as possible. Torrance had been right about trusting Ryland to keep his word. He was a man of honor and would do anything to keep his clan, his family, safe.

"One more thing before we take our leave," Nug said. "What brings you to these parts, Ryland?"

"A secret that may help settle this situation. But not one I am ready to discuss just yet. Now be on your way and I will be in touch with my usual cryptic messages for you to decipher."

While Nug and Knox went to Ryland for a few private words before departure, Dru went to Esme. "You've got courage surviving a marriage to the devil himself. But you have nothing to fear with Ryland. He is a good man. A bit commanding at times, but that comes from being a wise chieftain. You're safe with him."

Esme smiled softly. "Thank you for your encouraging words." She wanted to believe they were true, but once again she simply did not know what or who to believe or trust.

* * *

THE FIRE CRACKLED low in the hearth, its glow barely touching the thick stone walls. Shadows shifted and stretched along the high, soot-streaked ceiling. Dust clung to every surface, undisturbed for years, and cobwebs fluttered like lace in the draft. Esme drew her knees to her chest, wrapped in her cloak on a blanket spread out near the fire.

They hadn't bothered exploring the rest of the keep. Neither had the stomach to wander halls echoing with old grief. The Great Hall was enough of a haven for the night. More than enough.

Ryland sat close beside her, his body brushing against hers, staring into the fire like it held answers. Or maybe penance. He could sense she had more questions and ones he didn't want to answer. But he could understand her wanting to know, though he worried that knowing would only cause her more pain?

"You didn't tell me everything," Esme said softly.

His gaze didn't move. "About what?"

"What Torrance said… before he died."

He let silence linger between them.

She felt his hesitancy to answer her in the way his body tensed and shifted against her. "He said something about me, didn't he?"

Ryland didn't look at her. "Some things are better left unsaid."

"I want to know." She didn't demand. It was more of a soft plea.

Ryland struggled between her right to know and not wanting to hurt her.

She reached out and placed her hand on his arm. "You told me to trust you. I trust you to speak truthfully to me."

Her innocent touch sent a spark racing through him, igniting things in him that should not be on his mind right now. But nor should he tell her what Torrance said, but didn't she have a right to know?

The fire cracked, a sudden pop breaking the silence.

"I speak his words not mine," Ryland said, his voice low and rough. "He said you were a worthless wife that you couldn't get with child and that he intended to get rid of you and get a new wife. He told me that I was to carry through with his plan."

The words struck like a lash, though she had braced for them. Her throat tightened, her jaw clenched. But she didn't look away.

"You gave your word to him to do as he asked," she said, with a tremor in her voice.

His eyes met hers, solemn, unflinching. "Not about that. That I refused to do."

She blinked, stunned by the quiet weight of his words and what they could mean. The flicker of pain inside her chest softened.

"He never knew you. Never cared to get to know you. Torrance cared for no one but Torrance," Ryland said. "You are a beautiful, courageous woman who deserves so much more."

Her breath caught at his heartfelt words. "How did he react to your refusal?"

Torrance grinned. "He died cursing me since I told him I would do something he failed to do. That I would get you with child and not just one but many and that I would be a good husband to you."

Her mouth fell open, and her eyes went wide, he so stunned her.

Ryland took her hand in his. "I do not know how this situation will end. Whether I will have no choice but to remain Torrance and let Ryland die or if I can reclaim my life. If I must remain Torrance to keep peace, then I would be honored for you to remain my wife and share our life together. If I can return to being Ryland, then—" He shook his head. "I intended to give you a choice. Be free or wed me, but since we have coupled, we will wed."

"You would want me as your wife?" she asked bewildered.

"Why wouldn't I?"

She spoke truthfully. "I thought you didn't find me appealing."

"I found you appealing since the first day I saw you."

That shocked her. She never even imagined that he thought about her, though she had thought of him and his kindness to her.

"I always wanted to thank you for your kindness the day you were at Clan Glencairn and retrieved my shawl and spoke in defense of me. Though Torrance made sure I suffered for embarrassing him."

Ryland's eyes darkened. "What did he do to you?"

"Two days in my bedchamber with nothing but bread and water. Thankfully one of the servants took pity on me and snuck food to me."

"I am sorry you were punished for what I did, but it wasn't then that I found you appealing. The day I defended you was the day I fell in love with you."

Esme's mouth fell open, no words falling out. Had she heard him correctly? Had he said he had fallen in love with her? How could that be?

"I should explain," Ryland said when she remained speechless.

Esme nodded.

"I first saw you when I accompanied my da to your clan for him to speak with your father concerning trade. I saw you sitting under a tree hugging a kitten, kissing him on the head, smiling. I never saw someone as beautiful as you. I couldn't stop thinking about you. You were on my mind day and night. I finally told my father that I wished to wed you and to make an offer of marriage to your father."

Ryland turned quiet a moment. "I fear my offer spurred Torrance to make an offer of marriage for you since he forever felt in competition with me. I was furious when I found out what he did and that your father accepted his offer over mine. I confronted him and we fought, actually fought over it, and even though I bested him, it didn't matter. He laughed and said it was done, the agreement signed and that you would be his wife."

Quiet settled over him once again. "My first thought when I saw Torrance near death was that you would be free to wed again and I didn't intend to lose you a second time. When he presented his plan to me, it wasn't only my clan I wanted to protect… it was you."

Esme stared dumbfounded at him. "My father never told me. No one ever told me. I would have gladly accepted your offer. It has been so difficult thinking you two different men, finding that I enjoyed being with one and fearful of being with the other. To realize I cared for one and not the other."

"You care for me… for Ryland," he asked anxiously.

"I do and it shocked me to realize it, to favor your kisses, your touch… when you could be so cruel at other times.

He cringed. "I hated treating you badly. It tore at my heart." He reached out to rest his hand on her cheek. "I should have waited until you knew who I was to couple with you. It should have been your decision whether you wanted Ryland or not, but—good, Lord—it was torture keeping my hands off you. I want to love you so badly." He shook his head. "The way you challenged me that night sent me over the edge. But it was not the way I wanted it for us, especially after learning you and Torrance never consummated your marriage. It should have been your choice."

"It was," Esme said, turning her face so that her lips grazed his palm with a kiss. "My thought had been that if you were Torrance, I would least have the chance to get with child and if I was right and you were Ryland, I believed you an honorable man who would do right by me."

He leaned his head down and kissed her. "I will do right by you, Esme. I will love you more each day for the rest of our lives and keep you and…" He rested his hand on her stomach. "Our future bairns safe. I only hope someday you can love me half as much as I love you."

"Now that I know it is you, Ryland, I can care, feel for you without fear."

"Take your time, Esme, I want you to be sure that you love me, and not that you're just grateful I'm not Torrance."

"I more than care for you, Ryland, but Torrance left me wounded and I need to heal, to know you are not him so Torrance can never darken my life ever again."

"I understand that Torrance isn't out of your life yet. And that it doesn't help that you must continue to call me by his name and I must continue to treat you badly in front of others."

"But it will be different his time," Esme said. "I will know your words hold no truth and that you are Ryland, a good man, a good husband."

"But you cannot act kindly toward me, show me favor when it is fear people expect to see in you when dealing with Torrance."

"That shouldn't be too difficult, for when you snap at me, berate me, talk badly to me, I believe you are Torrance."

He lowered his brow to rest on hers. "Any unkindness or meanness I show you know that I will make it up to you when we are alone."

A tingle rushed over her. "And how will you do that."

"Like this." He lowered his lips to hers and kissed her.

Esme enjoyed the kisses she had shared with him, but they were not nearly as amazing as the way he kissed her now. His arm slipped around her back, drawing her up against him as his lips took command in such a way that she could swear she felt the love he had for her.

But then she thought how easily she could love him, the caring Ryland, and she kissed him with all the power such a love could feel. It was like being swept away in a haze of magic where everything felt just right, where two hearts beat as one, where silent promises could be heard, where fate was willingly sealed.

Ryland reluctantly tore his mouth away from hers. "You are mine, Esme, mine forever."

"Aye, Ryland, and you are mine forever," she whispered.

"Good, for I have no intention of ever letting you go," he said and wrapped his arm around her as his lips settled on hers once again.

The kiss lingered between them, warm and full of unspoken promise—until the sound shattered it.

A heavy, drawn-out weeping echoed from above. A

woman's sorrowful cry, raw and unrelenting, drifted down through the rafters like a chill wind.

Esme stiffened, her eyes lifting to the darkened ceiling. "That… that wasn't the wind."

Ryland was already rising to his feet, lifting her along with him. "Stay here. I'll go look."

"You are not leaving me here alone," she said, latching onto his arm as tight as a shackle. "I'm going with you."

His eyes met hers, the firelight catching the fear in their depth. "Alright, then we do this together."

Esme agreed with a nod. "Aye, together."

A torch that Ryland took off the wall sprang to life when he held it to the hearth's fire. He held it out in front of them as they climbed the winding stone stairs, the cold deepening with each step. Cobwebs brushed their arms, and the air felt as if it grew still. The upper level of the keep sprawled before them, shrouded in shadow. Old wooden doors lined the hall, some partially open, others closed.

Silence hung heavily around them as if whatever was here had heard their approach and grew quiet at their intrusion.

A creak sounded and was followed by footfalls, light but unmistakable, padding across a wooden floor and coming from just ahead, yet they could see no one.

Esme tightened her grip on Ryland's arm. They moved slowly, cautiously, past each door, peeking in the open ones and pushing open the closed ones. Dust floated everywhere and cobwebs were plentiful. Some furniture pieces had decayed while others stood the test of time.

But no one was about.

Then another sob broke the silence, low and heartfelt, coming from further ahead.

They followed it down the narrow corridor, the sound leading them like a pulled thread.

Something made Esme turn her head, and she gasped.

A shadow darted across the far end of the hallway, too swift to see clearly, yet it carried the shape of a woman, hair flowing behind her like smoke.

Esme clutched Ryland's arm with both hands, pressing herself close. "Did you see that?"

He turned fast, raising the torch above them. "See what?"

A strange heaviness suddenly descended on her, as if the sorrow of the weeping ghost had seeped into her chest. Her eyes stung, a lump lodged in her throat, and she could no longer bear it.

Ryland saw her struggle. "What's wrong, Esme?"

"Please," she whispered, her voice breaking. "Get me out of here. I… I can't stay up here."

Ryland didn't hesitate. He wrapped his arm around her and led her down the stairs, guiding her back into the comforting glow of the hearth. She trembled as she sank down onto the blanket.

After returning the torch to its bracer, he sat down beside her, pulling her into his arms.

She clung to him tightly, burying her face in his chest, seeking his strength, his warmth, cold having sunk into her bones.

The sorrow lifted slowly, like a veil being drawn back and the deep cold began to fade. Her breath steadied, but her voice was barely a whisper when she spoke.

"It was unbearable… like grief had taken root inside me. As if I'd lost someone, I loved so deeply it hollowed me out."

Ryland pressed his lips to her temple and held her closer. "You didn't imagine it, Esme. Something lingers here."

She nodded against him, her fingers curling into his shirt.

"I don't think it means us harm," she said quietly. "But, like you, it searches for something."

The fire burned strong, leaving shadows lingering in the

corners, but the weeping had ceased, leaving only the quiet crackle of the logs and the sound of their breathing.

Esme remained nestled against Ryland, his arms strong around her, anchoring her to the present. She could still feel the lingering echo of that sorrow, like the fading ache of a bruise on her soul.

"I wonder who she was," she murmured. "What loss broke her so deeply that it still echoes through these walls?"

Ryland didn't speak right away. His fingers slowly traced a soothing path along her arm. "Maybe someone who loved fiercely," he said at last. "And had that love torn from her."

Esme closed her eyes. "It frightens me, how easily sorrow can slip inside and steal your breath. For a moment, I felt like I couldn't bear it. Like I might never feel light again."

He turned slightly, his cheek brushing her hair. "I would never let anything happen to you. I'm with you now and always."

She pulled back just enough to look up at him. In the firelight, his features softened, shadows and flame playing across his face. There was something unguarded in his eyes, something he hadn't shown her before. A quiet kind of protectiveness. A tenderness she'd never known.

"I don't know what happens next or where it will take us," he said, brushing his finger against her cheek. "But I do know we will face it together."

Her eyes shimmered, not with sorrow from before, but something gentler and warmer now. She felt loved and that faded her worries, though not completely. Not that it was any fault of Ryland's. It was the damage Torrance had done to her, how inadequate he had made her feel, the games he played that left her frightened and unsure of herself. That damage lingered in her and while Ryland was far different from Torrance, he wore the same face. And she couldn't help but worry, try as she might, of it hurting her chance of true happiness with Ryland.

"Aye, together," she said.

Ryland held her throughout the night as she slept in his arms. He remained alert, dozing now and again but never letting himself fully sleep, keeping alert, ready to protect Esme. He could feel and see the worry in her. Though she said she would no longer let Torrance darken her life, he knew it would not be that easy for her. Torrance had a way of leaving his mark on people one way or the other. He had tried to do it to him but had failed. It takes time to erase, to be rid of such a burdensome mark. But Ryland had faith that the love he had for Esme would make all the difference and that time would heal the invisible wounds she had suffered, and Torrance would be nothing but a faded, powerless memory.

CHAPTER 19

Darkness pressed in from all sides. Esme stood on the upper floor of the keep, the walls long and shadowed, the air thick with unease. She didn't remember how she had come to be there alone, not seeing Ryland anywhere.

"Ryland?" she called out, her voice tight with fear.

Silence was the only response she got.

She moved soundlessly over the cold stone floor as she hurried from chamber to chamber, heart pounding. Shadows leapt and danced, fed by glimmers of unseen firelight, but she found no sign of Ryland. Why had he left her alone? He promised he would keep her safe. Her panic swelled.

"Where are you?" she whispered, her body beginning to tremble.

She suddenly found herself in the corridor where the weeping had echoed before, but now it was oppressively still. A chill wrapped around her, a warning, and she turned only to see an old woman standing there. The same woman from the celebration at Clan Rennoch. Silver hair hung around her shoulders like strands of mist and her dark eyes glowed fathomless.

"Ryland must find the healer," she said, her voice thin and

whispery, as if carried on the breath of the dead. "The one known as an Seann Bhean."

Esme opened her mouth to speak, to demand more, but the woman lifted a finger.

"Beware," she whispered. "Friends are foes... and foes are friends."

With that, she vanished, dissolving into smoke that curled around Esme like grasping hands. A low growl rumbled through the air. Esme's breath caught as the hallway dimmed further, shadows thickening into something solid. A dark figure surged toward her out of the gloom, no face, no form, only menace, and she screamed, the sound ripping from her throat as she threw her arms up—

Esme woke, thrashing in Ryland's embrace.

"It's me, Ryland. You're safe, Esme," he said, tightening his hold, his voice rough with concern. "It was nothing more than a dream."

Her chest heaved, the scream still lingering on her lips, the terror still clawing at her insides. She clung to him, trembling, her cheek pressed against the warmth and solidness of his muscled chest.

"Nay, it was much more," Esme whispered hoarsely, struggling to strengthen her voice. "She… the mysterious woman who spoke to me at Clan Rennoch, said you must find the healer called an Seann Bhean… the old woman. And she warned to beware that friends are foes and foes are friends."

Ryland stilled, recalling how the woman had told Esme that she had to go with him on this quest. Was this why her presence was necessary?

Tears slid down her cheeks unchecked. "It felt so real, Ryland. So real…"

He cradled her closer, his hand stroking her hair, his concern for her mounting, feeling her slim body tremble against his. "Then we will take heed, Esme, since I believe you are right. It was more than a dream."

* * *

DAWN HAD BARELY TOUCHED the sky when they left Purdom Keep behind, its silhouette swallowed by mist. Ryland held Esme close, her back pressed against his solid chest, his arm tight around her waist as if he feared she might vanish with the fog.

Silence lingered between them, though it was not born of distance but of weight, of dreams and warnings neither could ignore.

They followed a narrow trail into the woods, the trees arching overhead like cathedral columns. The forest breathed with cold, quiet purpose, and Ryland's every glance scanned the shadows.

Esme broke the silence, tilting her head slightly to look at Ryland. "Do you know where to find her? The Old Woman?"

His jaw tensed. "Nay, I have no idea, but someone must. We should come upon a village soon. I'll ask the questions needed… as Torrance."

She asked gently, "Are you ready for that?"

"Are you?" he asked, his eyes filled with concern.

"I want to say, aye, but it will be strange seeing Torrance return in you, and me being his target once again. He was a skilled marksman and just like his arrows hitting their mark, his words hit with the same precision and pain."

He adjusted his heavy cloak wrapped around them both, giving her a reassuring squeeze. "Remind yourself that he is dead and he cannot hurt you anymore and pay no mind to any hurtful words I speak to you, for they are nothing but lies. And do not let the name Ryland slip from your lips and, most importantly, remember how much I love you."

Esme's heart soared hearing those words. She had come to understand, seeing him with his friends, how fiercely he protected those he cared for, those he loved, and to know she was part of that circle, though probably more the center of it, calmed her worries.

They rode in silence a while longer, the trail twisting and narrowing through the thickening trees. A raven's harsh cry echoed somewhere ahead, and Esme shivered.

"This place feels... watched," she said softly.

"When you're being hunted or doing the hunting, everything feels as if it is watching you," Ryland murmured."

Esme shivered again and wondered which one they were... the hunter or the hunted.

The land began to change, the forest thinning and opening to meadows dormant in the cold and not long after, the sharp outline of rooftops emerged in the distance, smoke curling into the gray sky.

"A village," Esme said relieved, yet anxious.

Ryland slowed the horse, scanning what little he could see. "It's small and isolated. That may work in our favor. I'll speak to whoever leads there. Hopefully, someone there has heard of the Old Woman."

"And if they ask why you're searching for her?"

"No one is foolish enough to question Lord Torrance," he said, with the commanding tone of her dead husband. "You will stay close. With no warriors to have my back, I will take no chances. One false look, one whisper out of place, and we leave. I'll not risk your safety."

She laid her hand over his where it rested at her waist. "I will do as you say, Ryland, and I will obey Torrance's every word without question."

He kissed her, her lips welcoming and eager as if for that moment the world slipped away and there were only the two of them, then—reluctantly—he urged his stallion forward.

Torrance entered the village at a slow gait, keeping his arm snug around Esme's waist.

Heads turned their way and conversations faltered as the villagers watched the couple ride through the village.

A lad, his eyes wide, dropped the bundle of firewood he'd been carrying and rushed off after one look at Torrance.

A grizzled man leaning on a cane squinted at them, then blinked hard and stumbled back a step.

Esme swore she heard him whisper, "Lord Torrance."

They didn't travel much deeper into the village when the whispers began. The name slithered through the village swift and chilling, filling people with fear. Faces disappeared behind shutters. A pair of young men near the smithy made a show of turning away, though not before crossing themselves.

Esme leaned closer to Ryland, her voice barely above a breath. "They recognize you."

"They should," he said grimly. "Word travels far of bloody victories and evil leaders."

A hunched woman near a garden plot stared openly, the corner of her apron clutched in one hand and bravely spoke up. "We are a peaceful village, my lord?"

"Then you have nothing to fear," he called out.

Esme couldn't stop the shiver that ran through her, hearing the cold, heartless voice of Torrance. Nor was it easy trying to ignore the rumble of hunger in her stomach, it had been too long since they last ate.

A gentle squeeze at her waist reminded her it was Ryland, and she had nothing to fear from him. She realized it wasn't going to be as easy as she thought to undo the damage Torrance had done to her.

"Who leads here?" Torrance demanded, his powerful voice carrying throughout the village.

The door of a cottage that had seen better days creaked

open and an elderly man in a wool cloak stepped out. He bore the signs of age, a face weathered with wrinkles, yet he was sharp-eyed. He gave Torrance a long, wary once-over.

"Do you lead here?" Torrance snapped impatiently.

"Who's asking?" the old man demanded.

Esme spotted the lad who had dropped his bundle of firewood and taken off now leaning against the corner of the cottage. He had run to warn the old man of their arrival, or had he recognized Torrance?

"Don't play the fool, old man. It will end badly for you," Torrance cautioned.

"These old eyes aren't what they used to be," the old man countered with a reasonable excuse.

"Have it your way," Torrance said, and his chin shot up, his eyes narrowed, and he cast a glare around on all who stood near. "I am Lord Torrance of Clan Glencairn, and I seek information."

"Where are your warriors?" the old man asked. "Lord Torrance never travels without them. Too many enemies would gladly have his head."

"As I will have yours if you continue to question me," Torrance threatened.

Esme got the sudden urge to put distance between them, the guttural growl that followed his threat reminding her of a time when Torrance warned her of the same. And it made her wonder about Torrance's plan to get rid of her. How would he have done it? Would he have made her suffer?

"Quit your musing, wife, and pay attention to what goes on here," Torrance barked, startling Esme.

Once again, she felt the tender squeeze at her waist, reminding her that she had nothing to fear. Though another rumble in her stomach, louder this time, continued to caution how hungry she was.

Habit had her answering, "Aye, my lord."

"As for you, old man, my warriors are nearby and you will be the first I pass judgement on when I take over this village, unless your chieftain gives me good reason not to."

Gasps and whispers circled the few gathered there.

"Your next words better hold the truth," —Torrance's glance turned harsh— "or I will make you suffer greatly."

"Patrick is a stubborn old fool, the last of our warriors who looks to protect us, since we no longer have a chieftain to lead us," said the woman who had spoken of being a peaceful village.

It struck Torrance then. "You are part of Clan Purdom."

"Aye, a once fine and proud clan and still is—those left of us," Patrick said, drawing his shoulders back as best he could.

"Then it is good I have come here. You are now part of Glencairn," Torrance declared.

Esme felt a smile tempt her lips, but she kept them locked tightly. If it truly was Torrance speaking, she would worry for the clan, but knowing Ryland spoke, she knew he would see to their care. Not so Patrick, the old man.

"You don't want to do that, my lord," Patrick advised. "It is best you leave us alone."

"And why is that, Patrick?" Torrance demanded.

"We are cursed, my lord, and the curse will only bring you misery and defeat as it has done us repeatedly."

"That curse is about to be broken, Patrick. Now, my wife and I require someplace warm and food and drink," Torrance ordered, having heard Esme's stomach protesting its hunger and realizing it had been far too long since they last ate. "Then you will help me find what I seek."

"What is that, my lord?" Patrick asked.

Torrance kept a steady eye on the old man to see how he would react. "I seek, Seann Bhean… the Old Woman."

That brought silence so sharp it stung.

Then someone muttered, "Fool's errand."

Another said, "She's no one's friend."

"She is an old woman who doesn't mind her tongue, but healers revere her for her endless healing knowledge. Follow me to our meeting house where you will be provided with food and drink. I will have our healer fetched so you can ask her about the Old Woman.

"You are a good husband to see your wife fed," Esme whispered as he turned his stallion to follow Patrick.

He wore a scowl as he cast glances at the villagers they passed by, and he whispered to Esme, "I am nothing like Torrance. Always remember that."

Torrance bought the stallion to a halt in front of a shelter that appeared the size of two cottages placed end on end but had only one entrance.

Esme stretched her shoulders and back as soon as Torrance helped her off the horse. Not used to riding as much as she had done lately, her body ached.

"I will see we have a bed to sleep in tonight," he said, his hand at her back, caressing it for a moment before guiding her toward the door.

She almost sighed aloud with how soothing his strong hand felt along her back. She nodded at his remark while thinking what it meant to share a bed with him now, knowing he was Ryland. He loved her and that made a difference.

The firepit in the center of the large room heated the area well. That the village didn't have much was obvious by the sparse vegetable stew they were served, though it did fill and warm the stomach as did the hot cider. Along with that, four oat cakes were placed on the table in front of them and Esme wondered who would go without them, so the lord and his lady could be fed.

"Fill your stomach, wife, so I don't have to listen to it

rumble endlessly," Torrance ordered, seeing his wife's reluctance to touch the oat cakes.

She lowered her head embarrassed by Torrance's remark, then realized it was Ryland who made it. What was he trying to tell her? The answer came easily to her. Ryland would never let others starve if he could help it. He was telling her that he would see the village get more food and with that, she reached for an oat cake.

Patrick had not waited for Torrance to invite him to join them at the table, he sat opposite them. "I am warning you, my lord, do not bother with us. The curse will destroy you."

Torrance went to ask about the curse when the door opened and in walked a woman, plain features, brown hair streaked with gray, full shape, and wearing a gentle smile.

"Breann," Patrick called out. "Come join us. Lord Torrance wishes to speak with you."

Brenn hesitated before approaching the table, her glance going between Lord Torrance and Esme. "Word traveled, but I thought it was just rumors."

"Sit, Breann," Patrick urged, patting the spot next to him on the bench.

Breann ignored him, looking a bit dazed as she continued to stand.

"What rumors?" Torrance asked.

"That a lord and his lady would come looking for the Old Woman," Breann said. "Now here you are."

"And what message do you have for us?" Torrance asked.

Breann bit at her bottom lip as if biting back her response.

Torrance pounded his fist on the table. "Tell me now!"

Breann jumped frightened by his demand and hurried to say, "The Old Woman will only meet with the worthy one... the woman."

CHAPTER 20

"That is never going to happen," Torrance said, his voice as ridged as iron. "My wife will not meet with her alone."

Silence swept like a cold wind through the hall, shivering everyone.

Breann stiffened where she stood, her glance dropping to the floor and Patrick wisely held his tongue.

Esme lowered her gaze as well, though she could feel the heat of Torrance's stare pressing down on her. She didn't speak. Not yet. Not here in front of others to Torrance, a man she could not openly defy. Alone she could discuss the matter with Ryland, though she didn't think his response would be much different.

"You will not go alone, and I will hear no more about it," Torrance said, his voice sharp and commanding.

"The Old Woman summoned her and her alone," Patrick said cautiously. "That she made clear enough."

Torrance's gaze snapped to Patrick. "The Old Woman does not command me," Torrance said with an angry snarl. "I command!"

Breann dared a glance up, her voice tight with unease. "It's not the custom. The Old Woman summons who she wishes, no one dares approach her without being summoned."

"And no one commands my wife but me," he said with such force that Breann drew back, and Patrick turned his head away as if avoiding being struck.

Esme's fingers curled into the folds of her garment. She kept her voice calm, respectful. "May I speak with you privately, my lord?"

"Nay," Torrance snapped. "The matter is settled. We go together or not at all."

"Then the Old Woman will not meet with you," Patrick said.

Torrance turned his cold gaze on him. "We'll see about that."

The warning settled heavily in the room.

"I meant no disrespect," Patrick said, trying to make amends for his error. "Only that if your wife does not go meet her, the answers you seek may stay buried."

Torrance said nothing, only stared at Esme a long moment—long enough for her to feel it deep in her bones. He was worried. She could see it beneath the hardened mask he wore. And she understood now that it was because he loved her. It wasn't duty all those times he had protected her… it was because he loved her. And it would be so easy to love him, but she worried that Torrance would somehow get in the way as foolish a thought that was.

"I will have my answers one way or another, but my wife will not go meet the Old Woman alone." Torrance turned a scowl on Esme. "Do I make myself clear, wife?"

"Aye, my lord," she said softly. "I will abide by your decision."

He gave her a slight nod, but she could still see the storm brewing in his eyes.

The hall doors burst open.

A lad stumbled inside, panting, his face pale. "My lord! Warriors! They approach the village fast, two dozen from what I could see and armed for battle."

"Do they wear my colors?" Torrance asked, not moving from where he sat.

The lad thought a moment, then nodded. "Aye, they do wear the colors of your plaid.'

Torrance looked at Patrick. "My men. See them greeted and brought here to me."

Patrick nodded, stood, and left with the lad.

Breann turned to go.

"Did I give you permission to leave?" Torrance asked with a harshness that turned Breann pale.

Fear froze Breann, but she managed to say, "Nay, my lord."

"How do I get a message to the Old Woman?" he asked.

"She will get one to you," Breann said and shivered, fearful that her answer would disappoint him.

"We will talk again. You are dismissed," he said with a careless wave of his hand and when the door shut behind her, he turned to Esme. "We only have a moment before Brack, and my warriors arrive. We will discuss this matter when it is safe to do so. But know I meant what I said. You will not go meet the Old Woman alone.

"What if it is the only way?" she whispered.

"There is always another way."

"Nay, not always. Sometimes you have no choice but to make do if you want to survive."

"This is not one of those times," he argued. "I will not chance losing you."

His words were genuine as was the concern in his eyes.

He truly didn't want to lose her. Her heart and stomach fluttered. Never had her father nor Torrance expressed such true concern for her and though Ryland's arms were not around her, his words hugged her tightly.

Brack rushed into the hall, sword drawn, and his glance racing around the room.

"We are safe here," Torrance called out.

"This is Purdom land, no one is safe here," Brack challenged.

"Do I appear injured to you, Brack, and what took you so long to reach me?" Torrance demanded.

Satisfied no danger existed, Brack came to a stop in front of the table where Torrance sat. "I expected to find you at Clan Stott where you were to stay while in this area. I feared you were taken captive or worse dead since the tracker found so many different tracks. Until he finally found the ones familiar to your stallion."

Torrance scowled. "Then the tracker needs to improve his skills."

Brack sheathed his sword with a sharp motion. "Aye, I told him the same. This is no place for you to be, my lord."

"And my warriors should not have betrayed me," Torrance said, his scowl deepening.

Brack's jaw tensed. "And they will suffer greatly for it when caught and warning has gone out to anyone who may be harboring them or any Glencairn warrior who may be thinking to do the same. Betray Lord Torrance and your suffering will be never-ending."

"Have any been caught?" Torrance demanded.

"I have sent some trusted warriors out to hunt those who betrayed you, but the focus has been on finding you."

"Now that you have found me shift the focus on finding those who dared to raise their swords against me," Torrance ordered.

"Aye, my lord, as soon as I see you settled safely at Clan Stott."

"I am not going to Clan Stott," Torrance said, with such finality that it left no room for argument.

Brack argued anyway. "That is not what was agreed. Clan Stott is prepared to offer you shelter, warriors, whatever you need. It was arranged for your protection."

Torrance's eyes narrowed. "And you trust them completely with that protection?"

Brack's brow furrowed. "They have always proven loyal."

"You know as well as I do that loyalty can sour faster than milk left in the sun." Torrance leaned forward, his tone cool. "Gavin. Has he returned?"

Brack blinked at the sudden change in subject. "Gavin? I don't believe so. Last I heard, he had not been seen since you dismissed him and the others who failed you."

Torrance gave a noncommittal grunt and reached for his tankard. "See if that has changed."

"You believe he may have returned?"

"I asked if he has. Not what I believe."

Brack's gaze sharpened. "What aren't you telling me?"

Torrance's grip tightened around the tankard. "What I do or don't tell you is my decision."

Brack stepped closer. "Are you doubting my loyalty to you, my lord? My concern is and always has been for your safety, your life."

Torrance's fist tapped the table. "Then do as I order without question."

"It is my duty to question you, to challenge you," Brack snapped, the last thread of restraint unraveling. "You should be at Clan Stott. You're vulnerable here, exposed. Too many unknowns—"

"Then let me make it known now," Torrance cut in, his

voice suddenly low and lethal. "Where I go, where I stay, who I trust... that is my decision to make, not yours."

Brack bristled. "I've risked my life to keep you alive, my lord. I only speak because—"

"Because you forget your place," Torrance growled, rising slowly from the bench. "You may command the warriors, Brack, but not me. Never me."

The silence that followed was heavy, and Brack held his tongue only by sheer discipline. He gave a sharp nod, though the tension in his shoulders was obvious.

Torrance stood tall, every inch the feared leader. "You say this land is dangerous. Then prove your loyalty. Protect me and keep watch. But speak again as if you rule my steps, and you won't like the consequences. Do you understand, Brack?"

Brack inclined his head stiffly. "Understood, my lord."

Torrance sat, ending the conversation, but the fire in his gut hadn't settled. He'd seen Gavin speaking with Eagan and he wondered who else plotted against Torrance. And the elderly woman's warning whispered in his head.

Friends are foes and foes are friends.

"See that preparations are made for my stay here," Torrance ordered, wondering who to trust.

"How long—"

"Until I say otherwise," Torrance snapped. "Now go and do as I say."

Esme had remained silent throughout the exchange, knowing Torrance would never tolerate her interference. But now that Brack was gone, she went to speak.

"Not a word," he warned.

If she didn't know any better, she would swear it was Torrance who had spoken to her. And it did make her wonder if perhaps a bit of Torrance existed in Ryland.

Then he placed his hand on her thigh and gave it a gentle

squeeze and that was not something Torrance would do. He would have squeezed her thigh until she cried out in pain. So, she held her tongue and waited for a better time to speak with him.

* * *

EVENING FELL WITH A SLOW HUSH, the gray sky giving way to deep indigo as a thin flurry of snow drifted down like ash from a weary sky. The village quieted early, as if sensing that something—or someone—rested uneasily among them.

The cottage that had been prepared for Torrance and Esme stood at the edge of the village, its thatched roof rimmed with frost and smoke curling from the chimney. Inside, the warmth from the hearth filled the small space, casting a soft amber glow across the room. It was modest, no more than one room with a curtained alcove for sleeping, but it was enough.

Torrance stood near the fire, his hands outstretched toward the flames. He had not spoken since they'd left the hall, tension etched in every line of his body.

Esme removed her cloak and shook the light snow from it, hanging it by the door. She watched him in silence for a moment, the glimmer of firelight dancing over the hard planes of his handsome face.

"You're angry," she said softly.

His hands dropped to his sides. "Nay. I'm frustrated. There's a difference."

She stepped closer, folding her arms against her to warm them. "At Brack? Or me?"

He turned and stepped behind her, slipping his arms around her to stroke her chilled arms. "Never you, but everyone else."

Esme smiled softly, hearing the sincerity in his voice

while enjoying his gentle touch. "You didn't confide the truth in him about Chieftain Eagan. Do you doubt Brack's loyalty to Torrance?"

His jaw tightened. "Loyalty can be a fragile thing. But Brack is known to be fiercely loyal to Lord Torrance and if he discovers who I am, he will not hesitate to kill me. And he would no doubt believe that you had a hand in the plan., putting your life at risk."

A silence settled between them, the fire popping softly as such dire consequences settled in on them both.

With the realization of how precarious their situation truly was, Esme broke the silence. "We are not safe anywhere, are we?"

"Nay," he admitted. "But I'll keep you safe and if for some reason that becomes impossible, I will send you away where you will be safe."

Her eyes turned wide and her voice firm as she turned around in his arms to face him. "I'll not leave you."

"Aye, you will if I order you to," he insisted.

Esme was even more insistent. "We are in this together."

He tightened his arms he had settled around her waist. "I will not see you harmed, and you will do as I say and that means not going to see the Old Woman on your own."

"But if it is the only way—"

His expression darkened. "Nay! My word is final."

Esme rested her hand on his chest. "I am not fragile. I can do this."

"Your courage was never in question—" He bit back any further words, then as if he could hold them back no longer, he let them loose. "Fear like I have never known would eat at me and my heart would never survive sending you off alone. And if you never came back to me…" He took hold of her chin. "I do not want to live a moment without you, Esme. I have loved you from afar too long and now that you are mine, I intend to make sure you stay mine and let nothing happen to you."

He kissed her as if it had been too long since he last had and he lingered, having been eager for the feel of her lips. Her response told him that she was just as eager for his kiss. And just like him, she wanted more. He could feel it in the way she pressed her body against his and she no doubt felt his desire grow hard against her.

His mouth left hers and he looked into her passion-filled eyes. "Tonight, we seal a vow between Ryland and Esme joining us together us one."

"Aye," she whispered and was surprised when his hands began to strip her of her garments. Her hands quickly grabbed his. "What are you doing?"

"I want you naked and myself as well so we may enjoy each other."

"Is that proper?" she asked, the image of her being so exposed leaving her feeling vulnerable.

"Anything is proper between a husband and wife," he assured her.

"But we aren't husband and wife," she reminded him.

"In everyone's eyes we are and tonight the only eyes that matter, are yours and mine. But if it eases your worries—" He took her hand in his.

She pulled it away. "If we are to claim vows, I want it done the proper way for all to see and know we chose this. I do not want to take any chance of someone claiming it invalid and separating us."

"That will never happen," he said so fiercely that it caused Esme to step away from him.

Ryland reached out slowly, his arm going around her waist to ease her toward him. "I am not Torrance, but I am fierce and will remain so with anyone who attempts to take you from me. I love you, Esme. Trust me, I will never hurt you."

She leaned into him. "It is going to take time for me not to hear or see Torrance in you, especially since the façade must continue."

"But not when we're alone. When we are alone, we can love freely."

"I am not sure I know how to do that since with Torrance coupling was a duty," she said.

"With me it will never be a duty. You will realize soon enough that making love is something we both want, enjoy, and cherish."

"That sounds quite pleasant."

He smiled. "It is more than quite pleasant, and I can assure you that once you realize it, you will pester me to make love to you often."

She chuckled. "Are you bragging about your prowess in bed, my lord?"

"I could but I'd rather show you."

The way he attempted to ease her worry with a light teasing nature, so far removed from Torrance's cruelty, that it touched her heart.

He brushed his lips over hers. "Let me love you, Esme."

She returned his faint kiss. "Aye, Ryland, I want you to love me."

He went to remove her garments again and her hand stilled him again.

"Trust me," he whispered. "We make new memories tonight."

His remark startled her. He was right. They needed to make their own memories, and her hand fell off his, and he gently disrobed her.

CHAPTER 21

Esme shivered once she was naked even though the heat from the hearth caressed her body. She couldn't help but feel vulnerable, never having recalled ever being completely naked and certainly not in front of anyone. But then her attention was caught by how easily Ryland shed his garments in front of her. There was no hesitation in his movements, no doubt in his eyes, and for some reason that eased her worry.

When he stood naked, he immediately reached out and drew her slowly against him. She shivered again when their flesh touched, she was so shocked by how warm he felt. Her nipples tightened against his chest and when his hand caressed along her back down to her backside to give it a gentle squeeze, she felt herself grow damp between her legs.

"I love the feel of you," he whispered close to her ear.

Tingles ran through her from his warm breath faintly brushing her cheek. And she felt an overpowering need to touch him, but Torrance always warned her she was not to touch him without permission, but he wasn't Torrance.

Cautiously, as if she expected to be admonished, she let her hand roam over his back.

Warm, smooth, hard muscles that felt good to the touch and she smiled when she felt him shiver.

"Let's explore," he said and scooped her up in his arms and carried her to the bed in the alcove behind the curtain.

He laid her down, drew the curtain aside so the fire's heat could reach them, then joined her lying on his side next to her. "We will get to know each other. I want to see and touch every part of you, and I want you to know you can do the same to me when you're ready, when you feel comfortable doing so."

He kissed her, needing no response, knowing she was unsure yet willing to make new memories. And he intended to make a lot of new memories with her.

His kiss was tender, loving, purposeful, and Esme loved it, loved how he did what he could to make her feel comfortable, desirable, loved. She had never felt that before now. His hand began to roam over her body, his touch light as a feather, but it was when his mouth settled on her nipple that her passion struck hard and fast. And when he finished with one, he tasted the other and by then she was moaning with pleasure. And his hand? Good, Lord, he worked magic with his hand. He roamed and caressed intimate places she had never touched, having been told to touch herself was sinful. But his touch was anything but sinful… it was amazing.

The desire to touch him had her shifting and realizing what she intended to do, Ryland moved, freeing her hand to slip down and settle on his manhood, and her unexpected but welcome touch elicited a moan from him.

Her hand froze where it was. "I hurt you."

He rested his brow to hers. "Nay, Esme, just the opposite. Your touch feels wonderful."

His words encouraged her and just as he caressed her, she

did the same, finding she quite enjoyed the feel of him, smooth, hard, thick.

Passion grew quickly with their hands exploring each other and it almost tumbled him off the edge when Esme moaned his name.

"Ryland."

That Torrance's name never once slipped from her lips more than pleased him and he moved over her.

"I need you, Ryland," she said, her passion-filled eyes confirming just how much.

"You have me… always," he said and slipped inside her with gentle firmness and his thrusts were slow at first so as not to hurt her.

She cried out.

He halted inside her. "I hurt you."

"Nay. Nay. It feels unbelievably wonderful. Please. Please don't stop."

"As you say," he said with a satisfied smile and continued to please them both.

It didn't take long. Esme was close, so close, and yet she didn't want to let go, didn't want the pleasure to end, didn't want him to stop loving her. But his strong thrusts took her over the edge, and she couldn't help but scream his name.

Ryland saw what she was about to do and dropped his head down, his mouth capturing his name as he kissed her and dropped off the edge along with her.

He tore his mouth off hers when he realized his name lingered no more on her lips and he braced himself over her to urge the last bit of pleasure out of them.

Esme moaned softly, her hands gripping his taut arms. "I think you are right. I may pester you often."

"I'm glad I won't be the only one who pesters." He bent his head to kiss her when a pounding at the door startled them both.

"My lord," came the shout and Brack's familiar voice.

"Scream Torrance's name like you were about to scream mine before I stole it from your lips," Ryland ordered as he hurried off her and out of bed. "Now!"

Esme did her best to scream as if in the throes of climax. "Torrance!"

Ryland waited a moment, then yanked the curtain across, and went to the door naked and flung it open. "You dare disturb me, Brack, when I finally have her tamed enough to do her duty?"

"Forgive me, my lord," Brack said, keeping his eyes on Torrance's face. "But Gavin has arrived here and has news."

"How did he know to come here when he was ordered to return home and get help?"

"I sent word to Chieftain Eagan when we finally found your trail as to where we would be in case, we somehow missed you and you made your way there. Gavin waits in the meeting hall."

"I will be right there," Torrance said and shut the door.

He turned and, seeing Esme peeking out from behind the curtain, he pressed one finger to his lips and went to her.

He kept his voice low. "Forgive me for leaving you so shortly after such intimate pleasure when I want nothing more than to take you in my arms, hold you close, and tell you how much I love you."

Her heart thumped rapidly at his endearing words. "I look forward to that upon your return."

He kissed her quickly. "A very good reason for me to make this quick."

She shook her head. "Nay, take what time you need to discover the truth. The sooner this is done, the sooner the charade can end."

"Aye, and the sooner we can start our life together." He

hugged her to him, then released her with haste, worried he would linger, she felt so good naked in his arms.

As he dressed, Esme slipped into her shift. "Be careful."

"I don't like leaving you alone or trusting you to warriors I don't know if I can trust," he said once he finished dressing.

"I will keep the door latched and open it to only you."

"That helps me worry a bit less," he said, slipping his arm around her waist and lifting her up against him to kiss her.

She rested her brow to his when the kiss ended and whispered, "Go and be done with it, Ryland. I miss you already."

Ryland left, resuming his role as Torrance as soon as the door closed behind him. That she bid him good-bye as Ryland gave him hope that one day she would not see Torrance at all when she looked at him.

"See that no one enters... no one!" Torrance ordered the two warriors who stood guard at the sides of the cottage.

He walked off, two warriors following behind him to the meeting house.

The meeting house sat quiet beneath the late-night sky. Brack stood just outside the door, arms folded, a sour expression on his face.

"Gavin is anxious," Brack said as Torrance approached. "He claims he has news worth hearing."

"Let's see if his tongue proves as useful as his sword should've been," Torrance muttered, pushing the door open.

Inside the room, the firepit burned brightly, casting a good warmth throughout the large area. Gavin stood near the long table closest to the heat, his cloak damp and his boots caked with mud. A travel-weary slump bent his shoulders, but his eyes lifted quickly at Torrance's entrance, and he straightened.

"My lord," he greeted with a respectful nod, though his voice carried a tight edge, forced yet calm, perhaps even practiced.

Torrance said nothing at first. He took his time removing his cloak to drop on a bench, drawing out the moment as his gaze raked over the man. "You said you have news."

Gavin nodded, stepping forward. "I did. Keeping to the trees, on my way home as you ordered, I caught sight of a few riders. I followed at a distance." He paused, turning a quick glance toward Brack before continuing. "Mercenaries, I'd wager. The sort who fights for coins and little else or entices others with coins. I would not be surprised if it was them who caused the betrayal among our warriors."

Brack's brow furrowed, and he looked ready to speak, but Torrance raised a hand, bidding silence. He moved to the table, resting both palms on its edge, leaning slightly toward Gavin.

"That's quite the tale, Gavin. Mercenaries, skulking through the woods, plotting betrayal." Torrance gave a faint, humorless smile. "You must have followed them far to be gone as long as you were."

"I did. I thought it important," Gavin said quickly, too quickly. "They led me past the ridgeline. I returned as soon as I lost their trail."

"And yet," Torrance said with a hard gaze on the man, "I saw you."

Gavin's eyes narrowed. "Saw me?"

Torrance straightened. "At Clan Stott. You were speaking with Chieftain Eagan."

The room went still.

Brack stiffened beside him, turning sharply to Gavin, whose jaw flexed as if working through his next lie.

Torrance's voice sliced through the heavy tension like a sharp blade. "Strange, isn't it, how a man so busy tracking mercenaries ends up in conversation with a chieftain of the clan where I was meant to stay?"

Gavin opened his mouth but said nothing. The spark of surprise, or was it calculation, had already given him away.

Torrance held his gaze. "So go on, Gavin. Tell me again… about these mercenaries."

Gavin hesitated, his mouth parting slightly, then snapped shut again as if weighing his words.

"Don't keep me waiting," Torrance cautioned.

"Aye, I did pass near Clan Stott," he said at last, eyes darting between Torrance and Brack. "But only to see if they had any word of strangers in the area. Chieftain Eagan caught sight of me and summoned me. What was I to do? Refuse a chieftain and raise suspicion?"

Brack frowned but said nothing.

Torrance's jaw tightened. He stepped around the table, slow and deliberate, his boots thudding on the packed dirt floor. "I ordered you to return home and report what happened to Brack. Yet you saw fit to trail mercenaries and to pause long enough to chat with Chieftain Eagan.?"

Gavin drew himself up. "I serve Clan Glencairn. I did what I thought best."

Torrance halted in front of him, close enough to see the sheen of sweat beginning to bead at Gavin's brow. "Nay, you did what served you. And I want to know why."

Gavin's breath caught. "My lord—"

"Who gave the order?" Torrance barked. "Who bought your loyalty? Tell me who stands behind this betrayal!"

Gavin's face contorted. "Someone wiser than you is what I heard." His voice cracked with something twisted—bitterness, regret, guilt. "I followed orders same as every man there. You were never meant to survive the battle with Clan MacLeish."

Brack moved, startled, but Torrance's hand went up, stopping him as his eyes narrowed dangerously.

Gavin gave a bitter laugh. "You should have died. That's

what was promised. A clean end to a burdened legacy. But you lived. Damn you, you lived."

A heavy silence dropped, broken only by the slow, measured sound of Torrance's breathing.

Then he moved, seizing Gavin by the front of his tunic and slamming him back against the table. "Who gave that promise?" he snarled, his face close. "Who?"

Gavin stared at him, defiant, even in fear. "Ask your noble allies. Ask those who smile to your face and sharpen blades behind your back. You have no idea how deep this hate for you runs."

Fury raged in Torrance's voice. "I'll find them, every last one of them. And you'll tell me all you know, or I'll leave your bones for the crows."

Brack stepped forward, uncertain. "Torrance—"

"Secure him in a dwelling surrounded by trustworthy guards," Torrance ordered, his voice like ice. "He'll talk by the time I get done with him."

Gavin spat at the floor. "It doesn't matter what you do to me. I can't tell you what I don't know. And it won't change anything. You were meant to die… and some still mean to see it done."

Torrance didn't look at him again. His gaze was distant, fixed, as if seeing the battlefield all over again. Had he missed something? Had the answer been there in front of him all along?

Brack moved quickly, signaling two guards to seize Gavin.

Torrance turned away, jaw clenched, rage simmering beneath his skin. He meant to know who wanted Torrance dead. He had given the man his word and he would keep it. But what mattered the most to him was getting the chance to have a good life with Esme.

Brack fell in step beside Torrance as they left the meeting house. "You believe him?"

Torrance's mouth twisted. "Not a word. His lies were layered thick enough to drown in. I wouldn't be surprised if he was meeting with that group of mercenaries."

"He named no one."

"He didn't need to. He confirmed enough." Torrance's tone sharpened. "Someone wants me dead, and this person is using others to see it done… those who hate me and we both know there are many."

They walked a few paces before Brack said, "What now?"

"I find out who gave the order. And then I break every bond of loyalty that holds this treachery together."

Brack nodded once, grim. "You'll have my sword when the time comes."

Torrance paused at the edge of the path, his expression hard as flint. "I'll need more than swords, Brack, only the truth will see this done."

With that, he turned and headed toward the cottage as snow began to fall in faint, drifting flakes. The two warriors were as Torrance had left them, standing guard at either side of the door.

"One of you go and warm yourself with drink in front of the fire at the meeting house while the other remains here. When that one returns the other may leave and warm himself and rest. Do that throughout the night so neither one of you freeze," Torrance ordered and rapped hard on the door. "Open the door, wife, it is me."

The two guards stared at Torrance's back as the door opened and shut behind him. Then they stared at each other until the younger of the two smiled and nodded at the older warrior to go. With a nod of appreciation, he left, and the younger warrior shook his head, not understanding Lord Torrance's generosity.

Esme found herself taking a quick step away from Torrance when he entered, a shadow of anger on his handsome face that startled and frightened her.

It hurt Ryland's heart to see the fear in Esme's eyes as she hurried to step away from him. He silently cursed the resemblance to Torrance, but then if there hadn't been he would never have had this opportunity to be with Esme, to make her his wife. He would need to give her time, be patient, and show her that he wasn't Torrance.

A sudden spark in her eyes and a slight shake of her head, as if realization struck, had Esme saying, "Ryland."

"Aye, Esme," he said, tossing his cloak aside as he took a slow step toward her, aching to take her in his arms.

He didn't need to take another step, she rushed at him, throwing her arms around him, hugging him tightly.

His arms held her pinned against him.

She glanced at him. "You must tell me everything." She took his hand and hurried him toward the bed. "I tied the curtain back so, the heat could warm the bed for us."

He thought of a better and more satisfying way to warm the bed, but he didn't say, knowing how curious she was to hear what he had learned.

Esme got into bed and held the blanket back for him to join her.

Ryland didn't think twice, he shed his garments since he wanted her to get used to seeing him naked. Something he intended to do often when they were alone in their bedchamber.

She looked down at her own garment, but she didn't remove it and that was alright with Ryland.

Time.

In time she would learn and feel comfortable donning her garments in front of him.

Ryland got in bed, turning on his side to face Esme who

lay on her side, and he hooked his hand at her waist and drew her closer to him.

"Tell me," she said, her hand going to rest on his arm. "I am impatient to hear."

"Someone definitely wants Torrance dead, but Gavin insists he doesn't know who the person is behind it all," Ryland said and went on to explain all of what he had learned from Gavin.

Esme listened, commenting now and again or asking a pertinent question.

"What will you do?" she asked when Ryland had finished.

"Torture is the only thing left to me."

Esme frowned and moved away from him to lie on her back.

That disturbed Ryland. "What's wrong?"

"I hate when you must be so like Torrance."

"I have little choice if I am to see this plan through and even less choice if I want to make sure we are never separated and—" he leaned over her. "I will do what I must to make sure that doesn't happen." He kissed her as if his remark was a vow and the kiss sealed it.

Esme rested her hand on his cheek. "I fear Torrance's cruelty will stain you like it has me and I don't want that for you."

"Torrance could never stain such a beautiful soul. You may have been in his shadow, but you are now free of him. He can never harm you again."

"Yet his cruelty lingers, and he knew it would when he had you give your word to revenge him. You do as he would have done, what everyone expects of Torrance."

"Not in everything, but this one I have no choice. I must know who hunts Torrance." He moved away from her to lie on his back. "I would have it different if I could, but there is no other way."

Esme could not help but think that part of Torrance continued to live in Ryland and that troubled her. How could she help Ryland fight that?

Love.

The thought startled her. Evil had difficulty surviving against love. All she had to do was love Ryland and the evil Torrance left behind would die away and be no more. And loving Ryland would be the easiest thing for her to do since she already felt him deep in her heart.

She turned on her side and wrapped herself around him, pressing her body snug against him. She couldn't speak to him of love just yet. Her heart had more healing to do but it would come in time. For now…

"Together, Ryland. We do whatever must be done together," she said.

He wrapped his arms around her and held her close, his heart thumping since it felt as if she told him she loved him, words he had no trouble saying.

"I love you, Esme, and always will."

"And I will forever cherish that love." She smiled. "Do you think I could pester you or are you too tired?"

Ryland chuckled. "I was about to ask you the same."

He rolled her on her back, and it wasn't long before gentle touches and kisses turned to moans and demands until their passions exploded together and once again, they lay satisfied and tired in each other's arms.

Ryland drifted off to sleep soon after and Esme's eyes grew heavy, though busy thoughts kept her from sleeping… until an idea struck her. It would work. She was sure of it. She would only need to get her husband to agree.

CHAPTER 22

"Bloody hell, woman, are you out of your mind?" Ryland said, stunned by her suggestion.

"Nay. I think it is a most reasonable solution to the problem and one that could get us much needed information," she argued, the next morning while savoring the hot cider that had been brought to them.

"You want to walk into Gavin's cell and ask him to tell you, his secrets? That's your grand plan?" He shook his head, not believing what he was saying.

"I want to make him believe I wish to help him. That I, too, want to see Lord Torrance's rule ended."

His brow shot up. "And why would he believe that? He may be a traitor, but he's no fool."

"Because I will convince him I can no longer take the abuse. That I know someone wishes Torrance dead and me along with him and that I don't want to die that I want to be part of the plan to see him dead."

"You think he'll believe you would betray me that you don't fear me enough to be too frightened to do such a thing?"

"Aye, if I give him a good reason to," she said, setting down her cup and rising off the bench to face him. "If I tell him that Torrance treats me cruelly and that as his wife, I suffer endless bruises and tongue lashings, he's bound to consider it."

"MANY WIVES SUFFER that at the hands of their husbands," Ryland said. "Why should he care?"

"Because I will tell him that I want desperately to live and repeat that my life is in danger being Torrance's wife and that I discovered he intends to replace me with a new wife What other choice do I have if I want to live?"

Bloody hell if she didn't make it sound like a feasible plan that could actually work.

"This is nonsense," he snapped, turning away from her annoyed that he might consider it. "You think tears and a few whispers will loosen his tongue? He'll laugh in your face or worse... he'll suspect I have a hand in it."

"He'll believe me if..." she said, stepping closer, "you leave a mark on me."

He turned, anger simmering in his eyes. "What?"

"A bruise," she said calmly. "One he'll see the moment I walk in. A mark that says I have reason to want you gone."

He stared at her in disbelief. "You want me to hit you?"

"Nay," she said softly. "One small mark on my cheek."

"Absolutely not," he said through gritted teeth, trying to temper his anger. "How can you even ask such a thing? I would never strike you."

"I know that, but it's the only way—"

"Nay!" His voice thundered through the small dwelling and beyond. He took a breath, trying to calm the fury that rippled through him. "Your plan is one thing to consider, striking you is completely out of the question. You have no idea what you're asking. I will never lay a hand on you, not even for pretense."

Her voice dropped, steady and quiet. "You said you were willing to do what must be done."

"Don't twist my words," he warned.

"I'm not. I'm trying to stop you from becoming someone you're not. If you torture Gavin, you take a step closer to becoming Torrance. Let me do this for you… for us. Let me find the answer we need."

He turned away from her, hands braced on the edge of the table. For a long moment, he said nothing. There was no way he could ever strike her, absolutely no way.

The silence grew heavy between them.

Then, behind him, he heard a quick shuffle, then a tumble.

He turned just as Esme staggered and fell against the hearth, her cheek catching the edge of the raised stonework, and she cried out.

"Esme!" he roared, lunging for her, his arm hooking her waist before she could hit the floor and turning her around in his arms. Anger rose like a mighty beast in him as he saw tears shimmer in her eyes and she blinked them away.

His hand went to her face to tilt her head gently. A red mark had already begun to rise along her cheekbone.

"What the bloody hell have you done?" he demanded.

She wouldn't meet his gaze. "What had to be done."

He stared at her, his jaw clenched and his heart hammering. "You could have hurt yourself worse."

"I didn't," she said, softly but firmly as she finally met his eyes. "And now there's no debate. Gavin will believe what he sees."

A tear slipped down her cheek, and he brushed it away with his thumb, his touch reverent, careful not to press where her skin had already begun to swell.

"I hate this," he whispered. "Hate that it's come to this."

"I know," she said. "But if we're going to get answers, we must be clever. You can't always win by force, Ryland."

He looked at her, at the pain she wore like armor, and at the strength beneath it.

"You'd make a fearsome laird," he muttered, then hugged her gently. "Don't ever do something like that again. Not ever."

"I didn't want you to stop me," she murmured against his chest.

He held her tighter.

When he finally pulled back, his voice had found steel again. "Then let's make certain it wasn't in vain. I'll make sure Brack is busy so he doesn't see you and I will see that the guards have reason to leave their post so you can sneak easily into the dwelling where Gavin is being held. But you must promise me if at any time you feel you may be in danger… you will leave immediately. I will be waiting close by out of sight."

Esme nodded. "He'll talk. I'll make sure of it."

* * *

THE WIND WHISTLED around the small hut as Esme approached the unguarded door. Ryland had made sure the guards were called away, but she knew she didn't have long to see the task done. She opened the door and slipped in.

A low fire burned in a fire pit, not giving off nearly enough heat for the small space. Gavin sat on a narrow bench, his ankles and wrists chained. His head lifted the moment she entered, surprise flashing in his eyes.

"Lady Esme?" he rasped, rising slightly despite the chains. "What in God's name are you doing here?"

"We don't have much time," she whispered, pushing the

hood off her head and moving closer. "I slipped in while the guards were called away."

He stared at her, wary. "Why?"

"I need your help." Her voice trembled with urgency. "I know you've no reason to trust me, but I swear to you… I am not your enemy."

His expression hardened. "You're the wife of the man who put me in chains."

"I fear not for long," she said quickly, stepping into the firelight and letting him see the bruise blooming along her cheekbone.

His brows drew together, his tone sharp. "He did that to you?"

"It is not the first time and won't be the last. I know someone wants Torrance dead and me along with him for fear I carry an heir. But I've failed to get with child, and I learned that he has plans to be rid of me and get himself a new wife. My life is in peril no matter what happens, and I don't want to die."

Gavin studied her, his jaw tightening. "And you think I can help you?"

"Not you," she said, the desperation in her voice raw and real. "The person who wants Torrance dead. I thought if I could get word to him and let him know I would help him in his quest to see my husband dead that I could have a chance to survive."

Gavin remained silent, his gaze fixed on her, as though weighing her pain against his caution.

Then slowly, he said, "There's been quiet talk since Torrance's father's death, spread between those with growing concern for Torrance's cruelty and what it means for the future of the clan." He hesitated for a moment. "Then the truth revealed itself."

Her breath caught. "What truth?"

He leaned forward, the firelight sharpening the lines on his face. "That Torrance has no right to lead Clan Glencairn."

She blinked, confusion spreading across her face. "What are you saying?"

He held her gaze. "Torrance isn't the true heir to Clan Glencairn."

* * *

THE DOOR CREAKED as Esme slipped out of the small dwelling, the cold wind biting at her cheeks. She pulled her cloak tighter around her, but it did little to stop the tremble running through her. Not from the cold... but from what she'd just heard.

She barely took two steps before a shadow detached itself from the nearby trees.

"Esme."

Ryland's voice was low, but sharp with concern.

She turned to him, startled, and he was at her side in an instant. His eyes searched her face, and his hand gripped her arm.

"What did he say to you?" he asked, his voice quiet but urgent. "You're pale as death."

"I... I will tell you at the cottage," she whispered, glancing toward the village path. "Not here."

He nodded and without another word guided her away, his hand steady at her back as they walked. Their boots barely left tacks in the little snow that had fallen, and neither spoke during the short trek, though Ryland glanced her way more than once, the tension in him winding tighter with every step.

When they reached the small cottage, he opened the door for her and followed her inside. The warmth was welcome, but it did nothing to ease the tightness in her chest.

She stood near the fire, her hands trembling slightly as she held them out to the heat to warm them.

He didn't press her. He waited… impatiently… but he waited.

She finally turned to him, her voice hushed. "He said Torrance has no right to lead Clan Glencairn."

Ryland didn't move but his body turned rigid.

She stepped closer, searching his face. "He says Torrance isn't the true heir."

There was no shock in his eyes or expression, not even a touch of confusion, or humor at Gavin's ridiculous statement.

"Did you know?" she asked, her voice barely above a whisper.

He still said nothing, but something in his expression changed, it warned he knew something.

"Is that what brought you here?" she asked. "Is that the secret you've been searching for all along?"

"If I tell you what I know and the wrong people find out you know something, it could put you in extreme danger," he said.

"I can't help you if you keep me in the dark and I am already in danger just being Torrance's wife," she argued, still trying to comprehend what Gavin had told her and what Ryland might know. She urged softly. "Please, don't let anything come between us."

Ryland dropped down on the bench by the table, stretched his arm out, and snagged her around the waist to ease her down on his lap.

"Torrance's father revealed stunning news to him on his deathbed. He then warned me not to trust anyone with the news, or the consequences could be dire, and I had to agree with him. His father had little breath left in him when he told Torrance that someone might challenge him as the rightful heir to Clan Glencairn, that he could be older than Torrance and he was to make sure he didn't unseat Torrance."

"Did Torrance assume it was you? Is that the true reason he went to war with you?" she asked.

"He assumed we were half-brothers which was why he urged me to take his place so that the Glencairn bloodline would continue to rule the clan. But he told me to find out for sure if it was what his father meant or if his father's penchant for women produced another son who could be waiting to claim the title to Glencairn."

"Did Lord Randall give Torrance any indication of where to start his search?

"Nay, though I assume eliminating me was his first choice."

"Where to after that," she asked perplexed.

"Healers, midwives was the most logical direction, though it has been so many years I wonder if the woman who knew such information still lives."

"So, then the Old Woman, might know the identity of the healer who possesses such information and could possibly know who the true heir is to Clan Glencairn."

"I am assuming so since it is the only lead that I have found thus far. I am assuming whoever wishes me dead is the one who intends to lay claim to Glencairn. But—" He gave her waist a gentle squeeze. "He cannot prove it, so therefore, he has no choice but to see me dead, though he attempts convince others he will be a better, more tolerant leader than Torrance."

"How can he be a better more tolerant leader if he wishes me, an innocent in all this, dead as well?" Esme said, with a brief shake of her head. "I doubt many would care as long as it brought an end to Torrance's cruelty." She sighed softly and laid her head on his shoulder. "I wish we could leave, walk away from it all and have a simple life together."

"We could have a good life with my clan if this person proves worthy to lead Clan Glencairn and bears no ill will against Clan MacLeish."

"Those are big ifs, and a man doesn't always show his true nature right away, especially one who has so much to gain," she said, a yawn escaping her lips.

"You are tired. We can talk more about this in the morning," he said, lifting her in his arms as he stood.

"You know we have no choice?" she said softly.

He didn't respond. He set her on her feet by the bed and began to undress.

Esme hesitated. She shed her garments down to her underdress and got into bed, a chill already rushing through her and another yawn attacking her.

Ryland slipped into bed naked beside her and reached over to tuck her close to his side. No more talk," he ordered.

Esme yawned again and cuddled snug against him. "You can ignore the obvious all you want. But you know we have no choice... I must go see the Old Woman alone."

CHAPTER 23

Esme woke the next morning to intimate touches and gentle kisses and, at first, she thought she was dreaming and was extremely pleased to find out she wasn't. When she opened her eyes, she was startled, and her body grew taut. She had to remind herself that her husband was dead and the man who touched her with such love was Ryland.

"I love you, Esme," he whispered, and her body relaxed to his touch.

Ryland wanted to linger but he knew someone would arrive and disturb them soon and though it was quicker than he would have liked, it was no less satisfying.

They were barely dressed when a pounding at the door caused Esme to jump in fright.

Ryland's arm went quickly around her to hug her against him as he called out, "Who disturbs me!"

"It is Brack, my lord. Gavin has escaped."

Ryland felt his gut twist tight as he reluctantly left his wife's side to yank open the door.

"What happened?" he demanded, stepping aside for Brack to enter.

Brack strode in, his face taut with fury and frustration. "Two of the guards were temporarily reassigned per your orders. It was supposed to be for no more than a few moments. By the time they returned, Gavin was gone. Vanished without a trace."

RYLAND SWORE UNDER HIS BREATH, his mind already racing. It was a calculated risk he'd taken—one he'd justified in the moment for the chance to learn the truth. But now…

Brack's sharp gaze shifted past him, to Esme. She stood straight, shoulders drawn back, and her chin slightly tilted.

Brack's eyes narrowed. "Someone saw her, my lord. Slipping out of the hut just before the guards returned."

Ryland tensed, prepared to defend her. "That's not possible."

"She was seen, my lord. There is no mistaking that." Brack's voice held no malice, only a firm conviction. "You had the guards pulled away, and she was seen entering the prisoner's hut alone right afterwards. What I'd like to know, and what others will soon demand to know, is why."

Esme stepped forward before Ryland could stop her. "I went to speak with Gavin."

Ryland swung a warning look at her, but she continued, calm but deliberate.

"I went for answers. For my husband. I believed Gavin might say something to help him understand what's been happening. I meant no harm and certainly no betrayal."

Brack shook his head. "That bruise on your face tells me you displeased your husband, and he gave you what you deserve. Anger may have caused your betrayal, though I don't believe that you acted on your own accord. That you risk being seen, risk suspicion, just to help your husband? Forgive me, my lady, but that doesn't sound like loyalty. It sounds like manipulation."

Ryland's eyes turned stormy, and Esme could see the change in him as he stepped between them, the air around him bristling. It was Torrance who demanded, "Do you manipulate, wife?"

"Nay, my lord," Esme said, lowering her head. "I would not be so foolish, for you would see through it right away."

She could be part of the plot," Brack said. "She needs to answer for what she's done. Because if you don't hold her accountable, your warriors and they"—he motioned vaguely toward the village beyond— "will wonder why. Why she is spared when Torrance's punishments are swift and brutal."

Torrance's jaw clenched. The truth lodged painfully in his throat. He couldn't defend her without undoing everything. The fragile illusion. The plan. The name he'd taken to root out the treachery in Clan Glencairn.

Esme stepped forward again, her voice steady despite the tremble that ran through her. "Though I wanted only to help, I will take my punishment, so no one thinks less of my husband."

The room fell deathly silent. Torrance felt, though he didn't show it, like she had just torn something out of him.

"She tries to secure her place as your wife while she betrays you behind your back," Brack said to Torrance, eyes remaining fixed on Esme.

"And if she meant to help me?" Torrance growled, trying to contain his anger while trying to find a way out of this for Esme without causing her to suffer. "Then what, Brack? I punish her for helping me."

"And what will your warriors and others think if you

don't act," Brack asked bewildered that Torrance should question the obvious. "Will word spread that Torrance has grown weak, for if that should happen you leave your clan vulnerable."

"Never would I do that," Torrance snapped with a furious snarl.

Brack took a step back, surprised yet pleased by Torrance's response. "What do you intend then, my lord?"

TORRANCE DIDN'T ANSWER RIGHT AWAY. His gaze locked on Esme, heart pounding with dread and admiration. Then he turned back to Brack.

"She'll be confined to the cottage until I say otherwise. No walks. No visits. No speaking to anyone unless I permit it. And she will be given only bread and water to eat."

Esme remained still, showing no hint of protest. She knew Ryland would never let her starve. He would somehow get food to her. But why confine her?

Brack nodded, pleased with his decision. "It will be done."

"We have more pressing matters to see to, Brack," Torrance said, grabbing his cloak off the peg.

Brack's brow narrowed.

"If my wife speaks the truth, then it was someone else who helped Gavin escape, and we need to find out who."

Brack was quick to accuse strangers. "Someone in the village."

"Some in the village would have a key to the chains… unless the chains escaped with him," Torrance said, his blue eyes intent while waiting for an answer.

"The chains were found on the ground in the hut," Brack said, shaking his head.

"So, one of our own, yet again?" Torrance asked, his sneer

showing his disapproval. "Wait outside for me. I will speak to the men and discover who truly betrayed me."

"Aye, my lord," Brack said.

As the door closed behind him, Ryland pulled Esme into his arms, his voice a strained whisper at her ear. "You didn't have to do that."

SHE LOOKED UP AT HIM, fierce and unyielding. "Aye, I did. I needed to show myself I could be brave."

"It takes true bravery to go through what you have gone through with Torrance and with me posing as him. You are a courageous woman, Esme. And you must be even more courageous and remain in the hut while I search for the truth."

Her eyes turned wide, and she stepped out of his embrace. "That is why you confined me, so I could not go and talk with the Old Woman."

"I must keep you safe whether you like it or not," he insisted. "I have no time to discuss it with you now. We will talk when I return."

She let him know how she felt. "I'm disappointed."

"But you are safe and that is what matters. That is what keeps my heart steady and my stomach from twisting in fear of losing you."

The truth in his voice, the concern in his eyes, and knowing how much he loved her softened her disappointment.

She smiled softly and in a way of accepting his punishment, said, "I'm hungry."

Relief showed in his smile. "I will make sure you get food, and I will return as soon as I can if it is only to spend a short time with you. I am not leaving guards outside the door since

I trust no one. So, keep the door latched and open it to no one." He kissed her quickly and hurried out the door.

He was barely gone when the latch rattled, and she opened the door thinking he had forgotten something or had brought her much needed food.

"If you want to meet with the Old Woman, come with me now."

Esme stared at Breann briefly and didn't think twice. She grabbed her cloak and followed her into the woods.

* * *

THE MORNING AIR BIT SHARP, the thin layer of snow crunching under heavy boots as Torrance stepped into the open area in front of the meeting house. The sky hung low, gray and brooding, and smoke from the cook fires drifted like ghosts across the hard-packed ground. Warriors gathered slowly at Brack's summons, fanning out in a wary half-circle before Lord Torrance.

Silence reigned. Not a sound was heard from the gathered warriors, not even a murmur.

The cold crept into cloaks and stiffened hands, but it wasn't the weather that made them uneasy... it was him. Torrance's silence could cut deeper than any blade, and today, it hung over them like a drawn sword.

Brack stood off to his right, arms folded, his posture stiff.

"Gavin has escaped," Torrance announced, his voice carrying sharp and clear through the stillness. "He did not fly, nor disappear by witchery. Someone helped him."

Not a word stirred the air.

Torrance took a slow step forward, his gaze moving over each man. "The guards posted at the prisoner's hut were called off to tend to another matter—briefly. When they returned, Gavin was no longer there."

Still, none of the men spoke. Their eyes were careful, downcast or fixed on a distant point behind him. No one wanted to be the first.

"You all know what happens to traitors," Brack added, his voice colder than the wind. "And you know Lord Torrance does not suffer fools or liars."

One man shifted, his boot scraping the snow. Another adjusted the hilt of his sword with fidgeting fingers.

Torrance let the silence stretch painfully long before speaking again.

"I will ask once more and only once more. If any of you heard or saw something, anything, you will speak up now. If not, every one of you will suffer."

It took a moment before a voice broke the tension. "There was talk about..."

Torrance's stare froze the man in place and when the warrior remained silent, he demanded, "Finish what you will say."

"Lady Esme," the warrior said carefully, "was seen near the prisoner's hut, so says wagging tongues."

Another cleared his throat but did not step forward. "Aye, I heard the same."

Brack glanced at Torrance, then stepped forward. "Lady Esme has already been punished for whatever, if any, roll she may have played in this. She is confined to her dwelling with only bread and water until otherwise ordered by Lord Torrance. That matter is settled."

Torrance said nothing, letting that pronouncement sink in.

But then, from the edge of the gathering, someone spoke up. "Forgive me, my lord, but with respect... what if it was more than curiosity? What if someone convinced her to help him? Surely, the escape was planned, not something done on the spur of the moment."

The men were quiet again, some nodding subtly, others pretending not to hear.

"She was seen," the warrior pressed.

"And yet none of those who supposedly saw her has stepped forward here to say so," Brack said, his voice edged with warning.

The warrior offered a slight shrug. "Perhaps they fear being punished for speaking the truth."

Torrance's gaze stayed fixed on the warrior, unmoving. He wasn't young, more seasoned with a defined scar along his jaw to prove it.

"I will not have my warriors gossiping like women," Torrance threatened. "If any man has something worth hearing, he will say it with a name attached, not from shadows."

Not a single man moved.

"You will all be watched," Brack snapped. "Until we know who turned traitor."

Torrance scanned the line of warriors once more, his eyes lingering briefly, intentionally, on the seasoned warrior. Not accusing, simply watching.

"Go," Torrance ordered, and the men began to break off, some faster than others, boots disturbing the freshly fallen snow until there was barely any on the ground.

Torrance waited until the last of them disappeared from sight, then turned to Brack, "I didn't recognize the one who had the most to say... the seasoned warrior."

"A mercenary, Galen is his name, asked to join the clan after the battle with Clan MacLeish, pledged his allegiance to you and has caused no problems, up until now. He spoke boldly for one so new to the clan," Brack said. "Perhaps he wants us looking elsewhere."

"I thought the same," Torrance said. "If he is the culprit, he'll give himself away thinking he fooled us. We'll catch him when he thinks no one is looking." He turned and walked toward the meetinghouse, Brack following alongside him. "Has any word been heard from Hakon?"

"Nothing yet, but he's like a beast when a bone is dangled in front of it. He won't stop until he gets the reward."

"Una," Torrance acknowledged.

"He has his eyes and mind set on her. There will be no changing it. Una can be a troublesome lass. She won't be missed."

"So, you have made the decision for me?" Torrance snapped sharply.

"Nay, my lord, I simply see the obvious," Brack said. "And I believe you do as well, unless..."

Torrance stopped abruptly when he reached the meeting house door. "Why hold your tongue now? It never stopped you before. Say what you intended."

"You seem to be more tolerant of Lady Esme when before you believed her to be a poor wife and asked me to search for woman who would better suit you."

"It took time for her to realize her duties, but now that she has, and that there is a good chance she is with child, I intend to keep her. Perhaps, like my father, a mistress or two will suit me. But not until I can put this betrayal matter to rest."

"An heir would be good news for the clan, my lord, your father would be proud. There are a few warriors I believe trustworthy. I will speak with them privately and see if they have anything to confide."

"Let me know anything you find out," Torrance ordered and entered the meeting house.

The elderly warrior, Patrick, was sitting at one of the tables, his wool cloak wrapped around him.

"It is no good to starve your wife," Patrick said defiantly.

"News spreads fast," Torrance said, dropping down on the bench opposite Patrick.

Patrick scoffed. "It was your own powerful voice penetrating these walls that delivered the foolish news."

"You call me foolish?" Torrance asked with a cautionary tone.

"When the name fits—wear it."

"You're loose with your tongue."

"I speak the truth… do you?" Patrick asked with the quirk of his brow.

"First, you call me foolish and now a liar. Be careful, old man," Torrance warned. "I will only tolerate so much."

"You are like your father."

"Finally, a compliment," Torrance said, reaching for a chunk of bread, reminding himself that he couldn't wait too long to get food to his hungry wife. "You knew my father?"

"Aye, I knew the evil shite."

Torrance glared at him.

"If you want only lies, you are speaking to the wrong man." Patrick cringed with a bit of pain as he went to lift his leg over the bench to leave.

"Stay where you are," Torrance ordered, his tone angry enough to keep Patrick seated. "How did you know my father?"

Patrick looked at him strangely. "Do you not know that your mother was from these parts?"

Ryland failed to hide his surprise. "Nay, I did not. Nothing was ever mentioned of my mother's family."

Patrick scoffed again. "Being a Glencairn was all that mattered to your father. He disliked your mother's family and that was no doubt due to a snowstorm that stranded his wife at Purdom Keep, leaving the next heir to Clan Glencairn to be born there."

"That's not true. All heirs of Clan Glencairn are born in the birthing room at Clan Glencairn keep."

"That's a lie. A snowstorm forced Torrance's mother to give birth at Purdom Keep."

"I am to take your word over my father's?" Torrance asked annoyed, though such news made him wonder the truth of Torrance's birth. "Are there any of my mother's family left who could speak the truth to me?"

Patrick shook his head slowly. "They are all gone now."

"Then there is no way of my knowing what is true," Torrance said, his brow scrunching in frustration.

"There is one who may be able to help you, but you are being stubborn."

"The Old Woman," Torrance muttered, annoyed that everything seemed to point back to her. "She will not dictate to me."

"Be careful, my lord, she always gets her way," Patrick warned.

Torrance waited until Patrick left to stuff his cloth napkin with food for Esme. He was anxious to return to her and share what news he had learned and see if in any way, they could connect it to their present problem. And like it or not, he was going to need to consider having Esme go and speak with the Old Woman. His own orders might help with that. He could sneak her out of the cottage, have her meet with the woman, then sneak her back in. It was a thought, though not one that pleased him.

He kept an angry scowl on his face as he walked to the cottage so that no one would approach him and slow him down from reaching his wife. A light snow fell and with the air feeling colder than when he left the cottage this morning, he worried a snowstorm might alter any plans they might make.

He entered the cottage eager to see his wife, eager to talk with her, but mostly eager to take her in his arms and kiss her.

He entered, a strong wind along with him and he hurried to shut the door, then he turned with a smile. "I brought you fo—"

The cottage was empty, the curtain drawn back to show the bed unoccupied.

Esme was gone.

CHAPTER 24

Ryland stood unmoving in the middle of the small cottage, the fire in the hearth crackling cheerfully, mocking him. Esme's cloak was missing and so were her boots. Had she left of her own accord? He felt a punch to his gut. Or had someone taken her?

His hands clenched at his sides, fury twisting his stomach in knots. He didn't believe she would go without leaving a word, but if he was right that meant she hadn't gone willingly. And he didn't like that possibility at all.

He turned sharply, scanning the room again as if it might yield a clue, some sign of struggle. But there was nothing, only absence, the aching, hollow kind. This time he felt it in his heart, as if something clawed at it, the pain so overwhelmed him. He couldn't lose her again. Torrance had snatched her away from him before he could even make his intentions known to her. He would never let anyone take her away from him again.

A knock sounded.

He strode to the door and yanked it open, eyes narrowing

when he saw Patrick standing there, shoulders tight, face pale beneath the shadow of his hood.

"What is it?" Ryland demanded curtly, resuming the role of Torrance.

"A message for you," Patrick said.

"Tell me," Torrance said, his jaw tense and his mind racing with finding Esme.

"Lady Esme went with Breann to meet the Old Woman," Patrick said quietly, the news meant for Torrance's ears alone.

Torrance stepped away from the door waving Patrick inside.

"Lady Esme insisted you be told," Patrick said after closing the door.

"She shouldn't have gone without me."

"It's probably why she went. She knew you wouldn't let her go."

"She's right," Torrance growled. "I wouldn't have allowed her to go."

The silence stretched heavy with tension and worry.

"I am going after her," Torrance said.

"Is that wise when the Old Woman wants only to speak with Lady Esme?"

"Wise or not, I will not leave her out there alone when men want her dead along with me."

"You'll take your warriors?"

"Nay. I don't know who to trust among them."

"You can trust me, my lord," Patrick said with a bob of his head.

"For your sake I hope so," Torrance warned.

* * *

THE SNOW WAS FALLING HEAVIER NOW, BLANKETING the forest in a thick hush. Esme tugged her cloak tighter around her shoulders, the hood already damp from the wet flakes. She kept close pace with Breann, their boots leaving footprints in the snow that had turned heavy. The occasional snap of brittle twigs was the only sounds between them as they moved deeper among the trees.

"Are you sure my message will reach my husband?" Esme asked, worried what Ryland would think when he found her gone which was why she insisted Breann get a message to him to let him know where she went.

Breann didn't pause her stride. "It will. I trust the woman I gave it to, and she will see that Patrick delivers it since she would be too fearful to do so herself."

Esme nodded but unease stirred in her chest. Not fear exactly—but the sense of stepping off a familiar path into something unseen.

Decisions weren't something she was used to making for herself. Her father ruled any important matters in her life, then Torrance, and now Ryland, though with him it was different. While Ryland might get upset with her hasty decision, she did not have to worry about repercussion and punishment. He loved her and would never be cruel to her. And what she was doing would help them move closer to being free to have a life together, at least she hoped it would.

"What do you know of the Old Woman?" Esme asked, wanting to learn what she could about the woman before meeting her.

Breann slowed, brushing a snow-covered branch aside. "As I mentioned before, I've never met her. Few have."

Esme frowned. "Then how—?"

"Healers pass her messages around and share her wise words. I know only what I've heard about her. She has knowledge stretching far beyond most. She has strong opinions, and those who argue with her often regret it."

They walked a few paces more before Breann added, "It is said she can read a person down to the marrow of their bones. So, if you go to her hoping to fool or flatter, you'd best turn around now."

Esme blinked against the swirling flakes. "I go to hear what she wishes to tell me."

"Good." Breann stopped then, placing a hand on Esme's arm. "From here, you go alone."

Esme looked ahead. The woods thickened, trees standing close like silent sentinels, the light dimming beneath their snow-laden boughs.

"Follow the stream," Breann instructed, pointing to where water still trickled, the air not cold enough to freeze it. "It will lead you to a stone crossing. Go over it, and in the woods beyond, you will find her there."

Esme hesitated, then nodded. "Thank you. Will you be waiting here for me when I am done?"

"Nay," Breann said, pulling her cloak tighter around her against the snow. "But your husband probably will be here since this is where Patrick will track us to, though neither man will know where to go from here."

"You underestimate Torrance," Esme said, though she meant Ryland, for she was sure Ryland would let nothing stop him from finding her and that thought lessened her worry.

With that, Breann turned and melted back into the snow and trees, leaving Esme to the silence and the path ahead.

The trees thinned just beyond the stone crossing, giving way to a small clearing blanketed in snow. At its center stood a crooked hut, its thatched roof hunched beneath the white weight of winter, a thin line of smoke curling from its chimney. Esme hesitated at the edge of the trees, her breath misting in the cold and her stomach roiling anxiously, then she stepped forward.

The door creaked open before she could knock.

"Finally, you respond to my summons," the sharp voice said.

Esme's breath caught as her eyes took in the familiar face of the old woman who spoke to her at Clan Rennoch emerged from the shadows of the doorway, the same sharp eyes gleaming and her long silver hair plaited neatly.

"You," Esme whispered. "You were there…"

"I am always where I'm meant to be," the Old Woman said, turning and leaving the door open behind her. "Come, lass, and shut away the cold behind you. We've words to speak."

Esme stepped inside and closed the door. The warmth of a small fire greeted her, flickering beneath a blackened pot. Shelves lined the walls, cluttered with herbs, bones, stones, and things that whispered of old magic.

Esme didn't wait… she got right to the heart of the matter. "You summoned me. Why?"

"You have questions, and I have things to tell you," the Old Woman said, settling on a bench at the table barely big enough for two. "Sit and pour yourself some chamomile tea to warm you."

Esme kept her cloak on, too chilled, from the walk and snow to remove it. She gratefully filled a small tankard with tea, cupping it to warm her hands.

Esme spoke truthfully. "I have more questions than I can count, but I have been warned to listen and say little."

"Bah," the Old Woman said, dismissing her claim with a wave of her hand. "Spoken by the fearful and weak. You are neither. You have grown in courage and strength."

"I have my share of fear and weakness," Esme admitted.

"Most do, but few learn and grow from it like you have."

Her words sunk deep, Esme realizing there was truth to her words.

"I will speak my piece and then you may ask questions," the Old Woman said and took a swallow from her tankard before speaking. "Secrets run deep in Clan Purdom and deeper still in Clan Glencairn. They've tangled themselves in lies so long, even the liars no longer know what's true."

Esme tightened her grip on her tankard, her heart pounding, waiting to hear more, to learn the secrets.

"Beware. Vengeance will bring you nothing," the Old Woman warned, her gaze sharp. "What you need is truth. And truth lies with the one who was there. The one who saw it all."

Questions rushed out of Esme. "Saw what? Tell me who it is and how I find this person?"

Before the old woman could answer, the door slammed open behind her, cold wind rushing in.

"Esme!"

She turned to see Ryland filling the doorway, fury and worry etched deep across his handsome face. His eyes snapped to the Old Woman.

Her lips curled in disdain. "I made it clear that I did not wish to speak with you."

"I don't care what you wish," Ryland snapped. "I am here, and you will answer my questions." He shoved the door shut behind him as if it sealed his intentions.

"You think to command me?" the Old Woman asked with a chuckle.

"Must I?" he asked and turned his head briefly to Esme. "You should not have come here alone."

"I could not pass up the opportunity," Esme said softly. "I left a message. I knew you would follow."

"You are lucky to have such a faithful and kind woman love you from the depths of her heart," the Old Woman said and grinned at the surprised look on his face. She chuckled. "You didn't know that she loves you?"

Esme spoke. "I have felt it in my heart, but—"

"You don't need to speak of this here, Esme," Ryland said, though his heart soared that it could be true that she did love him more than he expected she would.

"Aye, I do," she said, nodding. "I do love you from deep in my heart. I have since you told me that you love me. I was too fearful to accept it for reasons I am sure you understand. But you have proven to me you are the man I can love without question, the man who will always see me kept from harm, a man who will keep an honest tongue with me, a man who will forever love me. A man I will forever love."

Ryland snatched her up off the chair and into his arms and kissed her with a strength that was meant to seal their love forever.

Their kiss ending, Ryland rested his brow to hers and said, "I will see that we have a good life together, Esme."

"Not unless you solve this mess that has been left to you," the Old Woman said, drawing both their attention.

Ryland kept his arm around Esme while his eyes focused on the Old Woman. "Explain what you mean."

"I do not take orders from you," the Old Woman warned.

Ryland's eyes turned stormy. "I will have answers."

Esme squeezed Ryland's arm gently. "My husband can be impatient. You were telling me—"

"Before he so rudely arrived uninvited," the Old Woman said with a tilt of her chain.

"My apologies," Esme said and gave Ryland's arm another squeeze when she felt him stiffen beside her. "Understandably, his concern was for me. He means you no disrespect."

"Is that true?" the Old Woman asked, her eyes glancing at Torrance.

He stared at the woman, Esme's grip on his arm warning him to watch his words. But the woman had asked if that was true and lying would do him no good.

"Nay, it's not true. How do you expect me to respect you when you summon my wife and command that she visits with you alone? I would be a poor husband to let my wife go alone to a stranger, especially when the information we seek concerns me, not her. Respect works both ways."

"A truthful tongue, surprising and confirming," the Old Woman said with sly smile.

His brow scrunched. "Confirming?

"Aye, your truthfulness confirms what I already knew. You are not Torrance. You are Ryland."

Ryland stiffened.

"Torrance never spoke the truth, and he would have burst in here and threatened my life if I didn't tell him what he wanted to know."

Esme's face betrayed her surprise as she spoke, "You knew Torrance?"

"I know of him and his family."

"What do you know?" Ryland demanded.

"There you go demanding again," the Old Woman chastised.

"And you not telling me anything, tells me you know nothing," he accused.

The Old Woman stood so fast the bench she sat on toppled back. She stood straight, her height impressive, no hunch to her shoulders, and a flare of anger in her eyes.

"Here is something you should know, Chieftain Ryland of Clan MacLeish… you and Torrance are twins."

The silence cracked like thunder.

Esme stared bewildered. "Twins?"

Ryland shook his head, stunned by her remark. "That's not possible."

"Isn't it?" the Old Woman asked, not that she expected a response. "You have never wondered why you and Torrance looked so much alike. Never gave thought to him being your brother."

"I can't say the thought hadn't crossed my mind a time or two that the rumors about my mum and Torrance's father could be true. But that would make us half-brothers, not twins." He shook his head again. "It makes no sense. That would mean my mum and da were not my true parents."

"Therein lies the secret that must be revealed if you and Esme are ever to know peace.

"Could there be another to claim the title?" Esme asked, recalling what Ryland had told her about Lord Randall's deathbed remark.

"Pretenders, liars, fools," the Old Woman said dismissively. The true heir to Clan Glencairn is the firstborn twin. With your brother dead, it truly doesn't matter whether you are the firstborn twin or not. The problem is… proving you are Torrance's twin and rightful heir to succeed him as leader of Clan Glencairn."

CHAPTER 25

"How are we to find the answer to a secret so long buried?" Ryland asked, still trying to comprehend the shocking news. "And why was Torrance and I separated?"

The Old Woman glanced at Esme. "Where do you think you could find such answers?"

Ryland turned his attention on Esme as if she had the answer.

It came to Esme without much thought. "I would start with the healer who delivered the twins."

The Old Woman smiled, though it soured when she shifted her attention to Ryland. "Pay heed to Esme, for she is wiser than most."

"It is why I don't hesitate to seek her counsel," Ryland said proudly, "and one of the reasons I love her so much."

That he believed she was wise stunned her and it showed in her expression, her eyes turning wide. She never thought herself wise. Her mum often reminded her to hold her tongue around men and pay them no mind. But when alone with her grandmother, she would tell her that her mum only got part of that right. She cautioned Esme to hold her tongue around men and pay heed to everything they said and learn from it. Perhaps she had gained more wisdom than she believed.

"You don't know who the healer was who attended the birth, do you?" Esme asked.

"It pains me to admit I do not know," the Old Woman said with a touch of annoyance. "All healers seek my help, not so this particular healer. But she may have been sworn to secrecy and healers do hold on to their secrets."

"If you can't find her, how can we?" Ryland asked.

"We start with Torrance's mum's family," Esme said, the slight scrunch of her brow and the brightness in her eyes a sign that her thoughts were churning rapidly. "We find out if she had any siblings and if so where we can find them. Then we find out where your mum gave birth."

"Torrance spoke about a room in the keep where all heirs to Clan Glencairn are birthed. I assume that was were Torrance and I would have been born, but Patrick informed me that Torrance was born at Purdom Keep due to a snowstorm that stranded her there." Ryland shook his head, still finding the news that Torrance was his twin brother difficult to digest.

"Then he could know more than he says, and other elders might know something." Esme said. "We need to speak to elders in your mum's clan who were around when you were born and see what they remember. Did Torrance ever mention his mum's clan? If not, maybe one of the elders would—" She stopped abruptly and looked to the Old Woman. "You know."

The Old Woman smiled but said nothing.

"Of course," Esme said with a wide smile.

"What am I missing?" Ryland asked then shook his head. "Purdom. She was from Clan Purdom, which is why you wanted to meet here, where it all began." He nodded this time. "Patrick is older, he might know something. He waits for me—"

"He returned home," "the Old Woman said, "before the snow stranded him here."

Ryland left Esme's side and went to the door and opened it. The snow was falling heavily. It would be foolish to travel in it. He shut the door and turned ready to demand to know why she didn't warn them.

The Old Woman didn't give him a chance to speak. "You two need time to talk, time to be alone without worry. The snowstorm has provided that for you. There is a small cottage just beyond this one. It is there for those in need. You are in need. I have told you all I know. The rest is up to you. If I learn more, I will let you know. Now go and find the secret of the twins' birth that will free you both."

Ryland drew Esme to his side the moment they stepped outside the cottage. Snow whipped around them in wild gusts, biting at exposed skin and blurring the world to shades of white and gray. He wrapped his arm around her, holding her tight to him, shielding her as best he could from the storm's fury.

"This way," he said close to her ear, his voice a low rumble against the wind.

Esme tucked herself into him, her head beneath his chin, her arms wrapped around his waist, trusting him to lead the way.

Their boots left tracks in the deepening snow as they made their way, and a layer of snow soon covered their cloaks, the snow was falling so rapidly. The cold seeped through layers of wool and fur as they made their way along the barely visible path.

Ryland pressed on, determined to get Esme to the safety and warmth of the smaller cottage nestled just beyond a

thicket of wind-blown trees. He was relieved when
spotted it and saw that smoke curled from the chi
slow, steady plume. Heat would be there to greet th...

He shouldered open the door and ushered her inside.

Warmth rushed over them, the fire crackling in the hearth, filling the space with much needed heat. The cottage was modest, a table and two chairs, a narrow bed against the wall, and shelves lined with crockery and baskets filled with root plants. It was a perfect sanctuary from the storm.

Esme stepped forward, snow trailing behind her, and held her hands out to the fire.

Ryland closed the door behind them, shutting out the wind and leaning back against it for a moment, watching her. Gone was the fear and worry of what might have happened to her when she left to meet the Old Woman with Breann as her only companion. Those meaning her harm could have found her, taken her, killed her. He chased the torturous thoughts away. She was here with him and safe, and though the Old Woman could be annoying, he was grateful she offered them sanctuary and grateful to the snowstorm that gave them this time alone.

Esme turned to him, her cheeks flushed from the cold, eyes bright. "Are you all right? I can only imagine how it feels to learn Torrance was your twin and separated from him."

He went to her and slipped her damp cloak off her shoulders then slipped off his and went and hung them on pegs by the door to dry. He returned to her and circled her waist with his arms to draw her back against him.

"I believe I am too stunned by the unexpected news to fully comprehend it."

Esme rested her arm over his at her waist, comforted by his strength. "What troubles me is how a mum could separate her twins, most likely, at birth. Unless she had no choice and if that is the case then my heart breaks for her."

"Torrance never mentioned his mum. His sole thought was on one day ruling Clan Glencairn."

"Did you ever think to ask either of your parents why you looked so much like Torrance?"

"I asked my da once since I didn't want to hurt my mum with such a question. He told me that some things just don't make sense, and one shouldn't waste time worrying over it. I did hear him mumble something when I was leaving his solar. "From sacrifice miracles are born."" Ryland gave her waist a gentle tug. "I didn't understand what he meant though I do now. The sacrifice that I made brought me a miracle… you."

She turned in his arms, her eyes misty. "I love you, Ryland."

"You truly meant what you said in front of the Old Woman?"

"Every word," she said softly then chuckled. "I thought I was going mad when feelings began to stir in me for Torrance. I couldn't understand how I could feel something for someone so cruel. It truly was a relief to find out that I had fallen in love with a good man."

His fingers slipped beneath her braid, brushing lightly along her neck, her silky soft skin stirring his desire for her. "I will be a good husband to you, Esme. On that you have my word."

"A word I can trust and that means much to me after so much deceit."

He leaned in, resting his brow against hers, his voice low. "Deceit is not something you ever have to worry about with me. I will be honest and sometimes bold with my words to you, like now when I tell you I want to strip you naked and make love to you."

His blunt words sparked her passion sending a shiver of

desire through her, and she whispered, "And what, may I ask, is stopping you?"

He grinned and went to kiss her when her stomach rumbled loudly, reminding him that he had left her hungry hours earlier.

"Ignore it," she insisted.

"I think not," he said, his grin turning wicked. "You will need fuel for what I have in mind."

Her cheeks flushed imagining what he meant, and she had no intention of waiting too long to experience such pleasure.

"I spied some root vegetables in the baskets on the shelf. If you can fill that cauldron," —she gave a nod to the black pot on the hearth stone— "with snow, then I can set a vegetable stew to cooking."

"That will take time and you're hungry now."

"Aye, but hungrier for your touch than I ever thought possible." Her hand rested on his chest and drifted slowly down lower and lower and…

Ryland grabbed her hand. "I'll fill the cauldron with snow."

He reluctantly left her, slipped on his cloak, then grabbed a large bucket and hurried to the door, saying, "I will be right back."

Esme grabbed a basket of root vegetables off the lone shelf and set them on the table. A bucket of snow to melt and have ready to wash her hands would be good and she could grab that before Ryland returned. He would know enough to pick a clearing where the snow would be the purest which would take him further from the cottage. Besides, she could use a quick, private trip outside before they settled in for the night.

She grabbed the bucket and her cloak and hurried outside, staying close to the cottage, barely stepping around its side to get done quickly when Ryland emerged from the falling snow and entered the cottage.

He kept his head bent, shaking the snow off his cloak as he walked to the hearth to hang the cauldron on the hook and push the hook back over the flames.

"The snowfall grows worse. We may be—" his words ended abruptly after throwing his hood back and seeing the cottage was empty. He cast a quick glance at the peg by the door to see her cloak was gone. And he could not think of any sensible explanation for her to risk leaving the cottage. Then he thought of one and grew furious, she didn't wait for him to go with her. She could easily get lost in the snowstorm, not find her way back.

Just then the door opened, and Esme entered, the bucket in her hand, and seeing Ryland sending there, fire in his eyes, she almost turned around and headed back into the fury of the snowstorm.

Instead, she reminded herself he was Ryland, not Torrance, who was upset, and she quickly offered an explanation. "I stepped around the side of the cottage. I thought for sure I would be back before you returned. I did not mean to upset you."

Ryland had seen the panic in her eyes when she looked at him and he silently cursed himself, for he realized what she saw… Torrance.

"You could have gotten lost in the snowstorm," he said more calmly than he felt.

"I made sure to keep my hand on the cottage wall and I truly needed to step outside for a moment," she said, hoping he would understand.

"The next time wait for me. You frighten me when you disappear like that. Promise me you will not do it again."

"I promise," she said without hesitation, realizing how much it had upset him.

"Hurry and get the stew cooking," he said, his anger slowly dissipating.

"Aye, it won't take long," she said, setting the bucket of snow near the hearth and after shedding her cloak, got busy chopping the root vegetables to add to the cauldron as soon as all the snow melted.

Ryland rid himself of his cloak and went and sat on the bed to watch her. She moved in a way that enticed, the gentle sway of her hips, the way her breasts bounced softly, the way her slender hands gathered the vegetables so tenderly in her hands, all had him eager to touch her and feel her touch.

Uncomfortable with the silence, Esme talked. "My grandmother insisted I learn to cook a few things, though my mother argued with her, insisting it was senseless that I would have servants to do that. But my grandmother told me that fate could be a fickle thing, and one never knew what it might do to them. I guess she was right, but then she was right about most things. Thanks to her, we won't starve."

"A wise woman," Ryland said. "You take after her."

She cast a glance at him, gone was his anger, though his eyes smoldered... with passion.

"Not yet, but I'm learning," she said, and seeing how much he desired her spiked her own passion.

"Hurry, Esme, I cannot wait much longer. I want you badly," he urged.

Her breath caught a moment, hearing a wicked passion in his voice, and she nodded, her desire for him soaring.

She no soon as dropped the last of the vegetables in the cauldron, then he summoned her with a firm command, "Come here."

She could feel their passion crackle in the warm air, and she caught his manly scent as she got closer to him. It enticed and flared her own.

He spread his legs so she could step between them and

his arms wrapped around her to draw her close. He pressed his face against her stomach as his hands slipped beneath her garments, stroking the back of her legs, then moving up over her soft backside and not able to resist squeezing it.

"Spread your legs," he whispered, and she did, his hand slipping between them.

"I love the feel of you," he said, his voice turning rough with passion.

She gasped and rested her hands on his shoulders as his fingers slipped into her to tease and excite. She was certain his touch held magic the way he enticed and drew repeated moans of pleasure from her.

She gasped again when he suddenly stopped, stood, scooped her up and dropped her on the bed, shoving her garments up. "I want you naked but there is no time for that, though there will be later."

He tucked his garment out of the way, grabbed her legs, and pulled her to the end of the bed and gripped her backside, lifting it enough for him to slip into her with ease.

"Wrap your legs around me," he ordered with a rough breath, and she did, locking unto him.

He kept firm hold of her backside as he plunged in and out of her and she moaned enjoying every powerful thrust. She needed this, needed him, needed to know he desired her, took pleasure in her… loved her.

Passion surged and raged like the mighty snowstorm outside, building in intensity, demanding attention, seeking the satisfying calm after the storm.

But Esme wasn't ready for the calm, she wanted to experience the very depths of it, feel it's tremendous power, revel in it until… she cried out so near the edge but not wanting to fall off it just yet.

"Don't stop. Please, don't stop," she pleaded, her sanity

nearly gone devoured by the passion that surged uncontrollably through her body.

Ryland had no intention of stopping, he couldn't if he wanted to, his need for her overpowering him. He feared he would never stop getting enough of her, never stop aching to slip inside her and never would he stop loving her.

He watched how she arched her body to meet his thrusts, saw the way they fit so perfectly, felt the immense pleasure surge through him and mount in leap and bounds.

His name tore from her lips. "RYLAND!"

It sent them both over the edge together, exploding as they tumbled in an endless abyss of pleasure.

It wasn't until the last bit of satisfaction faded that Ryland dropped down on the bed beside her, both their legs hanging off the edge, both too spent to care.

He reached out to take hold of her hand and her slim fingers closed around his giving it a gentle squeeze, her strength waned from their lovemaking.

"I never thought I would be so pleased with a snowstorm," he said, a chuckle in his voice.

She chuckled along with him. "I thought the same."

"We share much alike, but then I knew we would when I first saw you. It was as though I knew in that instance we were made for each other." He turned his head to her. "I just wish I had found a way to you sooner."

Her brow narrowed.

Ryland was quick to ask, "What's wrong?"

She felt the need to confess, for Ryland to know what she had done. "I fear I aided in Torrance's death."

His brow scrunched, confused. "You were not on the battlefield."

"Nay, but my prayers held weight… I prayed daily that he would never return to me that the battle would claim him and I would be free."

"It was a blade that took Torrance's life, but more so it was his own evil. He tormented and hurt people more than anyone I know. Your prayers didn't decide his fate... he made his own."

She turned to roll against him and his arm went around her. "I will never understand how two brothers, twins, could be so different."

"I had a far different father than Torrance. He didn't lead his clan with fear like Torrance's father did, nor did he tell me I was more important than others, wiser than others, a ruler who was to be obeyed. Torrance's father wanted influence and power. Torrance wanted more. He wanted to rule the Highlands, and he didn't care who he used or hurt to obtain his goal."

"And he feared you might stand in his way," Esme said, "and now you may get what he wanted so badly, to rule Clan Glencairn."

"If it proves true that I am Torrance's twin brother."

"The healer who delivered you and Torrance could confirm that and perhaps she will know why your mother separated you both."

"Unless it wasn't her choice."

Esme frowned. "The secret deepens, but we won't know unless we find the healer and hopefully Patrick can help us with that."

Her stomach rumbled, and they both laughed.

"Your hunger is one problem we can solve now," Ryland said.

They had barely gotten to their feet when the door burst open.

Ryland quickly shoved Esme behind him, but she didn't stay there when she saw it was the Old Woman.

"Hurry, you must leave," she said anxiously. "Mercenaries are headed this way, and they mean you both harm."

CHAPTER 26

Snow lashed at their faces like a thousand tiny blades. The world beyond Ryland's cloak was a white blur, shifting and howling, as if the storm itself were hunting them. Esme clung tightly to him, her arm looped around his waist, her cheek pressed to his chest. Her body shivered violently, and he tightened his hold on her, one arm wrapped around her, leaving the other free in case he needed to draw his sword.

He leaned his head down for her to hear him. "We need to find shelter."

"Or get to the village," Esme said. "We have walked for a while, maybe we're close."

Snow battered them from all sides, the wind howling like a wounded beast.

Ryland gripped Esme tightly, fearful he would lose her to the blinding snow. "It's impossible to know direction."

"Then it would be the same for the mercenaries," Esme said with a shred of hope.

"Unless they knew the area, knew where to go," Ryland

said, halting in his tracks and spotting a large stone formation. He headed for it.

It was a cluster of huge boulders, forming a small cave and he hurried Esme into it, following behind her. It was only big enough for them to sit huddled together, but at least they were out of the raging snowstorm.

Ryland tucked a shivering Esme close to him, wrapping his cloak around them both.

"What you said about the mercenaries knowing where to look for us would suggest they were told where we went," Esme said, grateful for what heat their entwined bodies provided.

"Aye, my thought as well," Ryland agreed.

"The only ones who knew were Breann and Patrick."

"And the woman who Breann had deliver the message to Patrick," he reminded.

"Then whoever wants us dead has hired mercenaries to help besides those who believe Clan Glencairn would be better off without Torrance."

"Which means he has coins to see it done or..."

"Or what?" Esme asked when he didn't finish.

"Or somehow Torrance made enemies of them and what they want is revenge."

Esme shook her head. "It seems revenge looms large in this matter, and I wonder if it is harbored in the secret as well."

Silence fell between them, and they sat huddled, Ryland stroking Esme's back in hopes that it would keep warmth running through her. It must have worked since her head slowly came to rest on his chest in sleep.

He kept alert, knowing they could not stay here. They would have to keep moving or chance freezing. He wanted to get to the village. It wasn't that far. He remembered seeing the rock formation on his way here. And while time can blur when walking in a snowstorm, Esme had been right. They had been walking for quite a while. If only the snowfall would ease, giving them a chance to find their way to the village.

The cold was creeping into his bones which meant they would have to leave soon, get movement back into their limbs. For a moment, just a moment, he rested his head atop hers, exhaustion finally taking its toll and unexpectedly fell asleep.

Ryland woke with a start silently cursing himself for dozing off and giving Esme a slight shake to make sure she stirred, and she did. He sighed with relief, and hearing his quiet sigh, realized the snowstorm wasn't howling.

He shook Esme a bit harder. "Wake up, Esme. The storm has eased."

He didn't know how long they had slept, though it was still night, but the snow was now a mere trickle.

Esme rubbed the sleep from her eyes. "I cannot believe I slept."

Ryland smiled and gave her a squeeze. "The coupling we did just before rushing into a snowstorm might have had something to do with it."

She returned his smile. "It has been a memorable night thus far, and I cannot believe I am saying this, but I look forward to my confinement in the cottage at Purdom. Though," she said, her voice firm. "I will need food." Her grumbling stomach confirmed that.

"You have my word on it," he said. "Now it's time we get out of here in case the storm should intensify again."

Ryland went first, looking around to make sure no one was in sight, then he helped Esme out.

"There is enough of the half-moon's light to help us find our way," he said, taking her hand. "And we will not be staying long at the village. We return home where I can keep you safe. We are too vulnerable here."

"We must stay long enough to find out what we can about your mother," Esme reminded.

The distinct crack of a branch halted them both and Ryland eased Esme behind him, his other hand ready to draw his sword until he spotted the person on the horse and more men behind him.

"Finally, I feared the snowstorm, or the mercenaries got you," Brack said, relief in his eyes and annoyance in his voice. "You cannot leave without telling me where you go or without protection, and she—" He nodded at Esme. "Needs to be punished for disobeying you and her selfish act that could have cost you your life."

"Watch your tongue, Brack," Ryland warned taking on the commanding persona of Torrance. "I and no other decides my wife's fate. Is that clear?"

"Aye, my lord, but—"

"Did I not make myself clear, Brack? Do I need to shout it in your face?" Torrance snarled.

"Nay, my lord," Brack said with a bob of his head.

"Esme will ride with me back to the village. We will talk after I see her settled and fed," Torrance said in a tone that left no room for anyone to challenge him for reversing his previous orders that she get nothing but bread and water until he said otherwise. But now, he was saying otherwise.

Brack waved his hand and Torrance's stallion was brought forward.

Torrance looked from the stallion to Brack. "It is good you had enough confidence in me that you brought my stallion. Otherwise, I would have questioned your loyalty."

"Never would I be disloyal to you, my lord."

"What I like to hear," Torrance said, the annoyance still noticeable in Brack's voice.

Esme didn't say a word until she was in Ryland's arms on the horse, then she whispered, "Friends are foes and foes are friends."

Ryland nodded at her reminder and held her close.

* * *

RYLAND WALKED to the meeting house, two warriors following him and several warriors stationed throughout the village. He had waited until food was brought to Esme to make sure he kept his promise that she would get fed and only then did he take his leave. But first he kissed her, a slow and easy kiss. He smiled as he licked his lips, the faint taste of the generous honey she had spread on her bread and eaten just before he had kissed her still lingering there.

He entered the meeting house to find Brack there alone, sitting at a table close to the firepit.

Brack stood as soon as he spotted Torrance and only sat after Torrance did.

Torrance took a strong breath, needing to make sure he spoke as Torrance would and that would be with annoyance or full-fledged anger. He chose annoyance since it might grow into full-fledged anger.

"How did you know mercenaries were in the area and that they knew where I might be?"

"They were spotted in the woods by a sentinel, four of them, taking a respite before continuing their mission. The sentinel heard a few words the mercenaries exchanged between themselves that this time they would catch Torrance unaware."

"And how did you come to learn where Esme and I were?"

"I wouldn't have needed to learn that if you made me

aware of your intentions," Brack said unable to keep the annoyance out of his voice.

"That's not what I asked," Torrance snapped, his eyes sparking with anger.

Brack took a breath, then spoke. "I gathered the villagers and threatened them if someone did not step forward and tell me where you went. They were silent at first until I warned that I'd start using a lash on the lot of them until someone spoke up. A woman stepped forward and told me that she delivered a message to Patrick that Breann had given her from Esme and it was to go Lord Torrance. Patrick was the most forthcoming with information since I left him no choice. By then the snowstorm had worsened and I couldn't search for you. Once it did, I came looking for you. Why did Lady Esme go see a woman who is believed to be a witch?"

"That doesn't concern you," Torrance warned with a heated glance.

"I cannot keep you safe if you keep me in the dark," Brack argued, frustrated.

"There are some things I trust to no one."

"You always trusted me," Brack insisted. "What has changed that?"

"Nothing," Torrance snapped.

"Then why not confide in me and let me help you as I have always done."

"Aye, you have supported everything I have ever done without question."

"Of course I have. It is my purpose to do so. Your father made that clear enough to me when he appointed me your counsel. He knew I could be trusted."

"How did he know that?"

Brack's eyes narrowed. "Do you forget my uncle was your father's righthand man?"

"That doesn't answer why you were chosen," Torrance said, Ryland, not having known that.

"I cannot say for sure. My uncle suggested it and your father agreed, understanding I would always, like my uncle before me, be a loyal servant to Clan Glencairn."

Torrance nodded as if he'd heard enough. "We return home as soon as the snow allows."

"A wise decision, my lord. You are better protected at Clan Glencairn."

"Where is Patrick? I wish to speak with him."

"He's recovering."

The anger in Torrance's eyes flared. "Recovering?"

"He was not forthcoming when I spoke with him, so I had to encourage him to talk."

"You beat an old man?" Torrance snarled.

"I did what you would have ordered me to do as always, my lord," Brack said, holding on to his own anger. "Your well-being was more important than his."

Torrance's fist came down heavy on the table. "How many times must I warn you not to make decisions for me?"

"No disrespect, sir, but only since you returned from battle have you grown annoyed at me for making decisions that you once preferred, I not bother you with. I do not know what goes on with you, my lord, but you are a far different man than the one who was victorious over Clan MacLeish."

"Men change," Torrance said, worried that Brack suspected something.

Brack shook his head. "Not like you have. You left a husband intending to replace his wife, sick of her after being wed for only six moon cycles, ready to move on to another woman, and returned a man intent on keeping her after she so displeased you. Any woman who cannot grow a man's shaft hard is worthless, your own words to me, sir. And the punishments you have handed out since being home show concern whereas before you relished giving out severe punishments. And you once would not hesitate to give Una to Hakon, yet you question whether you should. If I didn't know any better, I would say you are not Torrance."

"If not Torrance than who?" Ryland challenged.

"There would be only one man who could pass for Torrance… Ryland."

"That is laughable, Brack."

"Yet you aren't laughing, my lord."

"Because it is a ridiculous notion that has no sensible reason behind it. Why would Ryland do such a foolish thing and what of Torrance? Where is he?"

"Torrance would have to be dead for Ryland to assume his identity and Ryland would have to be a fool to do so."

"Exactly," Torrance said. "That begs the question why you would even think such a thing."

"I do have a simple answer for that," Brack said, a slight smirk to his lips. "I saw when Ryland visited Clan Glencairn how he looked at Lady Esme. Don't you remember? You saw it yourself, punished her for it, making her go without food or that one time giving her a good slap across the face, though she was unaware it was because of how Ryland felt toward her."

"Remind me what I saw," Torrance said, his fist tightening to think Torrance struck Esme when he was angry with Ryland.

"What we both saw… that Ryland loved Esme. You could see it in his eyes when he looked at her. But then you knew he loved her before you wed her. It was the reason you wed her, so he couldn't have her. Sometimes I think I see that look, Ryland's look, in your eyes, sir, when you glance at her."

"You are fool, Brack."

"You have called me worse, my lord, but I am loyal to Clan Glencairn and always will be."

"That is good to know, Brack," Torrance said, needing the conversation to end before Ryland could be unmasked. "Now where is Patrick. I wish to speak with him."

"He is probably sleeping, recovering. The healer looks after him. You might want to wait until morning to speak with him. You should get some rest before daybreak. I will send men out then to look for the mercenaries and see if they can be found and we can learn who hired them."

"You should rest as well, Brack. You know how much I count on you."

"Not as much since your return, my lord," Brack said, his eyes intent on Torrance.

Torrance stood abruptly, forcing Brack to his feet. "That is about to change very soon."

He walked out of the meeting hall without another word and went straight to his cottage, slipping in quietly so as not to wake Esme if she slept, and she was sleeping. He shed his garments and climbed beneath the blankets to wrap himself around her and she cuddled against him, though she didn't wake.

The conversation with Brack drifted back to him and worried him. He got the distinct sense that Brack knew he was Ryland. What that meant, he didn't know, but he was likely to find out soon.

CHAPTER 27

Esme welcomed her husband's intimate touches the next morning that swept her away in a whirlwind of passion. It allowed her to forget the problems they faced, the secrets yet to be discovered, and the fear of what might happen to Ryland when it was discovered he was not Torrance.

Ryland lay beside Esme in the afterglow of their lovemaking, his hand locked around hers. He warned himself that now was not the time to ask her, but the thought had tormented him so badly last night that he had difficulty falling asleep. This might not be the time, but he had to know.

"I shouldn't ask this now when we have just shared such pleasure. It is probably selfish of me, but I cannot hold my tongue." He turned on his side, facing her. "How often did Torrance raise his hand to you?"

Esme turned on her side, moving closer to him, his arm going around her. "A few times."

His gut twisted as he asked, "Did he hit you after any of my visits?"

She narrowed her brow in thought. "Come to think of it, he did."

"How many visits of mine did you suffer that?"

Another moment of thought and her brow rose in surprise. "All of them."

Ryland brushed his lips over hers. "I am so sorry you suffered because I could not hide my love for you."

"What do you mean?"

"Brack told me that he and Torrance knew Ryland loved you, that it was obvious when I looked at you. That Torrance got great satisfaction out of knowing that he had gotten you as his wife knowing I wanted you. He made you suffer because of my love for you, and I never knew, or I would have done something about it, gone to war with him if necessary. Like you praying for Torrance to die, I went to war intending to kill him, stop his evil madness… and free you."

"I never knew. Torrance never said anything."

"He wouldn't have. It was enough that he knew. Besides, he wouldn't give you the satisfaction of knowing that another man favored you."

"You're right about that. He told me often enough that I was lucky he wed me, that my father begged him to wed me since no one else wanted me."

He brushed his lips across hers again. "I wanted you more than anything in the world from the first moment I laid eyes on you, Esme. You haunted my thoughts and dreams since that day and when I returned to Clan Glencairn as Torrance, I was overjoyed to see you but heartbroken that I had to treat you as badly as Torrance did."

"But it's different now that I know who you are but more so that I know how much you love me." Her brow wrinkled. "Why did Brack tell you that?"

"He's suspicious of me. He questioned how I have changed since my return home and that if he didn't know any better, he would think Ryland not Torrance returned. He told me that I look at you the way Ryland once did."

Esme couldn't hide her worry. "What are we to do? If Brack suspects you killed Torrance to take his place, he may want revenge."

"We do nothing, at least not yet. We find out what we can so I can present the truth to the clan, whatever that might be, and decisions can be made."

"We shouldn't waste any time in talking to Patrick," Esme said, moving away from him to get out of bed to dress.

"Aye, and to make sure he is all right." Ryland followed suit, getting out of bed, but before reaching for his garments he pulled Esme into his arms. "Never forget that I love you."

"The same goes for you. Never forget that my love runs deep for you and always will."

The exchanged a quick kiss and began dressing.

"What did you mean about making sure Patrick is all right?"

"Brack told me he had to encourage him to talk."

"Surely Breann would have spoken up out of fear," Esme said.

"Breann was unimportant to Brack. Patrick was the one who received the message and the one who took me into the woods. His words were what Brack wanted to hear. We will go to the meeting hall for the morning meal and have Patrick brought there to join us."

Ryland draped Esme's cloak over her shoulders, then slipped his on once they were ready to leave and they stepped outside surprised by a flash of sun and rise in temperature. Snow was beginning to melt and children hurried to make snowballs while they could and toss them at each other laughing.

Ryland opened the door to the meeting hall for Esme to enter and raised voices greeted them.

"What goes on here?" Ryland demanded in Torrance's commanding voice, seeing Breann trembling as she stood before Brack.

"Patrick has vanished," Brack said, standing.

Ryland hurried Esme to the table where Brack stood, and food waited.

"Patrick is a warrior," Ryland said, assisting his wife to sit. "He would not confess his intentions to a healer." He turned to Brack. "Who discovered Patrick had fled?"

"I did, my lord," Breann said, continuing to tremble. "I went to his cottage to see how he was, and he wasn't there."

"And she did not report her findings to me," Brack said. "It was only when I went looking for him that I discovered he was gone and that she had known it and said nothing."

"I didn't know he had fled," Breann argued. "An empty cottage was no indication to me that he fled. He simply was not there."

"Or you lie and helped him flee," Brack accused.

Ryland took command of their exchange. "Need I remind you again that Patrick is a seasoned warrior and would need no help fleeing. If he has fled, then he has done so on his own. You may leave, Breann."

"Wait," Esme said and looked to Ryland. "May I speak with her privately, my lord, a small healing matter."

"A moment," Ryland said sternly and waved at Brack to follow him.

When the two men stopped by the door, Esme whispered, "Who has been here at Purdom the longest."

If Breann thought the question odd, she didn't show it. "That would be Ida. She has seen many chieftains come and go. She knows the history of Clan Purdom well. So does Patrick, the last of his family. And I truly do not know where he is, my lady."

Esme smiled softly. "I never thought you did, Breann."

"Is that all you wanted to ask me, my lady?"

"Nay, if asked, please say I wanted to know how long before I know for sure I am with child."

Breann smiled. "Did you miss your monthly bled?"

"It isn't due for a few days, but I suppose I am anxious," she said, realizing that now, finally, there truly was a possibility that she was with child.

"That is the first indication, tender, fuller breasts are another, and stomach upsets in the morning or throughout the day."

"Thank you again, Breann."

"I pray a child grows safely within you, my lady, and you can find Ida two cottages away from mine. It is the one with a fresh winter wreath on it. Ida's fingers may be gnarled with age, but she still makes the loveliest wreaths." Breann bobbed her head and headed for the door.

As Esme suspected, Ryland, though the stern look he wore spoke more of Torrance, stopped her. As Breann spoke, Ryland's eyes darted to her and Brack grinned like a fool.

Brack continued to wear the grin as he approached the table with Ryland.

"Some possible good news among such unpleasant matters is most welcome," Brack said.

"The news also leaves her more vulnerable," Ryland said annoyed. "Since there is no news to spread just yet, I want no word of this getting around."

"Aye, my lord, a wise decision," Brack agreed.

"Now take some men and see if you can find Patrick," Ryland ordered. "And we will not linger here. Prepare the men to leave tomorrow and send the tracker ahead to make sure no surprises await us."

Brack nodded, then hurried off.

Ryland swung his legs over the bench to sit next to Esme.

"Did you ask those questions because you believe you may be with child or to mislead?"

She smiled gently and took hold of his hand. "To mislead, though after I asked, I realized there is a chance now I could be. But I won't know for a while yet."

"I would be pleased to hear that you carry our child. It was something I thought about when I planned to wed you. That we would have many bairns together, sons and daughters," —he grinned— "since I knew I'd never be able to keep my hands off you, and also that our keep would be full of laughter and love."

"I would love that," Esme said, her heart swelling with the possibility of such a good life with him.

"As would I. Now tell me what you truly asked Breann."

"I asked about the eldest person at Clan Purdom and Breann told me it was a woman called Ida and that she has seen many chieftains come and go."

"Which means she would know about my mother," Ryland said, nodding.

"We'll eat and go speak with her," Esme said. "She might know the healer who attended your birth."

* * *

IDA'S FACE paled when she opened the door to see Lord Torrance standing there, though her worry eased some when she saw that Lady Esme was with him.

"How can I help you, my lord?" Ida asked.

"I have a few questions, if you don't mind," Ryland said and ushered his wife in, leaving Ida unable to deny him.

Ida stood staring at them for a moment, then closed the door. "Please sit, my lord and lady. I will get you a hot brew."

"Nay, Ida, you sit along with my wife while we talk and a

brew is not necessary since we just finished the morning meal," Ryland said and pointed to one of two benches.

Esme hurried to sit knowing Ida would not sit before she did, and the woman looked too frail to be standing yet there was a spryness in her eyes that suggested she had strength despite her advanced age.

"What can you tell me about my mother?"

Ida smiled, gently. "Lady Claire. She was a lovely woman, kind, generous, thoughtful to all in the clan." Her smile faded. "Her life was so sad. I wept along with others when she passed."

Ryland nodded to his wife, leaving the conversation to her, knowing Ida would talk more easily with her. He took a step back closer to the corner of the small hearth where Ida might forget he was there and speak freely to Esme.

"What do you mean, Ida, when you said that her life was so sad?"

Ida got teary-eyed. "When you're young, you dream about the future, how you see it, how you hope it will be." She shook her head. "It never turns out how you dreamt it. Fate has far different ideas. Mistress Claire fell in love with someone outside her station, but she dreamed her father would grant her permission to wed him. Her father had different ideas. He arranged a marriage for her, one that benefitted the clan. Lady Claire was heartbroken. She had no choice but to do her duty and our hearts broke for her again when we discovered that her husband could be a cruel man. Some believe it was his fault that she lost their first bairn."

Ryland's eyes turned wide, alerting Esme that he was not aware of that.

"Lord Torrance is not the first-born child of Lady Claire and Lord Randall?" Esme asked.

"Nay," Ida said, shaking her head. "She gave birth to a

daughter, though she barely took a few breaths. She had delivered her at Purdom Keep just as she did Lord Torrance."

"Lord Torrance was born at Purdom keep?" Esme asked, even though she was aware of it, wanting to hear all of what Ida would say.

"Aye," she said with a wide smile. "And we all celebrated the birth." Her smile faded once again. "Unfortunately, her life did not go well after that. Her husband refused to allow her to return to Purdom Keep and visit her family. Some say it was jealousy that she preferred Clan Purdom to Clan Glencairn. Others believe he was angry that she did not give birth at Clan Glencairn like generations before."

"Do you know why she gave birth at Purdom keep and not Clan Glencairn?" Esme asked, to see if her story would confirm what they had already learned.

Ida's voice turned whispery soft as if revealing a secret. "Some say it was despite her husband that she hated him and traveled to Purdom without his permission. By then, a snowstorm prevented her from returning to Clan Glencairn to deliver the bairn."

"Who attended the birth?"

"Let me think," Ida said.

"Was it the healer who delivered Claire's daughter?" Esme asked.

Ida shook her head. "Nay, she left the clan not long after." She scrunched her brow trying to recall, then she smiled. "I remember. It was Claire's mum. She had a wise healer brought here for the task fearful her daughter might lose another child, though I don't recall her name. I don't know if anyone knew her name." Her eyes widened. "Verna. She was a loyal servant to Claire and willingly went with her to Clan Glencairn. She might know." Her eyes turned sad, and she shook her head. "Though she may have passed by now, since she would have returned to Clan Purdom after Lady Claire's death and she hasn't been back."

Esme tucked that name away to share with Ryland, and asked, "Lord Randall must have been thrilled to have a son."

"If he was, he certainly didn't show it. He was furious with her when he arrived the next day. He raved and ranted and even swore at her. Lady Claire's mum had him physically removed from the bedchamber. Some believe that was why he forbid Lady Claire to see her family." Sadness filled Ida's eyes. "Poor lass, she looked so heartbroken when she left a week later. I think she was hoping for a miracle that would keep her home, but it never came." She leaned across the table and whispered again, "It was heard that Lady Claire forbade him to ever touch her again, the reason they never had more children, and in retaliation Lord Randall turned his son against her. But it was no secret he had his mistresses to please him. The poor lass had a moment of happiness with the man she loved and a lifetime of misery with a man she hated."

Ryland nodded to the door and slipped out, concerned the old woman would get upset when she recalled that he was there.

Ida shivered and hugged herself. "Did you feel that chill?"

"A slight one," Esme said as the door shut quietly behind Ryland.

"A chill haunts Purdom Keep along with Lady Claire. You can hear her weeping in the upper chambers, crying for all she has lost. Many believe we are cursed to suffer until her heart hurts no more." Ida shook her head slowly. "I pray that someday she finds peace."

"I pray the same," Esme said, her heart hurting that Claire's life was filled with such pain. "Thank you so much for the delightful chat, Ida."

"I quite enjoyed it myself."

Esme stood. "By chance, would you remember the name of the man Lady Claire loved?"

Ida shook her head. "She never let anyone know who it was. She feared if her da found out he might send him away or worse… harm him." She got teary-eyed. "She died of a broken heart, and some say it was his name she whispered before she died."

Esme couldn't stop the tears from filling her eyes. "Thank you again, Ida."

Ida grabbed her arm as she walked past her and whispered, "Don't let him hurt you like Lord Randall hurt Claire. Run. Run as far as you can to get away from him."

Esme stepped outside, a couple of tears rolling down her cheeks.

Ryland was at her side in an instant, his arm around her. "What's wrong?"

"Your mum. She had but a moment of happiness and it was gone." Another tear fell. "We can't let that happen to us. I don't want a fleeting time with you, little to no memories, I want to spend the rest of our lives together."

"We will. I'll make sure of it," he promised.

"I imagine the man your mum loved promised the same and she believed him, had hope, and then…" Another tear fell.

"Our situation is far different."

"Is it or do we follow in your mum's footsteps?" she asked fearfully.

He took firm hold of her chin. "Listen to me well, Esme. You are mine now and always, and I will let no one take you from me. We belong together and we will stay together."

She nodded, though she remained fearful, thinking his mum must have once thought the same.

"I never knew Torrance had," — he shook his head— "I have a half-sister."

"Two," Esme corrected. "Dru is your half-sister as well."

He shook his head and smiled. "Dru can be a handful, but I always wanted siblings."

"You know where one is. You just have to find the other, not an easy task, I fear. She could have been taken anywhere."

"Did Ida tell you the name of the man my mum loved?" he asked, slipping his hand around hers as they walked away from the cottage.

"She didn't know. Your mum kept it a secret fearful he would suffer for loving her."

"My lord," Brack called out, rushing toward him.

Ryland stopped. "What is it?"

"We found tracks. A sole rider met with maybe three or four others. I believe Patrick betrayed you. He sent the mercenaries after you and fearing he would be caught, he fled, joining them. Purdom was always a thorn in Clan Glencairn's side. It is time to remove it for good."

CHAPTER 28

"He's angry with you," Esme whispered, glancing at Brack, a sneer on his face as he cautiously surveyed the woods around them.

"His suspicion grows with every decision I make that is contrary to what Torrance would have done," Ryland said, too busy scanning the area to waste a glance on Brack.

Esme tightened her hold around his waist. She could feel the tension in him, the way his body had been taut with unease since dawn. They had left the village just after daybreak, not a bit of sun greeting the morn. Nothing but bleak gray clouds had followed the road they traveled along through the dense woods.

Brack had been furious when Ryland had refused to punish the villagers for Patrick's folly. Ryland had gone further and ordered a hunt to fill their larders. That alone had Brack ready to voice his disapproval, but he held his tongue when Torrance threatened him.

"Object to another decision of mine and I will cut your tongue out of your mouth."

That had settled that matter, hence the sneer but not another word was heard from Brack.

The trees thickened ahead, the path narrowing and the heavily snow-covered ground making travel difficult.

"Maybe we should have waited, at least until the snow melted some more," Esme said, eyeing the large snowdrift they had to make their way around.

"Nay. That bit of sun and warmth yesterday lolled us into believing we need not worry about more snow. The air turned bitter today telling us otherwise. We are too vulnerable at Purdom Village. We need to reach home where I can make sure you are safe. Besides, I am eager to speak with the woman Ida told you about, Verna. I don't recall Torrance ever mentioning her."

"Why would he?" Esme asked. "She was nothing but a mere servant to him and his mum's servant at that. He probably didn't even know her name."

"Quiet," Ryland urged with a hush.

How his body tensed more than it already had puzzled Esme and frightened her. Something was wrong and she watched as he tilted his head slightly and narrowed his eyes, as if he was straining to hear something.

Ryland slowed the horse, his voice a quiet warning. "We dismount. Now."

Fear rippled through Esme as he called out to Brack while he drew his stallion to a stop and nodded at him.

Brack acknowledged his nod with his own and silently alerted the men.

She tensed, her stomach tightening, and dread filling her. Ryland swung down off the horse first, then reached up for her, settling her quickly to the ground behind him. He moved her toward a pine tree.

"Stay here," he ordered. "Keep the tree to your back, and if things turn badly... run."

She went to argue, not willing to leave him, but thought better of it and nodded, worry flaring in her eyes.

Brack hurried toward them. "What is it?"

"We're not alone," Ryland answered, drawing his sword.

An arrow struck the tree beside them.

"Ambush!" Brack shouted, drawing his blade as men burst from behind the trees.

They came fast—mercenaries by the look of them. Ragged, armed, and intent on blood.

Ryland waited, sword ready. He would not go far from Esme. The first attacker lunged and was met with a brutal strike to the chest that sent him staggering back. Another followed, slashing at Ryland's side. Ryland ducked and countered, his blade slicing clean through the man's thigh.

Brack fought close to Ryland, covering his right flank. "Too many to be coincidence," he spat, parrying a blow. "They were waiting for us."

Ryland grunted, felling another man with a savage thrust. That meant that someone alerted another to their plans, or they were being watched.

Steel clashed and shouts filled the air as the battle bloomed. Ryland fought with grim efficiency, always aware of Esme's position behind him. He adjusted his stance to always keep himself between her and the fight, forcing attackers to face him head-on.

One mercenary broke past Brack and charged toward Esme.

Ryland's rage surged and he released a terrifying roar as he threw himself into the man's path. He caught him mid-lunge, blade striking hard enough to break through bone. The mercenary dropped, gurgling, to the forest floor.

Brack shouted, his voice raw. Ryland turned just in time to see Brack take a blade to the shoulder. He staggered, barely keeping his grip on his sword, but didn't fall.

Ryland was beside him in an instant, taking the man down with one swing.

"Bloody hell," Brack growled, his shoulder bleeding freely and though his movements were hampered, he stayed upright, fighting.

Ryland fought with the fury of a skilled and seasoned warrior, but still men kept coming, a steady stream of them. His warriors fought bravely, some falling never to rise again and others continuing to fight though wounded. It was like the battle with Clan Glencairn where the mercenary warriors completely flooded the battlefield. He didn't even have a chance to turn and see how Esme was, blades swinging all around him.

Esme watched with horror, one hand clenched around a fallen branch. It wasn't much of a weapon, but it was better than nothing. There were too many of them. They would not survive the battle. She did the only thing she could... she prayed for help.

It came quicker than she expected, a roar from deeper in the woods.

A troop of warriors thundered through the trees, Torrance's colors flying on their sashes.

The mercenaries faltered at the sight of the warriors charging, and within moments, the tide turned. The clash of swords rang louder, and cries of pain followed as the attackers were cut down or fled into the woods.

Ryland spun, chest heaving, eyes sweeping the clearing. "Esme?"

"I'm here," she called, rising unsteadily. She stared at the blood, the bodies, and then at him—unharmed, fury and worry in his eyes. She dropped the branch and ran to him.

His arm reached out and scooped her up around the waist, her arms going around his neck as he hugged her tightly against him. She felt his heart pound against her chest, though it could have been her heart it hammered so heavily. But it didn't matter. They were alive, they survived.

Esme gasped, catching sight of Brack leaning heavily against a tree, his hand clamped over his shoulder, both covered in blood.

Ryland turned lowering Esme to the ground as he did. He took her hand, and they hurried to Brack.

Brack grimaced as he tried to stand straight.

"Stay as you are," Ryland commanded.

Brack sagged against the tree. "I left orders for a sizeable troop to follow if we hadn't returned by a certain time. If all went well, I intended to send a message to rescind the order, but seeing how things were going, I thought it wise to leave it stand."

"You will be rewarded for your wise choice," Ryland said.

Brack's eyes narrowed before his questioning look turned to another grimace.

Ryland turned and signaled to one of his warriors. "See to his wound."

"I need it wrapped, that's all," Brack insisted.

Ryland ignored him. "See that he can ride. There will be only brief rests. We ride straight home."

"I am grateful, my lord," Brack said as Ryland turned away.

Ryland stopped and turned. "For what?"

"Saving my life. That was... *kind* of you."

"That I needed as many warriors fighting as possible, then I suppose you can say it was kind of me rather than practical. Now see to your wound. I am impatient to leave."

"It is difficult for a good man to hide his nature," Esme whispered after they were a distance away from Brack.

"He knows," Ryland said, annoyed.

"Or he questions like I did, unsure of what he suspects."

"This has gone on long enough. It needs to end and soon," Ryland said.

A warrior approached them cautiously.

Ryland waved him forward. "What is it?"

"We found one still alive, but he won't be for long."

"Show me," Ryland ordered and was about to tell Esme to wait there for him when she tugged his hand for them to hurry and follow the warrior. She was not going to be left behind.

One look and Esme saw that the man wouldn't live long. She also saw how Torrance's warriors watched him. Most looked fearful, but a few grinned as if in anticipation and Esme's stomach roiled at the thought of the pleasure they got from seeing another suffer.

"Who do you fight for?" Ryland demanded.

"Don't know…don't… care," the man struggled to say.

"You fight for coin?" Ryland asked.

The fellow continued struggling to speak. "The only… thing… that matters."

Ryland squatted down beside the man, staring at him.

The man squinted as if he was trying to see Ryland clearly.

Ryland leaned over and whispered something to him.

The fellow whispered something back and they exchanged several whispers before Ryland stood. He looked about to walk away when his hand went to the dagger at his waist. In one fluid motion, he slipped the dagger from its sheath, bent down, and slit the man's throat.

No one spoke and no one moved, and Esme paled.

"Move his body deeper into the woods away from the path," Ryland ordered, as if taking a life had not bothered him at all.

Esme found herself speechless when Ryland took her by the arm and continued to issue orders and in no time, she found herself atop his horse and in his arms. Once again, they were on their way.

Glencairn warriors surrounded them, the wounded riding double so they could be helped and the dead left to the forest animals. Esme could not stop seeing what Ryland did to the man. It was burned into her head. He had slit his throat without a flinch as if it didn't matter in the least to him. It was something Torrance would have done.

But he wasn't Torrance, something she needed to remember. Why then did he do it?

Esme raised her head, their eyes meeting.

Ryland saw the question in her eyes and kept his voice low as he said, "I knew him."

She let out a low gasp, suddenly understanding.

"He begged me to end his suffering quickly when I called him by name and reminded him what I—Ryland—had said the last time we spoke. He fought alongside Clan MacLeish against Clan Glencairn. He was a good man. He spoke the truth when he said he didn't know and didn't care who hired him. He only cared that Lord Torrance was to die and his wife in case she carried his child."

"You ended his suffering."

"It was the least I could do for him when he was a friend to Clan MacLeish."

Esme rested her hand against his chest. "There are too many who hated Torrance. They will not stop. You need to speak the truth and let everyone know who you are."

"Not until I can prove I have a right to rule Clan Glencairn. Once that is established, no one can object."

Worry for his safety, for their future together had her trying to make him see reason. "No one would object. The clan would be relieved to have you lead them."

"I must prove to them who I am, so I can secure my leadership, so no one can step forward and object, so I can make sure you are safe, and no harm can come to you or our bairn if you should carry one."

"Then it must be done quickly, or I will perish from the fear of losing you," she argued with a soft smile.

"Love me that much, do you?" he teased with a chuckle.

Her whisper was soft, her eyes intense when she said, "Much more than you can imagine."

His heart thumped against his chest and his love for her soared. "I want so badly to kiss you right now, but—"

"Torrance would not do that. He would wear his annoyance for all to see which you are having difficulty maintaining right now. So, turn your desire to kiss me to anger that Torrance is stopping you from kissing me." Her eyes widened with how fast anger flared in his eyes.

Ryland snarled. "Even in death, he touches you."

"I want badly to soothe you, but it will not help us. So, stay angry," she said, folding her arms across her chest and turning her head away from him as if annoyed.

Ryland took advantage of her small act of defiance and grabbed hold of her chin to turn her head to face him and spoke loud enough for those nearby to hear. "Watch your tongue, wife, or I'll see you locked away in your bedchamber."

Esme lowered her head. "Forgive me, my lord." She hurried to whisper, "You better be locked away with me."

He scoffed, for the benefit of anyone watching them, and she could swear she felt him grow hard against her. A smile hurried to her face, but she kept it from escaping, eager to get home and be locked away with him.

CHAPTER 29

The Great Hall was quiet but for the crackle of the hearth fire and the occasional rustle of servants moving about. Esme sat at a table near the heat of the hearth with her hands wrapped around a tankard of hot cider to warm her insides. They had arrived home late yesterday, and sleep had been the only thing on their minds. This morning Ryland got busy securing the keep and village, making sure no one could approach without warning. She had hoped they could inquire about Verna, the woman Ida had told her about, but he couldn't spare the time. She tried to inquire about it herself, but people were too fearful of Torrance to answer any of her questions. The cold had driven her back into the keep to get warm.

"You need this."

Esme turned at Brenna's raised voice, never having heard the soft-spoken healer raise it.

"Are you deaf, woman, I said I'm fine."

Brenna stood beside the high table, a cloth in one hand and a small earthen bowl of salve in the other, her gaze fixed on Brack as he sat stone still at a table, his expression stern.

"You are not," she pressed, stepping closer, her voice firm. "The wound—"

"You have done a fine job. It will heal well." He stood so abruptly she stumbled back a step, and he stepped closer, planting his face nearly against hers. "I don't need fussing."

Brenna blinked hard. "I'm not fussing." Her voice cracked, the hurt slipping through despite her best effort. "I just—I care if you heal well as any good healer would."

He turned to walk away, but her whispered plea stopped him. "Brack, please."

His shoulders tensed, but he didn't turn. "Leave me be, woman."

Then he strode from the hall, the heavy door closing behind him with a final thud that left silence hanging thick in the air.

Brenna stared at the door, the cloth and bowl still in her hands.

Esme watched her. She had seen clipped exchanges between the two and then there were the moments she had caught a tender look passing between them. She had had her suspicions, though she had said nothing to anyone. She thought her suspicions foolish just as she doubted thinking Ryland had returned as Torrance, but she was right. And she felt the same now, though she wondered how Brenna could love a man who made it known that marriage was not for him. Or did Brack wear a mask as well?

Brenna jumped when Esme placed a gentle hand on her arm and, tried of secrets, asked, "You have feelings for Brack, don't you."

Brenna shook her head. "Nay. Nay. He is—"

"A horrible, terrible man you could never love."

Anger sparked in Brenna's eyes. "Brack is a good man who must—" She gasped, then clamped her hand over her mouth.

"You can trust me, Brenna, I will keep your secret."

Brenna turned away and placed the untouched bowl on the table, before turning back to Esme. "We tried to be cautious. Quiet. A few stolen moments where no one could see. I thought we were careful."

Esme stepped closer. "Brack's afraid."

Brenna nodded slowly, tears slipping down her cheeks. "He's seen what Torrance does to couples who defy his rules. Those who dared love where he disapproved—he's separated them, punished them, ruined them. Brack has nothing good to say about marriage since Torrance had once told him when he decided to wed, he would choose a wife for him." She wiped away a few tears. It would break both our hearts if that was to happen. I am careful of not getting with child but Brack and I both long to have bairns, have a life to love freely."

Esme lowered her gaze, her throat tightening. "That's a fear I understand."

"I weep for you being stuck with such a horrid man. While I fear what Brack and my love could cost us, I am still blessed to be loved."

Esme hesitated, every word on the tip of her tongue threatening to expose what could not be spoken. Yet she wanted to caution her to hold onto hope. She swallowed it down and said instead, "You and Brack deserve to love openly. Don't give up hope."

"Hope was something I had when Lord Torrance went into battle," Brenna said. "I prayed God would be stronger than the devil, but the devil was victorious and returned home."

"There is always hope," Esme said softly. "You hold fast to what you feel, even if you must keep it hidden for now. The time will come. Wait and see. It will come."

* * *

THE WIND HISSED along the stone walls of the keep, a low, mournful whisper that crept beneath the doors and stirred the flames in the hearth. Esme sat alone in the bedchamber waiting for Ryland. She stared into the flames, her thoughts tangled with Brenna's tearful words.

"The devil was victorious and returned home."

If Torrance was so horrid that most believed him to be the devil, then who would dare go against him... those who believed they were deceptive enough, cruel enough to unseat him, to take his thrown or good people who wanted to end evil's reign?

She didn't want to think that Brack could be the one behind the attempts on Torrance and her life. But he was in the perfect position to do so, to convince Torrance's warriors to betray him, and being he loved Brenna, it would give him a strong motive to do so.

She stood and started pacing, her mind working rapidly. Then there was Clan Purdom, if any clan had a good reason for wanting revenge, it was Purdom. Could Patrick have waited all these years, gathered warriors who would help him, who had enough hatred for Torrance's father to see the son dead? And what of the various clans Torrance wanted to conquer, consume, force to align with him?

Her hand flew to her chest, a sharp pain striking her at the thought of how hated Torrance truly was and how dangerous that was for Ryland. How could one man instill such fear and cause such misery and suffering? Surely, his reign couldn't last... and it hadn't.

But it wouldn't be the devil whose life they took, it would be—

The door opened and Ryland entered. Esme didn't wait, she ran to him, flinging herself into his arms.

Ryland braced himself and caught her, her lips finding his and kissing him as though it was the last time and that frightened the hell out of him.

"Easy. Easy," Ryland cautioned, tearing his mouth away from hers. "What's wrong?"

"I can't lose you. You must tell everyone who you are," she insisted.

He scooped her up in his arms and carried her to the bed to sit, settling her in his lap. "What brought this on?"

She stared at his fine features, searching for something that would set him apart from Torrance, something people would notice and make them believe he wasn't Torrance. A mark. A small scar. Something. Anything. But she saw nothing but a face that was identical to Torrance.

"Esme," he said softly when she didn't answer.

She sighed and confessed her troubled thoughts, starting with Brack and Brenna.

"Wait," he said when she finished and went to move on to her thoughts on Patrick. "You're telling me that Brenna and Brack love each other and want to be together? How could I have missed that?"

"It wasn't something you were looking for and you don't know Brack well. If he kept it from Torrance, he certainly could keep it from you."

"True enough," Ryland said, nodding. "So, you think he could be behind this plot to see me and you dead because of his love for the healer?"

"It is a possibility."

"Then what if I give him what he wants? Give him Brenna to wed," Ryland said as if it was easily solved.

"I don't think that would solve the problem." She shrugged. "But you never know. However, there is more we need to consider."

She shared all her thoughts with him and when she finished, his first words were, "Bloody hell, I'm truly hated."

"Torrance not you, huge distinction, which is why you must let everyone know who you are before it is too late."

"Not until I can prove who I am and make sure I take rightful ownership of Clan Glencairn. I'll not chance someone getting what rightfully belongs to me and making right what was done to Clan Purdom and whatever sacrifice my mother made separating Torrance and me, and my sister wherever she may be."

"Then finding the proof takes priority over everything," Esme insisted.

"Aye, now that I have the keep and village secure, though I'm going to reach out to clans that have been loyal to Torrance for years—and hopefully they still are—to send some troops for added protection, then we can continue our search. Hopefully, Verna is still alive, and she knows who the woman is who delivered the twins."

"I was thinking," Esme said and gasped lightly when Ryland's hand found its way under her garments and slowly up her leg.

He grinned. "I was thinking as well."

"When I finish," she said, swatting at his hand.

"You better hurry. I can't help myself. You are just too irresistible." He nuzzled her neck with a playful growl.

His teasing sent gooseflesh rushing over her as well as igniting her passion.

She spoke as fast as she could. "If Verna was so loyal to your mum to leave her life behind at Purdom and go with her to Clan Glencairn, then—"

Ryland raised his head. "Then she no doubt was present for my birth."

"I would think so."

"We'll find out tomorrow if she's still with the clan,"

Ryland said and stood bringing Esme to her feet. "Now off with your garments," he ordered as he striped his off. "I intend to please the woman I love more than once tonight."

Esme smiled as she hastily shed her garments. "That is a promise I intend to see you keep."

* * *

THE NIGHT SENTINELS were finishing the morning meal, some having already left eager to get some sleep. Brenna had been summoned to tend one of the warriors who had suffered an injury to his ankle and Brack sat at the table on the dais discussing the day's duties with Ryland.

Ryland decided to test what Esme had confided in him about Brack and Brenna.

"Brenna."

His shout startled everyone at the dais and had Brenna dropping the cloth in her hand.

She stooped, picked it up, and before standing straight, he caught the way her eyes darted quickly and briefly to Brack and how his eyes held hers for a mere moment and his body stiffened.

"How may I help you, my lord?" Brenna said with a slight quiver in her voice.

Ryland tapped the side of his head. "I was thinking. You are a good healer. I am pleased with your work." He saw Brenna's shoulders lose their tension and Brack reached for his tankard as if needing a drink. "It is time I reward you. I have decided to find you a husband."

The ale spewed from Brack's mouth, and he coughed so badly that Brenna hurried to his side.

Esme jabbed Ryland in the side and turned a stern look on him.

He leaned down to whisper. "A little fun."

"Little," she repeated and jabbed him in the side again.

"I'm… all right. Don't… fuss," Brack said, brushing Brenna away while he continued to cough until he was finally able to speak without gasping for a breath. "It went down the wrong way. I have no need for your help. Be gone with you," he ordered when she hadn't left his side.

Ryland saw it then, the sadness on her face and he caught Brack's hand brushing over hers as if he was shooing her away, yet his fingers lingered a bit there. How had he been blind to this?

"A husband will do you good," Ryland said firmly. "Besides, the clan needs to grow. You'll need a virile man for that. One who will seed you with many bairns." He got another jab in the side for that one and he almost laughed.

Esme joined in. "Shouldn't Brenna be allowed to choose her own husband?"

Ryland rubbed his chin, then shook his head. "Nay, it is my duty to see she gets the perfect man for her. A strong, potent man."

Brenna's shoulders sagged again, and Esme feared she was about to cry. Feeling terrible for the uncalled-for misery, she kicked Ryland under the table.

"Ouch!" Ryland cried out.

"Forgive me, my lord," Esme said, looking repentant. "I didn't mean to kick you, a cramp got my leg, but it's fading now, and I am certain it will be gone soon."

Ryland got her clear warning and turned to Brack. "I know this is a lot to ask of you, but you are loyal to Clan Glencairn, and I am sure you will make the sacrifice. I want you to wed Brenna."

Brack stared at him speechless.

Esme jumped in. "Would Brack be acceptable to you, Brenna?"

The joy in her eyes was hard not to notice. "Brack is a

good man. I would not mind having him as a husband, if he will have me."

Brack suddenly found his voice. "I will sacrifice for the clan, though it will not be a difficult one since the healer is a good woman."

"Good. See it done, Brack. Send to the abbey for a cleric to wed you both before winter sets in hard."

Brack stood. "I will get one here right away, my lord."

"Walk with Brack, Brenna, so you both can talk and come to know each other better," Ryland ordered.

Brack turned to Ryland and stared at him, looking as if he was about to say something but didn't. He bobbed his head and he and Brenna turned to walk away.

"Wait, Brack," Ryland called out.

Brack and Brenna both turned, fear in both their eyes.

Esme understood. Torrance loved to play games, fill people with hope then snatch it away from them with a laugh. That's what they both thought was about to happen.

"By any chance, Brack or Brenna, do either of you know of a woman in the clan known as Verna? The name is not familiar to me."

Ryland saw it in Brack's eyes as soon as he said it. The thing that Brack had been waiting for… the proof to his suspicion. Ryland quickly turned a scowl on him, then shifted his eyes briefly to Brenna then back to Brack, a silent warning.

Brack nodded. "I am not surprised you don't remember her, my lord. They'd be no reason to. Verna was my uncle's second wife. They wed in their later years, not long after your mum's passing. Is there something in particular you would like to know about her?"

"We will discuss it later, Brack. Go see to getting that cleric," Ryland said.

When the door closed behind the pair, Ryland turned to Esme, his voice low. "He knows who I am."

Esme almost sighed with relief, and whispered, "Good, someone you can confide in."

"But can I trust him? Will he believe I didn't kill Torrance, or will he want revenge against me?"

"I believe that keeping his love for Brenna a secret is proof that he knew how evil Torrance could be and that you can trust him. You just allowed him to wed the woman he loves and hearing who you are and knowing Torrance won't be around to snatch Brenna away from him at a whim will no doubt be a huge relief to him."

"I do see the wisdom in that," Ryland admitted. "But with Verna dead where do we go next to prove that I am Torrance's twin brother?"

Esme slipped her hand around his, hugging it tight. "You may never get the proof you seek, and I don't know if it would matter to the clan. I believe that when you announce that you are Ryland, Torrance's twin brother, and will rule Clan Glencairn that the clan will be overjoyed with relief, believing they will finally have hope of a better life under your rule. And maybe it will stop attempts on our lives." She leaned closer. "You can't continue to do this alone. It is time to send for those you trust and bring this to an end."

He rested his brow against hers. "I know you're right, but once I announce who I am that leaves you—" He paused briefly, lifting his head, his eyes sparking with excitement. "Marry me. When the cleric arrives to wed Brack and Brenna, he can wed us. Do not refuse me. Do not tell me it is too soon. Do not tell me we must wait. You will wed me and there is nothing more to be said about it."

"But there is," Esme insisted.

"And what is that?" he snapped prepared to argue with her.

"That I accept. I would be honored to be your wife, Ryland."

The door rushed open and Brack hurried in. "Chieftain Roland of Clan Rennoch approaches with a troop of warriors.

CHAPTER 30

Word traveled fast in the Highlands—faster than even a horse could ride when rumor ran hot with talk of betrayal and blood.

Chieftain Roland of Clan Rennoch rode through the village with a troop of twenty warriors, their presence turning heads and causing whispers.

Ryland, still cloaked in Torrance's name and title, stood on the steps of the keep as Roland came to a stop in front of him and dismounted. His deep-set eyes gleamed with concern, but Ryland wondered what truly was in his thoughts.

"I heard of the attack in the woods," Roland said. "Word is… someone seeks your death. I have come to offer my support." He looked past Ryland to the keep, then to the warriors who stood as sentinels along the walls. "And prove that clan Rennoch is loyal to you."

"A wise decision, Roland," Ryland said and offered no hand in greeting. "How does your father fare in the dungeon?" A reminder that Clan Rennoch's betrayal still weighed on his mind.

"He suffers his punishment as best he can."

That news matched what Brack heard from the warriors Ryland had left there to keep watch over Rennoch since he didn't trust them.

"I've placed men beyond your sentinels—silent watchers hidden where none will see. If any troops approach, we'll know before they reach the village. The rest of my warriors will make camp along the outskirts." He nodded toward the line of men behind him, each heavily armed with weapons and ready to fight. "Better to be cautious, aye?"

Ryland gave a single nod. "Aye, see to setting up your camp. We can talk later."

Roland bobbed his head. "My lord."

Ryland watched until he disappeared behind the rows of thatched cottages. Then, with a glance at Brack, he turned on his heels. "My solar. Now."

They entered the room, and Ryland closed the door behind them with quiet precision. No guards to hear, just the two of them.

Brack leaned against the heavy oak table, arms crossed. "You don't trust Roland."

"Nay," Ryland said. "I don't. That attack at the celebration was meant to be victorious, meant to see me, Esme, and every one of my warriors dead. His surrender and compliance came too easily."

Brack arched a brow. "I agree."

"That matter can wait for a moment. There is something more important I need to discuss with you."

Brack straightened, prepared to listen.

"I don't think this will come as a surprise to you." Ryland paused, since what he was about to say would change everything. "I'm not Torrance. He is dead, killed by one of his own warriors." His words were steady despite the weight behind them. "I'm Ryland. His twin."

Silence followed his announcement. Outside, the wind stirred faintly, as if the Highlands themselves paused to listen.

Brack didn't move. Didn't blink. Didn't look surprised. Then he finally spoke. "Torrance is dead. You are sure of it?"

"I am sure. He was food for many an animal."

"Why did you take his place and what makes you think you are his twin?" Brack asked, continuing to show not an ounce of surprise or concern.

Ryland gave a curt nod at the table. "Sit and I will explain it all to you, though you don't seem surprised."

Brack sat after Ryland did. "I suspected… from the beginning."

Ryland frowned. "Yet you never said anything."

"I had no proof, only instinct. The change was obvious to me. You looked the same, but your manner…" Brack shook his head. "Punishment and suffering came easily to Torrance. He enjoyed it, fed off it. You showed none of that. So, I waited and watched. Tell me what happened."

Ryland explained it all from coming upon Torrance severely wounded yet finishing his attacker with a blade, to how Torrance urged him to take his place. That he believed they were somehow related, and his concern was that a true Glencairn ruled the clan for generations to come. And how Torrance had him swear to find out who was behind his death and revenge him.

"I know you were loyal to Torrance, Brack—"

"At one time there wasn't anything I wouldn't do for him, but over time Torrance grew worse than his father. My own uncle saw it. He told me Verna tried to warn him about it. She told him that Torrance's mother feared the son he would create, selfish with no thought for others, so power-hungry that he would lose his soul to get what he wanted." Brack shook his head slowly. "Torrance wanted his father to step down as leader of the clan, but Lord Randall refused. It infuriated Torrance. I don't know for sure, and I can't prove it, but I believe Lord Torrance poisoned his father. He never shed a tear and was impatient to see him buried. His father created the monster his mother feared he would."

Ryland had his answer as to why his mother separated him and his brother at birth… to give one son a chance. He couldn't imagine how difficult that choice must have been for her.

"What of Lady Esme? What will become of her?" Brack asked. "When Torrance told me to find him another wife, I knew he would want Esme dead. He cared nothing for her. He only wanted her so you couldn't have her. He never planned on remaining wed to her. My plan was to fake her death and send her away where she would be safe."

"She is safe, Brack… with me. I love her as you had once suspected when I visited here. And she has come to love me. That cleric you sent for will not only wed you and Brenna but me and Esme."

"That is good to hear. Lady Esme deserves a man who loves her. It disturbed me to treat her poorly, suggest punishments, but if I hadn't, I feared Lord Torrance would have believed I put his wife before him. Then he would have seen both of us punched. The reason I kept Torrance from finding out about me and Brenna." Brack scrunched his brow. "I thought we had hidden our love well. How did you know about us?

"I was oblivious. Esme is the one you should thank. She told me and kicked me under the table when I chose to tease you both."

Brack smiled. "Lady Esme is a good woman."

"That she is," Ryland said, his expression turning serious. "You will be loyal to me, Brack?

Brack answered without hesitation. "I have done what

was necessary to survive under Lord Torrance's rule and to keep Brenna safe from him. I feared for the future. You have restored hope for the future and for that alone, I will be your loyal servant. Mostly though, I will be forever grateful that you are allowing Brenna and me to wed and share a life together."

"I am pleased to hear the, Brack, though loyal friend sounds better than servant to me," Ryland said and held out his hand.

Brack took it. "I am honored to be your friend and will do whatever you ask of me."

Ryland shook his head. "I am not Torrance. I don't want you to agree with everything I say. I need you to share your opinions with me. No man is infallible. We all make mistakes sooner or later. Different opinions can help a leader make wise decisions."

"Aye, my lord. It will be a pleasant change of pace to speak my piece."

"Good now there are some things I need you to do. First, I need you to choose the clans most trusted warriors and ones skilled enough to avoid Roland's men."

"I know the perfect ones, my lord," Brack said and listened as Ryland detailed what needed to be done.

* * *

WIND SWEPT THROUGH THE VILLAGE, tugging at cloaks and hair, and rattling shutters. Gray clouds hovered above, low and heavy, as if they also bore witness to what was about to unfold. Unease rippled through the crowd that began to gather in front of the keep. They came hesitantly, husbands holding firm to their wife's hand. Mothers with bairns braced on hips, the elderly slow, some leaning heavily on walking sticks, and warriors with swords sheathed but close to hand.

They all shared one thing… uncertainty glaring in their eyes.

Ryland stood tall on the top step of the keep, Esme at his side.

"Roland and his warriors approach," Ryland said, seeing the young chieftain and his men keep to the back of the crowd. "Three days now he's been here, insisting he will remain as long as necessary. Is it loyalty or does he have something planned?"

"And will your announcement today make a difference?" Esme said, keeping firm hold of his hand, intending to remain by his side and show everyone that she not only supported him but also believed in him.

"We shall see." He turned his head, his eyes coming to rest on hers. "You give me strength Esme."

A soft smile graced her lips. "Nay, Ryland. It is you who gave me the strength to dig deep, to gain confidence, and find my strength that gave me the courage to love and be loved. And to stand by your side no matter the consequences."

He squeezed her hand. "Together—"

"Always," she finished with a whisper.

"My lord," Brack called out, climbing the steps.

Ryland turned.

"Everyone is here," Brack said and stepped to the side.

Ryland stood tall looking over the men and women who had suffered under Torrance's cruel rule. People who had bent under the weight of fear for far too long. They deserved the truth.

Ryland's voice cut through the murmurs like a blade. "Listen well."

The crowd instantly turned silent.

He kept his voice strong, confident. "I stand before you not as Lord Torrance, but my true self… Chieftain Ryland of Clan MacLeish."

Gasps and startled cries spread through the crowd, then whispers, mumbles, and several people shook their heads in disbelief.

"Lord Torrance died in the battle with Clan MacLeish. I did not kill him. One of his own warriors delivered the blows that claimed his life, though not before Lord Torrance swung a final blow that took the traitor's life. He told me to take his place, to be him, to revenge his death, to find out the truth if we were related so that Glencairn's bloodline could continue.

A few heads lifted. Others frowned.

"I recently discovered that Torrance and I are twins. Why we were separated at birth, I don't know but I intend to find out. With Torrance and I being twins… that leaves me to rule Clan Glencairn."

Glances darted at one another, tongues wagged softly, and people stared at Ryland, some shaking their heads.

An elderly woman called out, sharp with suspicion. "A lie, is it? A test to see who speaks out and who stays loyal?"

More murmurs followed.

A voice was raised. "He plays games with us."

An angry growl was heard. "To draw out dissent."

Ryland raised his hand, and silence followed. "I will never rule you with fear. That ended the day Torrance drew his last breath. I want proof as well as you do, and I will find it. But know this, I didn't come here to demand your loyalty. I came to earn it."

Eyes widened, some with hope, some uncertain, but most still fearful.

Ryland kept his voice strong as he spoke. "You've lived too long in silence. You've lost sons to Torrance's ambition.

Dignity to the never-ending demands he made and the cruel games he played. No more. If you fight, let it be for your future. Not to please a ghost."

He saw them falter. Hopes surfacing like fragile shoots in frostbitten soil. And yet... fear ran deep, and doubt clung hard.

Then it was like a voice calling out in the dark.

"I CAN PROVE WHO HE IS!"

Heads turned at the shout and a cloaked figure stepped through the crowd, moving with calm certainty.

Ryland watched the man approach, though a hood kept his face hidden.

The man stopped at the bottom of the stairs and drew back his hood.

Patrick.

Brack stepped forward ready to lunge at the man and while Ryland threw his arm out to stop him, it was the cry of a horn alerting the clan of attack that halted him.

"ATTACK!" several people cried out and those who didn't have weapons ran to get them.

Women rushed their bairns and the elderly to their homes to take cover.

Brack rushed down the stairs to Brenna. "Get in the keep and stay there."

"The wounded will need me," she argued.

"They will be brought to the keep. Now go," Brack ordered, shoving her toward the stairs, then ran off shouting orders to the warriors.

Patrick hurried up the stairs amid the chaos.

Ryland drew his sword and with his back to Esme, ordered, "Get in the keep and stay there."

Esme didn't move, waiting to see what Patrick would do.

Ryland raised his sword, ready to battle.

"I have no fight with you. I left when I did to see if I could find out who means you harm. It is the least I could do for the good son of the woman I loved with all my heart."

Ryland had no time to respond to the shocking revelation. Esme grabbed his arm.

"Look," she urged anxiously, pointing in the distant at the low rise.

Ryland's eyes shot wide. A large troop of warriors were charging down the rise and they wore the colors of…

"Clan Rennoch!" Ryland roared out and behind them rode Clan Stott.

"That is what I found out. Rennoch and Stott clans work together to see you and Esme dead, and Ryland too."

"Why? Esme asked.

"That I had no time to find out," Patrick said. "I thought it more important you knew who meant you harm."

Ryland searched through the chaotic crowd for Roland, but he couldn't find him. What he did see infuriated him. Roland's warriors were already raising their swords against his people.

"Get in the keep, Esme, and stay there," Ryland ordered again.

This time she went but not before she kissed him and demanded, "You will survive. I will have it no other way."

"Since you command it what other choice do I have," Ryland said, then rushed down the stairs, Patrick at his side, straight into battle.

Esme stood rooted on the steps of the keep, the chill wind biting at her cheeks, and the sky heavy with dark clouds that threatened to split open. She was unable to move, though Ryland had ordered her inside for her own safety. She could not take her eyes off the battle, not while the man she loved fought heroically and not while the fate of Glencairn hung in the balance.

She stared at the village. It had become a battlefield.

Men poured into the open square, warriors of Clan Rennoch and Stott flooding the village like a tide of fury, blades drawn, faces twisted with bloodlust. She could not tell how many, but she could see there were too many.

And yet Glencairn's people rose to meet them.

Blacksmiths, farmers, stable boys, men who had never known the feel of a blade beyond their everyday tools armed themselves with axes, pikes, swords, pitchforks, whatever was near and deadly enough. Something in Ryland's speech had stirred in them. They fought not just for their land but for the clan, for the hope of a better leader, a promise of a better tomorrow.

Her glance caught on Brack. He fought near the gate like a man possessed, his sword flashing as he brought down two warriors in rapid succession. His shoulder bled, but he did not falter. He moved with brute force, sheer will driving him forward with each blow, each block, each guttural shout.

And Ryland—

Esme's heart pounded with every swing of his sword. He fought at the center of it all, eyes cold with focus, movements honed and deadly. She saw him fell one man with a clean stroke, then pivot to parry another. Mud splattered his legs, blood streaked his cheek, and still he pressed on, never hesitating, never pausing. He was a storm in human form.

Patrick fought at his side, roaring with every swing, his axe cleaving the air and bone alike. His laughter, feral and fearless, rose even above the screaming.

Esme's fingers gripped the edge of the stone balustrade, her knuckles white. Smoke from cottages that were torched stung her eyes, or perhaps it was tears. She did not know.

All she felt was fear. It rose sharp and unrelenting.

This could not be won. Not with so many enemies. For every man that fell on the other side, another seemed to take his place. And Glencairn's warriors, fierce as they were, were fewer, outnumbered. Even the villagers who fought bravely were starting to fall back, retreating wherever they could.

She spotted a young boy, barely more than eleven years, swinging a broken spear and losing it in the fray. Another man, gray-bearded and limping, drove a pitchfork into the leg of a Rennoch warrior before being struck down.

There was no line. No formation. Just the raw crush of battle, steel against flesh, screams and roars and the endless, terrible sound of death.

And Ryland, her Ryland, fought on.

Esme pressed a hand to her mouth, barely stifling the sob that rose. *Don't fall. Don't fall. Don't let this be the day I lose you.*

Then she heard it... a horn.

It echoed across the hills and every head turned, even the enemy stilled.

Over the rise, they came.

First Hakon, his long hair wild, his axe raised high, his troop of warriors behind him roaring like thunder. Fierce men with faces painted and weapons swinging ready to battle. They poured down the hill like a flood let loose from the heavens.

To the side, to her shock and relief, came Knox.

His mount tore through the grass, and his warriors thundered behind him, blades drawn, battle cries fierce. His mare reared as he shouted to his men to go faster.

Then to her even greater surprise came the third wave.

A shout rose from the left, and down from the woods rode a dark-haired man, his expression grim, with a savage band of mercenaries at his back. They charged with blades and clubs, roaring curses and war cries, descending into the village like the hounds of hell let loose.

She knew by reputation it could be only one person---The Monk, the mercenary all mercenaries feared.

The enemy broke, fear and confusion sweeping through their ranks.

Esme's chest seized with something close to awe. Then she sobbed once, loud and sharp, full of disbelief and grateful relief. Ryland's friends had come to help him, and she realized then that he must have sent for them, feeling they might be needed. And they were.

Ryland and Clan Glencairn would not fall today.

She turned, breathless, eyes stinging, ready to enter the keep, and froze.

Roland stood nearly on top of her, blood on his face and garments, and a dagger in his hand.

CHAPTER 31

Roland stepped closer, his breath ragged, a smear of dried blood across his jaw. "Don't scream," he warned. "I'll cut you if you scream, try to run, or don't obey my every word."

Esme's heart thundered as she simply nodded.

One step and he was on her, the cold press of steel meeting her side as he grabbed her arm and forced her down the stairs.

"Move," he ordered.

She stumbled forward, nearly falling, the edge of the stone step slick with snow, if it wasn't for his hand like a shackle on her arm.

"You're going to be the price," he hissed against her ear, "for all of it."

She didn't answer. She would not give him the satisfaction of showing fear. Ryland still battled, believing her safe in the keep. She had been foolish. She should have listened to him. He would not know she was gone before it was too late. She had no choice. She had to find a way to escape. She had told him to survive, and she needed to do the same.

Enough snow covered the ground keeping them moving slowly as Roland dragged her around the side of the keep. They crossed the frozen garden path, heading for the stone wall that lined the rear courtyard. The woods loomed just beyond that, and she feared once they entered there, she might never escape him. She glanced back over her shoulder, just once, hoping, but no one followed. She truly was on her own.

But someone saw them, a shadow watching.

Roland didn't notice. He shoved her forward again toward the woods cursing under his breath as he slipped on a patch of ice.

He tightened his grip each time she tried to slow her steps, his fingers dug into her arm, forcing her to match his pace. The cold bit through her shoes. Her toes ached. But her mind raced faster than her feet. If she didn't act now, she'd lose her chance.

Just before they reached the edge of the woods, Esme wrenched her arm hard to the side and kicked at the snow-covered ground. Her foot struck a buried stone, and she stumbled, falling hard onto her side.

Roland snarled and lunged for her.

Esme scrambled, slipping, gasping, and surging up, bolting toward the keep. If she could get around the side—

A hand snared her cloak, yanked her backward, and before she could scream, she was slammed against a tree trunk, bark scraping her back through her garments.

"I said don't run," he growled, voice low, breath steaming the air between them. "I should cut you like I said I would, but that will come later. For now—"

He backhanded her.

Stars burst behind her eyes, and her cheek felt like it was on fire, but she didn't cry out. She wouldn't give him that.

She would not tremble in fear or plead for mercy. She would fight.

Once again, his fingers dug into her arm as he dragged her into the woods. "You're going to beg for death before I'm done with you."

The forest swallowed them, and Esme nearly lost all hope but the thought of never seeing Ryland again filled her heart with such pain that it revived her courage, her hope, and she kept alert, her mind turning with ways to escape and a silent prayer on her lips.

A voice suddenly rang out, sharp and sure. "Let her go."

Roland froze and Esme along with him.

From the shadows stepped Hakon, tall and broad-shouldered, his expression cold as ice, and a large axe angled low at his side.

"Let her go. Or die where you stand."

Esme's breath caught, her legs nearly giving out with relief.

Roland let out a cold laugh and turned, dragging her partially behind him as he faced the northern chieftain. "You came alone, then?" He cast a hasty glance around, then grinned. "Brave, but foolish."

"I came to end this," Hakon warned.

Roland laughed and lifted his chin. At his signal, eight men stepped from the trees behind him, Rennoch warriors, hard-eyed and armed, fanning out like wolves circling prey.

"You'll be dead before your blade swings, Northman."

Hakon didn't move, didn't show an ounce of fear. "She's not yours to take."

Roland pressed the dagger to Esme's side again, drawing a sharp gasp from her lips. "And yet I've taken her."

Hakon's grip tightened on the handle of his axe.

And just behind him, deeper in the woods... another shadow moved.

Roland's blade pressed harder to Esme's side, just enough for her to feel the threat behind his grin. "Nine against one," he said with a shrug. "That's poor odds, Northman."

Hakon didn't flinch. His eyes stayed locked on Roland, unreadable. "I agree. It is poor odds… for you."

One of the Rennoch warriors shifted just enough to draw attention, then lunged.

Hakon turned and swung, catching the man in the side with his axe before he could complete his swing. But the move exposed him for a single heartbeat.

A second Rennoch warrior darted in from behind.

A flash of movement, a quick jab to the neck, and the warrior staggered, then dropped.

Behind him stood Una, dagger in her hand, blood dripping from it. Her eyes never left Hakon as she muttered, "You're welcome."

Hakon grinned. "I knew you'd make a good wife."

"In your dreams," she called out as they both turned to face two more warriors.

Esme tried again to twist free, but Roland held fast, using her like a shield. "Kill him," he spat to the others, eyes darting, calculating. "And her, whoever she is."

A roar split the trees.

One of Roland's men spun, too slow.

Dru flew through the air like a hawk diving on prey, her arms snapping around the warrior's neck, legs locked at his waist. He shouted, flailed, and stumbled backward into a tree as she tightened her grip, fury in every muscle.

Esme gasped. "Dru?"

The warrior slammed against the trunk, trying to dislodge her, but she held on, growling, "You'll not get my brother's wife!"

Another warrior turned to rush her—

. . .

A VICIOUS ROAR echoed through the trees.

Knox barreled in from the side, sword high, eyes wild. He cut the first man down with one sweeping blow, then ducked beneath the second's swing to drive his blade into the man's ribs.

"Dru!" he shouted.

She released the warrior with a final jerk of his neck, and he collapsed. Dru dropped lightly to the ground, winded but grinning.

Knox delivered a fast blow to a warrior who stepped between him and Dru while Hakon and Una saw to the last two.

"Did I or did I not order you to remain home?" Knox said annoyed as he stepped over the fallen warrior toward his wife.

Dru rested her hands on her hips. "Sounds like you don't know for sure what you told me. So, it's a good thing I followed you."

Knox shook his head and grabbed his petite wife around the waist to haul her up against him when a shout rang out and he turned with her in his arms.

"Enough!" Roland's grip tightened on Esme.

Hakon went and stood beside Una and saw that her hand bled.

"You are hurt?" he asked.

"A scratch," she said, her eyes on Esme and yelled, "We won't let you take her."

He dragged her backward, panic beginning to slip into his voice seeing his men had fallen around him. "I'll kill her. Don't think I won't."

A voice, deep and deadly calm, rang out. "You won't get the chance."

Esme's heart lurched.

Ryland stepped from the trees like a shadow given form,

his sword already drawn, blood staining the blade from the battle. His gaze locked on Roland, dark and merciless.

Roland's smirked though it faltered.

"I should've cut your throat the day you attacked me at the celebration," Ryland said.

"You would have if you were Torrance. I didn't understand your generosity that day, though I appreciated it, and I understand it now, *Ryland*." He continued to grip Esme, keep her close, keep the dagger pressed against her. "Clan Glencairn belongs to me. With Torrance dead, it left only you and Esme to kill. I was thrilled to hear earlier that you made it that much easier for me with Torrance dead."

Ryland stood still, his eyes locked on him, wanting to keep him talking until he could figure out a way to get Esme free of him without her being harmed.

"What makes you think you have a right to rule Clan Glencairn?" Ryland demanded.

"I am a distant cousin to Torrance's father. With Torrance gone and you, too make sure you were no threat to my claim —no relationship—which it appears you are, I would be heir to Clan Glencairn. But if I cannot have it, I won't let you have what you obviously want."

Roland moved the blade to Esme's throat.

Ryland raised his hand. "Stop! Fight me for it. Win, and Glencairn is yours. You have my word on it and those around me witness to my promise. You will rule and Esme will return with me to Clan MacLeish."

"And you will claim allegiance to me for all to hear," Roland said as if he already tasted victory.

"Aye. You have my word," Ryland confirmed.

Roland didn't hesitate. With a forceful shove, he sent Esme tumbling away from him.

Roland roared, his eyes wild with fury as he charged at Ryland.

Their swords clashed with a jolt that rang through the trees, steel scraping as they locked and shoved. Roland fought with brute strength, pressing forward fast and hard, trying to overwhelm. Ryland didn't back down. He fought with the strength of two men.

Blades sang again.

Esme got to her feet, her heart pounding. Snow churned beneath their feet, their breaths harsh in the winter air. The others stood firm, Knox keeping Dru locked against him, worried she would dive in and help her brother. Una stood beside Hakon, both watching every twitch of Roland's blade, but no one dared interfere.

This was Ryland's fight, and he had given his word it was to be a fair one.

Roland struck low and Ryland blocked him.

"You never belonged here," Roland snarled, lunging again.

"I always belonged here," Ryland said, slamming his hilt into Roland's ribs.

The man grunted, stumbled, but recovered quickly.

A flash of his blade caught Ryland's side—too shallow to slow him, but it drew some blood.

Roland grinned, tasting victory and lunged.

With skill and speed, Ryland sliced across Roland's shoulder, blood blooming.

Roland roared and came in swinging, reckless and wide.

A quick duck under the blade and a pivot, had Ryland driving his shoulder into Roland's chest, sending him sliding back across the snow. Roland tried to recover, lifted his sword—but Ryland was already there.

Steel met steel one final time.

Ryland twisted his blade past Roland's pitiful attempt to strike him, stepped in close, and with a swift, brutal motion —drove his sword through Roland's gut.

Roland let out a sharp gasp, then a strangled breath. His sword dropped from his fingers, hitting the snow.

With the force of his blade, Ryland held him upright. "Your fatal mistake was taking the woman I love." He yanked the sword free.

Roland crumpled to the ground, the snow catching his fall and turning red beneath him.

Silence settled over everyone, their eyes on Roland, all except Esme.

She stood frozen, breath visible in the cold, Ryland's name soft on her lips.

He turned to her, his chest rising, blood on his tunic and he held his hand out to her.

She ran to him, and he caught her in his arms, hugging her tight.

CHAPTER 32

"Time to explain," Ryland said, looking at Patrick the next morning.

It had taken the remainder of yesterday to clean up after the battle, see to the wounded and dead, and the prisoners they took. Esme hadn't let Ryland do anything until Brenna tended to his wound that thankfully turned out to be minor. He, in turn, forbade her to leave the keep until he said otherwise, then thought better of it, realizing he sounded too much like Torrance. He explained his fear that someone might still wish them dead and she agreed to remain in the keep until he sorted things out, which he did easier than he expected.

Any Glencairn warrior who had betrayed Torrance, which included Gavin, had quickly fought for Ryland, when they learned it was him, relieved that he would lead the clan. It did much to soften any punishment they might receive. Much still needed to be worked out but time would see to that.

"Aye, hurry and tell us," Dru urged, looking down the

table at Patrick from where she sat snug against her husband in the Great Hall. "I am eager to hear how Ryland escaped the clutches of my selfish father."

The others there, Hakon, Una, Brack, and Brenna were just as eager to hear. The Monk was not there. He had left at daybreak, anxious to return home to his wife, Shade, though not to an angry Nug who he had ordered to remain behind to see Clan MacLeish kept safe.

"It is thanks to his mum that he did," Patrick said, "though it broke her heart to separate the lads. But she feared that once Randall learned he had twin sons, he would pit the lads against each other to see who would emerge the strongest to rule Clan Glencairn. She didn't want that for either of them, so she gave one to the healer who delivered the twins and told her to find a good home for him."

"Do you know which one, first or second born and why did the healer give the bairn to a family who lived so close to his brother?" Esme asked, her hand locked with Ryland's where it rested on the table.

"That was by sheer accident," Patrick said. "And it greatly upset Claire. She feared for Ryland's safety. As far as who was firstborn, that was Ryland."

"How do you know?" Ryland asked.

"The firstborn was born with a mark on the back of his neck at his hairline. I spotted it on you in the meeting room when you leaned over near the flames to rid your hair of the snow."

"And the accident that caused me to live near my brother?" Ryland asked, the fact that he was firstborn held no significance to him with Torrance gone, though it confirmed him rightful heir to Clan Glencairn.

"From what I learned, the healer delivered a stillborn bairn, a week later, when she stopped at a clan for the night

—Clan MacLeish—and she gave you to that woman. She did not tell her who you were, only that you were an orphan and needed a home. The woman and her husband were only too glad to accept you as their own. I imagine your parents realized the truth when they saw how you were identical to your brother. The parents who raised you must have loved you very much to withstand the gossip that your mum had an affair with Lord Randall. I do know Lord Randall tormented Claire about it, accused her of giving away his son, but she remained firm, insisting she delivered only one bairn that day."

"How terribly heartbreaking all of that must have been for her, giving one of her newborn sons away," Esme said.

Patrick remained silent for a moment, then spoke. "It wasn't the first time."

"What do you mean?" Ryland asked.

"I am the father of Claire's firstborn child. Claire and I gave our daughter to the healer who delivered her to keep her safe. Claire feared what might happen to her if Randall ever suspected she wasn't his daughter or what he would do when she came of age to wed."

"I have a half-sister besides a half-brother?" Dru piped up excited. "Do you know where is?"

"Claire's mum knew that many healers are asked to take unwanted bairns and ones who could face danger and find homes for them for their safety. The healer we gave our daughter to kept her as her own. I kept watch from afar until... she was taken from her clan after a battle loss. I planned to rescue her."

"We'll help you," Ryland offered.

"Aye, we'll get our sister back," Dru chimed in.

"Not necessary. She's safe now," Patrick said and, with tears misting his eyes, he turned and looked at Brenna. "You have your mum's beautiful eyes."

Brack caught the tankard that Brenna held, as it dropped from her hand.

"You're my da?" Brenna asked as if she didn't quite understand.

"I am and Lady Claire was your mum, though I will say that Sarah, the woman who raised you, was an excellent mum to you, and Claire and I are grateful to her for keeping you safe."

"You should talk with your daughter privately, in my solar," Ryland said, and Esme smiled, pleased with her husband's thoughtfulness.

"I get a chance to talk with her as well," Dru hurried to say.

"You'll get your chance, Dru," Ryland said, "but one question before you go. How did you get past my sentinels and Roland's men and reach the keep without being seen?"

Patrick's eyes got more than misty. "I found a way into Clan Glencairn without being noticed, unable to stay away from Claire until she begged me not to return. She not only feared for my life, but she told me she couldn't take the heartbreak she suffered each time I left." A tear rolled down his cheek. "Nothing stopped me from going to her when I learned she took ill and was close to death. I was grateful Lord Randall and Torrance were away conquering some poor clan. Verna kept all servants away and I held Claire in my arms until she took her last breath."

Ryland hadn't cried since he was a child, but he felt tears choking him, though he wouldn't let them fall. Not so, Esme, she cried freely as did Dru who sobbed against her husband's chest, and Brenna openly wept for the heartbreak her parents suffered, Brack holding her close to him. Tears ran down Una's cheeks and Hakon stepped closer to her, but she turned a warning look on him not to come any closer and he didn't, though he stayed where he was.

"Go and have time with your daughter," Ryland said. "You are just in time for her wedding."

"Wedding?" Patrick asked anxiously.

Brack reluctantly left Brenna's side to stand. "Aye, I wish to wed your daughter, with your permission, sir."

"You were Torrance's man," Patrick said with a sneer.

"Not for some time now. I am loyal to Lord Ryland," Brack said.

"I love him, Da, and he loves me," Brenna said, standing to take hold of Brack's hand. "And I am sure Lord Ryland wouldn't mind if you made your home here at Clan Glencairn with us."

Patrick's smile swelled then faded. "I am Clan Purdom's only warrior, the people depend on me."

Brenna couldn't hide her disappointment.

"Not for long," Ryland said, drawing everyone's attention. "Clan Purdom is under Clan Glencairn's protection now and will have a new chieftain." He looked to Brack. "You, Brack, are the new chieftain of Clan Purdom. You will reside there with your new wife and return the clan to its glory and keep it well protected."

Brack stood speechless, staring at Ryland and tears of joy ran down Brenna's cheeks.

Patrick got up and slapped Brack on the back. "I'm proud to serve the chieftain of Clan Purdom and have him wed my daughter. Come there is much for the three of us to discuss."

Brack led them to Ryland's solar, still speechless.

"That was generous of you," Esme said, beaming with pride at Ryland.

"I'm feeling even more generous," Ryland said and looked to Knox and Dru. "You Knox are now the permanent chieftain of Clan MacFadin. You and Dru will raise a brood of children there loyal to Clan Glencairn."

"A brood?" Dru turned to her husband. "You better get busy."

Knox slipped off the bench, scooping her up in his arms as he went. "I will see to it right away, wife." He hurried out of the room, Dru laughing all the way.

"I have been patient long enough," Hakon said firmly. "I'll have Una as my wife now."

"What if I don't want you?" Una snapped.

"You saved my life. Why would you save my life if you didn't want me?" Hakon asked, confused, then shook his head. "It doesn't matter. You were promised to me in exchange for a task, and I completed that task." He turned to Ryland. "I found those men who posed as monks and got them to tell me who hired them. I gathered more of my warriors and headed here to warn you about Clan Rennoch and Stott and fight beside you if necessary. I kept my end of the bargain, now it's time to keep yours."

Ryland was baffled as to what to do, knowing Esme would object to him handing Una over to Hakon.

"Why did you save Hakon, Una?" Esme asked.

"He was needed to fight, to help Clan Glencairn," Una said with a quick glance at Hakon.

"You have no desire to wed Hakon?" Esme asked and Ryland sat back and let her deal with it.

"The only thing I know about him is that he's a barbarian," Una said scrunching her face in distaste.

"I am not. I am a warrior," Hakon argued.

"Who has already been through two wives," Esme said.

"Two?" Una said, her eyes flaring with annoyance.

"Not my fault. The first died from an illness that struck the tribe. The second suffered an accident through no fault of mine."

"You're cursed," Una accused.

Hakon turned to glare at her. "I am not cursed. I may be stubborn, brutish at times, but I don't harm the woman who belongs to me, though some assumed I have, and wrongly so. Not that I need to explain that to you."

"You do if you want me as your wife. I will not abide you keeping secrets, or you slipping your shaft between another woman's legs or I'll cut it off, and lie to me and I'll—"

Hakon grinned, grabbed her, and planted a kiss on her lips that she eagerly returned.

"I didn't see that coming," Ryland said with a quick look at Esme.

"I had a feeling Una might be interested in him, with the way she squabbled with him, though why she is, I'll never know."

Hakon arm went around Una when the kiss ended as though he worried she might run from him. "So, it's settled then. Una is mine."

Ryland looked at Esme.

"You will wed Hakon of your free will?" Esme asked.

"Aye, I will, though I don't know why I find him appealing," Una said, bewildered.

Hakon grinned again. "You're the only wife who ever said that to me."

Una jabbed him in the chest. "I'm the last wife you'll ever have."

"That's fine with me as long as you please me in the marriage bed, and often."

Una scoffed. "Please you? And often? You should be worried about pleasing me. I don't want a man who dips his stick briefly and thinks he's pleased me."

"No worries there, my stick has stamina. You'll be sore by the time I'm done with you."

"There you go being wrong again. If you leave me sore, then you're not doing it right."

"Women don't know better than men when it comes to poking," Hakon argued.

"Oh yeah, you want to prove that?" Una challenged.

"Bloody hell, I do," Hakon said and scooped Una up over his shoulder and carried her out of the keep.

Ryland turned to Esme at the same time she turned to him, and both smiled and went to hurry off the bench and to their bedchamber when the door opened and in walked… a cleric.

He shook the snow from his cloak that covered his robe as he approached their table.

"It's snowing?" Esme asked.

"Aye, it just started, a light lovely snow, I hope that doesn't turn wicked and make my return journey difficult. I have been summoned to wed a couple, but I learned upon entering your village that you suffered a battle. Many have stopped me, requesting blessings for the dead and prayers for the wounded."

"I would appreciate it if you could spare us extra time. The clan will provide you with shelter and plenty of food while you're here and you can partake in a large celebration since it is three couples you will wed."

The slim cleric smiled. "I wouldn't mind a warm shelter and plenty of food, the abbey can be cold and the food sparse during the winter. I will stay as long as you need me."

Ryland ordered more food and drink to be brought to the table for the cleric.

Brack soon joined them, explaining, "I wanted to give Brenna some time alone with her da."

The cleric was soon in a deep conversation with Brack about healing plants, to Ryland's surprise.

Ryland leaned his head down to whisper to Esme about Brack knowing an awful lot about plants when he sensed her unease.

He went to ask her when, she whispered, "Could we take a walk outside?"

Ryland stood, drawing the two men's attention. "We will return shortly."

"Not too shortly," Esme said to Ryland, as he draped her cloak over her shoulders when they neared the door.

They barely were out the door when Ryland asked, "What's wrong? Are you not feeling well? I could get Brenna."

"Nay," she said, hooking her arm around his. "I had enough of people, of the chaos, of the problems that have plagued us. I wanted to be alone with you. I look forward to people being gone, leaving you and me to finally start our lives together as true husband and wife."

"Lord Ryland and Lady Esme of Clan Glencairn," he said proudly.

"What will you do about Clan MacLeish?" she asked as they walked down the stairs.

"I wanted to make Quint, The Monk, chieftain of Clan MacLeish, being he has done a fine job so far, but he refused. He told me that he was tired of battle, of disputes, of complaints, of always tending to others. He and Shade want nothing more than to return to her healing cottage in the woods and raise their daughter, which Shade is sure she is having a lass, there in peace."

"If not Quint than who will lead Clan MacLeish?" Esme asked as the snow fell softly around them.

"I thought of Nug, my good friend since I've been young, but losing Brack to Clan Purdom, I will need Nug, and I believe he would be pleased to join me here. Quint mentioned someone he thought deserved to be chieftain and I agree with him… Caleb. It was because of Caleb that I came across Torrance."

"The badly wounded warrior of yours who you carried

off the battlefield?" Esme asked, recalling Ryland mentioning him.

"Aye, that's him. He is a fine warrior, and his wife Ula is a fine healer. She learned the skill from Shade. I believe they both will serve Clan MacLeish well. And if any clan members wish to follow me here they are welcome to do so."

"It is finally done and over, isn't it?" She stopped abruptly. "But what of Chieftains Stuart and Eagan. What will their fate be?"

"You needn't worry about them. They are gone."

"Gone? Do you mean dead?"

Ryland shook his head. "Nay, a much worse fate. I gave them to Hakon. They are already on their way north with Hakon's warriors. They will never bother us again and they will forever rue the day they did."

Esme smiled. "I just realized something Ida had said to me about Clan Purdom being cursed and how it's believed Claire is the woman heard weeping in the keep. With her daughter returning home, raising a family in the keep, Claire should weep no more and happiness will return to the clan and the curse broken."

Ryland nodded slowly. "Aye, my mum will finally rest in peace."

Esme sighed with relief and eased herself against Ryland. "I never thought that Torrance could do anything good in his life, but he did good when he asked you to assume his identity and you did good accepting his offer."

"There was no way I could refuse when he was offering me the one thing I wanted so badly in my life... you. And when I told him I wouldn't get rid of you as he demanded but instead, I would keep you as my wife and we would have many bairns together, I could see the anger in his eyes as he took his last breath. He knew he died defeated."

Tears shined in Esme's eyes, happy tears. "Your love was strong enough to free me."

"To free us both of the past, so we could build a strong and loving future together," Ryland said and took her in his arms and kissed her.

THE END

NOTE FROM DONNA

Get in touch!

I love hearing from readers so drop me a note and give me your thoughts on the book, say hello, introduce yourself, let me know what you enjoy reading,
and any questions you have are welcome.
You can reach me at donna@donnafletcher.com

Newsletter

Consider subscribing to my newsletter. It goes out twice a month, more if there is some unexpected news to share. I keep readers updated on forthcoming books, future books, and alert them to giveaways, offer a free book now and again, share recipes, and leave you with a cute joke to put a smile on your face. So don't miss the fun... subscribe!

Reviews

Some people enjoy leaving reviews, others don't. If you like leaving a review it is immensely appreciated. If you don't like leaving a review, consider spreading the word to your reader friends about the books you've read.

Thanks for reading my book!

Donna

ABOUT THE AUTHOR

To learn more about Donna and her books visit her website.

ALSO BY DONNA FLETCHER

Highland Promise Trilogy

Highland Oath (Prequel)

Pledged to a Highlander

Entrusted to a Highlander

Oath of the Beast

Cree & Dawn Series

Highlander Unchained/Forbidden Highlander

Highlander's Captive

My Highlander

Cree & Dawn Short Stories

Highlander's True Love

Highlander's Promise

Highlander's Winter Tale/Highlander's Rescue

The Pict King Series

The King's Executioner

The King's Warrior

The King and His Queen

ALSO BY DONNA FLETCHER

Printed in Dunstable, United Kingdom

66022617R00201